MW00810161

000000000924202 1 prnt

RETURN BILLIONAIRE TO SENDER

ANNIKA MARTIN

Here's to Jess, Tam, and Sandy, my original girl gang!
Global girls FTW!!

1

Noelle

"Are you nervous?" my roommate, Francine, asks. "I'd be nervous."

I tuck a pen into one of the pen-holding slots inside the flap of my bag. I rotate it so that it's perfectly lined up with the other pens, all nestled in their slots, then I look up and smile, putting a brave face on it. "It's just another delivery, right?"

She snorts. "Ummm...it's a little more than that, I think!"

I shrug and review my pen-alignment situation, then I snap the bag shut.

When I look up again, she's beaming at me. Like she thinks I'm a heroic person.

It so helps.

I'm not a heroic person—in fact, I'm scared out of my wits, but I'm our last hope. It would probably be better for my friends if they had somebody else for their last-ditch effort to save our home, but they have me.

Maybe he'll listen. Maybe he'll rethink his wrecking ball plans. If there's one thing I've learned after seven years of being a letter carrier, it's that people sometimes surprise you, and more often than not, it's a good surprise.

Then again, the person we're talking about here is business mogul Malcolm Blackberg—the ultimate big bad.

Still.

I unsnap my bag and do one last check. In addition to my wallet and phone, I also have my iPad, two backup iPad chargers, extra lip balms, and my pepper spray—not that I'll need it, but I've gotten used to carrying it over the years.

I arrange my carefully curled hair in the mirror and then I clip on my favorite brown butterfly bow tie.

Francine comes up next to me. Her silky black hair is up in her ballerina bun, all ready to take and teach classes today. She groans at my reflection.

"Don't even," I say.

Two years I've lived here, two years my friends have teased me for wearing a butterfly bowtie whenever I have somewhere official to go. I know they see it as a total backwoods thing to wear in the big city, but I love how practical it is, like a cross between a small neck scarf and a bowtie, and I think it's pretty, too. Most of all, it's what I'm used to, and today of all days I need to feel comfortable.

Honestly, I find it unnerving to go new places alone when I'm not wearing my United States Postal Service letter carrier uniform, but I've figured out some non-work outfits in life that operate like my uniform, like the pantsuit and butterfly tie. I have several colors.

I like how uniforms take the guesswork out of dressing. For going out, I have a proven-cute skirt and top set that I copied from my friend, Mia—also in different colors. For staying home, I have a specific brand of yoga pants and T-shirts.

"Fashion-reeducation camp with armies of Tyra Banks

clones working round-the-clock to break you of those weird ties! That's what we need."

"We'll see," I say. "Maybe when this is all over…"

Francine's delicate features are suffused with sadness, making me wish I hadn't said that.

Everything we say about the future is suffused with sadness because of Malcolm Blackberg.

He sent us all eviction notices last week. His dreaded wrecking ball is scheduled. Our beloved building will soon be rubble.

People from our building have tried to get meetings with him, called him, sent emails and even letters; we've visited lawyers, petitioned the city.

Nothing. Nobody seems to be able to get to Mr. Blackberg.

I'm determined to try.

"Forget it, you look cute," she says. "You look like young Sissy Spacek." She hugs me and wishes me luck.

Two subway rides and five blocks later, the August humidity has flattened out my curls—I can see this clearly in the gleaming row of glass doors of Blackberg Plaza. I pause, looking up at the six stories of polished black marble with actual gargoyles on top.

I belong here just as much as anyone else does, I whisper to myself, though I wish I had my uniform on. A letter carrier belongs everywhere.

I straighten and tip my chin up and put my shoulders back —the posture I take when I'm trying to remind myself that I can face anything—and push into the lobby.

It's like a cathedral of black marble inside. The sleek and gleaming walls are caressed up and down with light from elegant black sconces, and there's a large fountain in the middle that features a massive, jagged black boulder that's maybe two stories tall. Is it also black marble? Did Malcolm Blackberg leave any marble for the rest of the world? How did they even get a boulder in here? Did a giant pop off the top of the building and lower it from the sky? Water streams down the sides in gleaming rivulets. Voices and footsteps create an echoing din.

I clutch my bag and stride across polished black marble, avoiding clusters of people while trying to look purposeful, making my way into the belly of the building toward the elevators on the far side.

Halfway in, I pause at the wall to examine the directory, just to gather my courage and to show I have business here.

I don't need to look at the directory, of course. This isn't my route, but I know that this building has six floors. I know that Malcolm Blackberg's firm, Blackberg, Inc., occupies them all. I know their zip code and their delivery office; I know they have their very own plus-four code.

All of a sudden, the din of voices quiets. Did something happen? Did a shooter enter the building? Did the giant pop off the top of the building again, wanting his boulder back? I spin around, alarmed.

That's when I see him.

I recognize his dark, elegant looks from the few photos of him that we could find, though I think I'd know him just from the way his people walk a little bit behind him, like fighter jets flanking the fiercest and most important jet.

I stand there stupidly, heart racing.

The photos didn't do him justice. They didn't prepare me for his beauty. Or let's make that his terrifying beauty.

His swept-back hair gleams dark as midnight, and the skin on his aerodynamically chiseled face seems to glow with health, or maybe annoyance—it's hard to tell. His tea-colored eyes shine with gorgeous intensity, focused ferociously on the elevator he's heading towards, as if it's not enough for him to merely reach it with his two feet as a normal mortal would. No, he must also mesmerize it with his darkly enchanting predator's gaze.

Onward he strolls, legs long, steps strong and purposeful. I should look away, but I can't.

The confidence he exudes feels like a physical thing, a phenomenon with mass and weight, the self-assurance of a man with total mastery over his environment.

Nervously, I clutch my bag. Why did I think I could even speak with such a man, no less get him to watch something on my iPad?

Did my butterfly tie cut off circulation to my brain like Francine always warns?

I find myself longing to be anywhere but here. Ideally at work, my happy place.

Unlike most of my girlfriends, I love my job. I love the routine of it—picking up my mail in the morning, planning out my route, strategizing deliveries with the boxes, settling letters and circulars into the proper boxes, tilting them just so for easy grabbing.

My boss couldn't believe I was actually taking a vacation day. I never take vacation days. Why would I?

There's an important-looking, briefcase-toting woman coming toward Malcolm from the other way. Malcolm stops her and issues a command that causes her to show him something on her phone, and then the exchange is over, and the groups proceed in opposite directions, like a businesspersons' Ice Capades. And Malcolm is the star, the Grand Master of Ceremonies, the harsh and unforgiving god gliding among trembling masses.

He nears.

This is my chance—my chance to go up to him. To ask him for a few moments of his time.

But my feet stay rooted to the ground. Malcolm Blackberg seems too big, too fierce, not of this world.

I remind myself that we're just two human beings, but it's no use.

Sweat blooms up my spine.

This whole caper seems doomed. Who thought it up? Wait, I did.

I remind myself of this trick that I do when I'm scared during a delivery, like if an area is super dark, or if a building looks creepy, I remind myself that people inside there are relying on me. I imagine their faces, waiting for an important letter.

Standing there in the Blackberg lobby, I imagine my friends' faces, waiting to hear if I'm successful.

I remind myself that I'm our last hope; if I don't stop Malcolm Blackberg from destroying our building, my girlfriends and I will have to move away from each other to lord knows where. Sure, we'll make an effort to see each other, it just won't be the same as being able to pop down the hall and unload about the minutiae of our days, knowing there's always somebody to commiserate with you about the man spreader you had to sit next to on the train or watch Bachelor with you.

The little community that we've built up and down the hallways of our seven-story brick building is like a family. Especially to me. And poor old Maisey—she'll lose the rent-controlled apartment she's been in for five decades. Same with John, always in his platoon hat, leaning on his cane, and first-floor Kara—who will watch her baby when she has to suddenly run out?

None of us will ever find a community like the one at 341 West 45th Street.

Cued up on my iPad is a video that Jada put together as a digital keepsake for all of us to remember the place by. It's mostly us telling the camera our favorite things about living in our building and talking about how much we love it, and love each other. She strung together footage she dug up of parties, building meetings, historical footage, all kinds of things. She screened it to the group of us the other night, and it made everybody weepy. There may have been bubbly beverages involved.

But it really was so emotional, this sweet video of everything that we'll be losing when our beloved building is knocked down. I've only been there two years, and even I can't imagine losing it.

And then at one point during the night, I stood up in front of the whole group and declared that if Malcolm Blackberg were to see the video, like if we made him watch the whole entire thing, he would never, ever, ever tear down the building.

"You are soooo cute," Vicky said. Mia declared that I definitely needed to live in the city a while longer. Tabatha and Francine just thought it was sweet and sad.

I didn't think it was sweet or sad or cute at all. I was dead serious and definitely on a freaking roll. In fact, I stood up there like Winston Churchill addressing the House of Lords. "When people know each other's stories, their hearts change. And Malcolm Blackberg is no different. And I'm serious, you guys— if we made him watch the video, his heart would change, guaranteed."

They all scoffed, but I felt so sure. Who could see it and not be moved?

"Didn't Rex even say that there were other ways for him to execute his plan without demolishing this building?" I asked. "If Malcolm Blackberg knew what this building meant to us, I know he would rethink his plan. I would bet any amount of money."

"Okay, Professor Higgins," Francine had said, throwing popcorn at me.

"It has to happen," I'd continued. "In fact, I'm going to make him do it."

Lizzie joked that the only way he'd watch it would be if I tied him up and propped his eyes open with toothpicks. People laughed at the idea of me doing that.

"I don't know how I'll get him to watch it," I told them, "but no way are you going to see me standing across that street watching the wrecking ball fly without having done everything humanly possible to stop it. The worst he could do is say no, right?" And I made a big show of having Jada send me a copy to put on my iPad. I would make him watch Jada's commemorative video right on my iPad.

I unsnap my bag. There's a little notecard in there where I wrote down my impassioned speech that would get him to watch Jada's movie, but as Malcolm nears, the words on the card feel irrelevant as alien hieroglyphics.

"Can I help you?"

I turn and find myself face to face with a bushy-bearded security guard. Can he tell that I don't belong here? "No, thank you," I say.

"Do you have business in this building?" he asks.

"I...I'm here to meet with somebody," I say.

The security guard motions toward the elevator area. "Visitor reception's on two," he says, seeming suspicious of me. "You'll check in there and get a visitor's lanyard."

I back up. "Thank you," I say.

"Miss!" He gets this alarmed look on his face. "Watch your—"

I don't hear the rest, because I run smack into somebody.

I spin around. Stuff dumps from my open bag. "Oh my god, I'm so—" The apology dies on my tongue as I find myself face to face with the obsidian glare of Malcolm Blackberg himself. "S-sorry," I say. "I didn't see where I was going—"

"To be expected when one walks backwards," he bites out in a cut-glass British accent, reminding me that I read somewhere he's from England. The accent adds to his strange viciousness, and also to the rate of my banging pulse.

Malcolm Blackberg is beautiful from afar, but up close he's heart-splittingly hot, full of dark allure with his regal, bird-of-prey nose and dark-rimmed eyes the color of iced tea.

I squat down to gather my things.

Much to my surprise, he squats down and helps. I'm nearly hyperventilating from what a larger-than-life presence he is—and madly muscular, too, judging from the way his pants tighten around his thighs.

This—this is my chance to say something. But my mind is blanking.

I place my things deftly in their exact-right slots in my bag, because even when I'm freaking out, it's against my hyper-organized heart just to slam everything in.

I look up and again our eyes meet. He regards me with a look that sears me to the core, and then—slowly—his eyes lower to my neck. What does he want with my neck?

He's staring at my dorky bow tie, of course. God, why did I not listen to Francine on the bow tie? What is wrong with me?

He has my phone in his hand, and he tucks it into the designated phone pocket of my bag.

I gasp, pulse racing.

How did he know?

And then I smile, because I can't help myself. "Bingo," I whisper fervently.

And then I think, did I just say "bingo" to Malcolm Blackberg? But it was just incredibly perceptive of him. And sweet, too.

I stand, clutching my bag. "Thank you, you're very kind," I blurt.

He just regards me and my neck all fierce and scowly, and somebody behind him sniffs, and he turns and goes.

Leaving me shaking in my worn brown loafers, awash in his powerful masculine energy.

Only too late do I realize that I just blew my chance to speak with him. I try to catch up, but the elevator doors close quickly. I look for the button, but there's just a blank pad.

"That's not a public elevator, miss." It's the bushy-bearded security guard again. He gestures toward a different set of elevators.

"Oh. Thank you."

"Second floor."

I nod.

2

Malcolm

IN MEDIEVAL LONDON, they put heads on pikes as a warning to people who might venture across the bridge. Beware. Watch your step. Figure out the customs and follow them.

Or else.

The heads sometimes belonged to criminals, though sometimes they were simply unlucky members of the unwashed rabble in the wrong place at the wrong time—such was the system of the day.

At any rate, heads on pikes. As signage, you really can't do better than heads on pikes, can you? When you have heads on pikes, there is no need for words. There is no need to spell out even a single word. Beware, for example. There would be no need to spell out such a thing when there are heads on pikes in the vicinity. It's a perfect communication, really, suggesting to all who come to stay out of people's ways. And by people, I mean me.

"You're very kind," my assistant Ted echoes dryly as the doors shut.

"So very kind." Lynette says. "Wrong building, Riding Hood."

I look down at my phone, spinning through messages, feeling unsettled.

Kaufenmeier joins us on four, and the elevator continues.

"So very, very kind," Lynette says again. She's one of my lawyers, one of my best, but still. I give her a dark look because I heard her the first time around. The smirk disappears from her face.

"What's going on?" Kaufenmeier asks.

"Mal had to rescue a damsel in distress," says Ted. "A little gray bird flew into him and dropped all of her feathers."

"And Mal helps pick them up, and she goes, 'You're very kind,'" Lynette says. "Didn't recognize him, I guess."

"Very kind," Kaufenmeier says, also finding it amusing. "*Kind* like the big bad wolf, maybe."

"Kind like the scorpion while he's getting his turtle ride," Lynette adds with a quirk of her brow, managing to make her reference to the fable sound utterly filthy.

"Do I not pay a small fortune for guards to keep the public out of the lobby?" I grumble. "How about somebody checks on what their policy is for letting people roam around down there without a clear purpose."

"Get right on it," Ted says.

I stare down at my phone, but I'm back to the girl in the lobby. She was annoying, not watching where she was going, but Ted has her wrong when he says she didn't know who I am. She knew precisely who I am.

I stay out of the spotlight as much as I can, but people still recognize me at times; I can always tell from the way they turn guarded, expression hardened. It's a small click on the dial, but one I know well, having seen it so often.

Sometimes it's in their posture. Sometimes they actually back up a step, unaware they're doing it.

People rarely know what they're doing. They rarely see what's in front of their faces. It's why I'm so rich and why everybody else is so pathetic.

So the woman. I saw the recognition in her eyes, but she just stayed there with a kind of wide-open and frank gaze. She didn't shut it down even when I got close to her, knelt close enough to overwhelm her.

You're so kind.

It was hardly kindness. It's just that she was so buttoned down and tied up, right down to the bow around her neck, scrabbling her scattered belongings into just-so order. I had this overwhelming sense of her—I can't quite describe it—but I was driven to grab her phone and I knew instinctually that pocket is where she'd want it, a theory I proceeded to test. And naturally, I was correct.

I like to stay sharp about people. It's how I win.

A test of a theory; nothing more. And her, she was an open book, barely guarding herself from the likes of me.

You're very kind.

Lack of survival skills. Not a good look on a woman.

With this I dismiss her.

Though I have to say, my colleagues' assessment of her as a gray bird is off, and shows how woefully inaccurate their reading of her was. A gray bird is a common bird and she was anything but. What's more, they had the color palette wrong; this woman was more like sandstone, pale and subtly golden, her hair just a shade darker than the freckles that cover her face like dusky constellations. Her nose curved just so, the faintest shape of a ski slope. And the quick, efficient way she moved her strong, slim fingers—they wouldn't have noted that. Her scent—something raspberry coconut. Probably shampoo.

And really, the prim little bow around her collar. For one long, strange moment I imagined undoing it.

Undo the bow. Undo her. Like opening a guileless little gift. Unwrapping her neck, pale and bare. And then a button. Another button. Freckled skin flush with heat. Fingers on pale skin, scattering every last one of her little secrets out of every last one of her hidden little pockets.

You're very kind.

What would it take to undo her? What would that frank, wide-open gaze look like all heated up?

More to the point, why am I still thinking about her? I have a million things to think about, and they don't include her. I need to be thinking about a certain merger right now—I actually budgeted this transit time for that.

I put my phone in front of my face. When I have any kind of screen in front of my face, that's a sign not to speak with me, my own version of a head on a pike. Because the other secret to my success is rigid time management.

I lower my phone and put my hand to my neck. "And what the hell exactly was that? What she was wearing? Around her neck?"

"It's called a butterfly tie," Lynette says. "It's a women's bow tie."

I wait for more. When more is not forthcoming, I say, "A women's bow tie." The secret to getting people to tell you things is that you repeat their last few words. There's nothing more stimulating to people than their own words.

As one of my lawyers, Lynette's seen me use that technique hundreds of times but she still falls for it. "A women's bow tie, very Kmart circa 1989. A little bit Korean schoolgirl, a little bit country-mouse-goes-to-Sunday-school. It's not something anybody would ever wear."

"Women are wearing bow ties now?" Kaufenmeier asks. "Can you all leave one thing to us?"

"No, she wasn't wearing a bow tie like a man wears," Lynette explains. "A butterfly tie is a largish bow with the ends trailing out. Imagine a slim-ish scarf tied in a bow around her neck, though I'd bet any amount of money it's pre-tied and she clips it on. That would be so gray bird."

I frown. The clip-on aspect definitely ruins my fantasy—you can't slowly pull the end of a clip-on bow and untie it. You cannot pull it clear of the collar with slow, taunting deliberation.

If she were mine, I'd demand that it be an actual long bit of fabric tied around her collar that I could untie, like untying the bow on a gift, the gift in this scenario being her complete and utter undoing. I'd pull it out from under her collar, slowly. Pull it away. And then the buttons, one, two, three. A scrap of a bra, white, no frills.

The elevator comes to a stop on six. We get off and I head to my office, mind spinning on the country mouse down there.

Is it a clip or a tied bow? A tied bow would also be best because once undone, the tie would be there. Always useful for sexual hijinks. I'd hold it up in the air to show her. Would her gaze change then? Would she finally feel wary?

Though there's something to be said for the pre-tied bow. Any woman that I could take seriously as a human being would clip on a pre-tied bow. Fashion is an incredible waste of time. A woman I'd take seriously would appreciate that. She'd be interested in efficiency and order and not wasting the time of tying the bow.

So now I have two too many sexual fantasies about some country mouse I'll never see again.

Or will I?

Who is she? What business does she have here? My business has a lot of different segments. Was she going to HR?

I pick up the papers on my desk. These are things I need to sign. There are tabs by the contract changes.

I grab my pen, imagining tracing my tongue along that coy curve of her nose. I imagine her sprawled beneath me, hair a sandstone halo around her head, and she's undone and panting, naked in my bed. Or naked except for the butterfly tie.

I swallow back the dryness in my mouth.

One of the admins comes in. "Oh, I'm sorry," he says. He's here for the contract.

"No, hold on." I look at the changes and sign, hand it over. "Tell me, is HR conducting interviews today?"

"Interviews for what?" he asks.

"Interviews for hiring," I say. "Find out."

3

Noelle

THE ELEVATOR I'm allowed in only goes up to the second floor. I get out and step up to the desk. A woman on the phone there holds up a finger, signaling that I'm to wait. She has red hair tightly coiled into a bun on top of her head with a little braid woven in and out. According to the little sign, her name is Anya.

"Can I help you?" Anya asks.

"I need to see Mr. Blackberg, please."

"Do you have an appointment with Mr. Blackberg?"

"I have something that I have to show to him," I say. "Regarding a property."

"Appointment?" she asks again.

"No," I say.

"You can't see him without an appointment. You'll want to call the main line."

I clutch my bag, feeling the outline of the iPad with the movie cued up. "I feel that he'll want to see what I have."

"You have to talk to his staff. The number's on our site."

"It's time-sensitive. It pertains to 341 West Forty-fifth Street, a property he recently purchased."

"In what way is it time sensitive?" Anya asks.

I suck in a breath. "In a way pertaining to the property. He needs to see it."

"You're going to have to give me more than that," she says.

"Something for his eyes only," I say. "Extremely important."

She regards me for a bit. She picks up a phone. "I've got a woman with something about 341 West Forty-fifth," she says, sizing me up. Then, "She won't say. Mr. Blackberg's eyes only? I don't know. She thinks it's urgent but she won't say."

She sets down the phone. "This way." She leads me down a hall past a row of cubicles. We pass another elevator. This one, too, has a black pad. Do the black pad elevators lead to the offices above? We arrive at a door bearing the name Janice West. The woman with the red bun knocks.

"Wait," I say. "It's Mr. Blackberg who I need to see. It has to be him."

A female voice. "Yeah."

Anya gestures me through the open door.

Janice West is a stately woman in her forties with a long neck, black hair, and bright red lips. "What is it that you have to show Mr. Blackberg?"

"It's exclusively for Mr. Blackberg."

"That's not how this works," Janice says. "I'll take a look at whatever you have that's so very urgent, and I'll decide if it seems important enough to pass upstairs."

"It's for him alone to—"

"The answer's no." She waves a hand for Anya and me to skedaddle.

"Come on, then," Anya says.

"No, wait," I say. "It's from the tenants. Things he needs to know about the building."

"There's nothing he needs to know about the building. He's knocking that building down, and that tends to get rid of the issues with a building," Janice says.

"No, we need him to know...look, we're losing our homes. There's just this small film I wanted to show him. It shows what the place means to us..."

"That would be a hard no," Janice says. "The hardest of hard nos."

"You're leaving," Anya says.

"But we're losing our *homes*."

Janice says, "There's nothing anybody can do about that."

I don't know why this makes me mad, but it really does. "Mr. Blackberg could do something about it. He could change his mind—I heard there are other ways he could execute this project. If he could just see it. Look...it's just us telling..." I open the small portfolio and turn on the screen and press play, tilting it so that they both can see it. I have it cued up to a part with Maisey. She's the most persuasive. She starts talking about what 341 means to her.

"Good lord," Janice groans.

"Come on, then," Anya says.

"A minute of his time?" I close the portfolio, cutting off Maisey's story.

"Here's what you need to understand," Janice says. "Bambi and Mother Teresa could chain themselves to that building and Mr. Blackberg wouldn't stop the wrecking ball. In fact, if Bambi and Mother Teresa chained themselves to the building, he'd take great pleasure in swinging the wrecking ball himself."

I grip my iPad. What kind of person would demolish a building more gleefully if Mother Teresa and Bambi were chained to it? This is who has our fate in his hands?

"I won't believe that," I say, remembering the way Malcolm Blackberg tucked my phone into the just-right little pocket, a small, kind gesture offered as I squatted there, dying of nervousness. I have the crazy thought that these women just don't get him.

"He'd take extra pleasure in demolishing it," Janice says. "Like it or not, I'm doing you a favor. Because if I sent you upstairs and by some miracle—and trust me, it would have to be a miracle—they let you through, and you showed him those few seconds of your little movie? He'd speed up the timeline. If there's one thing Mr. Blackberg hates, it's his time being wasted with things like this."

"Leave with me or be escorted by security," Anya says.

Defeated, I follow Anya and her bright bun back toward the front. She walks me right to the elevator and pushes the down button. There is only a down button.

The elevator dumps me back into the grand lobby.

This can't be it. It can't be over now.

I linger for a while, pretending to wait for an elevator. I can't run back home with my tail between my legs.

I watch a person wave a card in front of the black box that goes to the higher-up offices. The card hangs around her neck. What if I went and stood next to her? And just got on with her? I watch the doors open. She sees me watching and frowns. I lose my nerve and watch the doors shut.

I decide I'll try to join the next person. Somebody else waves a card in front of the box. I go up and stand next to him, try to look like I belong.

He glances at me and then forward. Then at me again. "Can I help you?" he asks.

I smile brightly. "Heading up to six."

"Where's your lanyard?" he asks.

I put my hand to my chest. "Oh...I don't have it."

"You work on six?"

"Uhh...no," I say.

He shakes his head. "Floor two." He points at the other elevator.

"Thank you," I say.

I catch sight of the security guard watching me. He has his phone out and he's speaking into it, watching me.

I head around the boulder fountain, toward the exit.

There's a letter carrier coming through with her cart. Something in me calms. I hold the door for her and she thanks me and continues on. I watch her as she moves across the lobby. The security guard meets her at the elevators. He waves a card in front of the black pad. The doors open. She gets on with her cart and smiles.

The doors close.

And now he looks my way.

He really is going to toss me out now. I turn and start walking. I burst out onto the bright sidewalk...with a shocking new idea forming in my mind.

4

Noelle

I TOOK ANOTHER DAY OFF, but I'm wearing my uniform, with my trusty blue bag slung around my shoulder.

I watch myself stroll into Blackberg Plaza. I could get in trouble for this, but I remind myself that life is too short not to do the important things, even if those things are scary and possibly deranged.

And there's nothing more important than my friends. They're my family.

Francine and Jada were so amazed when I told them my new plan. They think I'm brave.

More like desperate.

I round the fountain and head to the security desk. The bushy-bearded guard comes out. He doesn't recognize me from yesterday—yet. People rarely recognize letter carriers in their civilian clothes, and vice versa. When you put on the uniform, your identity is the US Mail, and you're welcome everywhere.

I show him the small package that I've addressed to

Malcolm Blackberg. This morning I put a red "registered mail" sticker on it, and then I added a blank sticker, where I wrote "restricted delivery" and "addressee only" in bold black ink.

Restricted delivery mail is to be delivered to the addressee only, though it can also be delivered to an addressee's authorized agent. I'm hoping they're not too familiar with that part of the rule.

He walks me to the elevator, opens it with his card, and gives me a smile with nary a whiff of recognition.

"Thank you," I say, clutching my bag. I examine the buttons and hit floor six.

"Excuse me," A pretty woman in an elegant red suit shows a card to the guard. "I'm from Bexley Partners. I have a ten o'clock on six that I'm running late for and they said to check in with you."

"Yup, they just called." The guard slaps his hand over the closing doors and pushes them open. "Go on."

"Thanks," she says, walking in with a tentative smile for me. She has short blonde hair and wonderful red and white heels

I nod and adjust my bag. My pulse races as the door closes and the elevator begins its ascent.

We ride in silence.

The secretaries and assistants will probably try to sign for it, but I'm planning on saying it has to go to Mr. Blackberg personally. I'll just insist and I won't stop insisting. The uniform carries a lot of weight, and I'm counting on that.

The elevator seems to be slowing, buttons lighting sluggishly from floor one to floor two to three. Just before it reaches the fourth floor, there's a loud crack above us. I clutch the rail as the car shakes violently.

It tilts and grinds to a halt. The whole car goes dark, then another light blinks on—some kind of emergency light from the corner.

"Oh, my god," the woman says, clinging to the rail on her side.

My heart whooshes in my ears. It's all I hear in the total silence. "Okay," I say, "it's not crashing."

"*Yet*," she says.

"They have a lot of safeties on these things," I say.

There's another creak.

"There should be an emergency call, right?" she says.

She's looking at me like I should know. I'm a New York City letter carrier. She thinks I should know things about elevators. She'd be surprised to learn that I rode an elevator for the first time in my life just two years ago.

I go over to the panel and squint in the dim light. The top button—a red one—has a raised image of a phone and some Braille next to it. I push it once. "Hello?"

Nothing.

The woman pulls out her phone and makes a call. She's saying she's going to be late to whoever is on the other end just about when a crackly voice comes through the panel. "Hey, this is engineering. Everyone okay in there?"

"Yeah," I say. "It's two of us, and we're fine. What's going on?"

"Nothing to worry about," the voice says. "Just electrical. You're in no danger. We've got a team on it. It'll be a few minutes. Are you good in there?"

I look over at the woman. "How long?" she asks the unseen person on the other end of the intercom.

"A bit."

She heaves a worried breath.

The guy asks for our names and we tell him. "Okay, Noelle and Stella, sit tight. We're working on this issue. Buzz if anything changes in there, okay?" With that he's off.

"If anything changes," she says. "What is he thinking might change in here? Like if we run out of air?"

"That won't happen," I say with more confidence than I feel. "He probably means in case one of us needs medical attention or something."

"Not exactly comforting." Stella slides to the floor and hugs her knees.

Clanking noises ring out above us. Stella winces with each clank, terrified gaze fixed on the elevator ceiling.

"Or in case of werewolf transformation," I add.

She turns a shocked gaze to me.

I give her a sassy little smile. "Appearance of vampire fangs?"

She laughs, relieved. "Oh my god, I thought you were serious for a sec," she says. "Sorry. Not my day. And I don't love elevators."

I get the feeling that this is an understatement. "We'll be fine," I say. I set down my bag and sit. "They really do have safeties."

The clanking stops. A drill begins to whir.

"Though I have a feeling 'a bit' is more than a few minutes," I add.

She sighs. "Actually, I'd rather be stuck in here than go to the meeting I'm supposed to be at. I'd prefer ice picks in my ears. Leeches sucking my blood. Kid Rock on endless loop."

"No," I whisper. *"Not that."*

She tips her head back on the panel. "You have a route to get to. Is this going to put you behind?"

I shrug. "I'll be okay. So, do you work here?"

"No," she says dolefully. "Or, I'm starting a month-long assignment here, so I guess."

"Sounds like you're not looking forward to it," I say.

"Understatement of the year," she sighs. "Don't say

anything."

"Of course not," I say.

She nods. People tend to trust the uniform. "And so begins the first day of many long days. Many long and excruciating days."

"That bad?"

"Worse," she says. "Six hours it took in traffic to get here this morning and now this. And the hell hasn't even started."

I give her a sympathetic wince. "Does your job always suck?"

"Kind of," she says. "You'd think it wouldn't. I'm an executive coach, which is technically a super cool profession."

"Executive coach?"

"We help executives build their skills. My area is soft skills, like emotional intelligence, building positive relationships, leading through inspiration, you know. The skills that enable a leader to aggressively build a business are not the same skills that allow them to be a good manager of people. Business-building is a transactional skill; management is more of a leadership skill. So we help them with that."

"That sounds like it would be really fulfilling," I say, though I'm surprised such a young woman would be teaching leadership to executives. She's a few years younger than I am for sure —twenty-six at the most.

"You'd think, right? And I'm with a really good boutique agency in Trenton. Very well respected." She hugs her knees harder to her chest. "Okay. I'm ready for the elevator to start. Now I'm dreading it even more, just sitting here. My first meeting would be underway by now. And afterwards I'd be out, walking into freedom. In the sunshine."

"Yikes," I say.

"No, I'm being negative. I love the material."

A drill *whirs* above us.

"So what's the problem? If you don't mind my asking."

"Here's the thing," she says. "There are two kinds of executives who get executive coaching from our company. There are the kinds that are excited to improve their skills, successful businesspeople who are fired up to be more effective leaders. They want to learn and grow. Unfortunately, I don't get to work with those kinds. My bosses take those jobs."

"What jobs do you get?"

"I'm the person they send when the executive has been on the losing end of a lawsuit and the person is" —here she makes quote fingers— "mandated by a court of law to undergo a program to be designed by an accredited executive coach to improve emotional intelligence skills." She sighs. "And guess who that lucky coach is?"

"Ouch."

"It's the worst," she says. "Like when some ragey guy gets into a fight and the court sends him to anger management. You think he wants to be there? You think he loves the material?"

"Uhh, no?"

"Right? The people who I coach don't want me. By the time I'm walking in, somebody on the leadership team has shown problematic behavior, and a mediator or judge has gotten involved. The training I do, it lets the company say they're addressing the issue, but they usually don't care if there's change. So yeah, I'm the punishment. I'm where they focus their resentment."

"Oh," I say.

"Oh my god, you seriously can't say anything. Not that I'd care if they fired me at this point," she says, checking her phone.

"Cone of silence," I say. "Everything stays in this elevator... except *us*. Hopefully."

There's more banging and whirring above us. Voices yelling back and forth.

"Like the people I work with—the *dudes* I work with, because let's face it, it's dudes we're talking about—they could not be more disdainful of the material. Basically I just try to do the minimum so that we both can say it happened. My firm gets paid...I don't know why I'm venting. It's just...not the job I envisioned when I did my training. I thought I'd help people, not be their hated punishment."

I nod sympathetically. Did somebody on Mr. Blackberg's leadership team get out of line?

"When they first sent me to do one-on-one coaching with a bigwig exec, I was so shocked. I mean, I have a psych degree and tons of coaching training, but no experience, and they're sending me to coach this C-suite guy? They put me right in on the A-list? Turns out I was on the grunt list."

"Is there nothing you enjoy about it?" I ask. "Maybe one nice thing?"

"No. You kind of have to be a self-starter, too. I think I picked the wrong job." She sighs. "Do you like being a mailperson?"

"Yeah," I say. "I love it."

"That must feel so good," she says. "To love what you do."

"It does," I say. "Having a job you love is amazing. And when life gets hard, having this one little area where you feel like you're making a positive difference means everything."

She looks at me longingly. "I wish I was making a positive difference."

"Aren't there other jobs you can get?" I ask.

"I feel like it's too late."

"Are you kidding? It's never too late to change. I don't care if you're thirty or fifty or seventy," I say. "What are you, twenty-six?"

"Twenty-seven."

"*Puh-lease.*" I tell her my story—how long I spent stuck in a rural town I hated, dreaming so hard of a different life, a better life, and never making it happen. Maybe it's just because she's a stranger in an elevator, but I even confess how my specific dream of having a clan of girlfriends in the Big Apple was inspired by reruns of *Sex and the City*.

I tell her how I'd look on Craigslist at roommate-wanted ads in New York and Brooklyn and dream of answering one of them. I'd even google the addresses and stare at the buildings, but I was so scared to make the move because I didn't know anybody, and also I had an on-again off-again boyfriend and a mother back in Mapleton. Then my mom got cancer. I tell her how hard I'd fought the insurance companies to get the care that Mom deserved, this special treatment that I wanted her to have, but they refused. And she died.

"And your dad?" she asks.

"Sperm bank. My mom was super independent—she was amazing. There was nothing she couldn't do. Until, you know..."

"I'm sorry," she says.

"Thanks," I say. "The point is, it made me aware of how short life is. And even though I was scared, I went home after that funeral and I looked at the Craigslist ads. And there was this roommate-wanted ad. The ad mentioned gourmet popcorn and watching Bachelorette with women from down the hall, and I went for it. After all those years I spent looking at Craigslist roommate ads and never answering them, wasting all this time in a place I wanted to leave, it took my mother dying for me to make the leap. And I'm so glad I did."

"I don't know if I'm gutsy like that."

"I'm not, either. Not at all! You just have to do it. Life is short, Stella."

"I don't think I can leave my job after investing so much time."

"But you hate it," I say. "And you said even if you get the

good jobs, you don't think you're good at it."

"True." She picks at a sticker on her briefcase. "And I hate my bosses for sending me to coach these assholes. And I don't even get insurance."

"Seriously?" I scowl. "No insurance? You work full-time with no insurance?"

"I'm technically a contractor. A way for them to get out of paying benefits. God, it's not a very good job, is it?"

"Tell me, Stella, if you could do anything, what would you want to do?"

"Quit. Give them the big FU and blow my entire paycheck on shoes. Or maybe a new outfit. No—a diamond tiara, and I'd wear it to the Plaza Hotel and drink an entire bottle of their best champagne all by myself and then pick up a hot guy."

"I meant a job. Think of what you'd do for work. Tomorrow. If you could wake up and have any career."

"I don't know."

"Think big," I say. "Pie in the sky."

"Wellllll...There *is* one thing I could do," she says.

"What?"

"My friend Jaycee is going to Estonia to teach English. She's leaving this week. She invited me, like they need teachers. I guess that's kind of my Craigslist ad, because she's invited me before, and I always turn her down, but I like working with kids, and I think it would be really fun. It's this girls school. I even looked it up on Google maps. It's this sweet little school. And I do enjoy teaching..."

"Hold the phone," I say. "You're telling me that you have an actual opportunity to do this cool thing instead of coaching some guy who's going to be a jerk to you, and you're choosing the jerk?"

"Well, I have a lease. Bills to pay."

"Hold out your hands," I say.

She regards me warily. "Why?"

"Hold out your hands. Show me your hands."

She holds them out.

"That's funny," I say. "I don't see any handcuffs there, do you? I don't see a leash around your neck. Looks to me like you're a free operator with your own freaking life."

She tucks her hands back in her lap, but I have her attention.

"Life is short," I say. "I know that's a cliché, but it's a cliché for a reason."

She turns and stares into the middle distance, blinking.

"I'm serious, Stella." I feel myself getting riled up. Sometimes I get overly passionate, but things with Stella seem so clear cut. "When this elevator starts up, you could choose to not get off at the sixth floor. You could hit that lobby button and get out down at the lobby instead. Wouldn't that be nice?"

"Yesssss," she says.

"Well?"

She looks longingly at the button marked L. "I couldn't."

"Stella, you have an actual job offer. You have an apartment? Fine. Go put your stuff in storage. Get a subletter, or just eat the deposit. Get a standby flight with your friend. Pay the bills from Estonia. I mean, there's actually a job for you doing this cool thing? And instead you're gonna spend these next how many beautiful days of your life with some jerk jerking you around? And you're not even getting health insurance?"

She's watching me, eyes wide. "And he really *will* jerk me around."

I shake my head. "You deserve better."

She blinks. "I *could* get a subletter. My asshole ex needs a place."

"There you go," I say.

She sniffs. "The overseas gig pay would be shit, but you get free room and board." She looks at me. "I would feel happy."

"Well?" I say.

"Shit," she laughs. "I can't."

"You'd rather go up there and coach the asshole?"

"No," she whispers, clutching her briefcase, blinking some more. "Oh my god, Noelle, am I going to do this?"

"Yes!" I practically scream.

"Yes!" She reaches out and grabs my hand. "Because, why not?"

"Right?" I say.

"I could leave this whole nightmare behind," she says.

I stand up and point to the lobby button. "This could be your next stop."

"Let me see if there's still room." She pulls out her phone and calls her friend and tells her she's thinking about going along. I'm trembling with excitement for her. Because her job sounds like it seriously sucks. Her friend's squealing—I can hear it through the phone.

She hangs up and tells me that her friend is gonna make some calls. There's still a need for teachers and there might even be empty seats on her connecting flight to Amsterdam. The friend is checking.

"I can't believe I'm stuck in this elevator with a letter carrier and you're telling me to quit my job."

"Why can't a letter carrier tell you to quit your job?" I ask.

Her phone rings. It's her friend, and it sounds like good news. "Okay, then, I'm in."

She puts away her phone. "Oh my god, I'm gonna do it. I am —I'm just doing it."

"Yay!" I say.

"And I'm going to quit with no notice. I'm just going to walk out and never look back as punishment for them sending me on the jerk missions."

"Are you sure you shouldn't let them know?" I try.

"No," she says gleefully. "Let them figure it out when I don't show up."

Inwardly I wince—I'm a total rule follower; I would never dream of walking off a job without giving some kind of notice.

We're stuck for a good twenty minutes more. In that time she looks up a storage unit place and calls some people to help get her stuff into storage. The overseas-English-teacher people are working on an expedited visa.

The engineers tell us they're finishing up.

She turns to me. "Thank you. I'm like, happy again."

"You're welcome. But you made the plan. You're taking the leap."

"But you gave me the push." She digs a business card out of her briefcase and hands it to me. "That email address won't work as soon as they figure out I'm AWOL, but the mobile's good. If you ever need anything, you got it. If you ever go to Estonia, you have a place to crash, sister."

"Send me a postcard," I say. I grab a scrap of paper and write down my home address and phone number.

"Cool beans." She takes it.

Finally, the car lurches to the next floor and the doors open. We get out into the cool air. It's the fifth floor, and guys with toolboxes and phones are waiting. They apologize profusely. One hands us waters. Another does some work on the button panel.

We're supposed to get into the other elevator to continue on to the sixth floor, but Stella informs them that she's going to the lobby.

I hug her and wish her luck.

Talking to Stella was a perfect diversion, but ten minutes later I'm back to reality, getting out alone on the sixth floor with my bogus delivery. I head for the front desk, grateful that there's no sign of Janice or Anya.

Like everything in this place, the front desk is sleek and polished and possibly made of black marble. The two men and one woman perched behind it are intent on their work.

"You got this," I say to myself, pressing my bag to my belly. If Stella can drop everything and go to Estonia, I can pretend Malcolm Blackberg's personal signature is required on a delivery.

My new plan is to tell him that he must watch the video as part of the delivery, that there's something he must see in it. I'm hoping that gets him curious enough to keep him glued to the screen. Curiosity will keep people watching something for a pretty long time, or at least, that's how it worked for me when we watched "Stranger Things."

I smile at the man at the end, the only one of the three people who makes eye contact with me. His dark hair is cropped short against his boxy head, and he wears wire-rimmed glasses.

"Another?" he asks.

"Yup. Addressee only," I say.

"Sure thing." He holds his hand out for the electronic clipboard that I don't have.

"Sorry," I say. "Addressee only." I show him the front of it. "Mr. Malcolm Blackberg."

"We're all authorized agents to receive for Mr. Blackberg." He keeps his hand out for the clipboard.

"No, this is a delivery specifically for Mr. Blackberg. Only he can sign."

"We always sign for Mr. Blackberg's stuff," he says. "There's nothing we can't sign for."

I'd be impressed if my heart weren't pounding like a jackhammer on a pogo stick. "Addressee only," I say.

"Nobody delivers directly to Mr. Blackberg."

Another receptionist comes up beside him. "We're authorized agents. We can sign for his deliveries."

"This one is special." I set down my clipboard and Stella's card and show them the front of the envelope. "It must go to Mr. Blackberg himself."

The third receptionist comes over. "What's going on?" She squints at the envelope. "This isn't how we usually get private stuff. The private stuff comes by courier. I don't understand."

"This delivery requires Mr. Blackberg's signature," I say. "It's very unusual, I know. It's a video he must watch."

"A video?" She frowns at me.

"My instructions are very specific," I say.

The guy picks up Stella's card. "Ohhhhh, I get it." He shows the woman Stella's card. "This is who it's from. She was in the elevator that broke down."

"Ah," she says. "You're late, Stella."

"Your office called," the first guy says. "Sorry about that."

"I'm not Stella," I say. "I'm the letter carrier. With a very important delivery."

The other receptionist winks. "Right, you're the letter carrier. With a special delivery. That happens to be a video."

"Right," I say, "but I'm not Stella."

An older woman comes and takes Stella's card. "I'll tell him you're here."

The guy screws up his face and leans near to me, voice lowered conspiratorially. "Just no on the letter carrier shtick. Mr. Blackberg hates gimmicks. *Hates.*"

"I'm really just here to—"

"Yeah, yeah, yeah," he says. "Your funeral."

The woman is back. "He's ready for you, Stella."

"I'm not Stella..."

"We got it," she says, annoyed.

The guy comes out from behind the desk and beckons me to

follow him.

It's here that I realize I should just shut up, being that nobody else has gotten anywhere near this far in the quest to see Mr. Blackberg.

Tabitha's billionaire boyfriend, Rex, even tried to buy the building from him at one point, and Malcolm Blackberg seemed to take perverse glee in turning him down without so much as granting him a meeting. There's some thinking that Blackberg even sped up the eviction timetable because of Rex's offer. Tabitha feels sick about it, even though we all assure her that it's not her fault.

I follow the man into a luxurious little room with a couch and a selection of snacks. I stop him before he knocks.

"Wait. Remind me...how long do you have budgeted for this meeting?"

"We slotted out the hour you requested, but he has an eleven hard stop that can't be moved. I know you were stuck in the elevator—just add more time to the back of the schedule or whatever you do and we'll approve it." With that he knocks.

"Thank you," I say, clutching the envelope with its rectangular bulge. It's ten forty. I have exactly twenty minutes to make him watch the video. It's twenty minutes more than I'd dared to hope for.

There's a grunt from inside—I can't tell what it means, but my guide seems to think it means *come in* because he proceeds to open the door to one of the most luxurious spaces I've even seen. Practically everything is black marble or steel.

The desk is a massive black marble slab atop a rough-hewn marble base that looks like it was forged by the axes of ogres.

There behind the desk sits Mr. Blackberg himself. He fixes me with a confused glower.

I'm a deer in headlights, gathering my wits.

"Stella from Bexley for your emotional intelligence training," he says, quickly closing the door and leaving me alone with him.

"I-I'm here with a delivery for you," I say, walking to his desk like a trembling virgin approaching a powerful god.

"*You're* to be the new executive coach?" he clips out in his English accent. "You?" This as if it might be the most bizarre happenstance ever.

"Seems I am," I say, taking a seat across from him.

"What was all that down in the lobby yesterday, then? Recon?" he asks.

He remembers me? One split second of interaction and he recognizes me, even when I wear the uniform? Nobody does that. "It's not important," I say.

"It's important to me. And what the hell kind of methodology is this?" he asks. "A letter carrier? Good god, tell me it's not to deliver a dose of reality or something." His accent makes everything he says sound more angular, somehow.

I suck up my courage—I have less than twenty minutes to get him to understand how much we cherish our building. "My methodology will not be part of the program."

I pull out the iPad, willing my fingers not to tremble. It's his stare. He has the fiercest eyes I've ever seen. True dagger-staring eyes. Make that longsword, crossbow, and battering-ram-staring eyes.

I set up amid the onslaught of his gaze.

"An iPad? That's your delivery?"

I punch in my code and Maisey's face fills the screen, telling how she's been in her apartment since 1972. She shows where she knits every evening. "This home is everything I have in the world," she says.

Malcolm snorts. "Is this some kind of joke?"

"No."

"What is it?"

"This is your training," I say, trying to sound in control.

"Please," he says, voice dripping with annoyance.

I stop the video, trying to remember the words that Stella used in the elevator. "This is your court-mandated session," I say. "Court-ordered."

"A video of some old lady? This is what I'm meant to watch? Hard pass."

Can he refuse like that?

I'm supposed to be training him, but it feels like he's the one in charge. The silence grows. A panicky feeling washes over my skin.

But then I remember this one time at the Bronx substation, when a police officer tried to bully me into handing over a postal customer's mail. The postal customer was a suspect in something, but the mail is sacrosanct. I informed the police officer that he couldn't take the mail without a warrant. The police officer kept hammering at me, giving reasons why I had to give it that minute.

I felt so scared and unsure, so I called my postal inspector and she told me it doesn't matter what anybody says or demands. "Just repeat what you know over and over," she'd said. "You don't need more argument than a rule. A rule is the end of an argument."

I jut out my chin and repeat Stella's words best I can, "You were mandated by court of law to undergo a program designed by an accredited coach to improve your emotional intelligence. Th-this is that program."

"I don't think so," he says.

"It's court-mandated," I say.

He just glowers.

I draw in a breath. "You were mandated to undergo a program to be designed by an accredited executive coach, were you not?"

His gaze burns at me. "And this is what you designed? What does whining about a building have to do with emotional intelligence?"

Repeat the rule, repeat the rule. "This is a program designed by an accredited executive coach," I say.

"And will the film be featuring Corman at some point? Telling the tragic story of being fired by me?" he asks. "I'll tell you right now—it was worth it. I'd do it again, lawsuit and all."

I blink, unsure what he's talking about, though I'm thinking Corman must have something to do with why Malcolm ended up with a court-ordered coach.

I've never met anybody like him. He's a powerful, world-class beast of a man who belongs in a powerful world-class beast of a city like New York. A man who thinks Jada's film is a joke. It's not a joke, and Maisey is not "some old lady."

Straighten up, make eye contact, speak from the belly, feel your voice resonate—that's what my actress friend Mia always says when she tries to get me to be more assertive.

I straighten up. "You were mandated to undergo a program to be designed by an accredited executive coach." I continue, feeling my voice resonate. "You are to watch it. Or...we'll add more time to the back of the schedule, the back of the court-mandated hours."

Oh my god. I sound demented. What am I even saying?

I hold my breath. No way will this work.

A muscle in his jaw fires. He gestures at the iPad. "Get on with it, then."

Wait, what? It worked? I can't believe it worked.

I start the iPad again. We have ten minutes left. Maisey tells about the time Jada cared for her when she got her broken hip. How the building is her only family. The movie cuts to Lizzie, telling how much she missed her family in Fargo. "All my friends in the world are here. This is my home," Lizzie says.

I feel his eyes on me.

I straighten. Speaking from my belly best I can, I say, "You're not watching."

"Yes, I am."

The video plays on. Jada really did a nice job on it—she's an actress but she's really interested in the filming side of things, too.

After a few more minutes, he says, "I have an eleven hard stop. Compelling as this all is."

It's ten fifty-two. Disheartened, I stop the video. "Those are people who live at 341 West Forty-fifth Street," I say. "Are you familiar with it? It is a building that you're about to tear down."

His eyes narrow, as if in confusion, and then he smiles. His smile is huge and beautiful and it lights up his face and sets my heart pounding. His smile is the sun, blazing with light and warmth.

Am I actually getting through to him?

"That woman was Maisey Belleweather," I continue. "She's seventy-three, a retired Macy's clerk. Without that community in that building, she'll be alone in the world."

"Very good, very good."

What?

He stands and leans in toward me. I'm aware of him the way I was in the lobby—his size. His heat. He whispers, "I know what you're doing, of course."

"What are you talking about?"

"Oh come off it. This isn't leadership sensitivity coaching or emotional intelligence training or whatever it's supposed to be. They mean to torture me."

I stare at him, stunned. "That's what you think I'm doing?"

He looks back. "I'd fire my employment law firm for agreeing to this if I didn't already do it."

"It's not torture," I say. "It's real."

Malcolm

ONE OF THE most diabolical punishments devised by the monsters who ran Soviet-era prison camps was to force an inmate to toil away for days on end digging a massive hole. As soon as the unfortunate prisoner had completed a big, beautiful perfectly-shaped hole, they would force them to fill the hole back in with dirt.

It was an awful punishment because there's nothing more repugnant to the human soul than wasted labor, squandered time. Time is one's most precious resource.

It's clearly this principle that Corman and his lawyers had in mind in devising this. No doubt they worked overtime creating a program that would be as maddeningly useless as possible. God, I can just picture them cackling over scotches.

Stella gives me a blank look and blathers on about 341 West 45th. Yes, I know the address; it's going to be part of the Square West project.

"Is something funny?" she asks.

"Not in the least," I say. I really do have to hand it to them—the video is nearly unbearable.

But they made one very large mistake: her.

My last coach was a humorless old buzzsaw, but Stella's hot —especially if you removed the boxy and clearly fake letter carrier uniform, which I would very much enjoy doing.

And what was up with the outfit yesterday? Was that butterfly bow tie part of the show? Or is that what she really wears? Is she an entry-level coach of some sort? A hot rube who took a few seminars? I study her eyes as she goes on about the rooftop, something about flowers on the rooftop.

Her eyes are army green. Army green is technically a drab color, or at least it's a drab color in fabric, but it's startlingly beautiful in her eyes. Her butterscotch hair is clipped back on one side with a simple golden clip that allows it to cascade over her shoulders like a quiet waterfall. She really is pretty in an understated way.

Is that part of the torture?

She's continuing to talk, but I can't be bothered to listen, though I'm definitely playing the part of a listener.

She won't stop talking about these people. Did she pre-watch all the videos and get whipped up into a lather? She seems almost passionate about these people's plight, like some kind of Joan of Arc. A pure and incorruptible warrior. Being riled up really does lend her an extra spark of something... there's this vibrancy about her.

Is it truly possible she has twenty-one hours of that footage? *Twenty-one hours?* People have been complaining about the Square West project. Is that where they got this footage? From the gang of people complaining? Corman wasn't in my real estate group, but I suppose he could've heard about the complaints and stumbled upon the footage, and from there, devised this program.

My buzzer goes off. I grab my phone and shut off the alarm. "It's eleven," I say. "We need to wrap up for today, much as it pains me."

"But what do you think?" she asks, eyes wide. "About sparing them. There are other ways to achieve your goal. Why not consider them?"

"Nope," I say.

"But...if you could achieve your goals while sparing this building..."

"If the rest of your ridiculous program is anything like this little intro, well, I just can't imagine the fun. I really can't." I grab my briefcase. "Poor old Maude whining about her hip. I can't wait for more of that. Solid gold stuff!"

She stiffens, annoyed. "Her name is Maisey," she bites out.

So hot.

"Maisey, then, excuse me. Maisey. Poor Maisey with her hip. And her home going to be knocked down by Scrooge."

Stella's nostrils flare. She's unbelievably delicious—she really is.

I almost wish I didn't have to be across town in thirty. I'd like to stand here and upset her some more. Don't send a boy to do a man's job—isn't that how the American saying goes? And you definitely don't want to be sending a hot little country mouse like Stella.

"Scrooge wouldn't have knocked it down," she says.

"Coaching *and* a literary discussion. I can't wait for more of your presentation, I really can't— four weeks of whining Mary Ann, or at least, one can hope."

I wait for her to take issue with the name again. But she just says, "Four weeks?"

"And then you'll get to put Blackberg Inc. on your resume. Quite the feather."

"Four weeks," she says, as though she hasn't comprehended that part of it.

I really should go, but I find that I don't want to. Getting a rise out of this one is more enjoyment than I've had in a very long time. I narrow my eyes. "Unfortunately, I will be bulldozing poor old Maimie's building at the end of it all." I gaze into her eyes. I set my hand on my desk, wrist down, fingers up. Slowly I begin to push a few things across, mimicking a bulldozer. "*Vrum-vrum-vrum,*" I tease.

She gets the strangest look on her face right then—that little spark flaring into an angry flame.

My pulse races. I have the improbable urge to kiss her, to consume all of that soft-looking skin and affronted purity.

"And regarding these negotiation sessions this week?" I continue, "I don't care what the settlement says or how tightly the board has my balls wound up, there's no way I'm having you tagging along in that Halloween costume. That is not happening. Yes, you get to observe and critique my soft skills and pass along what I'm sure is very road-tested knowledge that you have for how to run a company, but I will not have you making Blackberg, Inc. into a sideshow. You're supposed to blend in with the team during the sessions—zero disruptions—that is the agreement. So this postal bit? Right?" I point at her costume. "Not happening."

Shock lights her freckled features. Did she expect to wear it?

Lawrence pops his head in. "Bird's waiting."

I point at her. "Go. Figure it out with Lawrence." I point at Lawrence. "The costume bit?" I draw a finger across my neck.

"Come on, then," Lawrence says.

She gives me a bewildered look and scurries out after Lawrence, shutting the door softly behind her.

I grab my coat and head out the other way, getting Brandon on the phone as I take the stairs to the roof two at a time.

"What the hell is this emotional intelligence training? Are you aware of this so-called training program they've concocted for me?" I bark.

"Um..." I hear keys clicking in the background. "An associate from Bexley Partners was stipulated. You had the ten o'clock intro session today. Everything okay? I mean, as okay as it can be, considering..."

"Considering that they're wasting my time in the most outrageous way they could dream up? Somebody's messing around here, because I don't know what that training was..."

"Was it not emotional intelligence training?" he asks. "It seems like a pretty flexible descriptor but..."

"I can't imagine what just happened is what anybody would have in mind."

"Really," he says. "The agreement was fairly ironclad, but it did stipulate emotional intelligence training, and if we can prove that the training doesn't rise to that level, then maybe there's wiggle room to get a different executive coach. We can't get you out of it, but if you're feeling a personality issue and we can maybe make them send somebody else—"

"Wait! No, no, I was just curious." I stop at the door. I can hear my chopper on the other side. "Did Corman's people suggest this firm?"

"I don't know. I can find out. Do you want me to look into lodging a complaint?"

"No, no, wait." I pinch the bridge of my nose. What am I doing? Why did I call him? "Don't do anything. Better the devil you know."

"Depends on the devil," he says.

6

Noelle

I FOLLOW Lawrence up to the desk, heart thundering. I'm waiting for him to realize I'm not Stella and throw me out.

But it seems like I get to give him another lesson tomorrow. They all seem to be expecting it. I could actually make him watch more of Jada's film.

I told my friends that if he watched enough of it, if he got to know the people in the building, maybe he'd have a change of heart. I still believe it—I don't care what anybody says.

And more than that, I think there is kindness in him; I really do. I thought it from the first moment with us squatting on the floor, that strange moment where the hardness went out of his eyes and he tucked my phone into the correct pocket. Even my roommate, Francine, wouldn't think to do that.

It was...sweet. The gesture of one person truly seeing another.

"Everything okay?" Lawrence asks, heading around to the other side of the desk.

"Yeah," I say.

He hits a few keys. "You want your lanyard to say Stella?"

Gulp. A lanyard? With a fake name? That feels...so official. But if there's a chance I can show him more of the movie tomorrow, I have to take it.

I straighten up. "Have the lanyard say Elle," I say. "E-L-L-E." I choose that because it rhymes with Noelle. It seems like it would be easier to answer to. And it feels less like lying.

He holds up his phone. "Smile."

"What?"

He snaps a picture, takes a look, and laughs. His face softens when he laughs. I like his impish smile. "We better try that again. You look like you just saw a ghost."

I give him a polite smile and he takes a new picture. He seems happy with that one. He's doing phone things now and bustling around.

"What's the picture for?" I ask.

"Your lanyard. Security credentials." He bustles at the other end.

This is absurd—they actually think I'm his coach! Maybe I could do just one more session. Or maybe two. I bite back a smile when I picture the amazement on my friends' faces when I tell them I not only got into Malcolm's office, but I made him watch the video. And that I'm doing it again tomorrow. They'll die.

"How's the room?" Lawrence asks.

"The room?"

"You didn't check in yet?"

"Uh, no," I say.

"Mmm," he says.

"Six hours it took me to get here this morning," I hear myself say, echoing Stella's words.

"Ouch. You leave your bags with security?"

What bags? I make a non-committal sound.

He comes back waving a card in the air. "Gotta let it cool down." He puts a lanyard on the desk. "Clip those together." He returns to his screen. "Not that you'll need ID with the San Fran traveling team, but it's unlikely we'll be there the entire four weeks. I'm going, too." He smiles up at me. I smile back. Something dings and he looks back down. "Hold on a sec." He types something into his computer and then walks to the other end of the desk area.

San Fran? As in San Francisco?

What am I doing? I can't go to San Francisco with them.

But then I remember the way Malcolm imitated a bulldozer, pushing things across his desk toward me. Like it was funny to him. And I picture my friends all waiting back at the building, counting on me.

And I imagine how it would feel to stand there across 45th, outside the little Korean market, watching the wrecking ball smash into the side of our beloved home. Watching a bulldozer pile up the rubble. How could I forgive myself, knowing I had the chance to find some humanity in him, to change his mind, and I didn't take it?

And I do have more vacation days. Lots.

Can I pull it off?

But I already know I'm going to do it. My pulse races. It's so outrageous.

"So, about tomorrow," I say.

"We'll send the car at two," Lawrence says. "We'll call when it's on the way and you can go down to the lobby. And you heard his thing about no more postal costumes."

"Downstairs?"

"Not *this* lobby, the Four Seasons? Why would we make you come all the way back here?" He looks up, dubious about me, now. "It's all in your packet. We take off at around four."

Then a bad thought strikes me. "Wait, my plane ticket..." The plane ticket would say Stella's name. No way will they let me on without a driver's license with a name that matches.

"What are you talking about?" he asks.

"I don't know if I...brought my license and...the airport."

"It's a company jet," he says. "You don't need a ticket on a private jet. We know who you are, right?"

"Oh, right," I say. "Right."

"Have you even looked at the packet? The itinerary?"

"I'm sorry," I say.

He sighs. "You need to read it. And you need to be out there, ready and on time." He holds up Stella's card. "Is this the best number to reach you at?"

"No," I say. "Let me give you my personal phone."

He slaps down the card. I cross out Stella's number and write mine over it and hand it back.

"Don't be late," he says.

I assure him that I won't, and grab the next elevator, punching the lobby button. The elevator stops at the second floor.

Janice gets on.

Gulp.

She nods at me. I nod back. We both turn to look at the closed door in front of us. I wait for her to say something but...nothing.

Apparently the only person in the world who recognizes me in my uniform is Malcolm, for whatever strange reason.

I pull out my phone and look up the nearest Four Seasons. I'm going to have to check in there if I don't want to raise suspicions. Will they need my driver's license? I've stayed at plenty of roadside motels, but never a hotel.

As luck would have it, there's a Four Seasons two blocks away. That has to be the place.

My feet take me there. A smiling doorman opens the door for me. I fish out my last few one-dollar bills.

He gives me a confused look.

"Right," I say. I'm in uniform. He thinks I'm on the job.

The Four Seasons lobby is incredible—luxuriously hushed in contrast to the cacophony outside, and there's a fountain and posh rugs and chandeliers—a regular palace.

I go up to the desk.

The woman tilts her head. "Our ten o'clock was already here."

"Oh, no, I'm not here for the mail. I'm Stella Myers." Inwardly I cringe, hating to outright lie like that, especially when I have the uniform on. I show her the badge and lanyard that Lawrence created for me.

"Oh, you're in one of the Blackberg suites." She hands over a packet with two keycards, and runs through the things like complimentary coffee in the lobby from six to ten. She points me toward the elevators.

Minutes later, I'm flopped sideways on the cloud-like bed in my new hotel room. Just beyond is a picture-postcard view of New York.

I roll over and begin to study the packet that the lobby clerk gave to me, but it just tells about the hotel; I'm pretty sure it's not the packet that Lawrence was talking about.

Obviously I won't be able to function without that packet, but how am I going to get it? I could try to get in contact with Stella, but I can't imagine she'd be very happy about what I'm doing. Which maybe means I shouldn't be doing it?

I grab my phone and call Francine. Francine always knows what to do.

"Galpal!" she squeals. "How did it go? Where are you?"

"Well, Francine, I'm in my room at the Four Seasons," I say.

"What are you doing at the Four Seasons?"

"Funny story..." I tell her about the case of mistaken identity, and showing Malcolm the video, and tomorrow's travel plans, which apparently involve me.

"Oh my god, Noelle. What?!"

"I know. What am I even thinking? I can't fly to San Francisco with these strangers! I mean, what if they call the Bexley office? I need to get out of here."

"Wait, hold on, let's think this through. Why would they call the Bexley office?" she asks.

"I don't know! I'm just a letter carrier. I don't know the world of executive emotional intelligence coaching."

"Just don't do anything yet." Voices in the background. I can hear Francine talking to somebody. "...thought she was his executive coach and she went with it!" There's laughter. The story is repeated. "No way! *Noelle?*" Murmuring voices. Knocking. The story is told again. More surprise.

"Excuuuuuuse?" That would be Jada. I can hear Tabitha's laughter. And then Lizzie's.

I stand at the window.

"Look, sit tight," Francine says. "We're coming over."

"I feel like a hunted fugitive already," I say.

"We're gonna think it through," Francine assures me. "Together."

7

Noelle

JADA IS FLOPPED on my cloud-like bed with Antonio. Her bright blond hair is a perfect contrast to his rich dark curls, and her sparkly boots are on the quilt.

"Don't mess up the bed," I say.

"This is your room, you're supposed to mess up the bed," Jada says.

Antonio agrees. He swigs water from a plastic bottle.

"Antonio, where did you get that?" I ask. "You didn't take that off of the dresser, did you?"

"Noelle, those are complimentary," Lizzie says from the chair by the window. "It's fine. It would be weird if you *didn't* drink water or sit on the bed."

"I guess," I say.

"You are so cute." Francine pushes her red glasses higher on her nose. Her silky black hair is still in her ballerina bun. "You are such a Girl Scout."

I cringe.

"It's what I love about you!" she adds.

I snort, feeling my face redden. I lean back against the dresser, wringing my hands. "Seriously, how long can I pull this off? The Bexley people might be figuring it all out right now, as we speak," I say. "And then they call Blackberg? Or Stella? How will Stella feel about all this? Probably not a hundred percent. Oh my god, what am I doing?"

"Don't worry, Stella sounds like a serious screwup," Lizzie says. "Trust me, I'm a boss. It's hard to get good help. They're not going to expect her to call right in. And do you think she'll answer if the office calls? You think Stella wants to talk to the bosses that she hates? Probably not."

"Probably not," I echo.

We're waiting for Willow to arrive. Willow is going to try to hack into Bexley Partners' intranet and get the packet. Our little caper is moving really fast.

Lizzie comes over and grabs my hands. "Breathe," she says. "You did so amazing in there. And we would never want you to do something you don't want to do."

"I *do* want to do it," I say. "I really meant it when I said it—if he saw enough of the footage, it would change his heart. Nobody could watch that and not have a change of heart—I really believe that. And I do have way more than four weeks of vacation time stored up. My boss is on me to take it. I'll lose it if I don't use it. I just don't know…"

My friends stay silent. They would never push me into something that I'm uncomfortable with.

"I really do want to do it," I repeat. "But the whole plane ride and everything—I honestly don't think I'm capable of pulling this off. I feel like any one of you all could do better. Or Mia or Tabitha—one of those two could totally pull it off."

"Don't *even*." Francine says. "Seriously? Dude! Yesterday none of us could even get in talk to him. We'd all given up. And what did you do? You went and maneuvered yourself into a position to force Malcolm Blackberg to watch twenty freaking hours of us talking about our building." Francine jabs a finger at me. "*You* did that—not one of us, *you*. You see yourself as such a shrinking violet, always following the rules and never taking too much, but deep down, you're a fighter. You just don't know it."

"Twenty hours. I barely pulled off twenty freaking minutes. I felt like they were going to figure me out at any moment. I'm a terrible liar. And he already thinks the training we did is bizarre." It's not just that. It's him, too—the overwhelming handsomeness of him, his scathingly sexy accent, his gaze, hard and sparkling at the same time, suffused with intelligence.

"It sounds like he thinks it's part of a plot to punish him," Lizzie says, her glossy light brown hair shining in the afternoon light.

"Well, true," I say.

"So he's made a story for himself about why the training makes sense," Lizzie says. "What's the worst that can happen?"

"They throw me in jail?" I say.

"Doubtful," Lizzie says. "They'd kick you out and we'd buy you a plane ticket home. Don't forget, I worked in PR—trust me: nobody wants that news story. Think of it—a girl trying to save her home gets mistaken for the corporate coach and goes with it. And they fall for it? They would look like total idiots. Imagine if you last a few days—they would be a laughingstock, and it would bring negative publicity to their project. No guarantees, but I don't see you pressing license plates in Leavenworth. And worst case, if they did bring charges, who would convict you? You're alone in the world. You found this family. Trying to save your building."

"Agree," Jada says.

"You're probably right," I say. "But I could lose my post

office job—there's that. We are held to a certain code. I can't go around on my off hours being scammy."

Everybody's silent. They know how much I love my job with the USPS.

But then I'm thinking, for the umpteenth time, about how I backed off of the fight with my mom's insurance company too easily. I so regret not fighting to the end. And this is my family now—these neighbors of mine at 341 West 45th are the most important part of my life, though I might not ever confess that out loud to them. Because, pathetic much?

"However," I continue, holding up one lone finger in the air, "you know my favorite motto—through rain or sleet or snow..."

Lizzie claps.

Francine rubs my shoulders like I'm a prizefighter. "You got this."

Antonio pumps his fist in the air. "*Forza!*" he says.

I turn to Jada. "How many hours of that damn footage do you have? And don't forget, you have to edit me out."

"Will do!" she squeaks.

Lizzie gets a text. "Willow's here. Willow to the rescue!" She grabs a key card and heads out to get her. Willow Drummond is the sister of Lizzie's famous chemist husband, Theo Drummond, aka Lizzie's sister-in-law. Willow runs her own technology firm.

A few moments later, Willow is setting up on the beautiful cherrywood desk in my room. Her thick, dark hair is in a fun bob, and her T-shirt says "I paused my game to be here," which is probably true. She's given us all jobs; I'm plugging in cords, Antonio is adjusting her mobile hotspot, and Francine is opening one of the water bottles.

"No spilling," I say.

Francine rolls her eyes.

Willow sits, and suddenly her fingers are going like lightning over her keyboard as she tries to hack into Bexley Partners.

"Oh my god, I can barely watch," I say

"Nobody'll know," Willow says. "Sheesh, they have the ultimate small-potatoes system." She lectures us on using shitty passwords while she does her thing. Every now and then she goes, "Puh-lease," and then, "You can't make it just a little harder for people like me? You *wanna* get hacked? Yes, yes, little droogies, I think you wanna get hacked."

I widen my eyes at Francine, who does a little dance.

"Noelle," Willow says. "I'm setting you up with a new email address where all of Stella's emails will be going from now on."

"Really?"

She writes something on a Post-it and hands it over. "Why not check it now? Who knows, you might have email there right now."

The way she says it, I'm thinking I probably do. I sit on the bed with Jada and Antonio and check it.

"Yikes. This is all of Stella's work email from...forever," I say. "Oh, this is so wrong."

"We're not hurting anything," Willow says, still tapping at her keyboard. "So if you send an email, it will be coming from Stella's work email."

"Whoa."

Jada points to a subject line from a month ago with an attachment— "Blackberg info." I click it. There are a few attachments. I start reading.

"That is the motherlode," Francine says, reading over my shoulder.

I hit a file called backgrounder and we read.

"Oh, man, this backgrounder. Look—" Francine points to the bottom of the screen. "Malcolm didn't just fire this guy, Corman—he dragged him out through the lobby by his necktie and then punched him three times on the sidewalk. The emotional intelligence training you're doing gets him out of potential jailtime for misdemeanor assault. He's been brought up on assault before."

"Wonder what that Corman guy did," Antonio says.

Willow asks me for details on the town where I grew up. "Mapleton," I tell her. "Population 501. An old railroad town." I describe the hilly beauty of it.

"May I?" Lizzie motions at my iPad and I hand it over and answer more of Willow's questions.

"Okay, check this out," Lizzie says after a while. "This is the key to everything." She squeezes onto the bed next to me and Jada and Antonio and Francine, because at the Four Seasons, you can get five on a bed.

She has something new up on the screen.

"A link in the main packet led to this interactive form," she says. "This is your check-in. Every time Malcolm completes a session, you type a 'V,' and that makes a check mark. The only other option is to choose an 'X,' which I'm guessing is a fail. The blank box with today's date is where you'd give him a check mark for today's intro session. I'm thinking that's how it works."

I study the form. Today's session was supposed to last an hour and be about "setting expectations." After the intro session, there are twenty boxes. Twenty-one hours of training and twenty-one-plus hours of observation to be checked off.

"This is perfect," Lizzie says. "This is how you check into the office—by making checks and X's."

Willow comes over and takes my iPad, slides her finger around the screen. "It's more than that. This is everything. This is the job right here. This form is shared with two law firms and Blackberg HR."

She hands it back and we keep going through.

We find an info email that says, "Dear Stella, everything for the Blackberg job is enclosed, including co-branded shells."

"What are co-branded shells?" Antonio asks.

"Like stationary with both logos," Lizzie says. "Maybe she has to print out worksheets?"

"You have to make him do worksheets on the people in our building," Francine says, rubbing her hands. "He has to watch the videos and remember things about us!"

"What is the name of Tabitha's hamster?" Jada jokes. "What is Francine's Holy Grail as a dancer? What city did Antonio grow up in?"

Everybody is laughing now. Except me.

"What is the name of the cutest dog ever, according to residents of 341 West Forty-fifth?" Lizzie asks. "Five demerits if you get it wrong, motherfucker!"

"Be serious, you guys," I say. "This has to at least seem real. The man's not a dipshit."

"Incoming," Willow says.

More things appear in my mailbox. It's the instructional program Stella devised for Malcolm. A PDF workbook and discussion topics.

"It looks like she's just an independent contractor," Willow says. "They probably don't even have an on-site office for her."

"Yeah, she said she was a contractor," I say.

"I think as long as you keep checking off the boxes, you're good," Willow says.

"What about the comments area?" I ask. "I would never know what to put there. But I'm guessing Stella would probably just blow that area off."

Willow says, "Maybe you should check out the Bexley Partners website and read about Stella."

Jada's on it. She lets out a hoot of laughter. I lean over. My picture is on Stella's bio page. It says she's from a small town in Pennsylvania and is committed to the synergy of excellence."

"Synergy of excellence? Did you make that up, Willow?" Francine asks.

"Do you like it?" Willow asks. "I think it's hilarious."

"You guys, this isn't a joke," I say. "Also, you think the Bexley Partners themselves won't notice this?"

"Companies never look at their own websites," Willow says. "Trust me. I know. Entire sites are down for weeks and nobody notices. Did you read the bio? It's your real background, plus some fluff. I included some stuff about your postal carrier background. I'm gonna insert the name Stella in your high school graduating class and elsewhere. Just in case."

"Oh my god," I say.

"I really think you could pull this off," Lizzie says. "I really do. As long as you don't make it too painful, I think he'll just want to get it over with. Bexley just wants their money."

Jada says, "I have ten hours of footage total, but I can make more. Maisey alone would give me another seven."

Lizzie is laughing. "You're gonna make him watch twenty-one hours of us telling about our love for each other and the building." She pumps her fist in the air. "Yeah!"

"Wait, excuse me," I say. "There's something I need to do." I grab my iPad and enter a check mark in the box next to the introductory session. "There. Malcolm earned a check mark for today's session."

"Woo-hoo!" Francine unscrews a plastic top off a mini bottle of champagne.

"You'd better not have gotten that out of the mini fridge," I say.

Francine points at Willow. "She brought it. But I'm sure it's fine to take things out of the mini-fridge," Francine says. "You probably even have a meal stipend."

I widen my eyes. "A meal stipend that I would *never* dare use."

Francine rolls her eyes. Willow offers me a mini bottle of champagne and I take it. "Question—what if he refuses to watch Jada's footage? That sort of thing isn't in the packet. You should have been there, he was extremely uninterested in the footage." I don't tell them he called Maisey by five different wrong names. We all have such a soft spot for Maisey, our seventy-something galpal from the third floor. "Do I have the power to make him watch it? What if he really, really doesn't want to watch it? Because he really doesn't."

"He won't get a check mark, then," Lizzie says. "He gets a failing 'X.'"

"What happens if he gets a failing 'X'? Would he even care? Is it just a grown-up version of a frowny face sticker? Does he get three and then a demerit?"

We study the packet and the materials, but that's one of those obvious things that isn't written down.

"You'll figure it out," Jada finally says.

"I feel like there are probably a lot of other questions I should be asking right now, but I don't know enough to even know the questions," I say.

"That's easy," Willow says, "just frame every question like it's about their company culture. For example, 'What time do we arrive on site *vis-a-vis* your company culture? What is the dining situation *vis-a-vis* your company culture?' Like that."

"Like when you get a fortune cookie and add the words in bed?" I say.

"Exactly," Willow says. "And if you really feel like you're getting into trouble, say, 'That's proprietary,' and don't back down. Try it with me—That's proprietary."

"That's proprietary," I say.

"How are the worksheets graded?"

"That's proprietary."

"Where did you do your special advanced license training?"

I frown. What is she even talking about?

She frowns. "You can't tell me the school you trained at?"

"That's proprietary?"

"Yes!" She claps.

Willow asks my permission to clone my Instagram. I give it.

"I'm merging your past with Stella's present," she says. "One of my clients had a shady employee who did that, and it was quite effective. Until I busted the guy. Once Malcolm Blackberg starts getting curious about you, he'll look at your bio and then click the Facebook or Instagram link and then he's in my parallel universe. And he'll have his tech guys try to research you, but his tech guys are my bitches."

We go through my entire social media life and take out all of the photos that show people in the building or the building itself. Which leaves me with just arty shots I've taken on my route, a few inspirational sayings about courage, and random stuff from my past.

It impacts me here big time, how really empty my life is without these women. Without 341 West 45th.

8

Noelle

I'M HEADING down through the posh lobby at two the next day toting a chic brown fleur-de-lis suitcase I borrowed from Tabitha this morning. I packed one yoga pants lounge outfit, one fun going-out skirt outfit, and all of my pantsuits except the one I'm wearing, plus a selection of butterfly ties, because I think I'll be in business meetings most of the time.

For the plane ride I'm wearing my favorite pantsuit— maroon with a white shirt underneath, pulled together with my lucky clip-on butterfly tie with little hedgehogs, because hedge-hogs are my fave.

Francine had stopped me at the door and tried to get me to change. "Seriously, the pantsuit? It says sexy detective. But the lady-bow-tie? It says you're a sexy lady detective who miii-ight just have a collection of creepy antique baby dolls at home."

"One more word about my butterfly tie and I *will* start a creepy doll collection," I told her. "And it'll be the kind of dolls that don't close their eyes at night. And some might migrate to your room while you're sleeping!"

She'd laughed. And it was the first time we talked about the future without this gloomy cloud of sadness over us. Because what if this works?

Still, there's so much that could go wrong. I'm crossing so many lines. Willow says they'd never press charges, but how can she be sure? I try not to think about that as I wait outside in the muggy August air. Eventually a stretch SUV with tinted windows rolls up. A driver gets out, then Lawrence pops his head out the window and waves. "Stella!"

I wave back and head over, praying Janice or Anya aren't in there. Because they'd definitely recognize me now that I'm in a pantsuit again.

I hand the driver my suitcase, thank him, and pulse racing, I get in. "Hi, everybody!"

Four faces. No Janice or Anya.

I take a seat next to Lawrence, who introduces me around. "Coralee is West Coast—East Coast admin," Lawrence says. "Nisha is legal serving as liaison to the San Fran legal team, and Walt is Malcom's overall PA. I'm Malcolm's admin assist. We're the lowly rabble of the traveling team. The legal and accounting hotshots are already on site."

"Oh, stop," Coralee scolds, shaking her cute brown bob. "We're not the rabble."

"Li'l bit?" Lawrence says with an impish smile.

I don't know what to say about the rabble thing so I just smile. "I'm Elle from Bexley Partners."

"Oh, we know," Walt says. He has a friendly, weather-beaten face and a huge Adam's apple. "Malcolm's *new coach*," he says, emphasizing the words with extra drama. He bites his lip, as if to keep from laughing. "We hear that you'll be helping Malcolm learn to be *a nicer, kinder, gentler person.*" The phrase "a nicer, kinder, gentler person" not only gets extra emphasis, but also a widening of the eyes.

They're all smiling like it's the funniest thing ever. I smile back, just to be nice, and I adjust my tie, wishing I'd come more casual. The two guys wear casual sports coats and jeans; Coralee and Nisha are in casual jackets and some kind of space-age pants that look like business pants from afar, but up close they are really stretchy like yoga pants, and on their feet are comfy space-age boots. This is what business people wear for travel, I think. And probably for their downtime in the hotel.

Coralee has pale brown hair in a bob and piercing gray eyes. She declares that she plans to sleep. "Don't let me go on Twitter."

Nisha, pronounced knee-sha, groans. "I'll keep you off of there." Nisha has close-cropped dark hair and shiny pink hoop earrings and a cute pink briefcase, which makes me incredibly thankful that Tabitha made me bring her brown satchel, boring as it is. Otherwise I'd have my beat-up old bag, and I'd immediately be busted.

We arrive at the Teterboro airport, a private airport across the river from Manhattan. Mr. Blackberg's plane is a gleaming white jet with a silver nose. It's parked inside a giant airplane garage, and walking in, I feel like I'm walking onto an action-adventure movie set.

I follow my new coworkers up the mobile stairway and into the plane, feeling like a stowaway in a forbidden world.

The plane is like a really nice living room with velvety gray armchairs and comfy-looking couches arranged around various tables. Tasteful maroon accent pillows are strewn about; they match the fun little window curtains as well as the panel that separates the front and back areas.

I try not to react, but I so wish my friends could see, because...*oh my god!*

The flight attendant leads us right on through into the back section, which features a lovely and intimate little lounge, also with maroon accents. Malcolm sits, tumbler in hand, ice cubes clinking.

My gaze collides with his. He seems to be sizing me up, dangerous and elegant predator that he is. His lazy gaze lowers to my neck. The weight of it makes my pulse race, makes me feel warm and strange.

My belly whooshes with something like fear, or maybe just adrenaline.

"Back to the lady ties, I see," he says.

I put my hand to my neck. "Yes," I agree.

The flight attendant helps us stash our luggage in a back compartment. I can feel him watching. I'm sure my hands are shaking.

We settle into our seats up front. Lawrence and Coralee are on one side. I sit across from Nisha. Walt's behind us.

"So he rides back there?" I ask Nisha. "That's his half of the plane?"

"It depends, but generally he keeps to himself on trips," she says. "He would never socialize with the team, which is..." She ends her sentence with a half-smile and a little shrug, which seems to mean that it's a good thing.

I watch out the window as we line up at the runway, as we get up speed and lift into the air. People are tapping away at their computers.

"I have a sixty-minute session with him on this plane," I say to Nisha as we rise above wispy clouds. "It's scheduled for transit time, and this is transit, but I'm not sure..."

She waits for me to finish the sentence.

I'm not sure how to. Do I go back there and tell him it's starting at a time of my choosing? Or does he choose the time?

Am I waiting for him to appear? I'm here by court order. How much power does that give me?

"Not sure of what?" Nisha asks.

"How this works," I say, "*vis-a-vis* your company culture. I want to be respectful of your company culture in terms of scheduling."

"Oh." She nods. "Walt has his calendar." She twists around in her seat. "Walt, when does he have his coaching blocked out?"

"Never. It's four hours of prep time," Walt says.

"Elle gets him for an hour of transit time," Nisha says.

Walt's frown is big like his Adam's apple. "Hmm."

"Should I schedule our sixty-minute block with you?" I ask. "Or directly with him?"

He looks at me strangely. Was that a weird question? Am I giving myself away? He picks up his phone and texts. Is he texting Malcolm?

9

Malcolm

I FEEL DISTRACTED. Off my game.

I tell myself it's the upcoming negotiation with the Germantown Group, a large logistics firm with a massive network of
distribution centers, trucking lines, and logistics software. We
need to take over their network to make another acquisition
pay off.

I'm looking at background docs, but I'm thinking about
Stella. Will she still do her letter carrier schtick now that she's
back in a pantsuit?

And really, why a letter carrier? Was that her own twist?
Something so corny? Is it something this Bexley Partners trained
her to do, or is it yet more of Corman's fuckery?

Will we watch more of the insufferable amateur documentary? Not that it matters. At all. Really, I shouldn't be devoting
any more time to it than what my lawyers signed away, but I'm
feeling agitated because I like to know.

We're airborne. Out the window opposite us, you can see all

of Manhattan, looking like a thicket of trees rising from the shining Atlantic. The wheels retract below us with two heavy clunks.

I pull out my phone and find myself looking up Bexley Partners. I locate the coaching firm's *About Us* page. I like to know who's on my plane. And I'm going to need to find a way to buy her, because I'm not spending twenty hours being coached by some random country mouse; I don't care how hot she is.

I have things to do.

I'm disappointed to find only the barest of details underneath her photo. Stella grew up in rural Pennsylvania. Her bio notes that she's passionate about helping executives achieve a synergy of excellence and reach their full potential as leaders and humans.

Synergy of excellence? What kind of rubbish is that?

From her background, it looks like she grew up in a small town. She spent time as a letter carrier before taking her degree in psychology and moving to New Jersey. So that's where the letter carrier schtick came from.

Not that it matters. Corman is paying her to punish me. It means she can be bought. That's all I need to know.

I'll have to roll it out carefully, though. Maybe let her show the movie once or twice so that she can feel like she's giving it a go, because she does have that righteous warrior thing going on. I will make her job as unpleasant and useless as possible, then make the offer.

A text comes through.

Walt: Where do you want your training block with Elle?

Me: Stella?

Walt: It's Elle...

I punch in the word "now" and hit send. Being that I'm already thinking about it, best to get it over with. I stand and head through the door. "Everybody out. Bar's open," I say. "Snacks. Kitchen."

People drift to the back. Except Elle. She stands uncertainly. "Is here good?" She motions toward the table.

"Fine," I say.

She props up an iPad on the table in front of us.

I take the seat next to her. "So it's Elle? Not Stella."

"Yes." She hits play.

"Just going right into the movie?"

"Yes," she says, not taking her eyes from it. "We're back with the people living at 341 West Forty-fifth Street."

"I see," I say. "So is it supposed to be a documentary or something?"

"It's them telling how they feel about the building," she says, stating the obvious.

It switches between people. It's not bad work, technically. Did the discombobulated residents hire some sort of filmmaker? And then they sent this footage to my real estate acquisitions group and Corman somehow got hold of it? And decided this would be the perfect torture device? And then they found this junior coach to lean on?

That has to be how it came together. Because honestly— what else could explain this?

Twin boys now, with some old man wearing a platoon hat. The boys call him John and tell the unseen camera operator that John taught them both to shave. They live on the same floor.

I groan. Stella—or rather, Elle—shoots me a dirty look, and a strange trill of pleasure moves through me.

After a few more touching Norman Rockwell moments with John the elderly army vet guiding the young boys, we get some twenty-and thirty-something actresses one-upping each other on their love for the place. The women here—good lord! If there was a video presentation tailor-made to annoy me, this is it.

As if on cue, the old lady's face fills the screen.

"Oh, please, no, not her again," I say.

"*Shh*," Elle scolds delightfully.

Maisey's telling about how she broke her hip and her neighbors rallied to help her. I try to catch Stella's eye, but she's glued to Maisey.

After what feels like ten hours of Maisey and her hip, we return to John and his army-insignia hat. He's on the roof of the building showing off his crop of flowers, spindly little things that grow out of rusty old coffee cans arranged all in a row.

"Is this being filmed at the Buckingham Palace Garden, then?" I ask.

"*Shhh*," Elle hisses, annoyed. It's positively delicious.

Onscreen, a young actress goes into a long dramatic story about an abusive ex, and how she'd be alone in the world if not for her 341 West 45th family. It's quite the maudlin little video, all in all.

I study the slope of Elle's nose, the freckle-dusted curve of her cheekbone, her fine, glossy hair. I imagine removing the clip and sliding a ribbon of that hair through my fingers; it would feel silky to the touch—of that I have no doubt.

It's actually more honey colored than butterscotch, I decide. And she herself is no confection. She's straightforward and simple. Technically plain, but quietly beautiful. Most people wouldn't recognize her quiet beauty, especially not out here with so much flash out there to catch the eye.

Her tentative boldness adds to her attractiveness. The straight-up way she postures herself when she gives a command. How she sometimes seems to marshal forces from deep inside.

I want her to stop the movie and talk.

"Is there...literally four weeks of this footage?" I ask.

She hits pause and turns to me. "We'll see, won't we?" she says primly.

"Come on," I say. "This isn't real."

"It's totally real," Elle says. "A hundred percent real. That's the point here. Now please save the rest of your questions for after the presentation."

"It's not real," I continue, "meaning, this is about making the settlement as painful as possible. This is not a real program."

"No, it is," Elle says, jutting out her chin. "This is a program about empathy, with human stories about real people. You know, those two-legged things moving about on the streets below?"

A sassy outburst from Elle. Another unexpected treat.

Once again, she hits play.

John is back, talking about how his neighbors remembered his birthday. "I thought my days of people remembering my birthday were behind me," he says, holding up a brightly wrapped box.

I slide my phone from the table to my lap and scroll through my texts. It's all of five minutes before she notices what I'm doing.

"Hey!"

"What?" I say.

"What are you doing?"

"I'm reading an important text."

"Well...don't."

"Just a quick look."

She frowns. "You can't be looking at your phone."

"I can't be looking at it?" I ask, mirroring her, just to draw her out. Will she enforce even this?

Her nostrils flare. "You need to watch the program." Then, as if there might be some confusion on the issue, she adds, "This is a court-mandated program."

"But these are extremely important texts. How do I assure my team on the ground that I'm here for them whenever they need me if I can't respond to their texts?"

She frowns, thinking.

Negotiation 101: make your problem their problem.

I add, "How am I to give this movie my full attention when I know deep down that I might be missing important communications? How can we work together to allow me to stay in touch with my team?"

"You can't," she says.

I'm surprised, to say the least. I expected her to fold on this one. She's some kind of low-level worker who has presumably been paid a bonus by Corman to make the program extra annoying. What does she care if I look at a text? She gets her money either way.

My last court-ordered coach gave in on the occasional phone checking with no problem at all. By the end of three days, our sessions lasted all of a minute and a half—just long enough for him to give me an assignment that I could pass off to my assistant. It was perfect. Plausible deniability all around.

"You're asking me to be incommunicado for a full hour?" I ask. "I'm never unavailable to my people—not even when I sleep." The fact is, this text bit is one of the little battles I need to win.

She looks back and forth between my eyes—the left, the right, the left. We're close enough that I can see that the army green of her eyes is cut with pale gray striations. Like light shining through the cracks. Close enough that I can smell her coconut-berry shampoo. Close enough that I can almost feel her thinking.

She says, "No interruptions."

I tried to hide my surprise. "But all executives keep tabs on multiple things. What if there were an emergency?"

"Wouldn't Walt get you? He's your PA. Or your admin, Lawrence?"

"Not necessarily."

She blinks, unsure what to do with my resistance.

I wait, aware of this strange, excited energy in my chest, a sort of enjoyable lightness. What will she do now? What will she say?

She straightens up. "Can't you make it so? Like...one of those messages that says if there's an emergency, contact my assistant Walt? Just for the hour that we're in a session?"

"I really can't do that," I say. "I can't simply go dark."

"But my program requires your full attention," she says.

"Does it, though?" I ask.

"Yes, my program absolutely requires your full attention," she says.

"It's not complex material, Elle."

"I mean it. You have to watch it with your full attention."

I blink. Why fight me over such a small issue? Everybody checks their phones—even during the most important meetings.

She holds out her hand, palm up. She wants my phone.

Everything seems to slow.

I grin. It's not in any way funny, but I can't seem to help myself—it's just all so unexpected. I look from her slim hand to her eyes. Her suit is candy-apple maroon; the sky beyond her shoulder is a brilliant blue, but even those bright colors are curiously desaturated next to her flashing green eyes.

"You want me to hand over my phone?" I ask, incredulous.

She nods.

She was interesting before. Now she just got a hundred percent more fascinating.

"I can't do that, Elle."

"Then you have to turn it off."

"That's not something I can do, either." I'm addressing her

in my best negotiator's voice. Laid-back. Downward inflection. Nothing to be done. Too bad, so sad.

The silence drags on. No coach pushes back against me. No employee of any kind pushes back against me. In fact, I can't remember anybody outside of a business rival pushing back against me, and even that tends to be weak.

She straightens even more and juts out her chin; this is her power stance, I realize. I find that I love knowing that. Her and her prim little bow tie and her power stance.

"If I catch you on your phone again," she says, "I won't be able to check the box for today."

I narrow my eyes. "What does that mean?"

"The box in the online form that is shared between Bexley Partners and both law firms involved in the suit?"

Is she joking? I give her an easy smile, the kind I reserve for a difficult negotiation session. "You wouldn't be able to tick the box? Even if I can tell you everything that happens in the movie?"

She shakes her head.

I say, "Contrary to what you may have heard in the media, some people can multitask, and I'm one of those people. Business leaders who have gotten to my level are typically among the small percentage of people who can multitask very effectively."

She sucks in her lips. She's debating something. What is she debating? She says, "Do you know what happens when one of the boxes isn't checked off? Or *ticked off*, as you put it?"

"What happens when one of the boxes isn't ticked off? You're asking me, do I know?"

She hesitates, then, "Do you know what happens?"

I stiffen. Is she really going there?

"Do you know?" she asks.

I cross my legs. "This sixty minutes has already taken ninety minutes," I say.

She puffs up a bit. In negotiations, as in poker, everybody has a tell. Is this puffing up part of her tell? Trying to occupy space? For some reason, I'm thinking back to our earliest meeting. *You're very kind*, she'd said, labeling me with a positive emotion, proposing a preferred reality. Is she a wilier adversary than I'm giving her credit for?

"What happens if you don't get all the boxes checked?" she asks again.

"I presume we'll have to repeat that lesson."

"What if I don't want to repeat it?" she asks. "What if I have a timeline that I have to stick to? And the box would never get checked off?"

I feel this sudden and strange aliveness. "What would happen?" I ask.

"There would be an X there instead of a check mark," she continues. "Can you tell me what that would mean?"

My pulse races. An X in one of the boxes is the nuclear option. I narrow my eyes. My lawyers wouldn't agree to working with a firm or an executive coach with a history of playing hardball, but Elle seems to be doing just that.

Why play hardball? And I can't even check my phone? It's not like Corman and his lawyers have hidden cameras here.

She folds her napkin into a tiny triangle, and then runs a fingernail along one side, creating a straight edge.

She appears to be waiting for my answer, even though we both know exactly what an X would mean. It would mean I'm in breach of our agreement. If I refuse to comply with the terms of the agreement, I'm in breach, and Corman's lawyers could haul me back to court.

A judge in a certain mood could throw me in jail.

Corman's lawyers would work overtime to get such a judge. They'd call in every favor. Sending me to jail would be beyond Corman's wildest dreams.

I feel a smile spread over my face. "Are you...threatening me?"

She looks surprised. "I'm just asking if you know what happens."

I can't believe it. She is threatening me with possible jail time. She has a tiny little sphere of power and she's using it like a cudgel. It's so incredibly...unexpected.

I sit up. I wasn't taking her seriously before, but I am now.

10

Noelle

HE WEARS A WOLFISH SMILE—GORGEOUS and darkly dangerous, like he's biding his time, dreaming of a someday attack. "Let's get on with the training, then, shall we?"

Inwardly I sigh. Will I never find out what happens if he gets an X instead of the check mark?

I really want to know!

I turn the video back on. Jada promised me that she'd edited out all of the parts where I appear, but this part is the group of us painting the top floor community room and I nearly have a heart attack when my arm appears in the frame. My hand. My ring. I fold my hands in my lap. I think the ability to recognize an acquaintance's hand and arm is quite rare, but I wouldn't put it past Malcolm—he sees things, eagle-eyed predator that he is.

I risk a quick glance. Malcolm's lounging in his chair, an annoyed prince on his mile-high throne, legs carelessly crossed.

He seems to feel me watching, because he looks over at me

just then, eyes sparkling. In a confiding, almost conspiratorial tone, he says, "Surely you don't have twenty hours of this."

"No conversation," I say.

"Can't I ask questions? Isn't that how a student learns?"

"Save your questions for the end."

"You're honestly telling me you have twenty hours of this footage?"

I stop the video. "My lesson materials are not your concern."

"What does a documentary on some people in a building have to do with executive emotional intelligence?"

"It's important for you to see the lives that your project is affecting." The absolute truth.

"Why?"

"Because it matters," I say, perhaps too strongly.

"How does that affect my executive emotional intelligence?"

I swallow, unsure how to answer that, being that I have no knowledge of executive coaching whatsoever. I need to get a book or something.

"You can't be asking questions," I say. "We're not two colleagues discussing training methodology here. In this part of the program that I, as an accredited coach, have designed, you are going to learn about the lives that your project is affecting."

"What possible lesson am I to draw from footage of people painting a run-down building that will soon be torn down?"

"Why not try to look past that? It may not be the fanciest place, but don't you see how hard they work to make it beautiful?"

"Is that a line from Oliver Twist?"

I frown, chest raging with frustration—and something more that I can't define. "Are you ready to resume your lesson?"

"Is it just about torturing and punishing me?" he asks. "If

that's the goal, you should've shown footage of vintage golf clubs being run over by busses. That would hurt me a lot more."

"You're telling me you would care more about golf clubs being destroyed than people's lives being torn apart? This beautiful building that they've put their hearts into? The loss of this close-knit community, a group that's almost like a family?"

"Depends on the golf clubs," he says.

I glare at him, stewing.

Something flashes up on his phone just then. He looks down, then back up at me.

"You just checked your phone."

"You can't ask me to go dark. You just can't. I thought we'd established that."

Can I really not ask that? I need him to pay attention. I need him to learn about my friends. I want him to feel like he knows them, and then maybe he'll come to care about them a little bit. God, why did I think this would work? He's so powerful and so busy, and what do I have?

I suck in a breath. "You were mandated to undergo a program to be designed by an accredited executive coach, were you not?"

"Yes, yes, yes."

"This program must be viewed without multitasking. That is part of the program. If you look at your phone even one more time, I won't be able to give you your check for the day."

He watches me for a long, silent moment with that hard-sparkle gaze.

My heart thunders. What is he thinking?

But then—suddenly, miraculously—he turns off his ringer and sets his phone on the table. His phone is dark and sleek like him. "Take it."

I pick it up. It's cool, heavy—more heavy than it should be, somehow, the way I'd imagine a loaded gun might feel.

"Let's get on with it, then," he says.

"Great," I say brightly, setting the phone aside. Was that too easy? But hey, he's cooperating, right?

We watch the rest of it, much of which is taken up by Antonio practicing a monologue. Jada definitely loves filming Antonio. I cut it off at exactly the end of his session, just to show him that I, too, am respecting the rules.

I hold his phone out to him and he takes it. Our fingers brush momentarily, sending a crazy charge of energy skittering over my skin, a sign of how jacked up I am—that's what I tell myself.

He pockets his phone without so much as looking at me, because of course, he's unaffected. He stands, resting his large, muscular hand upon his now-empty seat back.

Nervously, I put away my presentation stuff. Is he waiting for something?

His voice, when it comes, is a rumble of cool velvet. "Do I get my tick?"

Is he mocking me? I can't tell.

"Well?" he asks.

"For today," I say.

~

THE PLANE LANDS and we're whisked into a matching pair of SUV limos that ferry us to the Maybourne Hotel in the San Francisco Financial District.

The Maybourne Hotel is every bit as glorious as the New York Four Seasons, with marble pillars and marble floors and huge skylights flooding the area with natural light. The seating looks like it came straight out of a French palace. I turn around, slowly, taking it all in, because apparently my soul can't consume the place from a stationary position. Maybe I'm embarrassing the team, I don't know, but they should be thankful that I don't drop my bags and twirl around and around, Sound of Music-style.

Once I've gotten my overall eyeful, I spot a table with drinking glasses arranged around a crystal bowl of water with bright green cucumbers floating in it. I put down my bags and go to get myself a glass of it, needing somehow to consume all of this luxury. The water is indeed very cucumbery. I close my eyes and let it fill me.

It tastes fresh and pure. It's not like I can't make cucumber water at home, but it's weirdly special somehow. I sip and take another gander at the chandelier and potted palms. It's like I've entered a storybook written in another century.

And then I look across the lobby and there's Malcolm, coat slung over his arm, gazing at me. The beautiful devil.

But I know he's not a devil, and I won't give up hope. Yes, maybe I'm clinging too ferociously to that one little encounter that we had, to that one little flash of kindness in his eyes, my intuition of his heart. Well, cling I will.

Lawrence comes up with my key card. "You're in 708. A few of us are meeting in the restaurant for dinner if you want to come."

"Right, it's way past our dinnertime, isn't it?" I say. It's nine at home but it's only six in San Francisco.

"So? Save you a seat?" He's waiting for an answer.

"Thanks. I'd love that."

He heads for the elevator. I take one last look back at Malcolm, who's heading for the elevators with Walt. I fuss with my water glass, letting everybody go ahead. I'm tired of being always on guard, of acting like I belong when I don't. I just need to be alone for a little bit.

Yet again, I have a room to myself, and it's beyond glorious. Right out the window I have a classic San Francisco panorama with trolley cars and steep streets and the Golden Gate Bridge beyond the rooftops.

I text Francine some pictures and then I call her with a quick update.

She can't believe I took away his phone. "I can barely believe it myself," I say.

"Maybe this can really work," she exclaims.

A wave of doubt twists through my rib cage as I recall Malcolm's dismissive attitude. Maybe this whole thing really is nuts. But then I hear myself say, "Yeah, maybe it can."

~

I SPOT LAWRENCE, Coralee, Nisha, and Walt ensconced in a corner table in the plush, candlelit hotel restaurant.

Lawrence waves me over. Nisha stands up to get a chair for me; she's in flowy pants that look like a skirt. Coralee wears a long black sweater over a brown tee that's the exact same color as her brown bob.

I sit, fingering my butterfly tie, feeling like a dork for having come to dinner in my pantsuit.

The waiter hands me a piece of paper and asks if I want a drink. Do people on work trips have drinks? Three of them have beers, but they could be non-alcoholic, and I can't tell what Walt is drinking. "What's that?" I point to Nisha's beer.

"A local ale. Really good."

"I'll have one of those, too," I say to the waiter. I really can't afford it; I don't have much in my bank account—I'm still paying off credit cards from Mom's illness, but drinking what other people drink is a good way to fit in. I noticed that when I first moved to the big city.

I study the paper, which seems to be the entire menu. It doesn't even have prices—a definite bad sign.

"This is our favorite table when we're here," Lawrence says. "It's good luck to get it the first night."

"I hope I'm not taking Malcolm's seat," I say.

They all smile. "Not likely!" Nisha says. Is the idea of Malcolm sitting down with them and eating with them so amusing?

"Did you get the backgrounder and the schedule for the week?" Lawrence asks me.

"Yes," I say, grateful for Willow's computer magic. There was a lot of factual information in the backgrounder. "Looking to buy the second-largest logistics company in the nation," I say, just to show I read it. I actually read it twice—and some of the more complicated parts three or four times.

Lawrence fills me in on the upcoming sessions that I'm to observe. From what I gather, part of my coaching duties involve watching him in negotiation sessions and offering tips. Right. I'll offer Malcolm Blackberg negotiation suggestions, and after that, I'll give Lady Gaga singing pointers and show Kylie Jenner how to use an eyebrow pencil.

The waiter brings two plates of steamed mussels in garlic sauce. It smells unbelievably good. We all place our dinner orders—I choose the vegetarian pasta, which should be the cheapest dinner.

"The firm's not actually for sale," Lawrence says as soon as the waiter leaves. "It's a family-owned business and the father wants to pass it on to the son."

"I don't understand. I thought these were negotiations to buy it." I pass on the mussels, even though I desperately want to try them. But if this is a split check and I don't eat any, maybe I'll get out cheaper. How did I not think of the expense of being here? What will I do when I run out of money? I know that my friends would help me out if I asked, but I really don't want to do that. They've given me so much already.

"The father says he's open to selling but he's not at all open to it, and everybody in the world knows it," Nisha says, pink hoops swinging. "He just wants to sit down with Malcolm and educate his son what a negotiation looks like. Basically, it's a free consultation session that the owner is trying to pass off as a series of purchase negotiations. We think he also wants to see what Malcolm might do with the company. Spoiler alert: Malcolm would break it apart, fire everybody, and use the infrastructure for his own purposes."

"And all the people would lose their jobs?" I ask.

"Yeah. But that's what the owner will have to do, eventually, too," Nisha says. "Trucking is dead. Most of those people will be out of work in five to ten years either way."

"Why is Malcolm wasting his time with this whole thing if he knows the man's just using the sessions to educate the son and pick his brain?" I ask. "Malcolm doesn't strike me as somebody who would be into..."

"Charitable acts?" Lawrence offers with his trademark impish grin.

Coralee chuckles.

"He's not," Walt says. "Malcolm thinks he can change the guy's mind. Pretty unlikely."

Coralee raises a fork. "Malcolm has done the impossible before."

Walt leans in and says, "Malcolm is an expert at getting people to do things that they never intended to do. Let that be a warning to you."

I nod.

A bread basket comes. It smells amazing. People pass it around without taking any, but I go for it, slathering on a creamy layer of butter and chomping right in like a barracuda. It's pure heaven.

"Malcolm negotiating is a thing of beauty," Nisha tells me.

"He'll try and reshape the man's thinking about the situation. Get it so that it's him and this guy collaborating together against the realities of modern trucking."

"Wow," I say. "He just doesn't strike me as a people person."

Nisha shrugs. "You know how some comedians and actors and musicians can be really shy, but when they get up on stage it's like they're a completely different person? It's like that."

"My advice to you, though?" Coralee says. "In terms of your work with him? Keep him out of your head. Once he starts repeating things you say and asking *how* and *what* questions, that's how he gets into your head. And then he reshapes your thinking and makes you his bitch."

"Oh," I say. "Yikes."

"Elle will be fine," Nisha declares confidently. "Don't forget —she's a master of emotional intelligence. He won't be able to reshape *her* thinking."

"Do you have actual lessons you're teaching him?" Walt asks. "Emotional intelligence type things?"

"Yes," I say. "I am definitely trying to raise his emotional intelligence...in a way..."

They're all looking at me, waiting for more.

"Malcolm Blackberg. Probably not the most eager student you'll encounter," Coralee says.

Walt snorts. "There's nothing wrong with his emotional intelligence. He just hates everybody."

Lawrence does that jokey thing people do when they put their hand to their mouth and cough and say some words really fast. "Cough-understatementoftheyear-Cough," he says.

Nisha smiles. "You have quite the job ahead of you."

It's subtle, but they're all letting me know that I can speak freely.

I put down my knife. "I know what I am," I say. I'm thinking here about what the real Stella said to me in the elevator.

"There are the coaches who help executives who want to build their skills, to guide leaders who are excited to learn and grow. And then there are the coaches who are sent in as a slap on the wrist. A punishment." I close one eye and tilt my head, giving them a fun smile—I'm channeling my friend Tabitha here. "Am I that second kind of coach? Yes. Yes, I am."

I can feel the group relax now that I'm talking real.

Nisha laughs. She has an easy, bell-like laugh that I love. "Erp!" she exclaims.

"Right?" I say. "So, yeah. I think Malcolm would rather have his skin flayed than endure my coaching."

"No doubt," Lawrence says.

"But even so," I continue, "my goal is that he comes away with increased empathy for the people who his business touches."

Coralee is grinning at me with great anticipation, like she's waiting for a punchline.

"Yeah, good luck with that." Nisha takes some bread. "Though you have to respect a man who fully is what he is. People expect Malcolm to be totally misanthropic, and he delivers, which is a weird form of integrity, but integrity all the same. He'll always be what he is. But, your empathy goals? Not in a million years. But you've probably figured that out by now."

I nod politely. I've figured out that that's what the world thinks. Am I crazy for thinking different based on nothing but my gut? My initial intuition of him?

"So let me ask you, why do you guys work for him?" I ask.

"Our resumes. He's the absolute best, hands down," Lawrence says. "Nobody can touch him. When they see the name Blackberg, Inc. on your resume, they know you can handle any type of personality."

"Yeah," Nisha agrees. "It's not easy to work for him, but on a professional level? They know you've had a front row seat to a master at work. We live for the after-session roundup where he asks us what we've noticed."

Walt nods. "He's trying to get information from us, like if we caught things he might not have caught. You always want to pay attention to the kinds of questions that he asks. If he responds to something that you noticed with a word like *indeed* or *interesting*, that's huge."

Coralee says, "One time when I made an observation, he just looked at me and he goes, *Helpful.* One word, but it was everything."

"I remember that," Lawrence says, nodding.

"Right? *Helpful!*" Coralee says. "But it's an opportunity to see what he thinks. What he's reading in the room and what he does with it. If he says *Hmm*, that's a good sign too, it shows it's worth thinking about."

"I'll always take a *hmm* over a nod," Walt says.

"Me, too," Nisha says.

"Isn't that turnover bad for a company? As soon as you get expertise, you leave?" I ask.

"Malcolm *likes* churn or it wouldn't be that way," Coralee says. "He doesn't like us to get too cozy."

"We're all just interchangeable to him," Nisha adds.

The discussion turns to whether he even has friends. Lawrence declares not, since Malcolm's always at work.

Walt, who apparently exchanges information with Malcolm's other assistants, tells me that Malcolm has gifts sent to business associates and random people from his past, but he never travels to see anybody, and he rarely even seems to go out to dinner with people, except that Kyra once in a while.

"Kyra's a shark like him, and they're both vicious and on again, off again," says Coralee, who seems to be most up on the gossip in the group.

"But no gifts for her," Walt says. "Or for family. He has

holiday cards sent to his father here in San Fran, but never any gifts. Interestingly—and you can't repeat any of this—but his instructions are that the father card should acknowledge the holiday, but nothing emotional or sentimental." Walt points his fork at me and Nisha. "And get this—even though he signs the holiday cards that go out to his business associates and old friends, he never signs the cards to his father. The unsentimental cards for his father are to be sent with no *signature*."

"Oh, wow, I didn't know that," Nisha says.

"The relationship with the father is *not* the best ever," Coralee says.

I frown. "Did Malcolm grow up here in California?" I ask. "Because his accent..."

"The family lived in England until he was five, or so," Coralee says. "And then they moved here, but they apparently sent him back for one of those English boys' schools where the boys are all cruel to each other. And the mother's out of the picture. Took off somewhere..."

"Australia," Walt adds. "No cards for her. No nothing for her."

Dinner comes and we dig in. My pasta is insanely delicious, but I feel strangely sad for Malcolm. The boys' school and the distant parents. And everybody who works with him is on their way to somewhere else. Even the guy he's negotiating with just wants something from him. Is that how Malcolm likes it? How could anybody prefer that?

The gang is planning a day trip to the wharf. They're all on their phones checking maps and schedules to see if there's a gap between negotiation sessions and work sessions.

"Guys," Lawrence says. "Don't look."

The mood transforms right then, like an electric current got shot around the table. Everybody's gazes are fixed on their food.

Even the noise level in the restaurant has plummeted, like

the diners all sense a predator has entered their midst, and they've lowered their voices, staying small and quiet.

I know without looking that Malcolm has arrived.

I glance over discreetly, and there he is, strolling past the hostess stand, heading for the bar.

He's in an elegant black dinner jacket with a bright white shirt underneath. The bright white of it lends intensity to his dusky complexion. His gait is casual, strides long and confident, the picture of self-assured mastery, beautiful and alone.

It's not just that he's alone, it's that he's *ragingly* alone. He's a fiercely isolated storm, speeding across the sky, shadowing the lands below, charging up the atmosphere with negative ions of fear and tension and something else, like some kind of aliveness.

"What's he doing here?" Nisha whispers, even though there's no way he could hear us. Still, she whispers it, like he has demon-level hearing. "Is he coming over here?"

"No way," Walt whispers.

He takes a corner seat at the bar and looks down at his phone like it's the most natural thing in the world to be by himself. I feel weird going into places by myself, but *alone* is Malcolm's natural habitat. His hair is parted severely on the side, but two chunks of it hit down against his forehead like soft black spikes.

Everyone is looking at Coralee, being that she's the master of gossip and the person who's worked longest at Blackberg, Inc. —going on two years, I think she'd said. Even Coralee seems mystified. "Don't look at me," she says. "He can get room service to bring him any drink that they have. Why descend from his suite?"

"Prostitute," Lawrence offers.

"Not likely," Coralee gusts out, risking a quick glance over there.

"Do you think he knows we're here?" Nisha asks.

"Oh, he knows," Lawrence says. "He always knows the room. He's a spider, and the whole world is his web, and he feels everything. Every little vibration in every corner. Every unfortunate little bug that flies into his web, Malcolm knows all."

"You're such a dork," Nisha says. "But then again, he kind of does..."

I steal another quick glance, and right then he looks in our direction—right at me. Our gazes collide, and the fine hairs on my skin stand on end—every tiny, invisible little hair is straining and craning.

Am I the little bug? Does he feel my vibration? Because I'm definitely in full vibration mode.

"Erp," Nisha whispers.

Walt raises his glass in a long-distance toast. Coralee nods. I copy Coralee, nodding at him from afar before I plaster my gaze down at my half-finished pasta, heart pounding.

"What is this strange madness?" Nisha asks. "Will he come over here, now?"

"Uncharted territory," Coralee mumbles through unmoving lips, as if there's even a danger of Malcolm reading lips.

Everybody is more subdued as we finish our meals. Even the topic of conversation—football—is tamer now, as if he might hear.

After dessert, Coralee announces she's going aspirational shopping at the boutique in the lobby. Nisha claps. Nisha's all in.

"What's aspirational shopping?" I ask.

"It's where we go to the boutique where they serve us bubbly while we try on designer gowns that we'll never be able to afford," Nisha says. "Come with. It's fun."

"That does sound fun," I say. Though it would be better if we were going shopping where I could afford things. I feel out of place in my business outfit. They'll think I'm weird if I keep wearing the wrong clothes to everything.

"I'll pass," Walt says.

Coralee throws a wadded-up napkin at him. "You're not invited."

The bill comes—separate checks. I take out my wallet.

"What are you doing?" Walt asks. "You didn't use up your per diem already, did you?"

I frown. What's a per diem? Is it the stipend? The way he says it, it sounds like it would be weird if I had used it up already. "No," I say. "But I wasn't sure...vis-a-vis your company culture..." I mumble as Willow taught me.

"Put your room number and it'll go toward your per diem," Nisha says. She makes me tell her my room number and then she scribbles it on my check with a nice tip and throws it onto the table. "Come on, let's go."

Coralee stands and grabs her purse. "We'll be passing by him on the way out, but don't engage unless he does," she says to me. "Follow my lead."

I follow her and Nisha down past the row of booths. The path to the door takes us right past the corner where Malcolm scowls at his phone in the candlelight.

He lifts his gaze as we near, expression mysteriously stormy, like he's just learned lots of mysterious things on his phone that he feels really intensely about.

Coralee nods as she passes and he nods back at her. Nisha exchanges nods with him, too. He catches my eye as I pass. I nod, ears buzzing like crazy. Luckily, my feet still work, carrying me ever forward.

Did he nod back? I don't even know, but I can feel the weight of his gaze on my skin as I follow my new coworkers out into the bright lobby.

Nisha grins at me. "Your cheeks are all rosy," she says. "When I drink, I just get puffy eyes."

"Red carpet time," Coralee says, grabbing our arms and leading the way across the glamorous lobby. High above, a strange glass sculpture glimmers in the light.

11

Malcolm

LYING to oneself is one of the most idiotic habits. *Just one more won't hurt. Maybe this time will be different.*

How gullible do you have to be to believe a lie that you yourself tell yourself?

Yet people do it. They do it a lot. It keeps them victims of their own ridiculous games.

So just to be clear, I didn't come down to the bar for a drink, though I could have tried to tell myself that. I didn't need to stretch my legs; I didn't feel like a change of scenery, nor was I up for a bit of a stroll.

I wanted to see her.

I've been unable to wrest my attention from her since the moment I collided with her in the lobby, and my inexplicable inability to ignore her only intensified when she turned out to be my coach. And then there's that maddening, tantalizing butterfly bow tie.

And the way she threatened me. Yes. She's got my full

attention now.

Her sitting next to Lawrence was not my favorite thing ever. But then she left with Nisha and Coralee while Walt and Lawrence stayed behind, huddled up in intense conversation—American football, knowing them.

I finish my drink just as a call comes in from Tokyo. I wander out to the lobby to take it, pacing around, guiding my software systems group across the ocean toward salvaging a deal. I'd assumed she'd gone up to her room, but some twenty minutes into the call, I spy her through a lobby shop window, or more, I spy a bit of her hair, partially hidden by mannequins. I'd know that hair anywhere.

I find myself drifting nearer, settling into a seating area on the boutique side of the lobby, giving marching orders to a team a world away, while being entirely focused on the scene through the window of a women's dress shop.

Coralee moves in front of Elle at one point. Coralee wears a gown of blazing sapphire, and Nisha's in a bright retro number with geometric pink shapes, but it's Elle who shines. She's in something subdued—a slim sheaf of light brown. A shade lighter than her honey-colored hair, it sets up a resonance—the gown enriching her hair, the hair enriching her gown.

Before I know what I'm doing, I'm on my feet, moving even closer, mesmerized. I'm close enough to see that the two of them are listening, enrapt, to Nisha. Nisha's talking and laughing and clapping. Nisha's a woman with a clap for every occasion; on this one, she seems to be emphasizing a humorous point she's making.

Elle turns to the mirror. She smooths her hands over her hips and turns this way and that, army green eyes steady on her reflection.

She likes the dress; that's clear enough, and really it is perfect in the sexy way it grazes her barely there curves, perfect in the way it hugs her breasts, the way the scoop of the neckline frames the regal collarbones that she hides under those ridiculous pantsuits. I imagine running my finger along her collarbone, from one side to the other. The line of her collarbone is my second-favorite line on her, second only to the coy slope of her nose.

She puts up her chin, straightens her back, and gazes at herself from where she stands at the corner of the shop, unaware of the world outside the store window, unaware of the fact that when a bad man stands in a certain place in the lobby, he is free to enjoy her secret communion with the mirror.

Is the chin-up woman the woman she imagines would wear this dress? She turns again, taking herself in from another angle, and I think it's most definitely bravery—that chin up attitude she puts on, as though she's trying on the feeling of bravery the way she's trying on an elegant dress. And in a flash of intuition, I know she's thinking of me, thinking of facing me down. I could be wrong, but I don't think that I am. I'm the dragon she's been sent to torment, after all. I'm the one she requires bravery for.

I drink in this unguarded moment, this private performance of bravery. Real bravery is tedious. But this girl's put-on bravery is vulnerable and fascinating and entirely unexpected, just like her.

I remember when I was first trying on my own look of bravery as a young boy; trying on bravery like an ill-fitting suit, a hard stare at the mirror, an invisible cloak, desperate for that brave feeling to become part of my very own exoskeleton.

She turns again, straightens even more. This time she narrows her eyes at her reflection, lips slightly parted. This new look—good god—it's demure and flirtatious and ever so slightly witchy at the same time.

The playfully witchy look is gone as quickly as it appeared. And I'm left panting. I need more of that look. I could feast on that look forever. Brave Elle, witchy Elle. I want to peel back layer after layer of her. I want to taste every inch of her.

Dimly, I'm aware of an annoying noise in my ear.

My Bluetooth. Tokyo.

"What?" I bark. "Say something worth saying and maybe I'll listen." I storm off in the other direction, shaking her out of my head.

THE NEXT MORNING she's standing with the team and two of our West Coast lawyers in the seating area nearest the lobby door. People stiffen up when I arrive. I never cared about that before, but I don't want Elle doing it.

Elle is wearing another one of her suits. We've seen maroon and green; today's is brown, but otherwise identical, aside from a new color of butterfly bow tie—this one simply black. I look hard, trying to determine whether it's a clip-on bow tie or some sort of a slim scarf, threaded under the collar. I find it infuriating that I can't tell.

Also infuriating: that I'm expending mental resources on it.

"Cars out there yet?" I ask.

"Both," Walt says.

I point. "Walt, Elle, Nisha, you're with me." I head to the cars. What am I doing? I need to be focusing on this inaugural session.

And why the iterated suits? I iterate my suits because I don't like to use mental bandwidth on something stupid as clothing—a black suit for each day of the week. Decision made. But Elle's in a barely skilled profession, regurgitating things she learned in some seminar. What does she need bandwidth for?

We settle in. Elle ends up next to me on my left, and I can feel her energy, her heat, her nearness in a strangely palpable way. I tell myself it's because she's different, an oddball here, a square peg for a round hole—if there's anything I hate, it's a square peg for a round hole.

I successfully force myself to stop thinking about the infernal tie, but that just leaves my wicked imagination free to focus on that witchy gaze she gave the mirror.

Then I'm running a scenario where she gives me the flirtatiously witchy gaze while I slowly draw the tie free of her collar.

I clear my throat. "What do you know about the meeting today?" I ask her.

"Not that much," she says. "A large family-owned logistics firm that is not keen on selling."

"Have you been instructed on protocol in the negotiating room? I have very strict preferences."

She swallows. "No."

"You will not react," I say, "no matter what I do in there. You understand?"

She nods, color riding high.

It's here that I realize she heard that sexy. I didn't mean it sexy, but knowing she heard it that way nearly destroys my mind. And before I can stop myself, I lower my voice and ask, "Is that a problem?"

"No," she whispers hoarsely.

And just when I need to be focused on the upcoming negotiation, I'm wondering furiously about her; what it would be like with her; what she would be like. In my mind I'm tracing the line of her collarbone. She's in my bed looking up at me, watching me with that deliciously witchy expression.

I lower my voice to a deeper register. "I might do some outlandish things in there."

Her expression is priceless.

"Things that might even shock you," I continue. "But they will be effective."

Her color deepens. "Okay," she says.

What am I doing? This is my executive coach, a woman sent to punish and torture me.

I straighten up. "However, it's far more likely I'll seem friendlier than you know me to be," I say. The truth. Hardball negotiation is for amateurs. "Let's see your bored face."

"My bored face?"

"Are you able to look bored? Can you act at all?"

Walt leans forward and says, "It's important to have a neutral face in there."

"Okay." She sits up and puts on a little pout. "Wait—No." She wipes the air in front of her face and tries it again.

"No, no, no," I say.

"Okay, hold on." She tries for a neutral face, but all I see is energy and excitement, badly hidden. And pale, freckled skin. There is one darker freckle at the edge of her lips, and I imagine tasting it, kissing it, or maybe just taking that entire side of her mouth into mine, and then I'd let her lips go and kiss her properly, full on. What would it take to turn her on? What would it take to get her to aim that flirtatiously witchy face at me?

"You're an observer," I say, forcing my attention down to my phone, "but the Germantown Group doesn't know that. They'll assume you're privy to inside knowledge, and they'll be watching your reactions every step of the way." I look up and meet her intelligent green gaze. "An undisciplined team can undermine a negotiator's strength like nothing else. Even if you don't understand what's happening, they won't know it, and they'll be looking at you for cues. I can't have you muddying the water. Your poker face...no."

She nods.

"They're going to give you a packet of materials when we get in there. Every time you feel eyes on you, every time you think something interesting's going on, anytime you feel anything beyond neutral, you're to look down at that material and don't look up. Look at the packet the whole time if you need to."

"Okay," she whispers.

"Good," I say. "I'm glad we understand each other."

Once again, her face blazes. She swallows, blinks. "Um, they say that h-he doesn't want to sell."

"Deep down, I suspect he does," I say, "but he won't take a deal that fires his truckers and repurposes his assets, and that is the only deal he will ever see. The deal he wants existed in 1989, but it doesn't exist today. And once his kid inherits, he'd be wise to break up the company first thing while it still has value, but Gerrold doesn't want to face that reality either."

"Well, wouldn't it be bad for the people to lose their jobs?" she says. "He cares about what happens to them. I think his loyalty is admirable."

"Whose side are you on here?" I tease.

"It's just...I'm imagining it from their points of view," she says.

"They haven't exactly kept the self-driving car a secret," I say. "Gerrold knew, the truckers knew, everybody knows it's a dying business, and it has been dying for a long time. Gerrold didn't see what was coming down the pike, or maybe he didn't want to see, because he needed them. It doesn't matter. I need his infrastructure. His distribution centers, his logistics, all of it."

"And he wants to teach his son to negotiate," she says.

I'm pleased to see she's gone to school on the situation. "Exactly. A bit of schooling for Junior."

"So why are you indulging them? Why waste your time?"

I lock on to her army green eyes, pinning her with my gaze. I need to stop this madness, but I don't seem to be able to. "You can't win if you don't play."

She swallows. Nods. Freckles strewn like stars.

12

Noelle

THE NEGOTIATION TAKES place in the Kendrick building, a gleaming tower in downtown San Francisco that seems to have been rented out for this specific purpose. Our conference room is on a high floor with glass windows all around that overlook the city.

We all sit at a long table carved from a huge piece of wood, polished to a high gleam. Our team—Walt, Nisha, Coralee, Lawrence, and I—is on the fringes, and Malcolm and five people I haven't met—the legal and money people, I'm guessing—sit in the middle of our side of the table across from Gerrold Jespersen Sr., owner of the Germantown Group, and his son, Gerrold Jr., and their people.

Gerrold is a sixty-something man who wears one of those black Greek fisherman's caps. He actually looks like a fisher-man, burly and bearded. His son, Gerrold Jr.—Junior, as Malcolm calls him—is in his forties, thick like his father, but clean-shaven.

I imagined a negotiation to be a tense affair, but on this first day, it's more a getting-to-know-you session. Everyone even goes around and says their names, and some even tell a little bit of personal stuff, like one of Gerrold's lawyers just moved out from Texas. Another of them explains his broken arm is from competitive tennis. Walt figures out that he and Gerrold's accounts person have the same alma mater. I say I'm with HR—I was told to say that, and it's more or less true. Training and coaching is considered an HR function.

Gerrold talks up his business—the amazing service, the human touch, the state-of-the-art distribution centers. I expected Malcolm to pooh-pooh the value of the company—isn't that what you're supposed to do in negotiation? Act like there are problems with the thing you want to buy? Like kicking the tires on an old automobile? But Malcolm seems to have genuine appreciation for different aspects of the company. Now and then, Gerrold looks over at the son; it's hard to tell if the son is following along; I half suspect he's looking at his phone under the table.

There's even beverage service—you can order café lattes and espressos and things like that by text—and there is a giant platter of pastries in the middle of the table.

People don't seem that interested in the pastries, but I am—all I had for breakfast was some coffee in my room and one of the apples from the bowl that the hotel puts out in the lobby.

Maybe it's silly, but I can't justify spending that *per diem*/stipend thing. I feel bad enough that I'm here under false pretenses, staying in a room on their dime. No way am I going to go living it up at restaurants.

I don't know, spending a bunch of Blackberg Inc.'s money on meals just feels like crossing a line.

I take a croissant at one point when I feel like I'm falling asleep, and it turns out to be the most delicious thing I've ever tasted. I'm still in way too much debt from my mother's illness to justify expensive taste treats in my everyday life; the most I'll do is throw in for pizzas with my girlfriends. But that's more than food—spending time with my galpals is a lifeline to me.

So I'm staring at the croissants, thinking about taking another. But nobody takes two—it seems like the culture of the meeting. Also, when I count them, it's clear that they have one for each person, so it's possible it's against the rules.

Even so, I spend my time identifying the exact one I'd take—it's bigger than the rest, with way more almond paste in it, from the looks of it.

It's hard to focus on the negotiations and not the remaining almond croissants nestled among plain croissants and berry scones. I just want to eat them all.

I force my attention off of the tray and onto the session I'm supposed to be observing.

Gerrold and his son are supposedly running this session, but if you pay attention, you see that Malcolm is in control. What's more, Gerrold and his people tell Malcolm lots of things, revealing themselves to him, whereas Malcolm reveals nothing of himself, yet he seems deeply engaged all the same, all questions and lively interest.

That's a true kind of power, I think, where you're running things and people don't even know it. Though he's just as comfortable using his overt power, especially outside of the negotiating room. The power of him growling at people and sending them scurrying. He's so intense and mercurial. The center of every room. A magnificent beast.

Two hours in, we get a break. I'm standing outside on the rooftop balcony with Nisha and Walt. Walt's sneaking a vape that smells like cherries.

"He's so different," I say. "Malcolm down there."

"This is a point that we frequently discuss," Nisha says. "Is it an act? Or does he save up all of his goodness for the negotiation room?"

"I think he saves it up," Walt says, blowing the vape cloud away from us. "Coralee thinks it's an act."

"Nah, it's too real to be an act," Nisha says. "I think, it's like, if a farmer has a hundred acres, and he robs all of the nutrients and minerals from ninety-nine of his acres in order to give all of the goodness to one favorite acre, that's Malcolm. All the goodness that he has goes to that negotiating table, to the deal-making process. But the rest of his crops completely suffer."

"Wait, you think that he uses his goodness up in business negotiations and doesn't have any left for the rest of his life?" I ask.

Nisha shrugs. "My humble opinion."

"I don't see goodness or being friendly as finite," I say. "I don't think a person only has a specific amount of friendliness to spread around like nutrients in a field. I think goodness is unlimited. One of those things where, the more you use it, the more you have. Like laughter."

"Huh," Nisha says, unconvinced.

"The more you use it, the more you have," I say. "That's what I think."

"But then why would Malcolm utilize it only in this small segment of his life?" Nisha asks. "If he has it available to him elsewhere? Why go around trying to get everybody to hate him?"

"Mmm," I say. It's a good question. Why?

"Nah," Walt says. "He hates everyone and everyone hates him, and that's how he rolls. But he also likes to win, so he pulls it out in the negotiating room."

They analyze Malcolm's personality some more. For how much they seem to fear Malcolm, they're definitely fascinated by him, and they have elaborate opinions about him.

The session finally ends, and I'm back in the limo. Malcolm isn't riding with us, but my seat is oriented so that I see him walking across the road with his lawyers and money crunchers in his preferred fighter jet formation where he's flanked by people, yet excruciatingly alone.

It's hardly a shock that those who work for him are fascinated with him. He is fascinating. It's hard not to look at him, hard not to watch him, hard not to wonder about him.

In every way.

Have you been instructed on protocol in the negotiating room? I have very strict preferences.

OMG, it was so wrong to take that sexy. I should never have gone to see that *Fifty Shades* movie with Mia!

"Elle! Earth to Elle," Nisha says.

I turn to face her. "I'm sorry. What?"

"What do you think? Will you make him be all good now with your empathy program?"

Walt and Nisha are grinning, because Malcolm having empathy is such a joke to them.

"I'm telling you" —I point at each of them, from one to the other and back— "goodness. Empathy. *Not* finite. No way."

Nisha claps. "Hah!"

"A wild-eyed optimist," Walt says. "Watch out, Mr. Blackberg!"

"Yeah, watch out!" Nisha exclaims. "She's gonna beat you over the head and drag that goodness right out of you!"

Walt is laughing.

I snort. "How did you know my plan?"

"So obvious," Nisha says.

Walt finds sea salt dark chocolate treats in the snack pouch and passes them around. I try not to gobble mine like a freak.

Am I a wild-eyed optimist? Is it just stupidly optimistic and idealistic that I'm thinking I can change his heart?

I remind myself that people's hearts change sometimes.

Back at the hotel, Malcolm gathers the team in a private room, fully back to his grumpy self. "What did you observe?" he asks, or more, demands.

Nisha thinks that the lawyers are unhappy to be there. Malcolm wants to know why she suspects it and she gives her reasons, mostly having to do with facial expressions. She suspects they're giving him a deal on their hours because he's an old client.

Malcolm nods. "Legacy client. On retainer. Nobody thinks there's going to be a deal here."

"Exactly," Nisha says.

"You might be right," Malcolm says.

Nisha beams.

He wants to hear if anybody noticed when people perked up. Nobody noticed anything, including me, but you can see what Malcolm noticed, and it's fascinating.

Lawrence informs him that he caught the son on the phone a few times, and that Gerrold noticed it one of the times, and looked displeased.

Malcolm nods at this. "If Junior had his way, Dad would never get anywhere near a negotiating table, anywhere near somebody who wants to buy the place. Junior thinks that if he breaks it apart himself, he'll get more money. On the off chance we reach a deal, he'll try to nix it. So why is Gerrold here? What does he want? Maybe it's not about schooling Junior. Gerrold's not an idiot."

Walt says that on Facebook, Junior says he wants to start some kind of sports marketing operation. Walt theorizes that Gerrold is working to build the son's skills for that, perhaps. Malcolm nods, and Walt practically grows two inches. Other people give their opinions.

Malcolm soaks it all in. Listening. Watching. Quietly curious.

∾

TODAY'S COACHING session is scheduled for 3:30 p.m. in the "Blue Flame" conference room, which turns out to be a small, elegant lounge with a picture window that overlooks building tops and distant hills. There's no long table, no projector or screen, just five comfy chairs arranged around a low table.

It's more like a place to have after-dinner brandy than a business meeting spot. A mod fireplace at one end features just a strip of blue flame.

"Hence the name," Malcolm says, and I spin around to find him leaning in the doorframe, eyes sparkling. "There's also a Green Flame room and an Orange Flame room. God save us from luxury hotel naming conventions." He sits. "Take a seat, I'm across town at five."

I take the seat next to him and set up my iPad on the low table.

Malcolm's not smiling or anything, but he seems like he's in a good mood. "So do you have any coaching for me on my negotiation style?" he asks, like it's all a joke.

"No," I say.

He leans back and crosses his legs. His big, brown eyes would look kind if it weren't for his villain's eyebrows arching over them, dark and severe. "You're missing an opportunity to annoy me. You could open up a whole new avenue of torment with instructive commentary about my negotiation performance."

"I'm not here to torment you," I say.

"So what did you think? Why do *you* think Gerrold's at the table?"

"The negotiation process isn't my area of concern," I say.

"And what is your area of concern?" he asks, and I have the uncanny feeling that he's looking right through me, like he knows about my area of concern as well as my forbidden fascination with him.

I keep my face carefully devoid of expression. "You know what area," I say.

His eyes twinkle darkly.

Oh my god! Did that sound sexy? "My area is the video program that I have designed," I clarify firmly.

"It's entirely possible that you're a better negotiator than I am," he says. "You don't know how much money I'd pay to avoid watching any more of that footage."

"Why?" I ask. "Because you're starting to see those people as human?"

"No, because it's just so bloody tedious."

I frown, thinking of all of my friends that are on that footage.

"Come on, now, aren't you a reader of body language? Doesn't that sort of thing fall under emotional intelligence or soft skills or whatever it is that you're doing here? You have no theory on Gerrold and the negotiation?"

"Maybe Gerrold wants his son to see the beauty in what he built," I suggest. "To see the human value in it instead of looking at it coldly as a commodity to be destroyed."

"Yes," Malcolm says sarcastically. "I'm sure that's it."

"We need to get to the session here," I say.

His phone makes a soft chime sound.

"Your phone," I say.

He shuts it off completely and slides it over to me.

"That's okay," I say. "Just keep it off."

"No, no." He picks it up and holds it out to me, gaze fixed on mine. "Take it."

My pulse kicks up. A phone is such an intimate thing—almost like a part of a person. I'm pretty sure that if I said no, he wouldn't push it, but some perverse part of me wants to hold it in my hand again, like a talisman or an orb or something. Is that warped?

I watch myself reach my hand out, watch myself take it from his fingers. I curl my fingers around it, enjoying the cool heaviness of it. God, I barely even recognize myself anymore.

When I look up, Malcolm is watching me.

"And what did you think about Gerrold as a person?" he asks. "How does he strike you?"

"I thought he seemed nice," I say. "He reminds me of a fisherman."

"A fisherman?" he asks, interested.

"With the cap that he wears. And his weather-beaten skin. I could imagine him in a ratty knit sweater, casting the line."

Malcolm asks me more questions about what the fisherman's cap says, things like that. Malcolm seems interested in what Gerrold hopes to say about himself to the world. For being such a misanthrope, he really is quite the student of human behavior.

"You think you'll get a deal?" I ask him.

"We'll see," Malcolm says. His brown eyes look extra translucent in the natural light. "My guess is that Gerrold'll be begging for me to buy in the end. My goal is always that they end up begging me to do exactly what I already want to do."

"Another tick for self-esteem—and not the bug kind, either!" I say brightly, reaching for the iPad, willing my hands not to tremble. I have today's video all cued up. I press play and there's Jada and Antonio in the elevator telling elevator stories. I'm grateful for the way the footage reminds me of my goal here, which does not involve falling for the fierce allure of Malcolm Blackberg.

Antonio tells a funny story that involves gorilla costumes and a pizza delivery guy. Jada chimes in, describing the show Antonio was in at the time. I try not to smile, remembering the whole thing. This is my family.

"Question," Malcolm suddenly says.

I pause the video and turn to him, full of hope. Is he going to ask a question about Jada or Antonio? "Yes?"

"What are your specific instructions? Regarding this training, that is."

I'm not sure what to say—what are the instructions they give to coaches? I raise my chin. "That's not your concern."

"You're to play the video for me, that much I've gathered," he says.

"That would be one element," I say.

"You're to ensure that I sit in front of the video while it's playing. Not looking at my phone."

"Yes," I say.

"How about this, then," he says. "You'd set me up in front of the video and press play and then go about your business. I'd assure you that I'd sit in front of that screen for the full hour." He brushes a bit of invisible lint from his sleeve. Two dark chunks of hair fall to his forehead, soft spikes grazing the top of his dark brows. "You'd have that promise from me."

"Wait," I say, "you're asking me to let you watch it on your own?"

"You'd have my assurance that, wherever I am, it would be playing the entire time. Isn't that what you're here for? To play me this video? To see that I am present while it's playing?"

"So you can turn off the screen or the sound and do other things the whole time?"

"You'd be able to say with complete confidence that I was

present the whole time it was playing," he continues, as though I didn't just make a major objection. "And you'd tick off the box on your little form each and every day with a clean conscience, knowing that you've executed your duties perfectly. And I'd give you a nice tip at the end. Say, twenty thousand dollars. Very nice tip for a job well done."

"Wait—what?" I feel my eyes widen. "Are you bribing me?"

"I think it's customary to reward somebody for a job well done, don't you?" he asks casually.

I gasp. "You *are* bribing me."

"I'm simply suggesting an alternate way to run this course. One that would benefit us both."

"Oh my god," I say, realizing that I probably sound completely naive, what with my utter shock. Also—*twenty-thousand freaking dollars!*

It's a lot of money, but even if I took it and spread it around between my neighbors, it really wouldn't do anything. Forty units, that would be five hundred per unit. We'd still have to move out. Maisey and John and some of the other older people would still lose their rent-controlled places. And worst of all, we'd still lose each other. Some of us have talked about getting a major house together somewhere in one of the boroughs, but nowhere really works, considering our different jobs and needs.

"Well? What do you think?" he asks, as though he's wondering about my opinion on the color of his tie or something and not offering me a *bribe*.

No amount of money will get me to sell out my friends, not that I can say that to him.

"No thank you, that's what I think." I push play and focus on the film. Kelsey's telling about strange elevator conversations that she's had, and then Antonio reminds her about the no-sex-in-the-elevator rule that was recently instituted. I bite my lip, remembering when that happened. There were some very bad offenders in the building, and let's just say, you could always tell.

"Question," Malcolm says.

I pause the video. "I hope you know, Malcolm, every time I pause the video, time gets added to the end."

"Fifty thousand," he says.

My mouth goes dry. "I'm not one of your negotiation foes."

"Please. I'd never increase an offer by two hundred and fifty percent in a negotiation setting."

"Yet you're doing it for me."

"Dedication should be rewarded."

"You need to stop trying to get out of this," I say.

"I wouldn't be out of it. You'd have assurances that I'm playing it for myself while I'm present in the room, and you'd be able to report as much to your boss."

"Except maybe you're watching...but with the sound off and the screen black, right? And working or having a conference call on Bluetooth the whole time?"

He studies my face. "They can't be paying you more than that. Fifty thousand. For a four-week gig?"

"It's not happening."

If he's surprised, he doesn't show it. But then he's a master of the poker face. "Sixty. And that tip won't be on the table for long."

My mind reels with what I could do with that much money. I could get a decent place. I could get out of the credit card debt I accrued during my mother's illness—I was spending money like a drunken sailor back then, paying for every little thing that I thought could help her or make her more comfortable. Or I could help a few of my friends with their down payments on new places. But sixty thousand isn't enough to help everybody— not by a long shot. And no amount of money is worth trading in the only family I have—these amazing women who took me in, who've added love and meaning and endless joy to my life. "You would be wise not to bribe me again," I tell him.

"Why?" he asks. "Why would I be wise not to do that? What are they paying you? Can you tell me that?"

"What Bexley Partners pays me is proprietary," I announce.

"Come on, now," Malcolm drawls, looking highly amused. "You know who I mean."

My pulse races. Everything is so weird and complicated—why did I ever think I could pull this off? I need to get back to familiar ground.

I suck in a breath, reminding myself that I'm in charge here. Malcolm's not in charge; I'm in charge. "I get it—you're a billionaire. But guess what? That doesn't mean that you get to go around bribing people and doing whatever ridic thing flies into your mind."

"Whatever ridic thing flies into my mind?" His brown eyes become warm as he smiles. "I don't know, most days being a billionaire does mean that."

"Are you ready to resume? You don't want to be late for your five o'clock," I say.

He sits up, baffled. "Come on, now. You're not really turning that down."

"Yes, I am," I say. "Are you ready to get back to it?"

His stare hits right down to my core. "They couldn't be paying you more than sixty."

"That's not your concern," I say.

He blinks, studying my face. My blood races. Was it crazy to turn that down? I feel like he's on the verge of figuring me out. I wish so badly that I could consult with Willow right now. She'd know what to do. Or Jada. A lot of people who aren't me would know what to do.

He says, "If there are other requirements, we could work together on that. Nobody will know."

What does that even mean? I swallow. "The clock is ticking," I say.

He tilts his head as if he needs to get a look at me from a new angle, like this angle isn't making sense. "It's my strong recommendation that you take it."

What will happen if I don't take it? He seems so in control—I feel like, at any moment, he could get up and walk out. Dare me to tell on him. Have me hauled away.

He's waiting.

I fumble back to what I know—the only thing I know for sure: "You were mandated by a court of law to undergo this training. A court of law."

His eyes sparkle. "Wait, *what* kind of court?"

"Not funny," I say.

He smiles, and it does something to my insides. I've never been near a man so magnetic—his pull is nearly physical.

"What is it that you want, little country mouse? If it's not money."

"For you to watch this video," I say.

"That's not what you want. Tell me what you really want. Let's find a way to get you what you really and truly want."

For a second, I'm tempted to tell him—I want you to spare the building. Please, please, please don't knock it down.

"There must be something," he says.

I say, "I want you to watch this video with complete attention. And an open heart."

He's studying me with keen interest. "It can't be just that."

"I want you to see these people. Really see them," I say.

He grins like I must be joking. Anger rushes over me—anger that this man has our fate in his hands and it's all a big joke to him. Anger at myself for lusting after him in spite of it all, like some naive schoolgirl. Anger that I find him sexy even now.

"It's got to be something more," he says. "Tell me."

I realize that I don't have to answer his questions. I'm the coach, right? I meet his gaze with a hard stare. "If we don't get back to the video," I say, "you'll be in danger of missing your appointment."

He looks amused. He looks extra gorgeous when he's amused, like he's lit from inside. "So you'll just leave it on the table?"

"Leave what on the table?"

He blinks, as though my question defies comprehension. "Your *tip*," he says.

"Well...that wasn't a tip, it was a bribe," I say. "I suggest you refrain from further bribery attempts. Now are you ready to get on with it?"

He studies my face, still with that glint of humor, and slowly his eyes fall to my neck.

My cheeks heat with shame. *Country mouse*, he called me. Why didn't I listen to Francine about the bow tie? I'm sure he thinks I have a collection of creepy dolls with eyes that never close now.

My heart thuds.

Is he going to figure me out? Will he realize I'm a fraud and kick me out onto the streets of San Francisco...or worse? Oh my god, what was I thinking?

Even the way he's looking at my butterfly tie now—he knows I'm out of my depth. He knows he has all of the power.

"No more questions?" I ask—or more, plead. *No more questions. Pleeeease no more!* That's what it sounds like in my head. I move my finger near the "Play" button. I need for him to watch it, and then I need to get away from him so that I can think straight.

"Hmm," he says, like he's pondering, but I'm sure he's just saying that for the pleasure of watching me sweat. Maybe he's trying to get into my head like Nisha warned. "And will we get any more letter carrier wisdom?" he asks suddenly. "Or is that part over?"

I sit up, grateful that he's brought me back to familiar ground. There's nothing I can't overcome to deliver the mail, obstacles large and small. I can do this. And I know everything about being a letter carrier.

I cross my arms. "As a matter of fact, Malcolm, this is a perfect time for some letter carrier wisdom. Thank you for that idea. I have a little quiz for you."

13

Malcolm

"A QUIZ," I say. "I didn't know I'd be quizzed on the material." I cross my arms, still reeling from the fact that she turned down so much money. From what I reviewed of her background, she doesn't come from money. She grew up in a hardscrabble rural Pennsylvania town. She worked as a letter carrier while attending the local community college, graduating with a degree in psychology.

Exactly how much are they paying her? More than sixty thousand? Does she get a bonus at the end? Is she a better negotiator than she appears to be?

That wasn't a tip, it was a bribe. She really seemed surprised. She's impossible, and so delicious. And her program—it's a hundred percent ridiculous. And now she has a quiz?

I'm a hundred percent fascinated. People so rarely surprise me.

Slim, nimble fingers move up to straighten her little tie. She wears pale pink polish on her short, carefully shaped nails.

Everything about her is pitch-perfect in a way I can't quite articulate.

"This quiz is designed to provide you with a very important lesson," she says. "Don't worry, it's multiple choice."

"You think I'm that kind of student? That I need multiple choice?"

She smiles a genuine smile, and I find it strangely pleasurable. "No comment," she says.

"This had better count toward my hour," I grumble.

"Letter carriers encounter three types of dogs," she begins, "big dogs, medium dogs, and small dogs. Which of these three kinds of dogs does the letter carrier consider far and away the most dangerous?"

"First of all, you can't imagine how delighted I am that we're back to the letter carriers again," I say.

"Well?" she asks primly. She seems to be taking the quiz very seriously.

"This feels like a trick question," I say. "Is the obvious answer the wrong one or the right one?"

"Why not just tell me what you think is the correct answer without being fancy," she says.

I study her eyes for a clue. "Clearly the big dogs. All dogs are territorial, but the larger breeds—your Dobermans, your Rottweilers, your German shepherds—those would have the more lethal bite."

"Oh, I'm sorry, Malcolm, you flunked that quiz completely." Here she grins. "Letter carriers consider small dogs to be the most dangerous. You see, large dogs are confident dogs. They know that they can hold their territory, and they play by a certain set of rules; for example, they nearly always give you a warning growl before an attack. Letter carriers know exactly where they stand with a large dog."

"Is that so?" I ask, wondering where she's going with this.

"The medium dog is the same way," she continues. "Medium dogs will play by the dog rules, too, though they have less ability to back it up. But the small dog?" She shakes her head sadly. "Small dogs look cute. But they cannot be coaxed with treats. They cannot be reasoned with. I think it's something about their being small. The one thing they have in their arsenal is the ability to be unpredictable, to go completely crazy for no apparent reason when they feel threatened."

My blood races. Is she doing what I think she's doing?

She continues, "One minute they're just looking at you with their sweet little faces. And the next thing you know, razor-sharp teeth are attached to your leg!" Here she fixes me with a playful look. "And they *do not* let go! When a little dog attacks, they attack with everything, like a wild banshee."

"Is that so?" I say.

"Yes. Letter carriers carry pepper spray in their bags, as you know," she continues merrily, pretty eyes sparkling, "but good luck with that. Once a small dog is in attack mode, all bets are off."

"I see," I say, blood racing.

Her face glows with aliveness and a look of pleasure that's beautiful on her—or would be if she weren't threatening me. She looks downright amused by her clever little threat.

"Are you the little dog in this equation? Are you going to attack me with no warning?"

"No, the moral of the story is that you should never underestimate little dogs, that's all I'm saying. Maybe they have something to teach you."

"And if I don't behave, they'll bite me?"

She shrugs. "Ready?"

"For more of the video?" I ask.

"Yes," she says brightly.

"I'm jumping out of my skin with eagerness."

She turns on the video and we watch it. Or at least, she watches it. My face is pointed in that direction, my ears are open to the ridiculous conversations on the screen, the answers that the people give to the probing questions thrown out by the unseen filmographer who seems to know them all, but my attention is all on Elle.

～

THE NEXT DAY'S negotiation session is uneventful, or at least, on the surface it is. I'm getting to know a lot more about Gerrold and his son.

Our executive coaching session is also uneventful. Elle has gone back to her maroon suit, though she wears a new butterfly tie with tiny hedgehogs on it, and she starts the video up right away and allows no chitchat, shutting me down whenever I ask a question in the faux-bold manner of hers that I so enjoy. She's so intent on her program, so serious.

Today's program features a woman who bakes stupidly themed cookies; later, John, the Korean War vet, voices approval of the building's boiler system. I'm buckling in for a lot of jibber jabber, but then the unseen filmmaker asks him to describe a typical day overseas in the Korean War, a seemingly innocuous question that has him telling a moving story about a dear friend of his.

Elle ends the session as soon as the hour is up, escaping the Blue Flame conference room like the place is on fire.

The Germantown negotiation rolls on a third day. We're talking about side issues, and Gerrold Jesperson and his son are revealing a great deal of themselves.

In the world of negotiation, a *black swan* is a term meaning an unknown, unseen factor at work behind the scenes. A black swan is something like a hidden corporate history, an owner's secret belief, an unknown need that drives the negotiator. In current events, it's typically an unexpected circumstance or a catastrophe that radically changes everything going forward.

People have black swans too—a person's black swan might be a secret burning desire, or a trauma that drives them. Understanding a person's black swan gives you insight into why they do the things they do, and lets you predict what they'll do next.

So in this part of the negotiations, Gerrold and his son think they're telling me all about their company, but they're actually telling me about themselves, and hopefully revealing a black swan.

I need their black swan, no doubt about it. I made a massive acquisition last year that will be a total loss if he doesn't sell. In other words, I stand to lose a pile of money if this doesn't go my way. Nothing like an uphill battle, right?

So I'm in these sessions bleeding out tens of thousands of dollars a day to keep the team on site, needing to be on my A game...and what am I spending my mental energy on? Thinking about Elle. Wondering about Elle's black swan. Imagining the different ways in which I'd pull off that bow tie, which seems to be my new obsession.

If the bow tie's a clip-on, well, it ruins things slightly. At some point, I'd need to find a way to make her replace it with a regular women's bow tie, just so that I can have the pleasure of pulling it off. It comes to me that I should buy one, just to be ready. Like having a condom at the ready.

And after I pulled it off, I'd undo a button and kiss her neck. And I'd gather up the silky softness of her hair, closing it greedily in my fist as I press my lips to that side-of-the-mouth freckle, after which I'd devour her mouth.

"Boise," Gerrold says. "Boise, of course, would be an exception."

He's watching me, waiting for my response. What was he

talking about? How is it that I wasn't listening? "An exception," I say.

Luckily this puts him back on the road of what he was talking about. "Yes, exactly," he says, and he proceeds to re-explain his point in greater detail, allowing me to catch up. He wants me to fully grasp the breadth of the network, I suppose. I just need that black swan. What drives him? What keeps him up at night?

What keeps Elle up at night? Why turn down so much money?

I force my focus back on the proceedings.

I can feel Walt at my right, shifting feet, bored. Across the table, Junior's bored, too, if not downright hostile. He's useless to watch, as are Germantown's minor players—admins and lawyers. They give me nothing. It's possible there's nothing to see.

My gaze slides to Elle, sitting four seats to my left. She's staring at the tray of pastries again. She always takes one almond croissant during each session; not quite at the start, mind you; she stares at it for a while first, but then, inevitably—most often when people are fussing or gathering papers—she rises demurely from her seat, takes the tongs, and deftly trans-fers one to her small plate, then quietly sits back down. She eats it slowly, tearing off little bits, chewing with intense concentration—or so it seems; I can't fully see her from where I am.

Sometimes after she's finished eating her croissant, she seems to fix her gaze back on the pastry platter, as if she wants to take another one, but she never does. Why not take another one? Does she have a sweet tooth she's trying to tame? Is it out of some sense of propriety? Nobody ever takes two; most people don't even take one, but that doesn't mean it's forbidden. Is that why she didn't take the money? An idea that it's forbidden? It seems improbable, but Elle *is* improbable—deliciously improbable.

Silently I will her to take another.

Of course she doesn't. It's not like her to give in to temptation, but I think she wants to. God, what I wouldn't give to watch her yield to desire, to cross a line just once.

I have a lunch meeting after this, and then Elle and I have yet another afternoon emotional intelligence session scheduled for the Blue Flame room.

Will we get another postal-themed quiz or anecdote? I'm trying to think how to goad her into that. I need to know about her—not the people in that building. It's possible that Corman warned her not to let me ask too many questions. He knows what I can do.

I glance at the time. Our session is in just under three hours —a hundred and sixty-five minutes from now.

I straighten up right then. Am I literally counting the minutes until my court-ordered executive coaching session instead of finding my opening with Gerrold?

I call for a break at the next acceptable interval and order an espresso to be brought to me on the roof. I drink it up, sucking in the cool air, hoping to cattle-prod my psyche back to the business at hand. Energized, I head back down. I get the guys rolling on my business vision and close out the session soon after.

I arrive at the Blue Flame room to find Elle already there, taking pictures of the view out the window. Who does she send them to? Or does she post them? She wears the same business suit as she did in this morning's negotiation session. Does she wear her business suit while lounging around in her own hotel room? Does she take off the jacket? What about the tie? I close my eyes. The goddamn tie!

I settle into an upholstered armchair. "Did you have a nice lunch?" I ask.

She spins around, smiles. "More or less," she says mysteriously. She sets up the iPad on the table in front of us.

"Quite the view here, isn't it?" I say. "Different from New York. Or the rolling hills of rural Pennsylvania."

Her gaze snaps to mine. "Somebody's been nosy."

"Wouldn't you be more surprised if I hadn't looked?"

"I suppose," she says.

"What inspired you to move away from there? A small-town girl moving to such an urban part of Jersey, working in the big city. That's a major move."

"Not much need for executive coaches out on the rolling hills and potato fields."

"So you moved to the big city for the plentiful executive coaching opportunities?" I doubt that would be her reason, but sometimes when you offer the wrong reason, a person corrects you.

She frowns. I can see the thoughts, back and forth behind her eyes. Should she correct me? Is this a conversation she wants to indulge?

"I suppose it was always a dream of mine—bright lights, big city. Somewhere bigger, anyway," she adds quickly. "And to have lots of girlfriends near me. Fun things going on."

"Fun things going on?" I ask.

She smiles. "If you think you're running out the clock on your session, I should remind you that this conversation does not count as part of it. We have the video program to get through."

"I know," I say. "Did you find what you were looking for?"

"Yes," she says. "I very much did." She sounds almost wistful.

"But," I offer.

She furrows her pretty brow. "Are you ready?"

"But what?" I ask.

"But we have an hour-long program to get through," she says.

Room service arrives right then. A woman pushes in a tray with domed platters, plus a pitcher of lemonade with two glasses and a small stack of plates. She comes to a stop next to Elle's chair.

I stand. "Thank you," I say, handing over a tip.

"What is this?" Elle asks.

"Refreshments." I pull the lid off of a pile of almond croissants—I had them bird-dog the Kendrick building's bakery source. There are almond and chocolate arranged around the edges. The other platter holds an assortment of fruits, crackers, and cheeses.

She's staring, wide-eyed as I pour her a glass of lemonade.

"You ordered food?" she asks. "Didn't you have lunch?"

"Snacks. Fix yourself a plate," I say. I fix myself one with cheese and a bunch of grapes and a croissant and settle in.

She's frowning.

"Surely eating doesn't count as multitasking," I add.

"We'll see." She hesitates, turns on the video—without taking a plate, though she does her fair share of consuming the food with her eyes. She clearly wants it. What's stopping her?

"Nothing for you?" I ask. "Not hungry?"

She says, "Every time you talk, I'm restarting this thing from the beginning."

I pantomime my lips zipped and pop a grape into my mouth.

Today's program features the world's most monotonous voiceover. The unseen filmmaker seems to have specific feelings about each washer and dryer; she goes through an excruciatingly tedious monologue about what happens when you set the far end dryer to air dry.

"Is this a joke?" I ask.

"*Shhh,*" she scolds. The movie rolls on. Still she ignores the food.

I pretend to keep watching as the unseen auteur launches into the fascinating mystery of the "dryer-lint bandit." Apparently there's a rule that you're to clean the lint from the screen after you dry your clothes and one person wasn't doing it. There was sleuthing involved, but the culprit was never caught. Maisey is back again with her own interpretation—that people simply forget.

"Maisey's an optimist," I say.

"Shhh," she says. She's looking back over at the cart. I pretend to focus intently on the screen, but I'm really looking at her reflection in the window. Warmth spreads across my chest as I watch her take one and set it on a plate. She picks it apart and eats it in her bird-like way. At one point, she closes her eyes in pleasure. It's a rich pastry, and she's enjoying the forbidden hell out of it, and I'm enjoying the hell out of her.

She glances over again once she's done with the pastry. Will she have another? "Not hungry?" I ask.

"Oh...I don't know," she says.

"Not a fan?" I ask.

"Shhh," she says.

On screen, people theorize endlessly on how to uncover the identity of the person who doesn't clean a dryer lint screen. They're laughing and joking; they really do seem to know each other well in this building, right down to the details of who uses what detergent. There are ideas on how to set traps for the offender, but they're all good natured.

Is this how people in groups live? They collaborate on silly projects? They regale each other with endless details of their lives? They empathize about friends lost in wars decades ago? Growing up, I got a lot of my information about how groups and families operate from TV, and from being over at my neighbor Howie's. Scant information. And then I was overseas at school.

Onscreen, the case of the lint screen bandit rages. They're saying nice things to each other, now.

Something grinds in my gut.

I finish my plate and I wander over and load a bit more food onto my plate. "You do realize your presentation has devolved into people literally discussing dryer lint, do you not?"

She smiles.

"*Dryer lint.*" I take her plate, load it up with an assortment of pastries and cheeses, and set it back down in front of her.

"What are you doing?"

"It would be a shame to let it go to waste," I say, settling back into my chair. "I've never seen a group so animated about dryer lint. They really need to get lives."

She stops the presentation. "Quiz."

I grin. "Please let it be about mail delivery."

"It's about dryer lint. Why do you think this group is so interested in the whole dryer lint situation?"

I groan.

"You need to take my quizzes seriously," she says.

"Fine, I'll take your quiz seriously." Casually, I cross my legs. "Most of these people are theater people. Emoting dramatically is what theater people do. Especially Antonio and Mia. Those two are super emoters."

"Can you think of any other reason?" she asks.

"Are you telling me my answer was wrong?"

"It's not the answer I was looking for."

"But it's the right answer," I say. "Have you been watching this footage? Have you seen how they all mug for the camera? The pink-haired one."

She's grinning, building a cheese and cracker sandwich. "Can you think of any other possibilities?"

"Insanity?" I try.

"Come on." She's eating one of her cheese and cracker sandwiches. She goes on to another.

"Let's see," I say casually. "Do they want an excuse to use the homemade guillotine that they've been building in the basement?"

She laughs, covering her mouth to keep from spitting crumbs. "Stop. Give a real answer."

"Or what?" I ask. "Will you give me an X?"

Right then, that witchy look comes over her face. "Maybe," she says.

My pulse races. God, that witchy look from the dressing room—like a sexy secret coming up from deep inside of her. Country-mouse Elle, eating all the snacks, tormenting me, inventing her little quizzes.

This nearly irresistible compulsion to grab her hair and kiss her washes over me. I force my gaze to the screen, though out the corner of my eye, I can see that she's building another open-faced sandwich with a cracker, two giant hunks of cheese, and several grapes. A French sandwich. You can't build a proper French sandwich on a cracker. I should have ordered French bread. Next time I'll get French bread.

"Well?" she asks.

"Give me a moment, I'm trying to think," I say as she chows down. I wait for her to finish it, and then I say, "I give up."

She dabs at her mouth with a napkin. "It's because they care about the place. They love that building and each other."

"But there is a saboteur in their midst," I say, "who must be unmasked."

"That's not the point. Look how deeply they care about every little thing in that building. Imagine the effect that knocking it down will have on these people."

"I'm to get all of this from their fervent—and might I add, slightly insane—hunt for the dryer screen bandit?" I say.

She shrugs. "It means a lot to them," she says.

I smile. "Spirit," I say with Shakespearean enunciation. Dramatically I hold my hands in front of my face, shielding my eyes. "Please, spirit, I can't bear to see anymore. Remove me from this place!"

"W-what are you talking about?" she asks.

"You're the ghost of Christmas present, showing me the lives I'm ruining. Will I be treated to Christmas future after this? Will Tiny Tim yet live? Just to be clear, I'm Scrooge in this formulation. I'm entirely comfortable with that, you know."

She hits play. Discreetly, I watch her eat, watch her pink tongue dart out to lick the powder off the side of her lips.

She turns to me. "Are you even watching?"

"How could I tear my eyes away?"

"I feel like you're not watching."

"You want to give me a quiz?" I ask. "Go ahead and give me a quiz. Or maybe I'll give you one."

"You'll give *me* a quiz? Regarding the people there?"

"I certainly will." I raise my pointer finger. "What secret is John keeping?"

Elle hits pause. "You think that...this John fellow has a secret?"

"I don't *think* that he does; I know that he does," I tease, pleased she hasn't figured it out. Most people wouldn't.

"Well...he wears that hat from the army a lot," she says. "You think it has something to do with the army?"

"Nope. Something contemporary. Regarding another resident."

This perks her up. "What is it?"

"You have to guess."

"*Tell me,*" she demands, beaming at me.

Something lifts in my chest, and I just want to grab her and kiss the little crumbs off the side of her mouth and then devour her like an almond croissant.

She leans in closer. "Tell me!"

"Or what?" I tease. "Will you give me an X?"

She's grinning outright now. "Maybe I will," she says.

I shrug. "He's in love with Maybell, of course."

She straightens, studies my face. "What? You think he's in love with...Maisey?"

"You can't see it?" I ask.

"No," she says. "Looks to me like they're just friends."

"Back it up. To the part where all of those people are in the lobby with the pink-haired girl. When she's giving the announcement." Elle backs it up and finds the place I mean. "The way he looks at her. Everybody watches Pink Hair except John. He watches Maymie. He always watches Maymie."

"Maybe they've known each other a long time or something," she says.

"He beams at her when she talks," I say. "The woman rambles like nobody I've ever heard, but John could listen all day."

"Maybe they're just friends is what I'm saying."

"The way he looks at her? Come off it," I say. "Anyway, men being just friends with women? Very rare. Go to that roof part. I think it was in yesterday's highly instructive emotional intelligence program."

She goes to the part I mean.

"Do you see?" I say. "Maybelle is absolutely insufferable in her rambling, but John can't keep his eyes off her."

"Hmm," Elle says.

"I'm sorry, that's not enough for you?" I take the iPad and navigate to the beginning, pause it on Maisey's shirt. "What is this pin she wears? With every outfit."

"Gerbera daisy."

"She wore a belt buckle with that same kind of daisy, too, one time—in that dull pink color," I say.

"Salmon," Elle mumbles.

"Now, I've only seen a few days of footage. I'm gonna go out on a limb and say the salmon gerbera daisy is Maybelle's favorite flower. And let me ask you, what sorts of flowers does ol' John grow in those pathetic little coffee cans up on the roof?"

Elle takes control of the player and rewinds to yesterday's section of footage. When she gets to the John-and-his-sad-flowers-growing-out-of-coffee-cans section, her lips part in surprise. "God, that is so observant of you," she says. "He grows the flowers that Maisey likes."

"Do I get my tick now?" I say.

"You are really observant," she says, stunned.

"I know," I say. "Maybe I'll use my amazing powers for ill and make a billion dollars someday. Oh wait, I already did."

"No, it's amazing," she says. "You really see people."

"All the better to crush and destroy them on my way to the top."

She looks at me, challenge in her eyes, lips pursing and then un-pursing, as if she wants to say something, but isn't quite sure what. Maybe she wants what I said not to be true. Unfortunately, it is true.

I could never be one of the people in that video, all fun and laughing in a group. I don't like people. I don't like being around people, and vice versa.

"Can we wrap it up now?" I ask. "You can take the rest of the food to your room if you want. They're just going to throw it away."

"Wait—you haven't watched the whole hour," she says.

"Come on," I say. "I feel like I won emotional intelligence today. I get nothing for that?"

"Talking doesn't count. The hour is only you watching the video," she says.

"You understand, don't you, that the more of this video I watch, the more convinced I am that this is a piece of property that should've been torn down long ago. I think it'll be good for these people to be out of there—the place is a dump."

"It's not at all a dump," she protests. "All of those vintage details? The moldings? The chandelier?"

"The way I see it, I'm doing them a favor. It's called reality feedback."

She goes still for a moment—she even looks a bit pale. I wait for her to reply; it certainly seems as though she wants to, but then she scoots her chair forward, and without a word, she hits play, or more, stabs it. I can only see the back of her head now, and I can see that her arms are crossed.

"Buildings come down and buildings go up," I say to the back of her head.

"What about Maisey and John?" she asks. "You would tear them apart?"

"If they want each other badly enough, they'll find a way to be together. That's how it works."

"How would they have a chance of being together if they never even saw each other ever again? It's not as if they're going to find rent-controlled apartments in Manhattan," she says, trying to keep the emotion out of her voice. "More likely, they'll end up miles and miles from each other and never see each other again."

"Or John finally realizes he has to act, and he declares his love and Maybelline reciprocates and they get a little place together on Long Island or in Florida or something, which they never would have done if the building remained. Humans thrive on challenge. It's how we're designed. Maybe they've become too comfortable in that place."

She turns to me. Hotly, she asks, "Is that what you tell yourself? When you throw people from their homes? That they've become too comfortable in their places?"

"No," I say, picking up my glass of lemonade and swirling around the ice. "I tell myself that I'm going to make a whole boatload of money while improving the city."

She regards me dolefully, then turns away from me and hits play yet again.

14

Noelle

I START the video back up, trying to keep my hand from trembling.

Am I making things worse? Are these videos making Malcolm want to knock down the place even more? I've never met anybody like him.

"The entire neighborhood will improve," he adds.

I grit my teeth. Nisha and Coralee and those guys warned me not to let him get into my head, and he's definitely in there, now. More than in there—he's rooting around like a warthog in a china shop.

I hate that he's in my head. I hate that he saw things about John and Maisey that I never did. I hate that he's brought me all this food and it's so delicious, and now I just want to eat more, and it's not just because I'm hungry, it's that I'm tired in some soul-deep way that I can't define.

I hate how his voice gets me so stupidly quivery inside. I hate how muscular he looks under his sexy suit and how I have to exert actual energy not to imagine what it would be like to climb onto his lap, to press a kiss to his lips, to feel his hands clamp around my hips, solid and strong.

"What is it that you want, little country mouse?" he asks softly.

"For you to have empathy for these people."

"Negotiation one-oh-one," he says, "never ask for something that a person doesn't have to give."

"All humans are capable of empathy," I say. "Including you."

A deafening silence hangs in the air.

You sure about that? That's the question between us now. He doesn't even have to voice it.

"Even if I were capable of empathy, nothing would change. I would still knock down any building I see fit to knock down, including John and Maisey's." He watches me strong and steady, like he really needs me to get this. "Inspiring a person to feel empathy for those whose lives he might upend only works on somebody who cares, who wants to avoid being a villain. Me? I know what I am. I'm a bad man, Elle, and I'm perfectly comfortable with it. I'm the villain in everybody's story, and I always will be."

Chills come over me. "I don't accept that."

"Which part of it?" he asks.

"The whole thing."

He narrows his eyes. "You didn't know me before," he says. "You didn't give a shit about my empathy or emotional intelligence or moral fiber a month ago, and you won't give a shit about it in a month. What do you really want here?"

I swallow back the dryness in my mouth. "Your empathy."

He seems to find this amusing. "Come on, now, think big, Elle. What is it really? Tell me. Who knows, maybe you'll get it.

Tell me what you really want. Make a list. Ask for more than one thing. Be outrageous. Go for it."

I shouldn't play his game; I shouldn't allow his question to sink into my heart, but I do.

I want him to see the beauty in the building. I want for him to love it the way I do. But there's so much more—maybe it's something about eating the rich treats, but images of *him* crowd my mind...images of him watching me with that intensity that he has. Images of large, rough fingers skimming my cheek, my neck, my bare arm.

He's watching my eyes, looking back and forth from one to the other.

It's exciting and addictive, because I'm not used to it; people never even give me a second look. I'm used to being part of the furniture, always there in the background, and here is this man focusing on me, on what I want. And this is a man who sees people. Sure, he claims it's for ill, but I'm reveling in it.

And I would smooth my hand down his scruffy cheek, and I would help him off with his suit jacket and I would slide my hands over his shoulders and I would tell him that he's not a villain. I would whisper it in his ear. I would tell him that I knew from the first that he has a good heart. It's that good heart of his that enables him to see people like he does.

"I know there's something," he rumbles. "Let's see what we can do to get us both what we want."

"What I want," I force myself to say, "is for you to complete today's video with no more side conversations."

"Oh, how incredibly boring," he says.

"It's not boring to me."

He glitters. He's a nuclear reactor of sexy power, and I'm the nobody who will never contain him.

Quickly I turn and hit play. He watches the rest of the program—as much as he ever does, anyway.

I get out of there quickly as soon as it's over.

I observe yet another negotiation session the next day, observing him slowly and methodically spinning a web of friendly engagement and even charisma around the unsuspecting room. His keen interest cuts under the surface of everybody, makes people want to tell him things, to give him things.

He has one of Gerrold's lawyers proudly sharing their contrarian opinion on something about domestic interstate transit; he gets the son talking about a pit-smoked barbecue place near the Austin distribution center that the crew is crazy over. He has Gerrold sharing intimate business details like they're old colleagues.

Will Gerrold be able to hold out? Will he give in and beg Malcolm to buy as Malcolm so jerkishly predicted? Sometimes I send Gerrold silent bursts of ESP—stay strong! Don't fall for Malcolm's fascination and charisma!

I skip meals most days so as to not abuse the per diem, though I still go down and sit with the group. They all seem to think I'm on a one-meal-a-day diet, which is somewhat true, I suppose. And that one meal seems to be during sessions with Malcolm where he rolls in the treat cart. It really is hard not to feast off the treat cart. I tell myself that the food would go to waste anyway, so it's not like I'm taking more than I ought from this company, but I also sort of know that if I refused to eat the treats, Malcolm might stop ordering them. Or would he? Not that it matters.

Not only am I completely starving by the time our sessions roll around, but the selection gets better and better with chocolates, champagne grapes, freshly baked breads.

One day, an assortment of bruschetta is there, and I learn that this is Malcolm's favorite food, and I tease him about that before confessing that it's my favorite food tied with chocolate chip cookie dough and cheese.

Cookie dough arrives in a small crystal dish with a spoon the next day.

"You are evil," I say excitedly. But I really do want it. And, I have to keep my strength up. And hey, I'm still making him watch the videos.

I start up the video before I dig into the dough.

Malcolm is his usual incisively perceptive self. He guesses Francine's a dancer before it comes out in the footage. He thinks one of the second-floor residents seems depressed, and when I talk to Jada that night she promises that she'll invite her to watch Bachelor and get Maisey to tie a little baggy of homemade caramel corn on her door. That's Maisey's thing—tying little baggies of homemade caramel corn on people's doors when they've been nice to her, or just when she randomly feels like it. I've gotten my share of caramel corn baggies as the letter carrier for the building, and it always touches me, not to mention being utterly delicious and decadent. I'm scared to ask how much butter she uses.

My friends think it's amazing that Malcolm is so observant. They think it's a good sign. I don't tell them the part where he claims to use it only for ill.

I won't believe it. I refuse to.

Sometimes Malcolm peppers me with questions about the town where I grew up, and it's not just about how far Mapleton is from Pittsburgh or Philly or New York—he wants to know about the people, the culture. I dig out shots of the ridiculously tiny school I attended. He digs out pictures of the boys' school he attended. I tease him about always being in the back of the group pictures, never a smile.

"Oh I always sat in the back—whenever I could," he says.

"I always sat in the front," I say.

"That's perfect," he says. "With your pencils sharpened."

"And of course you sat in the back," I say.

"Where else? The front always seemed so far away. After a while, it was, I suppose." He sounds almost wistful.

"Would you have *wanted* to sit in the front?" I ask.

He declares the question unanswerable, and he teases me about always sitting up front. As the days wear on, I find that I'm showing him parts of myself I didn't expect to show him. Our sessions get longer and longer.

"No more questions; it's time to watch the video," I say after a lengthy exchange on favorite music—it turns out he's into classic UK punk rock like The Damned and Generation X. I'm more of a Sia girl, but I also like folk singers like Frazey Ford. He wants to hear more about Frazey Ford, and I tell him the music talk is over. "Time for the program."

"Will there be no more postal quizzes? I like those quizzes," he says.

"I can't believe you don't prefer the movie. When I was in school, people were glad when the teacher showed a movie. It meant you didn't have to do anything."

"People were glad," he says. "But you?"

I try not to feel flattered when his observational skills turn on me. The truth is, I always secretly hated having a movie instead of classroom instruction or quizzes. Before I know it, he's wrangling out of me what a nerd about school I was. I did all my homework, I helped out when I could. I was a Girl Scout well into high school. I always know where my keys are. I love accounting software and day planners. Suddenly I'm pulling my day planner out of my bag in order to show him my system of stickers, including stars, lightning bolts, and hedgehogs. I don't know what's come over me—it feels intimate, like showing him a piece of myself, the secret of how I run. And I want him to see.

"I hope you don't think this shortens your session," I say, shutting it and nestling it back in my bag.

"The point of chatting with you has nothing to do with my

sessions," he says, and I feel the truth of it, and my belly does its weird fluttery thing. But hey, chatting like nice, normal human beings is a good thing. Chatting is a key part of building empathy, though when I'm honest with myself, the way we're talking is feeling like a date. A really fun and promising date.

"It's time." I push play.

In the days that follow, we fall into a pleasant little routine. We meet in the Blue Flame room and feast and chat, but then it's onto the video. It's not easy to limit the chat but I do my best. And even though he acts grumpy about it all, he keeps paying attention.

He seems to really like Antonio, and he's happy when Antonio appears onscreen to tell a few neighbors that he landed a minor role in "Aladdin."

On another day, Malcolm laughs when Mia comes into the frame wearing the cat suit she has to wear for her delivery job—that particular video was from a few years back, when she first got the job. "Takes a lot of nerve to walk around Manhattan dressed like that," he says.

You have no idea how she hated it, I want to say, but obviously I don't. I do really wish I could tell him about the big break she got recently. And I have a funny story about her delivering sandwiches to her high school nemesis while wearing the costume. I hate this deception—it just isn't me.

But he's starting to see my friends and neighbors as human beings, and I don't care how hopeless he makes it sound, I'm going to take that as a great sign. That's how it was with Scrooge, right? Once he really looked at Tiny Tim, his heart opened. Maybe this is working.

I dine with my traveling team buddies, which is to say I have a drink and laugh and chat with them while they eat. Afterwards I take a walk down Pine Street toward the Embarcadero.

That's when the call comes in.

I don't recognize the number, but sometimes I answer unknown calls because I just never know if it's somebody from the building.

"Is this...Stella?" the woman on the other end asks.

I freeze...is it the Bexley office? I've been dreading a call from the Bexley office. "Can I help you?" I ask.

"Is this Stella?" she asks again.

I wince. "Who is this?" I ask.

There's a long silence on the other end. "It's Stella," she says. "The real Stella," she adds.

"Oh." My pulse pounds. "Um...oh."

"Who are you?" she asks. "What are you doing? What's going on?"

"Um, okay, it's kind of a long story," I begin. Am I really saying that?

"I think I'd like to hear it."

"I don't mean any harm—I swear. Do you remember in the elevator at the Blackberg Inc. headquarters? The letter carrier you were stuck with?"

"Wait, what? Is this..."

"Noelle," I say. "Please, Stella, I'm so sorry. I didn't mean for it to go this long. I mean you no harm—I swear."

"Wait, what? You're the letter carrier I was trapped with? You took my place? Oh my god, did you talk me into quitting so that you could take my place?"

"No, I swear! I wanted to get in to see Malcolm Blackberg— I was trying to see him, and I had your card in my hand from when you gave it to me. They thought I was you."

"Why let them think that? You're the letter carrier. I don't even get it..."

"I am a letter carrier, yes..." I tell her the story in one long ramble, how I was there to beg him to save 341 West 45th. How

I had video to show him. How I let them think I was her and magically, he thought he had to watch the footage.

She's laughing by the end of it. "Hold on, let me get this straight. You're making Malcolm Blackberg watch interview footage of people in an apartment building? And he thinks it's the coaching? I'm stunned he's going along with it."

"Well, I told him if he doesn't watch it, he'll get an X for the day."

"No."

"Yes," I say.

She practically screams with laughter. "Oh my god, you're threatening a client with an X? Oh my god, you are off the chain!"

"I'm sorry," I say. "I swear I'm not trying to steal your identity or anything like that."

"Wait, wait, hold on," she says. "I only called because I just got a new paycheck deposited into my account. I thought it was a mistake, being that I haven't shown up at work since that day we met —like I flew out here and I haven't looked back. I was wondering why they never called me to see why I didn't show up. And I logged into the intranet and I see you've been updating the checklist and things? And this phone number. You have quite the operation."

"We're trying to save our building. I know it all sounds outrageous."

"You clearly found the packet," she says.

"Yeah," I say sheepishly. Is she going to turn me in?

"Did you know that you got a glowing performance review from the client?"

"What? I did?" I ask, stunned.

"They don't think we can see them, but we can. If you know where to look," she says. "I can't believe he gave you such a good review for making him watch those videos."

"Trust me, he wants to get out of watching the videos." I tell her how he offered me money. She's shocked I didn't take it. "I know it's wrong what I'm doing," I say. "I don't want to get you into trouble."

"Wait," she says. "I'm in Estonia, right?"

"Are you enjoying it?" I ask. "I hope you're enjoying it."

"It's the best decision I ever made," she says. "I'd be miserable right now. And I really always hated traveling with the client. Like, god. I'd be stuck in that hotel."

"It's not so terrible."

"It's a gilded cage," she says. "To me, anyway. But, here's the thing. You want to keep working as me? You understand I'm getting your paycheck, right?"

"I don't care about the paycheck. I meant it—that's not why I'm doing it."

"Okay..." she says. "So I'm being paid for the work that you're doing. Umm, why would I object to that?"

I stop at a corner. "You're okay with it?"

"Dude, you're working as me and I'm getting the money. I'm good with it. Just don't let them know I know. Maybe I'm out here not giving a second thought to my life in the US. And if there's extra money that magically gets in my bank account from them paying me for work you're weirdly doing...it's not like I'm even looking at my bank account, right? I don't know anything and I'm not in on it. That's my position."

"Oh. Okay," I say. "Wow, thanks."

"Just write a letter of resignation at the end of it. Email it to HR saying you quit as of whatever the date is. They'll never have to be the wiser."

"Wow, thank you," I say.

"Hey, thank you," she says. "I mean, seriously."

"Okay. Wait—what's up with the per diem?"

"Blackberg gives you a hundred and fifty bucks a day for

meals and incidentals. You can get shit delivered from online stores and charge it to the room if you want. A per diem is money for whatever you need to sustain your existence there."

"I would never need that much."

"Well, you should spend it. It's there for you. Why not go crazy?"

"I'll think about it," I say diplomatically. "So you're really okay with me doing this?"

"Let's be clear: I don't know you're doing it. I have no idea. We never had this conversation. I'm just teaching English in Estonia. The risk is not mine."

"Okay," I say.

"I mean, how am I supposed to know you're doing this? Who would ever do such a crazy thing?"

"I *know*," I say. "What kind of freak?"

She snorts. "And one thought," she says. "Maybe somewhere along the line, you figure out you should write a few lines about the progress of the client in that blank space to the right of the participation field. Did you see it? That comments field to the right of the checkbox field? Maybe not every day, but it's common for us to say things like, one hour of relationship-building skills completed. Conversation about points of view. Positive reinforcement. I'm not officially telling you what to do, but it's what I do. Go google soft skills and use some of that language."

"Oh, wow. Okay," I say.

"They won't bother you as long as you don't screw up. Wow," she says. "Good luck with saving your building. I mean it."

"Wait—one more question. What *does* happen if I give Malcolm an X?"

"That's why it was so hilarious that you were threatening to give him an X—an X means willful non-compliance. You seriously can't give him an X."

"But what would happened if I did?" I ask.

"Malcolm Blackberg's program is court-mandated, right? So if you gave him even one X, he's basically refusing to comply with a court order. The lawyers for the party that brought the suit would see that X and they could haul him back in to court if they wanted, maybe throw him in jail. Once you hit submit, the X goes out to everyone. It's a nuclear bomb, my friend."

"I had no idea," I say.

"I know, which is totally hilarious. Do you know how many times I fantasized about putting a big fat X in that square? Sometimes when the clients are being impossible, I pull out a notepad I have and I write something in, like I'm giving a bad report, but that's the closest I ever came. I never imagined threatening them with an X. Blackberg must've been shitting. Seriously, Bexley Partners would never give an X. Even if there was an interruption or scheduling snafu, we let them make up the work the next day, or double up an hour if they can't extend. I mean, if Bexley Partners' coaches were running around giving clients Xs, the firm would never get any business."

"What if you entered it by accident?"

"You have a few minutes to edit your grade and your comments after you hit submit. But then it goes out. And this conversation? Never happened."

"Got it," I say. I thank her and hang up.

Get Malcolm thrown in jail? That's what I was threatening him with?

It's so not me. But Malcolm thought that's exactly what I was doing. I smile, leaning back on a building, watching the sunset, phone in hand, admiring the woman that Malcolm seems to think I am.

15

Malcolm

IT'S A DAY OF MEETINGS, morning to night.

I find I'm excited for it.

I haven't felt this excited about my business in a very long time. Or maybe it's just life. I don't know. I'd felt bored in the past year or so, and now I don't.

I make Elle ride in the limo with me—that's the only way I can fit in my sessions with her. Twenty minutes here, ten minutes there.

She settles into the back next to me. Being in this small space with her is more intimate than the hotel. I feel like we're alone together, cut off utterly from the world, even though my driver is on the other side of the security panel. Somehow that makes it hotter.

Out the window, the city glides by, but my attention is homed in on the freckle on the side of her lips. I draw in her sweet, bright coconut-berry scent, letting it fill me. The tips of her eyelashes, I notice, are covered in clumpy black mascara, but up close, you can see the pale roots of them, sandy brown like her hair. Every detail of her is more delicious than the last.

She's wearing one of her pantsuits and yet another butterfly bow tie, and something else that's new: a raincoat with a criss-cross line design, but when you look closely, the lines are made up of tiny hedgehogs. It looks worn, well loved.

This is definitely a woman who doesn't do a lot of shopping, but it's not that she doesn't enjoy fine things—I have a front-row seat for that during our coaching sessions when our treats cart comes. And I saw the way she drank in the grandeur of the hotel lobby that first day, mesmerized by the luxury. And from time to time I still overhear her gushing about how comfortable the bed in her room is. Nearly two weeks we've been here and she's still into it.

Yet she didn't take the money.

Why not take the money? So much about her just doesn't add up. I find it strangely thrilling.

"*You're* in a good mood," she says.

"I have a lot of meetings today," I say. "And one negotiation. And I'm expecting them all to go very well." I'm also, perversely, looking forward to my session with Elle.

"What is it about meetings and negotiations that you enjoy so much?"

"The interaction. The challenge, I suppose," I say. "The element of the unknown. I like to predict what people are going to do, but they sometimes surprise me."

"You enjoy when people surprise you?"

"Are you doing my technique on me?" I ask.

"Yes," she says, smiling.

"I enjoy finding out about people. I suppose most people walk into a negotiation seeing potential foes and obstacles arranged around the table, but I see a kind of journey of discovery. As annoying as they are, people really are kind of fascinating sometimes."

"Is it possible you're a people person and you just don't know it?" she asks.

"Nope," I say.

She snorts. "Is it possible you are just so full of bull?" she asks prettily.

I grin. "Nope," I repeat, because *nope* is just the kind of answer Elle would hate. Elle is a cat who doesn't like a closed door.

True to form, she rolls her eyes, frustrated.

"It's called a business skill," I add.

"You tell yourself that. Just a business skill," she says, ever hopeful. This woman, always looking at me like I might be a good person.

"Is that a requirement of coaches, to be perversely optimistic about people based on no evidence whatsoever?" I ask.

"You are amazing with people," she says.

"In *negotiations*. I'm amazing with people in negotiations. It's a strategy. It's not reality," I say.

"Maybe it is reality," she says. "Maybe the real you emerges in the negotiation room."

"Is this something like, maybe the thing you dreamed last night is real life? And all of this waking life is a dream?" I say. "Spoiler alert—it's not."

She shrugs.

"Or maybe, the Hitler who was really nice to his German shepherd is the real Hitler? And the rest of the time he wasn't the real Hitler?"

"What?" She turns to me, face lit with shock. "You can't compare yourself to somebody like that. You are not like that. Just...don't." She shakes her head, as if to shake out the idea. "You can't talk about yourself like that. God!"

Her passionate protest has my pulse racing. I don't know what to make of this woman taking my side like this. As if she thinks I need a champion or something. Who does that?

"It was an analogy; not a comparison," I say lightly.

"Oh my god!" she says, still staring out the window.

I want her back. I want her to be back looking at me. "The first meeting should only take an hour or so," I say.

"An hour?" She turns back to me. "I don't understand. What do I do while you're in these meetings?"

"Enjoy yourself," I say. "Have the driver take you to a nearby bakery or a deli. My treat. Walk in the park. Go out boozing and blow off the lesson completely. You have my permission."

She snorts at this last option, and I wonder suddenly what it would look like—her blowing off her duties to indulge herself. What would she do, left completely to her own devices?

"Or maybe you could use the time to think up more postal carrier quizzes. You know how I enjoy them. Or maybe there's a hedgehog-themed boutique nearby."

For a split second, she looks surprised. Then she shakes her head. "We need to start," she declares.

I grab a sparkling water and take one for her, setting it in her cup holder, because Lord knows she wouldn't take it for herself.

Elle puts down the bolster between us and sets up her little iPad on the pull-down surface in front of us. She sips her water as the residents of 341 West 45th ramble endlessly—I've never seen a group more focused on the smallest details of an apartment complex and each other's lives.

Now and then she gets the sense that I'm not paying attention, and she seems stunned and surprised. "Malcolm!" she'll say and she'll give the screen a stern nod.

There's really nothing quite like the sound of my name on her lips. When she pushes against my resistance, she transforms in a way that is endlessly hot. Or maybe it's more like her real character is revealed. She keeps her bravery hidden like a squirrel with a nut, burying it deep. Sometimes I think she keeps her bravery hidden even from herself.

On screen the most insufferable painting party of the century drags on.

"Will we also be watching the paint dry?" I ask. "Is that something I should be looking forward to?"

She looks over with narrowed eyes. "Do I have to stop the video?"

"I'm just saying, a few hours of paint drying would certainly go with the style of this documentary...or whatever you want to call it."

"Shut the bruschetta hole," she says.

I stifle a grin. "What did you just say?"

She points at the screen. There's some historical footage from the 1990s. After that, the woman who sometimes wears the delivery cat costume complains at length about pizza with caramelized onions. The building definitely has a lot of women in their twenties and thirties, and there's a kind of fondness that comes over Elle's face when they carry on about whatever they carry on about. Is she getting attached to these women who keep appearing on the screen? Is she the one developing empathy? Is she being hoisted with her own petard?

I'd googled her address in Newark, New Jersey back when I went to school on her background, and I studied her Instagram, too. You can never know too much about a person. Elle lives in a small, drab, dark basement apartment. I can't imagine she likes it. With sixty thousand dollars, she could move somewhere nicer. Why not take it?

What does this woman want out of life?

I'm thinking back to what she said about moving to a more populous area, her desire to be around women her age where things were happening. I'm assuming she found that in her neighborhood in New Jersey—maybe that's why she tolerates the shitty apartment. The building in her video program seems to be right up her alley. Too bad I'm knocking it down in a couple of months.

"Are you even watching?" she asks.

"They're so friendly with each other. Is it anything like your neighborhood?"

She stiffens. "What do you mean?"

"That was part of your inspiration for moving out of the boonies—to find more women your age. Fun things to do. It's like a goddamn sorority at 341."

"Those women do seem to love it there," she says. "It seems like a wonderful place. A really nice place..."

"Go ahead and finish the sentence," I say. "A nice place that the big, bad wolf is going to knock down. Or Scrooge, rather. Can we have a big, bad wolf named Scrooge?" Just then my driver buzzes. "Ah, hold that thought," I say. "We're at the Ling Tower."

She frowns. "Wait, what? You're leaving already?"

I look at my phone. "Seventeen minutes down." I slide out. "I'm expecting this meeting to run no more than fifty minutes. I'll ping you and the driver when I'm out."

She looks affronted as I shut the door. Frankly, I'm glad for the interruption. Something about the proximity of her tends to put me off my game. The scent of her. The sound of her sighs. Her nimble movements.

I stroll into the cool lobby where my accounting team awaits. They're recapping strategy, but I'm thinking about Elle.

What could she want beyond sixty thousand dollars? Presumably Corman paid her something to torture me with this footage. She took his money; why not mine? Is it possible she's holding out for more? It doesn't feel like her to hold out for more, but if it's not money she wants, what is it? Is it love? Is it possible she's involved with Corman? No way. She'd be loyal like that, but she's not Corman's type—not at all. Is it possible that she's involved with one of Corman's lawyers?

The idea bothers me intensely. I tell myself it couldn't be true, but there really is something that doesn't add up about her.

I hate the idea that she could be involved with somebody, but I can't get it out of my head.

My thoughts race back to her Instagram feed. I would've noticed if there were signs of a relationship. And then there's the fact of our strange chemistry—chemistry as strong as ours would feel like cheating to somebody like Elle; she simply wouldn't allow it. I don't know much about Elle in terms of her life, but I know a loyal person when I meet one.

We do another twenty minutes of video between my next two meetings. She's not happy about the interruptions. I enjoy knowing that, when I'm up there in the meetings that she's waiting for me down in the limo. I find myself looking forward to rejoining her, of once again resuming our strange dance. I enjoy her when she's charged up, as if something essential emerges from her, as if she drops her guard.

We're finally heading home.

"Twelve minutes left," I announce.

She's frowning—stewing, really, and it stirs something in me. Honestly, I cannot get enough of this woman.

"Ready?" I ask.

She folds her arms in a huff.

"What is it, little country mouse?"

"First of all, I'm not a country mouse; I am your coach. And second of all, from now on we'll have dedicated sessions. You will not bend me around your schedule like a Gumby doll. You'll bend your schedule around me."

I almost don't hear her words or make sense of them because

she's doing her chin-up thing and it kills me. I want her so bad I can't think. Maybe it was a bad idea to bring her in the limo.

"Are you even listening?" she says. "No more chopped-up lesson time."

I say, "I don't recall any stipulation that the lessons have to be held over one continuous hour."

"Well, they do have to be," she says. "The interruptions ruin the whole flow of everything."

"I can't do that," I say in my most finalistic, nothing-to-be-done voice. "Some days the lesson will have to be like this."

"Surely you can find one uninterrupted hour," she says.

"Not on days like today, I can't," I say. "And there will be more." And also, it's just too enjoyable to annoy her.

"We need an uninterrupted hour." Her face is bright with emotion, just this side of pink. I imagine brushing my fingertips over her cheek; would her skin feel warm to the touch?

She frowns, and visions of kissing that frown crowd my mind. "You have to find an uninterrupted hour. You have to find one."

"Or what, little country mouse?" I ask, pulse racing.

She straightens, brow furrowed. "Okay, then," she says, slipping a second iPad from her bag. She opens the hedgehog-themed cover, and fires it up. Deftly she punches in a code and navigates a few screens to some sort of grid hosted by Bexley Partners.

"Do you see this empty square?" she asks.

I'm barely listening.

She turns to me, chin up, so determined to hold her ground. Wildly, I imagine cupping that chin between my thumb and forefinger. Tipping her face to me. The idea has my blood racing.

"Do you see it?" she demands.

"I do indeed."

"That is where I put your check marks...*when* you earn them."

"Uh-huh." Is she doing this again? I should probably be annoyed.

She straightens up, seeking to occupy her full height. "If you can't agree to uninterrupted sessions, I'll be forced to give you an X instead of a check mark."

I swallow back a smile. She's totally bluffing, of course—no way will she follow through on her threat, but it's hot that she's trying. "You wouldn't do that," I say confidently.

"Wouldn't I?" she taunts.

I'm ready for her threat this time. I spoke to my lawyers about this. I inform her of what they said. "Companies like mine wouldn't agree to use companies like yours if they had a history of flunking clients. My lawyers would've insisted on a different firm."

"Maybe that was true in the past," she says, "but it's a new day. And if you do not complete the lessons properly, and that includes not having them presented in a chopped-up fashion, I will put an X here. And then I *will* hit submit."

"And then your employer would fire you," I say.

"Maybe I don't care about that," she says. "Maybe this program is just that important to me."

I smile. So unexpected. "A good girl like you? Not caring if you get fired?"

"That's right," she says. "If you are unable to agree to uninterrupted sessions, you *will* get an X in this box. Once I hit submit, the X is sent to several parties. Do you know who those parties are?"

She's breathtaking—she really is; David to my Goliath—if David had been quietly sexy, and Goliath had been, let's face it, a bit more competent. She's standing up to me with everything in her, magnificent and vulnerable at the same time, and it makes me want to consume her—her lips, her skin, her neck. I'm a vampire, driven to devour her goodness.

"No?" she asks. "Is this you not agreeing, then?"

I give her the smug smile that seems to get under her skin.

The air between us sizzles with energy.

She reaches out her forefinger, the deft little finger that she uses to hit play but she's hovering over something on the pad. She taps something and a large X appears in the box. I grin. She's taking it all the way to the edge. She won't hit submit though.

She wouldn't.

She hovers her finger over the blue SUBMIT button, taunting me.

"You won't," I say.

"I will." Her eyes flash. "Unless you agree to unbroken sessions."

"My day is too busy to carve out an hour, I told you that."

She taps *submit*.

I gasp. "What did you do?"

She taps again and the X disappears. "Aah. Retracted just in time."

"What are you doing?" I ask.

"Hitting submit on the X that you so richly deserve," she says. "Now, is this an agreement on unbroken sessions? Or..." She lowers her finger, getting dangerously close to the submit button.

I sweep in like lightning and snatch the iPad from her grip and set it on the other side of me out of her reach.

"Gimme that," she says.

"No," I say.

She's laughing. "Now you really are going to get an X!" She clambers onto me, trying to grab the device. "I'm *so* giving you an X!"

"Not in this life," I growl.

She laughs, reaching for it. A wild rush of pleasure fills me.

I hold the thing over my head, now, and she's laughing, going for it with renewed energy. She's practically on top of me, trying to reach across me, chest pressing against mine.

She's the perfect weight on my lap, and I breathe in her sweet scent, soaking up her soft curves with the unforgiving planes of my body. All at once she stills, color high, breath coming fast.

I set aside the iPad and fit my hands around her waist.

I expect her to maybe laugh and pull away with some snarky comment about giving me another X, but she stays. Her eyes gleam. Slowly, her gaze lowers to my lips. Heat rises between us.

"An X," she whispers. "Unless you can persuade me otherwise."

I blink. Did she just say what I think she said?

She smiles her playfully witchy smile, and there's no more guessing, no more hesitation. I yank her to me, taking her lips in mine with a hunger that surprises me.

Deft fingers burrow into my hair. She's warm and sweet, arching against me, and I'm devouring her, forcing the seam of her lips open.

My tongue invades her mouth.

"Nnng," she says. "Nnnng."

I'm reveling in her soft *nnnngs*, in the desperate way she bunches my lapels into her fists, tightening and loosening as though her very fists are undulating under my wicked kiss.

I slide my hand up her arm and cup her chin, repositioning her face for a gentle kiss, now—a simple brush of my lips over the center of hers, and then a quick kiss for my favorite freckle.

She pulls away, seeming to come to her senses.

I loosen my grip on her, watching to see what she'll do.

Her gaze falls to my lips.

She sucks in a breath as I draw near for another kiss—her lips, her nose, her brow. Badly painted lashes flutter against my hungry bottom lip. I kiss her other brow.

And then my driver's voice sounds over the intercom, informing me that we've arrived at my next meeting.

With that, the magic is broken.

"I'll make the uninterrupted hour," I say.

She gives me a wary look. "Really?"

"Yes."

"Then I'll consider a check mark for you. *Today*."

I grin.

She leans over, snatches her iPad, and takes her seat just as my door is pulled open by my driver.

I ORDER ROOM service in my room that night, but my attention is still in that limo; my entire mind and soul are still in that limo. I should be preparing for the next day's session but I can't stop thinking about the way she felt, eyes dark with desire, pulse a drumbeat in her smooth throat.

Unless you can persuade me otherwise.

I keep replaying the moment. Everything in her turned just then. Rose up, somehow. She was hot before, but shy Elle being sassy and demanding is mind-blowingly sexy.

I grab my phone, telling myself I'll review new intel we have on the Germantown legal team, but I find myself studying her Instagram again. I'm looking more carefully this time, reassuring myself there aren't other guys in her life. I've officially gone mad.

There are lots of pictures of a city—is it Newark? Manhattan? There are very few people in the photos she takes; she seems partial to colorful signs, ephemera on hidden corners, and random images of hedgehogs that she spots on street pole signs and so forth. What happened to the girls' squad she was longing for? Did she not find one?

I would find that incredibly sad.

I use Google Maps to determine that quite a few of the earlier shots seem to be in The Bronx—did she visit there at one point? Did she have friends there?

When you go even earlier, you get to her Mapleton roots. Rolling hills. Landscape panoramas that show rivers catching the light like shining slashes through wooded valleys.

And of course, more postal-themed shots. Whereas most of her newer pictures are of things, these older pictures feature more people, including a number of shots of a woman in her late sixties with dyed white-blonde hair who could easily be a relative. Is this Elle's mother? She plays a banjo in one of the shots. She's rather frail in later shots—not entirely healthy looking, but she has Elle's defiant green gaze.

After dinner, I try again to crack into her locked-down Facebook page—unsuccessfully.

And then I wake up. This was an evening specifically earmarked for negotiation prep, for gaining insight into Gerrold's team. What am I doing?

16

Noelle

I'M in a daze of shock—at myself!

Not only did we kiss; I instigated it. It was so surreal, us fighting over the iPad, and I was laughing, and feeling just so happy, and I practically threw myself onto his lap, and suddenly I was right up against his body, looking into those eyes, the color of tea in the sunshine, his gaze soft beneath the harsh dark slashes of his brows.

And he was so...everything, all muscle and whiskers and infuriating Malcolm, right there under me.

And I wanted to kiss him. It was all I wanted, but it also seemed somehow impossible and even dangerous, like kissing a god who has lightning bolt-throwing powers.

But I felt like I was going crazy, that's how much I wanted him. And then I said that thing about him persuading me, and he kissed me, and the kiss he gave me turned me inside out.

I never knew a kiss could be like that.

It's a good thing he had to go to a meeting, because I might not have stopped. And honestly, what was I thinking? Kissing Malcolm Blackberg?

I'm here on a mission and kissing him is not part of it.

As soon as the door shut behind him, I told the driver to take me back to the hotel. I told the driver that I had important business, and that the session would be marked as complete. But really, I just didn't trust myself to see him again while the kiss still buzzed through me.

And oh my god, what would my friends say? I came here to inspire Malcolm to have empathy, not to encourage him to have bow-chicka-wow-wow sexytimes with me.

Even so, our sizzling hot kiss is all I can think about all night, and it's the first thing I remember in the morning.

I worry things will be weird between us. Will there be strange sexy undercurrents that everybody detects? Will he expect me to fall into his bed now that we've kissed?

Well, he definitely has the wrong idea there. "You can think again on that count, mister," I say into the mirror.

I plan to be focused on my mission entirely from here on in.

MY FEARS about sexy weirdness turn out to be entirely unfounded. Malcolm is subdued the next day at the negotiation session, even surly. Was it our kiss? Does he regret our kiss?

Do *I*?

He's not paying even one iota of attention even as he sits down, as I start up the day's footage. He's barely there, even as my skin prickles with awareness of him.

You'd think this would be okay with me, being that I was worried about sexy weirdness, but it's not okay.

And I'm not saying that just because of the kiss, just because I've given it every ounce of my attention while he clearly can't be bothered—it's more that the section of video I'm showing him is one of my favorites for displaying the beautiful camaraderie within our building—the trip to the Grand Bazaar to pick art to spruce up the walls. He needs to be paying attention.

Finally I hit pause. "You're not paying attention."

"I'm watching it, aren't I?"

"You're not paying attention," I say.

"How can you think that I'm not paying attention?" he asks. "This thing is just distracting enough that when I'm watching it, I can't think of anything else whatsoever. Kudos."

"You need to change your attitude," I say. "It won't work if you watch this in a negative frame of mind."

"There's nothing in the settlement that stipulates the frame of mind with which I'm to undergo your training."

"If your attitude is extremely poor, the lesson is wasted," I say.

He gives me his dark look. "Will you give me an X?"

Heat comes over me, remembering the hungry way he kissed me, his body hard against mine. "I want you to have a better attitude, that's all."

"A person doesn't change their attitude with the flip of a switch."

I frown. As long as he thinks of this as punishment, his heart won't be open to saving my friends and neighbors.

"Instead of punishment, try looking at it as something like a human interest thing?"

"Attitudes don't change just like that."

I sigh. He's so surly! "I know what you need," I say.

"What?" he grouches.

I fold my hands in my lap. "When I worked as a letter carrier, there was this total asshole on my route," I say. "Stanley Manchette."

He rubs his hands together. "Another letter carrier anecdote."

"If you're gonna make fun of my lessons, we can just go back to the video," I say.

"No, please," he says with a wave.

"Stanley had this dog, Chuckles," I continue. "Chuckles was this old dog, kind of a grouch like Stanley. He was a bulldog with a frowny face."

"Ironically named," Malcolm observes.

"Yeah," I say. "Chuckles didn't like to be petted or anything."

"But on the upside, I'm imagining he wasn't unpredictable and crazy like those little dogs."

"Nice to see you're at least learning something. And yes, Chuckles was cool. He'd never bite me."

"Am I Chuckles the dog in this story? Or am I the asshole Stanley?"

I give him a warning look.

His eyes sparkle. "Do go on."

"Anyway, one day I found Chuckles wandering around in this subdivision miles away. My route covered a lot of territory, and I was surprised to find him there—I couldn't imagine how he'd gotten so far. I was thinking he must've gotten out of the fence, like maybe it wasn't latched, I don't know. I picked him up and I brought him back to Stanley's place on my way home, just quietly let him back into Stanley's yard. A day or two later, I found Chuckles somewhere else—a different direction. I brought him home and knocked on Stanley's door, thinking to let him know Chuckles was getting out, but Stanley was gone, so I just left Chuckles in the yard again."

"Chuckles is a little escape artist."

"That's what I thought," I say. "But a week later I ran into Stanley at the grocer and I asked him how's Chuckles? And he's like, 'The damndest thing. That dog, I tried to get rid of him. I'd bring him miles and dump him out, and he'd find his way back—back inside the fence. I never thought that dog liked me, but he must've been running at top speed to get back to me. So I decided I'd best keep the old varmint. I didn't realize he wanted to be with me so bad.'"

Malcolm blinks, stunned, it seems.

"I know, right? How horrible was Stanley to do that? When you get a dog, you are taking on the obligation to care for that dog for its entire life. That dog was depending on him."

Malcolm gazes into the middle distance with a stunned look on his face, as if he's suddenly spotted tiny elven folk there, doing the macarena.

"What?"

"Stanley didn't want the dog because he thought the dog didn't appreciate him," Malcolm says.

"Exactly. Granted, Chuckles didn't seem to like anybody. I mean, he was like Stanley in that way. But you don't just dump a dog," I say.

"No—true. There's a special place in hell reserved for people like that," he mumbles, still with that strange expression.

"What?" I ask.

"Stanley thought Chuckles didn't love him, didn't want him, so that made Stanley not want or love Chuckles. But when Stanley thought that Chuckles loved him, his entire disposition changed."

"Exactly. It was a shift in his thought, a shift of perception. And that's what I want you to understand. This video isn't a punishment. It's an opportunity—"

"This is incredibly...interesting," Malcolm says in a reverent tone.

"Are you being funny now?"

"Quite the opposite," Malcolm says.

"I think you might be just patronizing me."

"Did Stanley say anything else? Are there any other details?"

"Are you trying to get out of the video?" I ask.

"No, I like that story, I really do. Are questions not allowed?"

"Other details. Well, around a year later he showed me this trick he'd taught Chuckles, so they were clearly bonding. I mean, after Stan's attitude shifted, he actually had a better relationship with Chuckles. Nothing changed with Chuckles—nothing about the dog changed, but everything changed with Stanley's attitude, and suddenly their relationship was great. And that's how this footage could be for you."

"Only the story Stanley told himself changed," Malcolm whispers. He seems really taken with that aspect. "I'm Chuckles," he says.

"What? No!" I say, surprised that he'd be so dense about it. "You are Stanley and the video footage is Chuckles. The point is, this video isn't a punishment if you don't relate to it as a punishment. You need to stop telling yourself that it's a punishment and it won't be one."

Malcolm seems so happy. "Perfect." He sits back and crosses his legs. "Let's go on, then, with the video," he says.

"This seems too good to be true," I say.

"No, your anecdote really did change my attitude."

"Okay," I say, warily, but I still don't push play.

"What now?" he says. "I'm eager to get on with your video. What more could you possibly want?"

"I feel like you're maybe eager to get it *over* with."

"F for self-esteem," he says playfully. "You told me an anecdote in the hopes that it would improve my attitude in some way, and when it does improve my attitude, you find it suspicious."

I am suspicious, but he seems so buoyant, and he's asking to watch more of the video. I push play.

The footage is an all-building meeting from last year. It was such a sweet meeting, all of us together trying to make things great. Is Malcolm seeing what I'm seeing? Is it too much to imagine that his attitude really is better now?

Malcolm is still in his good mood when the session ends, and he disappears right after.

I head down later to sit with the team for dinner, and Nisha and Coralee are the only ones who show up. They tell me that Malcolm has Walt and Lawrence in a working dinner due to some project that just came up. All Nisha knows is that the creative team from the New York office is involved.

17

Noelle

PEOPLE LOOK sleepy the next day. Lawrence has an extra tall coffee with a shot of espresso in it, and Walt's hair is lopsided until Coralee fixes it in the limo on the way over. Malcolm is riding in the other limo, still wrapping up the finishing touches on their mysterious rush project.

We arrive at the Kendrick building, and the session starts as usual. I don't see what all of the preparation could've possibly gone toward until the two teams hit some random sticking point, and Malcolm suggests they look at some of the "backgrounder" that the Blackberg team has prepared, as that will clarify some point.

Gerrold furrows his bushy brows. "Backgrounder?"

Walt pulls up an iPad, pulls down the conference room screen, and dims the lights.

And the so-called backgrounder begins to play.

It starts out with black and white images of a milk delivery van. Gerrold laughs and claps, looking all around. "Where in the world did you get this? That's my grandfather delivering milk!" Apparently his grandfather delivering milk is how the company was started.

After that, there's a voiceover narrating the evolution from one milk truck to five. There are pictures of the first garage, a small place down in Millbrae.

"How'd you get these images?" Gerrold asks, stunned.

"Local archives," Malcolm says. The footage rolls on. There are more shots of the budding company.

"Look at that, would you!" Gerrold exclaims. "Pause it there, if you would." Walt pauses the video. "Remember that, son?" Gerrold says to Junior. "Look there—we used to take you there summers."

Junior doesn't remember it. "Neat," he says.

"You'd do your homework at that bench on the side," Gerrold says.

There are interviews with past employees, and then it comes to the section on how much the company grew under the leadership of Gerrold himself, beginning in 1981 when he took over. "Oh, that old Corvette. You remember that, son?"

Junior grunts his yes. There are shots of Gerrold getting awards, pitching in with supplies after an earthquake, employees talking about their pride in the company.

"This backgrounder is more extensive than our fiftieth anniversary retrospective," Junior says. He tries to make it sound like a compliment, but it's pretty clearly a complaint. Gerrold doesn't care. He's enjoying it.

Is this what they were up to all night?

Gerrold is delighted to see old Betty in the front office, and a guy with giant 1970s sideburns sitting atop their first semi-trailer hauler. There are quotes from locals about the importance of the Germantown Group to the local economy. Gerrold sometimes stops the tape and tells us extra things, like we're at a barbecue instead of a negotiation.

And right then, I see it all. I see exactly what's happening. A chill comes over me.

Gerrold had been rejecting Malcolm, believing that Malcolm doesn't love or respect him or his company. Thinking that Malcolm only wants the company for its parts.

Malcolm is Chuckles, changing the story by showing his appreciation for Stanley—aka Gerrold and his firm.

My pulse races. Malcolm is going to do this thing. He's going to buy the company, and he's going to throw those people out of work.

And it's all because of me and my dog anecdote.

I look over at Malcolm to find him gazing at me with that evil, sexy look of his that always makes my skin feel too tight.

Arrgh. I force my gaze back onto the screen, where there are images of the two logos side by side—the heraldic Germantown Group logo alongside the Blackberg Inc. black mountain.

I glower.

Junior glowers.

The session ends. Gerrold is warm in saying goodbye. He wants a copy of the "backgrounder" and Walt promises to send it.

I go up to Malcolm when we're all filing out to the hall. "What have you done?" I whisper.

Malcolm smiles innocently. "What?" His phone pings. "Sorry, I have to take this and then I'm headed across town."

I grit my teeth. I can't believe I ever kissed this man!

"Oh, and we're going to have to do a dinner session tonight," he informs me. "I'll have Walt text details when we're en route, but I'm thinking seven-ish."

"What?" I ask. "Since when do we do dinner sessions?"
But he's already gone.

~

OUR DINNER SESSION is to take place at the nicer of the
onsite Maybourne Hotel restaurants—the one my new
coworkers avoid because it costs an arm and a leg.

But this is to be Malcolm's treat, according to the instructions Malcolm's NY admin texted me. The instructions are also
to dress for dinner.

I only brought my work pantsuits and one of my going-out-
with-the-girls skirt outfits.

I decide I'll wear my work pantsuit, complete with a blue-
and-white striped butterfly tie, in order to demonstrate to
Malcolm that this is a work thing, and that we are not in any
way socializing.

And I apparently need to demonstrate that to myself, too,
because I still can't stop thinking about that kiss.

I walk in. The place is elegant in a minimalist way, with
white walls and ornate plaster ceilings and candles flickering
like scattered diamonds.

I'm led across the main dining room to a small side room off
the main dining area. The side room contains a few candlelit
tables, but only one is occupied—the farthest one, nestled
against the far wall near the corner. And there sits Malcolm,
relaxed and darkly elegant in a casual black suit jacket and jeans
and a white shirt with no tie.

He stands as I approach, eyes falling to the tie at my neck. I
can't read his expression, but I'm sure he's disappointed that I
chose not to follow his dress code and instead arrived in my
dorky business suit.

Good. If he thinks this is some sort of celebration for his evil triumph, he's so wrong.

"Don't you look lovely," he says.

I sit, setting the iPad on the table, further signifying to us both that this is a business meeting.

He touches his neck. "The blue with white stripes. It's one of my favorites."

Is he messing with me? "Whatever you say." I fire up the iPad. If he wants to eat dinner, it's fine with me, but he will watch his hour while paying keen attention. And I'm not telling him any more post office anecdotes, either. Or kissing him.

The waiter appears, fills my glass with something bubbly, and leaves.

"Umm..."

"You don't like champagne?"

"Yes, but we're at work right now."

"Oh, come on, now, you won't let me treat you to a nice dinner session? A bit of a thank-you? Your story was brilliantly helpful. And this is the best champagne you'll ever have." He lifts his glass. "I was Chuckles after all. How about that?"

"I didn't tell you that story for you to be Chuckles."

"Why not? I'm happy to be Chuckles. Chuckles was the most dynamic character in your story. I had something to offer Gerrold that I didn't realize I had—a new story about the two of us. He wants the cow butchered by somebody who will honor the cow. That's all he ever wanted."

"Why in the world would I toast to the fact that all of those people that work for Germantown Group are a step closer to losing their jobs?"

Malcolm does his weary sigh, like I'm being entertaining in a tiresome way. "They were always going to lose their jobs," he says.

"They'll lose them sooner now. Why should I be glad about that?"

He takes a sip and sets down his glass. "Because it shows what an excellent executive coach you are. You should give yourself a little credit. And that observation you made the other day after that negotiation session—you said, 'He wants his son to see the beauty in what he built. To see the human value in it instead of looking at it coldly as a commodity.' It was a good point, though I didn't know how to act on it until the dog anecdote. You really are brilliant, you know."

I frown. I meant that about our building, I want him to see the beauty in our building, in our community.

"You are really very good. It's as if you can't *help* but be insightful and helpful, even though you were sent to torture and punish me—and not to worry, you are doing a fine job of it, what with the videos—you nevertheless helped me to get a little bit closer to attaining one of my most vital business objectives of this year. Never in my wildest dreams—"

"I told you, I'm not here to punish you." I swig a full half of my drink and put it down. Francine always says not to swig the bubbly, but I don't care. "My goal as your coach is for you to have empathy. To see people as humans with hopes and dreams just like you. Trying to do the best that they can and—"

"That part is an especially good touch," he says. "Here to turn the devil good! To bring heart to the heartless."

Miserably, I rotate my glass. Am I making everything worse? I didn't come here to make everything worse.

"You're not the devil," I inform him. "And you're not heartless. And that's final."

Malcolm wears a ghost of a smile, meaning his lips don't actually smile, but his eyes twinkle and his cheekbones become more gorgeously defined. The ghost-of-a-smile look is unbelievably hot on him. But then, most looks are unbelievably hot on him, being that he himself is unbelievably hot.

And the fact that he thinks he's heartless makes him even hotter. He's forlorn and dangerous at the same time, a beautiful wounded beast.

Sometimes I have this crazy impulse to put my hand to his chest just to feel his heartbeat, to let him see in my eyes that I feel his heart beating the same as anybody's heart.

And then I would draw my lips to his ear and whisper that he is not the devil.

And maybe I would kiss him.

Gah. What is wrong with me?

I straighten up. "Also," I continue, "wanting you to have empathy is not a *touch.*" I glance down at my phone as my mind crowds with images of pressing my palm to his heart. And maybe I would close my fist and grab up a bit of his shirt and maybe I would twist a little bit. Maybe I would pull him to me.

It's as if the grumbly gravity of Malcolm and his tragic dark thoughts about himself are turning me into a freak of lust. A predator in my own right.

I ball my non-phone hand into a fist, as if that will keep my libido bottled up inside me. "Seven twenty-two. I hope you don't think our session has officially begun. Because it hasn't."

"Do you like seafood?" he asks. "They have some of the best here."

"I like seafood," I say. "Unfortunately, I'm not here for dinner."

"That is unfortunate, being that a delicious dinner is on the way."

Right then, the waiter comes with a steaming plate of fried calamari and something that looks like raw tuna encrusted in sesame seeds, plus a plate of bruschetta with red sauce and shaved manchego.

"Your favorite food," I observe.

"If I recall, it's one of your favorites too," he says.

I sigh. It does look delicious. And I *am* hungry. I force myself to picture my friends back home, counting on me to save the building. But the food looks and smells delicious. And Malcolm is wearing his ghost of a smile again, beautiful in the candlelight.

I press the starched-white napkin into my lap.

18

Malcolm

I LIKE PEOPLE TO make sense. Everything I do in life is based on my ability to understand what drives people and to turn that knowledge to my advantage.

But I still can't make sense of Elle.

If I didn't know better, I'd think she really *is* invested in the empathy thing, but that doesn't add up. The kind of person who takes money from Corman to torture me is not the same kind of person who cares whether I have empathy or not. And the person who cares about my having empathy doesn't force me to watch an endless documentary about some building.

And then there was that kiss in the limo. Stunningly, mind-blowingly sexy. Elle is mind-blowingly sexy. How the hell does this country mouse have me seeing stars?

"What?" she asks.

Was I staring at her? "Dig in. The video's not going anywhere," I say.

"Though we are on a schedule," she reminds me primly.

"Have you eaten?" I ask.

"No," she says.

"You're going to need to keep up your strength if you're going to be battling the dark forces for my sorry soul." I pass a plate. "Bruschetta?"

She rolls her eyes.

"No?" I ask.

She hesitates, then takes one. She's excited about the food, though she struggles valiantly to hide that fact.

I pretend not to watch—my country mouse doesn't like to be onstage. She takes a bite and chews briefly. Her eyes flare, a private little reaction that sends a strange ripple through my chest. She finishes it, eyes unfocused, lost in pleasure.

I'm more thrilled by this than I should be.

"Calamari?" I ask. She nods. I put a few of the plumpest rings of calamari on the plate in front of her, and pass over the sauces.

I focus on my food, barely tasting it—that's how hard I'm monitoring her pleasure. "The bruschetta really is one of the perfect foods, don't you think?" I say. "A tiny pizza, except with more artistry."

She nods. "Or a really amazing sandwich without all the bread."

"Yes, exactly," I say. "A sandwich is slapping paint on the side of a barn, whereas the bruschetta is a perfectly crafted miniature."

She grins. "And a pizza is a mass mail circular, whereas a bruschetta is a carefully chosen and thoughtfully written post-card to a specific person."

"I've always wondered," I say, "do letter carriers read the postcards?"

"Never," she says. "We would never read somebody's private mail."

"Not ever?" I ask.

"It's the mail," she says. "It's *private*. That would be—" She shakes her head as though she can barely contemplate such a thing. It's so her. I love it.

We fall into a comfortable silence, enjoying the food. Since when is silence so comfortable with her?

"I really am curious, though," I say. "If you really were concerned with me developing empathy and/or saving my soul, how do those videos fit in?" I say. "What exactly is the methodology?"

She blinks, looking caught out. She doesn't answer for a long time—long enough that I think she might not answer at all. Then she says, "My methodology is proprietary."

My heart races. She is so perfectly maddening!

"In fact, we should get to it," she says.

"No," I say.

"No?" she asks.

"I'm done with the video," I say. "It's ridiculous. I'm done with it, Elle."

She stiffens. "What do you mean? You have fifteen hours left..."

"Let's stop this. No more games."

It's time.

I throw my napkin onto my empty plate and pick up my water. Elle has a bottom line just like anybody. A price just like anybody. It's simply a matter of finding it.

"A hundred thousand," I say.

Her eyes widen. "What? What do you mean..."

"You know what I mean. A hundred thousand for me to watch the video in my own way on my own time," I say. "We'll enjoy the rest of the dinner and I'll watch the video in my room."

She blinks. "A hundred thousand? You're telling me you'd pay me a *hundred thousand dollars?*"

"For me to manage the video portion of the lesson myself. You'd have full deniability."

"A hundred thousand, and you'll play it with the picture and sound off while you shave or something."

"The video will be playing with me right there in the vicinity. Surely that meets whatever job description you've been given. You will still be making me watch the video, in a sense. Postal anecdotes and conversation, fine, but the video. No more video. Enough."

"I can't do that," she says.

I say, "I'm being serious."

"I know," she says. "Still."

I'm stunned. She's turning down a hundred thousand? "Why not?" I ask.

"Because you have to watch it," she says. "In fact, we should get to it." She's setting it up.

I sit up. Did she really just turn that much money down? "Two," I say. "Double. Two hundred."

"No, thank you," she says, not as quickly, though. She's fast-forwarding the thing, locating the spot where we left off.

A chill comes over me. What does it mean that she's turning down this kind of money? Suddenly I can't stop. I need to know her price. "Three."

"No."

"Five."

She frowns. "Do I have to give you an X for today?" she asks.

"Are you not taking me seriously here? Because I assure you, I'm being serious," I say. "You understand that, right?"

"I'm just not interested," she says. "Not everybody is interested in money."

I narrow my eyes. She's not unaffected—that I can tell. "This offer won't keep getting better. It may start going away."

"Good," she says. "I *want* your offer to go away. It's bribery. It's illegal. It's wrong." She looks around the room, gazes through the open doorway. You can see clear through to the plate glass window in the main room, and the lights of the city street beyond it. There's a couple in the far corner in the main room, heads bent over their meals. "Is it okay that we're doing this in here?"

Really? That's her concern? "This restaurant doesn't close for hours and there's nobody in this entire section. Nobody would hear it. I think they're fine with us sitting here."

She adjusts the angle of the screen.

"That was five hundred thousand," I say. "Dollars. Just so we're clear. Cash, silently appearing inside whatever bank account you name. It wouldn't go through Bexley or the lawyers. Nobody would know."

"I don't want it." With that she hits play.

I stare, dumbfounded as the screen fills with images of people on the street outside 341, some with bikes. They're rambling on about bike racks, and the perils of locking their bikes up to street signs.

"Did you sign something swearing you wouldn't take money from me?" I ask.

"No. And that's the last question you get. You'll save your questions until the end of the presentation."

My mind is spinning.

Why won't she take the money? And if it's not money, what does she want?

"You could do a lot of good with that kind of money," I try.
"Shhh."

"It wasn't a question; it was an observation."

She gives me a dark look, monitoring me until I pretend to

be watching. She is not a wealthy woman. I know where she lives. I know where she came from.

The video rolls on.

What am I not seeing? Nobody is incorruptible—not even her. I was there in the limo when she gave in to that kiss, kissing me back, breathlessly indulging herself. She wanted the kiss every bit as much as I did—of that I am sure. She crossed a line then. Why the hell not cross this one?

"Are you even watching?" she asks.

"My eyes are pointed that way, so I'm technically watching, but really I'm thinking about something else."

"Do I have to start it over?"

"God, no," I say.

"Then you'd better watch or you won't get your check mark for the day," she says.

"But my thoughts are so much more interesting."

She backs up a few minutes and makes me watch it over. A discussion about bike racks.

"Don't you want to know what I'm thinking?"

The way she blushes gives me a good idea of what she thinks I'm thinking. She's pretending to watch the video, but I think she's not. I can see the drumbeat of her pulse banging in her neck.

"Elle," I pursue. "Wouldn't you like to know?"

"Quit interrupting or we'll start the hour over."

"What do you want? Tell me that."

"I'm gonna delete yesterday's check mark if you don't pay attention."

My blood races. What I'm about to do is crazy, even for me. But I have to know—can she truly not be bought? Is it possible? "A million dollars."

She hits pause and turns to me, pretty lips parted. "*Excuse* me?"

"A million. All for you. Set for life."

She frowns, bewildered. "You would pay me *a million dollars* to stop making you watch these videos? You hate them that much?"

"Yes, I hate them that much. And I'm offering you a million dollars to make it stop."

"Is it because you feel bad that these people are going to lose their homes?" she asks.

"What?! Why does it matter?" I say. "The point is, I'd watch them as discussed, and you can report back with a clear conscience. You'd be able to report back that you forced me to watch them."

She shakes her head. "That doesn't work."

"What do you mean, that doesn't work?" A million dollars doesn't work for her?

"It just doesn't," she says.

"Why?"

"Because you need to do the program that I have created."

I laugh. "Is this a joke? A million, Elle. Come on. It won't be on the table forever."

"Good," she says. "How about we get it off the table right now?"

"No," I say.

"Do you want an X?" she asks.

"What exactly is your deal with Corman?" I ask, mystified. "Does he have some kind of leverage over you? Are you in legal trouble or something?"

"Is it so stunning to you that somebody would care about something more than money?" she asks.

"In a word? Yes," I say. "And if you care about those people so much, I just offered you a million dollars. You could buy the residents of the building their own condos."

"There are forty apartments in there. A million divided by

forty is twenty-five thousand dollars per unit—maybe half that per person. That's moving expenses, a down payment and a few months' rent. They'd still lose their beloved homes."

"Out of curiosity, is there any price that would work?"

A strange look comes over her face. She picks up her glass and contemplates the bubbles rising lazily up through the bright amber liquid. Then she turns her attention to me. "What would it cost to buy the building?" she asks.

"The building's not for sale."

"I thought everything was for sale," she says.

"Well, there is a price but I won't pay you that."

"How about just to stop the project," she says. "You keep the building as a landlord, and you let the people have their homes."

"Why do you care what I do with this building?"

"You asked my price and I told it to you."

"Is there a hidden camera somewhere here?" I joke.

She glares.

"The project cannot and will not be stopped," I tell her. "People have offered to buy the building and I've already said no. Think of something else."

"Why can't you stop the project, or at least, redesign it, sparing the building?"

"Why do you care?"

She sits up straight. "That is the program that I created," she says. "You were mandated to undergo a program designed by an accredited coach—"

"Yeah, yeah, yeah," I say. "So if I promise to not knock down the building, you'll graduate me? You'll tick off all of the boxes on the form? No more video?"

She stills right here, seems to consider her words carefully. "Yes. If you spare the building, I would consider you to have completed the course successfully."

"What kind of program outcome is that?"

"My program is for you to have empathy. Saving the building would demonstrate to me that you have empathy for those people in the video, and that would be a...sufficient leveling up of emotional intelligence. I don't see what's so stunning about it all. This is the outcome I have set my mind to."

"But what if I spared the building because I hate the videos?" I say. "What do you want more? The empathy or the building?"

She frowns. "You need to stop asking questions about my methodology. I just told you how you graduate from my program."

"Why ask for something impossible?"

"Nothing's impossible," she says.

"This ask of yours is impossible," I say. "The 341 building is coming down. I own most of the block that's bordered by Forty-fifth and Forty-sixth Streets and Eighth and Ninth Avenues. I'm planning a massive redevelopment and 341 sits right at the center. If we didn't knock it down, we'd have to redesign the complex to curl around the building on three sides, creating a chockablock look, and the hotel would have to be entirely redesigned and expanded on the side."

"So you *could* design around it," Elle says, "but you'd rather not redesign the complex."

"I could redesign it, yes. I could also get a Hello Kitty facial tattoo as well. Neither thing will be happening. The redesign you're proposing would be wrong on every level. It would be excruciatingly wrong."

"It's their home, Malcolm," she says.

"Things need to die for new life to appear," I say. "It's the circle of life."

"It's not my circle of life," she says hotly.

I lean in. "It's called progress. It's why New York City isn't full of rickety, three-story death traps. When you really think about it, I'm the one with empathy, and you are truly without pity."

She frowns. "The point is, the project could be completed without the destruction of their homes..."

"I'll watch the videos before I allow this brilliant project to become visually incoherent."

She looks crestfallen.

Why does she care? I find myself wondering again: does she know them somehow? Does she have some stake in the building?

But even if she did know the people, it's a million dollars. Who passes up a million dollars? Even if that had been her own actual home, it still wouldn't explain passing up a million dollars to stay living in a shitty building like that. She could buy something beautiful with that money. Several beautiful things.

"What do you really want?" I ask.

"For you to spare 341."

"No—341 is just some random building to you. But for whatever reason you're fixated on me seeing it enough to what? Love it? And if I love it enough, will I spare it? What does it mean if I spare it? What does it mean to you? Tell me that much."

"What would be meaningful to me is if you would put yourself into Maisey's shoes and think how Maisey feels. How about if you do that?"

"You want me to put myself into Maisey's shoes? Fine. Maisey doesn't want the building—not really. Maisey doesn't care about a decrepit pile of bricks. None of those people do—not really. For every one of them, it's something else. Love. Security. Happiness. Feeling successful. Being enough. For some, it's about overcoming some sort of fear. It's the old man's desire to be free of that horrible memory that gets him in the pit of his stomach. The black-haired dancer—it's escaping that dread of the future that haunts her while she's waiting in a line at the bank or whatever. The thing that comes to her before she can push it away. What people want—it's never truly an object."

She looks impressed; she shouldn't be. What people want makes them vulnerable. It's my stock in trade.

I say, "What you want, it's not money and it's not the building. It's not your excellence at this job. What do you get when I spare the building, little country mouse?"

She watches my eyes; for a fleeting moment, I think I've hit a nerve. "I want for you to have empathy," she says. "And I want for that empathy to move you to save the building. And the video isn't ridiculous."

Without so much as waiting for my reply, she wakes up the screen and hits play.

A million dollars.

Is it possible that she's just that passionate about achieving this outlandish goal that she has set for me? Is this the dark genius of Corman and his lawyers? Instead of paying somebody to torture me, they simply found the most idealistic, impossible-to-buy executive coach in existence? And she designed this program specifically for me?

Her absurd program will never work, but people believe in absurd things all of the time. All you have to do is look at Facebook to know that's true.

My heart pounds. Is that what she is? A bloody true believer in the value of empathy? And getting me to feel empathy is actually more important to her than a million dollars?

Wildly I think of everything that I know about her. I know that she doesn't take a lot for herself—I see it every day. Never more than one croissant from the Kendrick building pastry tray. Never a new outfit. Not even a million dollars, apparently.

I'm accustomed to people shrinking away from me, scurrying away from me, worrying about me, hiding from me, but this?

This bizarre coaching is worth more to her than a million dollars?

I stare at her, utterly baffled. She clearly understands the offer. And she's turning it down. This woman with her perfect breasts and her bell-like laugh and a thing about hedgehogs and the postal service, and the bizarre idea that reform works through documentary videos.

What is going on? What are the hidden variables in her calculus? What is this woman's black swan? It's so rare that a person baffles me. It's infuriating.

And exciting.

And sexy as hell.

I should be offended. How would she feel if I created a program designed to corrupt *her*?

The minute I get the thought, I can't shake the idea of corrupting her. What would she look like seduced, fully corrupted? My imagination runs wild, picturing her lying in my bed, hair tangled around her head, on the edge of coming, greedily enjoying everything she's ever denied herself.

I lean back and study the demure slope of her nose. The sly curve of her cheekbone. That butterfly bow tie. My country mouse was hot before, but now she's irresistible.

I'm thinking about her in that dress shop. That witchy look she got on her face when she tried on the dress, when she thought nobody in the world was watching.

I want her in my bed wearing that witchy look. Begging for me with that witchy look on her face. Mine, utterly and completely.

She stops the video. "Are you even paying attention?"

"Very much so," I say.

"Okay, then, because I'm turning it back on. We have forty-seven minutes left. Fourteen hours and forty-seven minutes."

I grin. Fourteen hours and forty-seven minutes. Only Elle would say that.

Only Elle.

19

Noelle

I TURN ON THE VIDEO, heart racing.

A million dollars. It was a huge gamble to turn that down. If we end up getting kicked out of our building, at least I'd be able to offer people something to help. But that would mean giving up on our home, giving up on Malcolm.

Was it foolish? Sometimes I feel like, spending all this time with Malcolm, it's making me lose sight of things that once seemed so clear. Even sitting on the same side of a table like this, watching the presentation, it does something to my judgement.

I should have put a table between us. Except it's easier to watch together this way, and it is kind of exciting to have him right next to me. Sometimes he slides his gaze to me—discreetly —thinking I won't notice.

I notice, that's for sure. Nobody ever looks at me the way Malcolm does. As if he's fascinated with me.

Who in the world has ever been fascinated with *me*? Nobody.

It's intoxicating.

I love the way he talks to me, too, so worked up and agitated and passionate, like velvet running over my skin, against the grain.

It's just that I'm always taking care of others, staying carefully away from the spotlight. When I'm at work, I'm the US Postal Service, delivering mail to the proper boxes, making the time to get to know the people on my route. I'm the trusted uniform, keeping a watch out for when elderly customers stop picking up their mail, for when children seem to be in distress. I know more about most people's neighborhoods than they do.

Outside of work, I'm shy Noelle, the girl who disappears into the background. The one who never rode an elevator until the year before last.

And then here's Malcolm—this beautiful, funny, scathingly clever man—focused so intently on me and me alone.

I try to concentrate on the video, a re-enactment of the great bicycle rack debate of 2019, but I can feel him looking at me. If Francine or Willow were here, they'd turn to him and be all, what the hell? But to me, Malcolm's bright gaze feels like sunshine after a long, dark winter.

I scowl, forcing my mind back to my mission. When I feel I have my wits back about me, I turn to him, eyes narrowed. "Are you even paying attention?" I demand.

"Of course I am," he says, eyes sparkling with mischief. "Is that a clip-on tie?" he asks.

"Yes," I say. "Why?"

"Wondering."

My gaze falls to his lips, remembering our kiss in the limo. I've been kissed before, but never wildly, madly kissed.

He's doing his sexy ghost-of-a-smile thing now. Does he sense what I'm thinking?

"You are not at all being a model student," I say.

"I know," he says. "And I think you absolutely love it," he says.

I snort. "In your dreams."

He just grins.

"Are you ready to watch the video anytime soon?" I ask.

He lowers his voice to a deep, rumbly tone that seems to caress my lady parts—that's how deep and rumbly it is. "I really want to kiss you again," he says.

Electric shivers skitter over my skin. "Well, you can't," I say.

"Why not?"

"It was a mistake before, and it would be even more of a mistake now."

"Even more of a mistake," he says. "Why even *more* of a mistake?"

"Workplace impropriety in a public place."

"I'll grant you that it's improper, but this is a private room in a public place," he says.

"A semi-private room where anybody could walk in."

"It's not as if kissing is X-rated," he says, leaning in, lips drawing near the shell of my ear. I close my eyes. The pleasure of feeling him this close is almost too much to bear.

"Kissing me while you view your lesson for today qualifies as multitasking," I breathe.

On screen, Lizzie makes an impassioned speech about bike racks.

Underneath the tablecloth, light fingertips settle onto my thigh.

My heart pounds like crazy.

"Is it multitasking if I just set my hand here?" he rumbles.

"I think it is," I breathe.

My mouth goes dry as he settles the entirety of his hand onto my thigh. His large, capable, unpredictable hand. It feels deliciously dangerous.

He squeezes gently and I nearly explode in a multi-layered orgasm—just from that—that's how wound up I am. "What do you think about the way I'm multitasking now? What do you think? Is this an acceptable form of multitasking?"

"Maybe," I whisper.

The video plays. It's not actually the great bicycle rack debate; it's a reenactment of it. Jada is running out of footage, so there have been some reenactments. In this reenactment, Tabitha has extra sparkles on. Francine put on her big eyelashes. Jeremy from the first floor, who ultimately lost the bike rack argument last summer, is way more jovial.

Malcolm moves his hand another quarter inch up my thigh.

I suck in a tiny breath. "You're not paying attention," I say.

"Lest you forget, I'm a CEO," he rumbles. "I'm a master multitasker. You're the one not paying attention. But maybe you've seen it before. Have you?"

I don't know how to answer that. It doesn't feel important. His hand moves nearer to the apex of my thighs. My belly fills with butterflies, excited, eager, fluttery.

"Do you watch these things ahead of time?" he asks.

"That's proprietary," I say.

"Whether you watch them ahead of time is proprietary?" he asks, moving his hand up, up, nearer my sex.

"Yes," I breathe. "Yes."

His hand reaches my pussy and he cups me through my pants. I gasp as the bright pressure of his touch flows through me, promising wonderful things.

Into my ear, he whispers, "Undo your slacks."

I exhale through my nose, a breathy snort. "I can't."

"Go ahead."

I cast a glance at the open doorway. Those two faraway diners are still bent over their table under the two-story plate glass window.

"Even if somebody came in," he says, following the train of my thoughts in his usual uncanny way, "the tablecloth is there, isn't it? Nobody sees. Nobody would know. This, for instance." He presses just one finger to my core now, sending ripples of pleasure through me—the feeling is so powerfully good, I nearly choke on my own tongue. "They would never see this."

"I'm not undoing my slacks for you," I say.

"Then undo you slacks for yourself," he breathes. "Take something for once. Take this one little thing for yourself. You work so hard, but you never take anything for yourself, do you? Always behind the scenes."

I swallow. How did he know to say that? It's true. I never even take up too much space. But then, that's what an executive coach is. A person who supports another person to shine and excel.

And now his finger is stroking my clit through my slacks and it's not enough. I need more.

"What does it matter?" he whispers.

"Because I'm your coach," I say.

"I'll still do the work. You know I need those ticks. But you can't be my coach twenty-four seven. What are you the rest of the time, country mouse?" He kisses the side of my mouth. "What do you want to be the rest of the time?"

Something dark seizes my mind. What do I want to be? What do I want? The video rolls on in the vague distance, and I can't even with it.

"Undo your pants," he says.

My pulse races. I want my pants to be undone for me. I really, really want him to undo them.

It's on the tip of my tongue to ask it but I hold back. Usually when I ask for things, there's a whole solid, sensible basis to it that I could explain if need be. I would never request a thing just *because* like some mad queen, but I really do want him to undo it...just because.

"Elle," he says.

"Umm, can you do it?" I force myself to say. "I want you to unzip my pants, please," I say.

I wait, sure he's going to think I'm a freak, but then he groans this deep, caveman-ish groan. Wicked fingers move around my waistband all the way to the side, unlatching the latch, unzipping the zipper.

"Like this?" he asks.

"Like that," I breathe.

He urges my hips up, and I comply. Together, we tug my pants loose from my crotch, a nifty cooperative project that gives him extra space to work.

His fingers are sliding around the loosened waistband of my pants, pressing to the bare flesh of my belly beneath, and down on the inside.

"Grab the table edge," he whispers, and I do it—anything to keep him doing his magical multitasking.

I swallow, thrilled and stunned, when he reaches the elastic of my cotton panties. Maddeningly, he moves his fingers over my cotton-clad mound.

His lips hover at my cheek, right in front of my ear, not quite touching, though now and then, there's a brush of whiskers that I feel down to my toes.

His breath is warm puffs, hot secret caresses that suggest he, too, is affected. I'm panting softly, in time with him.

I gasp when he hits the damp spot over my clit. "Fuck," I say, which is totally not a thing I say.

His breath fans over my cheek, now. His fingers steal under the protective panel of my panties, making blunt contact with my madly aroused core. "This," he says, apropos of nothing.

"That?" I say.

Whiskery lips curl into a smile against my cheek. And then his finger begins to move. Slowly—inexorably—across my clit.

Voices from the video sound out as if from light years away. The bench beneath me seems to tilt as he strokes. I can hear breathy sounds that can only be coming from me. He's reduced me to something I don't recognize—a creature who is beyond right and wrong, beyond empathy and evil, existing on the tendril of a dream.

I'm all need, and I need him.

I don't even care.

I push my pelvis into his hand. He strokes me with confidence, like he knows how I do myself, and he's bent on doing it better, overachiever that he is.

My breath has gone ragged. I'm being taken over by the devil and I love it so much.

"More?" he asks.

"Yes, more!" I whisper, so close to the edge. "Faster."

"Hmm," he says, and it definitely means something different in this context than when he says it during those post-negotiation huddles. I like what it means in this context. I like that he enjoys my telling him what I want. I liked how he seems to think it's the best thing ever.

And he does it, which I think is the best thing ever.

I'm panting hard. He moves deftly, adding pressure.

My orgasm ignites out of somewhere deep inside me, filling me with pleasure all the way up to my eyeballs.

I'm gripping the table edge, panting, coming, strung out with pleasure.

Malcolm slows his hand, leaving it in place, like he's soaking up my orgasm through his fingers. Then, slowly, he withdraws. "You are so beautiful," he breathes. He smooths my waistband, a gesture toward putting me back together, though it'll take a lot more to put me back together than that.

"I feel completely undone," I whisper. It's a piece of honesty; I feel undone and disorganized and all messed up. I like to present myself as put together, and I never admit when I'm not, but there's something between us now that feels like secrets in the night.

He presses his face to my cheek, whiskers like sandpaper. "You're beautiful when you're undone." He kisses me there and then pulls away.

"Umm," I breathe, dazed. I don't know what to do or say. I turn to him, look him in the eye.

He brushes back my hair. "I suppose you're going to insist I watch the last bit over," he says. "I'll admit to missing a lot of what just happened."

The video is still playing, I realize dimly. I'm glad he didn't catch what happened. I'd hate it if he truly had been multi-tasking.

"I guess I'll let it go," I say, looking around. I need to put myself back together, somehow. I feel like I have a wet spot the size of Texas between my legs.

"I should...I need to...excuse me."

"Of course." He's back to his dapper, wicked self. "Don't worry. I'll keep watching."

I point at him. "You'd better." In truth, I barely care at this point.

I head into the main room, to the far corner where the ladies' room is. I fix myself up and wash up and then I look in the mirror, expecting to see myself disheveled. And granted, my hair isn't perfectly smooth anymore, but also, my cheeks are rosy, and my eyes look brighter, and my lips look somehow fuller, and my face seems to be glowing. I have this sense, oddly, that I look like a mermaid.

I gaze at my reflection in wonder. The whole world feels magical.

I take out my hair pin and smooth my hair, refastening it, slowly but surely coming to my senses. What the hell am I doing? I'm here to save our building and instead I'm letting him seduce me!

I go back. The video is still playing. Has he actually been watching it?

I sit.

"Dessert?" he asks.

I give him a stern look. "I think we've gone crazy enough tonight, don't you?"

Malcolm studies my face. "We have three minutes left."

"I'll let it slide."

"Do I get a tick?"

I snort. "We'll see." I grab my purse. "I should go."

He's impossibly handsome in the candlelight, mischief dancing in his eyes.

"And if you think this is how future sessions will be..." I shake my head.

"You didn't think that was a good session?" he asks. "I thought it was a great session."

IT'S nine thirty West Coast time and twelve thirty in the morning New York time when I get back to my room. I call Francine, and I'm so grateful when she answers.

"I don't know if I can do this," I gust out. "Why was I thinking that I'd be any match for somebody like Malcolm Blackberg?"

"What happened?" she asks. "Last time you called, he was actually watching Jada's videos. Is he not watching the videos anymore?"

"No, he's still watching," I say.

"That is an amazing accomplishment right there, Noelle! You are getting him to watch the videos, like a boss. You are *doing this*. By the way, we've been discussing his John-in-love-with-Maisey theory. He may be onto something."

I flop back on the bed, reliving the way he touched me. I can still feel it in my veins, like the remnants of a magical potion. "I feel like I'm losing control of the situation, Francine."

"Noelle, you are doing this. It is mind-blowing, how far you've gotten. We are all completely blown away. You're this brave warrior for our building. The worst that can happen is he tears down the building. He was already gonna do that."

"I know," I say.

"Are you feeling nervous or homesick?" she asks. "Oh my god, is he being just a complete asshole?"

"It's not that..."

"None of us would blame you if you felt like you had to come home," she says in a small voice. "If you wanted to come home, we'll buy the ticket. You're all alone in a strange place—"

"No, it's not that. It's more that I feel like, it might be a lost cause. He's pretty into his development going the way it is, and my resolve might be weakening."

"Wait, what?" Francine barks. "What have you done with Noelle? You have the most resolve of anyone I know."

I object, but she keeps on, talking over my protests.

"You set your mind to things and you make them happen," she says. "It's what you do. Nothing stops you from doing what you set your mind to. You have the most resolve of anybody I know. Think of how you fought for your mother. Think of how you moved out to New York all alone. And as a letter carrier, you're out there braving all kinds of weather. Like that Christmas Eve blizzard you told us about? And it was a crazy amount of snow, and you were stranded in some cabin, but you ventured out to deliver that last package?"

I close my eyes. I did do that. Half the mailboxes were drifted so deep, no way could they be served without a shovel.

"You said you just started in and kept going. And you made it happen. That's what you're doing now, and we're all so freaking proud of you."

Would they be proud of me to know I was getting hand jobs from Malcolm?

I make her tell me the latest news from the building. Jada and Antonio are an official item now—not a surprise to any of us. Mia's show is getting raves. Maisey made caramel corn for the new letter carrier. The updates help.

I'm about to wash up for bed when I notice that I have messages from Nisha and Coralee—the traveling team is going out dancing.

It's ten at night, a bit late to go out, but maybe dancing would be a good way to blow off steam. I'm definitely not tired.

I text back.

Me: I'm into it! Have you left yet?

Nisha: We're in the lobby waiting for the Uber. ETA?

Me: I'll be there in seven!!

I change into my skirt outfit and rush down. We pile into an Uber and head out to a club with pink strobe lights where the people are packed into a thronging mass.

Nisha and Coralee and Lawrence and I do shots and then head out onto the floor where we make a fearsome foursome. It's totally fun, and I'm thinking, maybe things aren't so out of control. Maybe I can do this. I just have to find a way to get us back on track of him focusing on the videos and on my neighbors.

My phone is buzzing in my pocket. It's nearly midnight—who would be calling?

I pull it out and see that it's a New Jersey number. I have a mini heart attack. I don't think it's Stella's number, but it's the same area code, and I have this feeling like it might be bad news. I see that the same caller has tried me three times in the past hour while I've been dancing.

But there are no messages.

What does it mean? Have I been found out?

The call goes to voice mail and again, no message is left. I wish I'd answered—I'll agonize about it until I know what's going on. Or should I call the number back?

A fun song comes on.

"Come dance!" Nisha screams from the dance floor. Lawrence waves. Coralee rushes over to where I am. "Come on, Elle!"

My phone starts vibrating yet again. I hold it up and point to it. "I have to take this." I rush up the stairs and around the corner into a quiet hallway that leads to the restrooms. "Hello?"

"Stella?" It's a man.

I swallow. "Excuse me?" I say. "Who is this?"

"Is this Stella?"

"*Who* is this?" I ask again, pulse racing. It's the middle of the night on the East Coast. What is going on?

"I need to speak to Stella of Bexley Partners. It's very urgent. About her current assignment."

"What about it?" I ask.

"Is this Stella, then?" he asks.

"What is this regarding?" I ask.

"Don't freak out," he says, softening his voice. "I'm just pulling your leg. I know you're not Stella. Actually, Stella told me all about what you guys are up to. She told me to tell you hi from Estonia. She says the teaching's going well. The students' understanding of past tense, not so much."

"Oh, okay," I say. "What is it?"

"This whole thing with you taking her place and all...have

they shown any awareness that you're not her yet? She wanted me to ask you."

"Everything's fine," I say, trying to be vague.

"None the wiser?" he tries.

"I'm sorry, who is this?"

"A friend of Stella's—not you, the real Stella."

It's here I remember what she said about her asshole ex subletting her place. "Are you the one subletting her apartment? Is there a problem?"

"Yes, actually. AJ Doyle at your service. Here's the problem that we have—you're committing fraud." His voice is no longer friendly.

Cold shivers bloom up my spine. "W-what?"

"Don't act stupid," he says. "You're in San Fran pretending to be her? To a client? Stella may be okay with that, but I might not be okay with it."

"How is it even your concern?" I say. "I don't see how it's any of your business." It's so strange to talk to somebody in this tone. A month ago I wouldn't have taken this tone.

"Man," he says, "old lady Bexley is *not* going to be happy when she finds out about this little scam you two are running. Or that client? Blackberg Inc.? I hear the guy's an A-one prick. Imagine what he'll do when I tell him what you're up to."

I grip the phone as the music pulses below.

"I could see somebody pressing charges," he continues, "charges against both of you. But luckily for you, I'm in a good mood."

I frown. I have a definite feeling that I'm not going to like this.

"Here's the thing, I've been a little stretched thin lately. And you know that sweet little per diem you're getting? It would really help me out."

"You want me to...pay you?"

"That would be nice. A hundred fifty bucks a day. That's the cost of my silence." The exact amount of the per diem.

"But it doesn't come in the form of money," I say. "It's there for when I want to sign for meals and things."

"You can order shit from Amazon, though. Off your per diem? What you do is you order gift cards, and you email them to me. Don't worry, Stella's done it before, when I was in a bind."

"They'll think I'm stealing."

"That's your problem, not mine. Gift cards in my inbox by ten in the morning Eastern time every day from now on. Or else. I'll text you the email." He hangs up.

I stare mutely at the *call ended* message on my phone, pulse going crazy. What am I going to do? It's morning in Estonia. I give the real Stella a call. She picks up all groggy from sleep, but when I tell her what AJ is demanding, she wakes up really fast.

"Uh," she says. "I'm so sorry. He's such a devious piece of shit."

"What should I do? Will he follow through? Will he tell on me if I don't pay him?"

"I'm so sorry," she says. "There's not a lot AJ wouldn't do. He's not a good guy. I'm fine, I'll play dumb, but you need to either disappear or pay him. It'll probably be okay."

"What does that mean?" I ask.

"He's always broke—he'd be stupid to kill the golden goose," she says.

I hang up the phone, not entirely reassured. My web of lies is starting to feel like a noose around my neck.

Briefly, I consider fessing up to Malcolm, but how could I do such a thing? I'd be abandoning this project, my friends. And I'm not ready to put an end to my time with Malcolm. I don't know what it means, but I don't want to walk away from all of this now.

But if I stay, I have to pay AJ. And sure, I can go without the per diem. It's what I've been doing already. But paying it all to AJ feels like stealing.

I head back to the bar and find Lawrence. He buys me a shot of tequila, and I slam it, and then I buy him one.

The shots make me feel more confident. I'll brazen it out, I decide. Maybe it can still work out.

I head out onto the floor and dance like mad.

20

Malcolm

I WAKE up at dawn feeling energetic, and set out for a nice run through Golden Gate Park in the crisp San Francisco morning.

Usually I stop thinking about a woman the minute she leaves my sight. What is there to think about? Either I'm actually spending time with a woman and we're talking or eating or screwing or I'm doing other things that don't involve said woman.

Talking and eating and screwing does not require a lot of extracurricular thought. There are no decisions to wrestle with, no strategies to develop. And I would definitely not reminisce. What point would there be to that?

But all bets are off when it comes to Elle. I pound the trail, passing under trees collected from all around the world, every imaginable shade of green, reminiscing about soft gusts of pleasure, and intelligent eyes gazing sideways. The rush of excitement I felt when she made it clear she enjoyed my hands on her. The warm, coconut-scented silk of her skin under my lips.

I want you to unzip it, please.

The nervous-brave combo is definitely working for her, or at least it's definitely working for me—that naïve vulnerability of hers mixed with steely determination, the peanut butter and chocolate of the world of women.

God, I loved how she asked it, her voice wavering a little, like she was striding out of her comfort zone, but there was this determination inside her words. I felt like she was showing me something intimate. Like a gift of trust.

Foolish of her—a gift of trust is not really something anybody should be giving to the likes of me. But still she gave it.

I don't know what to think of it. It turns me around in my head to think of it.

I can't stop going back to things she said. And of course, there's the million she turned down. The absolute gobsmackery of that.

I get back, shower quickly, and hop on a call with the New York team, but I'm thinking about her blue-striped tie the whole time.

I could've unclipped it and cast it aside. Or better yet, I could've made her remove it. And then I undo a button.

Briefly, I imagine it as the non-clip-on kind, and conduct thought experiments designed to answer the question of whether it would have been more satisfying to pull it free with speed and efficiency, or to draw it from her collar slowly and provocatively.

All in all, not the most productive use of a conference call.

Those ties. She has no idea.

Or does she? She's smarter than she looks. She's *more* than she looks in every way. Does nobody else see her but me? It's difficult to imagine, but I also prefer it. I wouldn't like the idea of other men seeing her the way I see her.

I prepare for today's negotiation, turning our conversation

over in my mind—the money, the tie, even that video and the drama of the bike rack, which I have definite opinions on, and if I were keeping that building, I would locate it in the obviously perfect place that the dancer picked out. A couple of the first-floor guys wanted it in the back of the building and it's just an obnoxious place for it.

I have my New York PA make a reservation at my favorite place on the bay for the next night. It won't be easy to get, but I've given her leeway to spread some money around.

I get down to the lobby early, looking forward to seeing her and having the secret knowledge between us. It's a new feeling for me.

I'm surprised when she's not there; my country mouse is primly punctual in addition to being secretly full of heat. I frown, not liking that. I see Lawrence coming and I take out my phone. I want to talk to Elle, but not anybody else. Luckily, Lawrence has his phone out, too.

The rest of them come. I stay apart. I want to ask about her, but I don't want to show extra interest in her.

Coralee is the one to finally turn in the brilliant observation that Elle, who is typically the first to arrive, is currently late. I stay fixated on my phone, ears perked up.

Lawrence is laughing. "I'll be surprised if she shows up at all," he says.

I frown. "Elle not coming?" I mumble.

Nisha is glaring at Lawrence, trying to shut him up it seems.

"What's going on?" I demand.

"Nothing," Coralee says. "We went out dancing last night, that's all."

She went dancing? With Walt? Lawrence? The team?

"And it got late, let's just say." Lawrence seems to be trying to conceal a smile. *Late?* What the hell does that mean?

"Yes. Late," Coralee agrees.

Finally Elle appears, fast walking across the lobby, complexion green, dark circles under her eyes, toilet paper stuck to her shoe.

"Hey, soldier," Walt says.

She mumbles her hello. She can't even look me in the eye.

So she went out after we were together and got drunk? A wave of unease blooms through me. Was our dinner that upsetting that she had to go get drunk? And now she can't look at me? How drunk did she get? Is she okay? Did she think to hydrate?

I should ignore her—I really should, but I can't. "Elle and Coralee, ride with me." I head toward the cars and get in, determined not to pay any special attention to Elle. I'm usually having to remind myself to pay *more* attention to women, to remember to ask about their well-being and what they've been up to.

We start rolling and I sit silently, willing them to talk about their night, but employees never talk about their personal lives in front of me. Why start now?

"Night out at the club," I say.

Coralee seems alarmed. "We just wanted to check out a big club, that's all. See some of this famous San Francisco nightlife we've been hearing so much about."

"And? Was it all it's cracked up to be?" I ask blithely.

She looks at me, surprised. "Pretty amazing."

"Very amazing," Elle says, expression carefully blank. What is up with her? Coralee goes on about the décor and the lights, as if that's the part that I'd be interested in.

The car drops us at the curb in front of the Kendrick building. "Elle, a quick word on today's proceedings."

"Catch you later!" Coralee says, heading up the steps.

Elle clutches her brown bag to her chest. She has on her most somber of butterfly ties, a light brown affair with black dots.

"What's going on?" I demand.

"Nothing," she says. "Personal matters. A situation that I found out about—just a bit upsetting. I didn't think that I would be able to sleep."

"Personal matter," I echo, burning to know what it is.

"And I might have had a drink or two. I'll be fine."

"Fine?" I say.

She simply nods—she's not falling for my repeat-the-last-words trick.

I can't stand that she might have some dire situation, and that she's feeling hungover, or worse, remorseful about what happened between us.

"Come on," I say.

She looks alarmed. "What?"

"A ten-minute detour."

Her eyes widen. "We can't. We can't...not anymore," she says.

"A juice," I say. "I can't have you going into the session looking like you're about to pass out. You need a juice and there's a juice bar..." I point down the block. "What did you think I was proposing?" I text the group that we're ten minutes out. I head down the block, steps hard on the concrete. She catches up. "Are you going to tell me what's wrong?"

"I'm fine. Late night. You know."

"What's really going on?"

"Nothing that concerns you, I swear it." We get in line at the juice shop. I wait for more. "I got a call after our thing, that's all," she adds. "Upsetting news."

I frown. What was her upsetting news? Her mother died a few years back. Her father lives out West somewhere...he doesn't seem to be involved in her life, but I suppose it could be him. Or a friend thing. Or is it a medical situation with her? But doctors don't call at night. Does she have pets back home? There's so much about her that I don't know.

Why, upon learning upsetting news, would she go out and drink with the traveling team? Were my lips on her cheek and my fingers on her pussy just minutes before not sufficient demonstration of my interest in her?

Is it not clear enough to her that I'm a powerful billionaire who can solve most any problem with money? People love to say you can't throw money at a problem, but in my experience, it works well. And where money doesn't work, threats tend to come in handy, or perhaps a discreet application of foul play. Soulless corporate marauders such as myself really can be effective allies.

Yet my country mouse decides that getting drunk with the traveling team is the superior solution?

But I've learned over the years that you can't bark these sorts of questions at a woman, and you're not supposed to second-guess a woman's problem-solving methods. You're supposed to hold yourself back, much as you might want a crack at the problem.

She just stands there looking weary. Can she stop being maddening for one instant?

I grit my teeth. "Are you sure there's nothing that I can do? I hope it's not related to your tenure here as my coach." I make a mental note to give another good report.

"No, just, there's a problematic person, but I'm dealing with him."

I stiffen. *Him?*

"Does somebody need a visit from the fist of Malcolm Blackberg?" I say it as a joke, but it's not. Long experience has taught me that it's best to say the iffy things as jokes.

She turns to me with the strangest look. "It's under control," she whispers fervently.

"It's not under control from the sounds of it," I say lightly, studying her face. "Say the word."

"No, thanks," she says. Naturally. She would never send me after a person.

"Unless the problematic person is me," I say. "I draw the line at punching myself."

She smiles, finally, and it swells something in my chest.

At the corner I buy her an alkalizing green juice plus an orange juice. I hand her the green juice first.

"Thank you," she says politely, as if nothing but a client.

"Drink it," I command.

She's still staring at the drink.

"Now," I growl.

She sips. Makes a face.

I want to fix her, and I don't know how. It makes me crazy. I felt so in tune with her during our dinner session, and I don't get in tune with people all that much. I'd planned to ask her on a proper date, to that restaurant on the water, but now I'm not sure.

"Drink. All of it. The whole thing," I say.

She gulps it down. I take the empty glass from her and give her the orange juice.

"Thank you. So sweet—you really didn't have to."

I let up on the interrogation on the way back, allowing her to point out features of buildings. She seems to be feeling better.

The negotiation is unremarkable; it's not uncommon to have a sleepy session after a breakthrough session like yesterday's.

Mostly this one is a *what if* session—we're not at a deal, but we're exploring it. We spend the two hours imagining what it might look like together. Gerrold wants things for his people he'll never get, like job training and placement for fired workers. He needs to get the asking out of his system, though. He needs to be able to look at himself in the mirror and see the person he saw in the video that we made—the caring steward of the company, handing it off to another caring steward. He needs to be able to tell himself that I feel some kind of tribal allegiance that will lead me to sacrifice my own profitability.

Is that what a good person does? Is that what the people in the 341 building do? No doubt. And they probably talk about it *ad nauseum,* too. *Got your back!*

On the way back to the hotel, Elle makes it known to the group that she's going to take a "nice nap." And not with yours truly—that's clear.

"We have our afternoon session scheduled," I say.

"I'll email your assignment," she says. "You're to use our time slot to do the assignment. It'll be a work-at-your-own-pace session."

"Ah," I say. Two weeks ago, I would've been elated for us to have a work-at-your-own-pace session, and I would've promptly turned it into a Malcolm's-assistant-works-at-his-own-pace session.

I go back to my own room to work on the Germantown proposal. Sure enough an email comes. She's created a PDF worksheet with questions about the people in the building, and links to a few of the videos in case I need to brush up.

As if.

The questions are simple, mostly revolving around people's professions and professional aspirations. Elle's unorthodox training has given me a lot of knowledge about the people in the building, and while this hasn't translated into any executive soft skills, it has definitely resulted in an unhealthy fascination with my executive soft skills coach.

Did I move too fast? Did I scare her off?

And then instead of being caring and tender, I made her drink a disgusting beverage. But what was I supposed to do? She wasn't communicating with me. She was clearly upset. She gave me no other ways to fix the thing.

My team is texting me about the proposal. I tell them to figure it out, and I go back to Elle's worksheet, elaborating on my answers. I make a few observations on the power of Tabitha's sunshiny attitude and Mia's dogged determination. I praise Antonio's ever-growing acting skills—Elle will enjoy that I noticed.

Never have I put so much energy into winning over a woman. Usually it's enough to just want them, but the harder ones require a dinner or maybe a diamond trinket.

Elle would hate a diamond trinket, so here I am. But I do have a lot of opinions on the people, and I think it will be fun to discuss them later. I casually toss out that I have a theory about the identity of the dryer-lint-screen bandit. I don't tell her my theory, only that I have it.

Which is sure to drive her crazy.

I wish I could buy her a little something and have it sent to the room.

Maybe fresh-squeezed juice and fresh flowers, but that's something she could get for herself. Well, I know what she would most want—the building saved. Documents converting it into a co-op. I imagine her pretty lips parted in shock, her green eyes wide. There's something irresistible about the idea of giving her what she wants.

I'd put it under John and Maisey's joint management—that would be the icing on the cake. It would almost be worth it, just to see the shock on her face.

Almost.

Even if I were willing to go that far, which I'm not, I don't see how saving this random Manhattan building would be specifically important to a pretty young executive coach from New Jersey, aside from the fact that it's some sort of stretch goal that she seems to have chosen for herself, connected to this video that found its way into her hands by whatever means.

I frequently set my own stretch goals—a certain acquisition, presence in a specific city, running so many miles in a certain amount of time. It's always more about hitting the goal than the goal itself. Goals on their own don't make people happy.

Also, why would I want to end our sessions?

A dark thought hits me—does *she* want our sessions to end? She wasn't at all affectionate today; I chalked it up to the hangover and that mysterious bad news, but what if it's something else? Did I push her too fast?

I think back to the way her eyes fluttered with pleasure, the breathy *yes* she repeated as I moved my hand toward her pussy. The way she asked me to unzip her pants.

Is she rethinking the whole thing? Regretting it?

Is there something I should be doing now that I'm not doing? If I want to keep our interactions going—and I find that I very much do—I need to at least make a gesture toward something that looks vaguely healthy-relationship-ish.

I'm not entirely sure how one works, and I'm hardly capable of developing any such thing, considering my role model, but some gesture...

It's here that I find myself thinking about my old friend Howie. His family lived next to ours growing up, and he was my main source of information on normalcy before I went off to boarding school. I returned to California on and off in the years that followed, but we were never especially close—he was always a Boy Scout type, more likely to be serving omelets at shelter kitchens than throwing eggs at cars with me. These days he's a wholesome family man with a cabinetry business, but we've kept in touch.

WWHD: What would Howie do? Would he try to get her

on a nice date? But what if she won't go on a nice date? Then what would Howie do?

I give Howie a call.

"Malcolm!" Howie sounds happy to hear from me. "What's new? Are you in town?"

"I'm in town and I thought we could get together," I say. "Let me take you out tonight."

"We're grilling," he says. "The kids are excited for it. But you're welcome to come by for a steak."

"Hmmm," I say, not loving the sound of this. I was hoping to get him drunk and soak up some of his secrets, and you can't exactly do that with kids around demanding attention.

"You can finally meet the rug rats, and you haven't seen Clare since the wedding. It's a nice evening—what do you say?"

Reluctantly I agree—I suppose it's a bit much that I haven't seen his home or met his kids in all these years. I'm assuming he's invited me over before this—my New York assistant is responsible for filtering and turning down social invitations. I get her on the line and I learn that Howie has twin girls, both ten years old.

I arrive at Howie's place at seven sharp with a nice bottle of red, per my assistant's suggestion. The girls are cute, though their presence makes for underwhelming dinner conversation, to say the least.

Clare and Howie seem delighted with them, and with each other. Clare sometimes watches Howie with adoration, even when he talks about something as simplistic as his predictions for the Giants and his failure to get the girls interested in baseball. The girls tell what they don't like about baseball, Howie tells the girls to ask me what I call an elevator, a car trunk, a truck, and I dutifully play the Brit, though I've long since adopted the American words for those things. I learn many fascinating things like, they can only feed the dog at its bowl, and he howls at fire trucks.

It's as if they're this enclosed little social unit with their own little rituals and stories. They even have their own language; the entire family is endlessly entertained, for example, when one of the girls asks me to pass the bloop-bloop and I just sit there mystified. In Howie's family, bloop-bloop means the ketchup.

Endlessly entertained. I stare down at my plate pushing around bits of corn with the tines of my fork. Everybody could fall off the face of the earth and Howie's family would be content, just with each other.

It's strange to see children actually wanting to be with their parents and vice versa, and it's not an act for company.

My own family, which is to say, my drunk of a father, would have been happy if I'd fallen off the face of the earth. Especially after my mother made her escape to Australia.

Clare brings out cookies on a vintage platter. There are carvings around the edges of tall ships. Howie always loved tall ships. Clare's smiling at me expectantly now, as if she's waiting for me to break into song.

"Anything look familiar?" she asks.

I look down at the cookies. Am I supposed to recognize the cookies? "Familiar?" I say playfully, adopting her tone.

"Yes!" She grins, still with that air of happy expectancy. "Really so thoughtful. We love it—it's a prize piece in this house."

What?

"Well," I say. "Excellent…" I stuff a cookie into my mouth as Howie looks on, amused.

Clare looks confused. "I'm not just saying that, you know."

Howie grins, like something is suddenly hilarious. "How did you ever come up with it, Malcolm?"

"Come up with it?" I ask.

Howie's laughing.

"What?" Clare looks back and forth between us. "Are you giving him guff, Howie? Stop giving him guff. It was thoughtful."

"He doesn't know," Howie says. "He doesn't know what we're talking about."

"Oh." The fun expectancy is off her face. "Well, that doesn't mean it wasn't thoughtful."

Howie's laughing outright now. "It's exactly what it means."

"Howie," she says, catching his hand, giving him a look of fond warning. He gives her a look back. Just that small, wordless exchange contains worlds—she loves him, and she's scolding him, and he's showing her something back. Love and interest. He's saying, I know, I hear you, it's all good. And she squeezes his hand harder, widens her eyes. She's coming to my defense— this I realize with a distinctly unpleasant feeling.

Clare thinks I need defending.

I swallow. Before I can say anything, Howie speaks. "I'm his oldest friend," he says. "If I don't give him guff, nobody else will." He pins me with a look. "The platter that you gave us as a wedding gift?" He angles his eyes down at it.

"Oh," I say. "I'm so glad," I say. It's exquisite, and probably worth four figures, and I have no knowledge of it. That's my assistant for you.

"We love it," Claire says. "It's our family's favorite serving dish. And your clever little response to our thank-you note?" Her smile falters.

Howie smiles. "Mal's got good people."

"Well," Clare says. "Either way, we love it." Another warning look at Howie. But it's not shaming, it's full of love. She's on Howie's team. She doesn't want him to be hard on his friend. She lifts him, and he lifts her.

"My assistant really is good," I say. "She's not to bother me with anything that's not a death." A confession. I don't know why I make it.

"You must've provided some input," Clare says, "or how would she have known about the tall ships?"

"She would've looked at Howie's Facebook page and figured it out," I say.

"So I'm assuming that wasn't you congratulating me on the pennant win," Howie says.

I wince.

Howie just laughs. "Only you would outsource your friend-ships," he says.

It's situations like this where I'll usually say something like, *oh I'll be sure to dry my tears on the monogrammed towels I had made for my superyacht—hashtag priorities.* But that's not something I say to Howie.

"Well, if it works for you," Clare says brightly.

But it would've meant so much if I'd picked it out myself. It's the thought that counts, they say, but this gift is everything *but* the thought.

And then one of the twins, Vivian, comes and sits on Howie's lap and eats a cookie and traces an outline of the ship. "This one's mine," she says.

"The green one's her favorite," Howie says. "What do we do, Viv? What's our dessert game?"

"Where are they going today?"

It turns out that they made a whole game out of the tray that I couldn't be bothered to know about. They're all on each other's sides, imagining journeys together.

Howie and I have cigars on his deck after dinner. I want to ask him how to do what he does, but honestly, I can't think how to form the question.

"It's nice," I say. "You have a nice family."

"Is everything okay?" he asks.

"Why wouldn't it be?" I ask.

"Showing up here. Not that you're not welcome."

"Maybe I've come to plunder the secret to your relationship success," I say.

He gives me a look and I think that he realizes that is my question. "A relationship is just about showing up," he says. "It's all you can really do. Show up. Say things. Hang in there. Do your best."

As advice goes, it's vague. "That's it? Don't go into relationship coaching, my friend. Showing up is what gets people into trouble."

"No, showing up emotionally," he says, as if I'd know what the hell that means.

In the back of the car on the way home, I think a lot about that platter, and the game that the girls made out of it. It meant something to them and it made them feel closer to me—or it would have if I had known I'd given it to them.

I call my personal shopper on the way home in the car. It's late, but I don't care. She makes a mint upcharging me for the shit she finds. "I need a gift," I say. "I need it tomorrow."

"Okay," she says. I can hear rustling. "I just need the occasion, price range and social media leads on the recipient."

"It's a thank-you gift, but I want to be involved. It's for a woman."

"Great! Okay..." she says.

I'm never involved in the gifts, and I doubt she thinks it's great. "Let's brainstorm something. Where do we start?"

"Usually I do some research to see what the woman is into."

"She loves people. She has a quirky fashion sense," I say. "Hedgehogs. She'd go for homemade over designer labels. Anything having to do with the US Postal Service. Earth tones. Nothing showy."

"How personal? If it's jewelry, I need to study her style on social media."

"No jewelry." I think about Elle's bag. She once called it boring. Not really her style. What if I got her a bag that was her style? "She needs a new bag for her notebooks and iPad and things."

"Purses and bags are hard," she says. "High risk for women."

"Can we get some kind of postal-themed bag? But it can't be cheap or...inauthentic."

"What do you think about a vintage postal carrier bag? There is a market for those out there. Hold on." She starts sending me links to images. None are right. "I'm confined to vendors who can deliver overnight," she says.

"Money is not an object," I say. "Everybody delivers overnight for a price."

"Shit," she says. "Homemade?"

"Yes."

"Motherfucker. This is going to cost you, but I just sent you a link of a vintage postal carrier bag with a hand-done monogram and stitch flowers.

I take a look. "I don't know."

"Think about her stuff. You're matching her stuff."

"She wouldn't want a monogram," I say. "What are the chances I can get a few hedgehogs on there?"

"So the job is, overnight the bag to an artisan in San Francisco who will sew or stitch a hedgehog on it and courier it to your hotel by lunchtime."

"Can you do it?"

"It'll cost you," she says.

21

Noelle

I HAVE JUST over one hundred fifty bucks in my bank account, and I use it to pay AJ—I buy him the gift certificate with it. I don't know what I'll do tomorrow. Who knows, maybe I'll be busted tomorrow, but for today, he'll stay quiet.

I buy a soda at the bar and go sit down with the team who is already at dinner. Everybody is still talking about the historic backgrounder. I nab some of their bread.

The next day's session feels like it goes on forever, possibly because I had no breakfast and I'm starving.

After holding out as long as possible, I take one of the almond croissants and I eat it slowly, ripping off small pieces, savoring each and every bite, making it last. It tastes better than usual. I save the most almondy bite for last. I pop it into my mouth and pretty much let it melt, let the goodness suffuse me.

Then I look up and meet Malcolm's thunderous gaze and I freeze, because it's so intense, and it makes me feel so strangely alive. Then somebody asks a question and he looks away to answer it.

I swallow the last of it and wipe my hands, turning my attention to the PowerPoint, but it's not long before my attention is back on the pastry tray.

I torture myself wondering if they throw them all away once the session is over. I toy with saying something about feeding them to the birds, but I can only imagine Malcolm's dim view of that.

Malcolm is his usual engaging and personable self, interested in everything, enchanting people into divulging their secrets. I really do think he likes to learn about the people around him. God, if AJ told him who I really am, he'd be so pissed off.

I need to figure something out about AJ.

Does somebody need a visit from the fist of Malcolm Blackberg?

For a short, wickedly indulgent moment, I imagine Malcolm turning his dark power to AJ. Malcolm would be angry to hear that I'm masquerading as his executive coach, but something tells me that he'd be angrier if he knew that AJ was blackmailing me.

In fact, Malcolm would hunt him down if he knew. Yeah, Malcolm and his fist would so hunt him down. Shivers go over me.

Malcolm is all about tormenting me, but he would definitely draw the line at allowing AJ to torment me. This is the pathetic direction of my thoughts as I stare at the plate of pastries.

God, what is happening to me? I get control of myself, turn my full attention back to Gerrold and his son, and I keep it there for the rest of this session.

Malcolm asks about our coaching session plans on the way

back. I decide to make him do another session in writing, in order to have time to collect my thoughts.

He seems disappointed. "Did you read my answers on yesterday's quiz? I thought they were very comprehensive."

"Not yet," I mumble, and I escape to my room.

Am I being a coward? All I want to do is turn off my phone and hide—hide from AJ, hide from my inappropriate feelings for Malcolm, even hide from my girlfriends.

After all, I'm supposed to be saving our building. And what am I doing? Falling for Malcolm and doing sexy things with him. And now I'm hiding in my room. How many more chances will I have to show him the video?

But it feels more and more wrong to be posing as his coach. It was easy not to care about him when he was a bad guy with a plan to tear down our building. But up close and personal, there's something tragic about his ferocity, like he's lashing out at the world, fumbling toward some kind of solace that he never quite finds. And he's funny—honestly, he might be the cleverest man I've ever met.

And yes, he's fierce and even a bit frightening when you don't know him, but there's this hidden sweetness to him.

And I think he really does care about people...in his own compartmentalized way. He wouldn't see people the way he does if he didn't care. Why, then, is he so fiercely solitary? Surrounding himself with temporary people, in and out of his life like leaves in the breeze?

Humans are social animals who need each other; it's how our hearts are built. Malcolm is no different.

I flop down on my bed and stare at the ceiling.

I came to force him to see our humanity, instead I'm seeing *his*.

What am I going to do?

I'm not without an exit strategy—I could give Malcolm all of the check marks, declare him to have passed the course, and inform Bexley that I'm going to Estonia. And slip silently back into my real life.

It would be a completely effective transition—unless people started comparing photographs, and why would they?

I'd go home and start packing.

But then I imagine myself standing out there on the sidewalk across the street from our building while the wrecking ball flies. I picture us all crying, stuffing our faces with sad cookies that Lizzie made. And deep in the pit of my stomach, I'd know that I didn't do everything I could have.

Nothing's impossible—I don't care what Malcolm says.

There's a knock on the door. "Room service."

I didn't order room service. Do they have the wrong room? I open up and there's a uniformed woman with a cart.

"You must have the wrong room," I say. "I didn't order anything."

"I know this is the right room." The woman points to a small envelope on the cart. The envelope reads Elle, room 709. "Are you Elle?"

"I am," I say. "But..."

"Then this is for you." She pushes the cart into the room.

There are two of those silver-domed plates and a bottle of sparkling water next to a glass of ice. There's also a large gift box the size of two or three stacked pizza delivery boxes, and it's wrapped in silver paper printed with pink hedgehogs.

"Thank you," I say. "Wait, let me a..." I turn to scan for my purse.

"Tip's taken care of." With that, she leaves.

I pull the top off of one of the silver domes. It's a plate with three almond croissants and two bowls of crackers. Under the other dome are mounds of blackberries and raspberries and an assortment of cheeses.

Malcolm.

I take a croissant and bite in. It's just so incredibly thoughtful, I want to die. But first things first. I finish the croissant and move on to the cheese and crackers, telling myself I need to build up strength to open the present, because it might be amazing, which will complicate things more than they already are.

It's not until I've made my way through two croissants, the entire wedge of Brie, and most of the crackers, that I bring the gift to the bed and sit down next to it, running my fingers over the bright paper. Hedgehogs. An accident? Or did he notice that, too? I slip off the bow and carefully untape the edges, pulling the paper off and folding it neatly. I remove the lid, part the tissue paper, and gasp.

It's a vintage postal bag—a midcentury one, my favorite era for postal bags—and it has little hedgehogs embroidered along the edges of the flap. I run my fingers over the stitchery, pulse racing. I open the flap and explore the interior. How did he ever find such a thing? It's a bit beaten up—enough to show that a real letter carrier once used it, which makes me love it more. And the stitched hedgehogs. A sob of gratitude clogs my throat; for a moment, I almost can't breathe. I've never had somebody give me such a gift.

I stand and swing it over my shoulder and take a look at myself in the mirror. It's the most fabulous thing I own.

Not that I can keep it.

I can't keep it.

I hold it a moment longer, then I take it off and nestle it back into the box and replace the lid.

"I can't take this," I say when I get Malcolm on the phone. "It's sweet—thank you—but I can't. You have to have room service come back and get it. I can't accept gifts." I'm hoping maybe this sounds like an official Bexley Partners policy. I'm sure they have such a policy.

"It's for you. So you have to keep it," he says.

I argue with him a bit. There's another knock on the door. Is room service back? I open it.

It's him, looking beautiful as usual, elegant jacket unbuttoned, shirt crisp and white over his T-shirt. Is this what he lounges around in his hotel room wearing? Rummaging around in the mini-bar, spinning through the cable channels, always looking like a GQ model?

He strolls into the room, phone in hand.

He sits down in my chair and crosses his legs, giving me that piercing brown-eyed gaze. "The bag is custom-embroidered, so I won't be returning it. You're going to have to keep it. Or throw it away. Or donate it to a homeless shelter. That would be nice, wouldn't it?" he adds with a devilish gleam.

"Maybe I will," I say.

"Come on, at least give it a spin before you donate it."

"I have given it a spin."

"Have you, though?" He takes it from the box and comes to me. I can feel his body even before he touches me. We're alone, and I can feel everything about him. He holds the bag up by the strap, as if to measure it against me, then adjusts the strap and hands it back to me.

I clutch it, pinned by his gaze, breath speeding.

"You have to take it back," I whisper, even as I clutch it.

Again he takes it from me, and this time he puts it over my head, drapes it over my shoulder, cross-wise. "Is that the way a letter carrier would wear it?"

I switch sides so that it hangs over my left hip and turn to the mirror. "Like this when you're right-handed." I pantomime extracting a letter.

In the mirror I watch him come to me. My skin is all hungry fire, craving for him to touch me. And then he settles his heavy hands over my shoulders, holding my shoulders as if to fix me in place. Our eyes meet in the mirror in front of us.

I'm struck by how much larger he is than me, easily a head larger, and so much more dramatic. I'm pale pastels and he's a photograph with the black-and-white contrast pumped up, hair sooty, whiskers thick as night. My pulse whirs as he lowers his chin to my shoulder, sets it there, still holding me, two faces side by side.

The feel of being held in place by him is confusingly thrilling. I'm a fragile bird in a giant's grip, and I just want to stay—I want to forget my troubles and be held.

"What are you doing?" I hear myself ask.

"This." Rough whiskers nuzzle against my ear, sending a delicious shudder through me. He kisses my cheek, a brush of a kiss, light as feathers.

I'm breathing hard, possibly even panting. It's possible that I might melt from the pleasure of just that kiss. "It's improper to accept a gift like this."

"So improper." He kisses my neck, sending another shudder of pleasure through me. "Am I going to have to complain to your home office?" he rumbles.

Alarm shoots through me. "No," I say, maybe too quickly.

He kisses me again.

"You just can't be giving me gifts," I say.

"Or what?" Another kiss. "Or what will my little country mouse do?" His question is a warm fingertip tracing tender skin.

"You just can't, is all. It's inappropriate."

He slides my collar aside, baring a new patch of skin. He presses a warm kiss there. "Inappropriate like this?" he asks.

"Like that," I mouth, barely a whisper. "Yes."

He slides more of my shirt aside, claiming a bit more of my shoulder with his lips. Warmth flows over me every time he presses his lips to my skin. I feel wild and unhinged. I have this vision of pulling him to the bed, which would be so unlike me. But I want the bag. I want another croissant. I want him.

Completely and utterly want him.

I want to have sex with the man who is going to destroy our homes.

What is happening to me?

He kisses another part of my shoulder. "Like this?" he asks, voice thick.

"We shouldn't," I gasp.

"Probably not," he says, planting another whiskery warm kiss. "Like this?"

"Like that," I gasp. Men never make me lose my good sense. I'm the most practical woman in the world. But now I feel wild, and 341 West 45th Street feels worlds away.

"What happens if you take more than your share?" Warm, rough lips brush a kiss over my neck. "What if you take too many croissants? Too many bags? Too much pleasure?" He slides his hands down over my hips. "Does the world end? Does it all come crashing down?"

I swallow. "I think you're trying to tempt me," I say.

His laugh is a baritone rumble against my neck. "What would make you say that?"

I fix him with my sly gaze—it's the gaze I imagine an elegant, confident woman would have. An arch gaze. Very un-countrymouse. Very unlike me.

He stills, eyes riveted to mine in the mirror.

"What?" I ask, because he's looking at me strangely.

"I like that," he says. "When you look a little bit witchy like that."

"Witchy?" I say. "Watch out or I'll give you an X instead of a check mark," I warn playfully. It's like a whole new side of me comes out when he's around.

He's still fixated on my gaze. Which I intensify. His lips curl in a shadow of a smile. "You wouldn't," he says.

My pulse races. This shouldn't be fun. "I already decided," I tease. "You'll be getting an X for inappropriate behavior."

Still standing behind me, he takes the bag off my shoulder and sets it on the dresser. I'm shivering with excitement. He slides his arms around to my front and begins to unbutton my shirt.

"Don't think you can change your grade, either," I whisper.

He undoes another button as I watch in the mirror. "I do think I'll change my grade. That's my whole plan."

"I'm not susceptible to bribery, as you've already discovered," I tease, surprised I can form sentences at this point.

He turns me in his arms to face him now and pushes down my yoga pants. I press my hands to his chest, thanking my lucky stars that I happen to have good underpants on, because I have some bad underpants in my suitcase for sure.

Heat blooms through me as he kneels and pushes them down lower, past my knees. I should stop him. I should.

Will I?

No. Freaking. Way.

"I'm not going to bribe you. I know you don't like to take things." He presses a kiss to my belly. I watch him—watch us—as if from a mile above. "I know you don't like to take too much. I see you, country mouse." He kisses my right thigh and then my left thigh. He's sliding down my panties, hands skimming the sides of my legs, past my knees, my calves. "No bribery. I'm thinking more of extortion." He presses a kiss onto my mound.

I shove my hands into his hair, dizzy with desire. "Extortion?" I mumble. He could say devil worship at this point, and I'd probably go along with it.

He kisses me again, and I gasp from the sheer pleasure of it. Just a kiss and I'm all electric nerve endings. Before I know it, he's hoisted me so that I'm sitting on the dresser, and he's got me pretty much naked aside from my bra and open-hanging shirt, while he is still dressed. Just how he runs his negotiations. Stripping the person bare.

Moi? So good with that.

He kneels in front of me, with perfect access to my sex. Warm, dull waves of pleasure wash through my body as he kisses me between my legs, even kind of makes out with me there.

And then he sticks his tongue inside of me. I gasp.

Hard fingers dig into my thighs, pressing my legs apart, and he kisses me again, and again I gasp. And then he licks me. And I gasp. I'm a regular Pez dispenser of gasps.

"Omigod," I say, trembling, shoving my fingers deeply into his hair. He's licking me shamelessly now. It's nearly surreal that this is Malcolm Blackberg—supposedly dark, evil, misanthropic Malcolm Blackberg, licking my pussy.

So. Amazingly.

His tongue is hitting all the perfect bits of me, rearranging my mind.

Every stroke seems to ping my very soul—*ping!* So amazing. *Ping!* Malcolm fucking Blackberg. *Ping!*

I'm lost in pure pleasure for a good long time, but then I come to my senses and realize that he's being left out. It feels constitutionally against everything in me to take this kind of pleasure without giving anything in return.

I grab his hair and pull him up toward me. "Come here," I say. "Come up here."

"No," he says into my pussy, and then he finds an even better angle, and I nearly swallow my own tongue.

I grab his hair harder. "Do you have a condom?" I ask.

"Yes."

"Don't you want to..." I nudge him upwards. My one long-term boyfriend only did this to prime the pump, so to speak. He never just kept on and on. It seems like a wild luxury, totally one-sided.

Malcolm just growls into my pussy, which feels so good, I might just lose my mind.

"If you keep going, I might not let you stop," I say.

"Are you ready to quiet down and enjoy this?"

"You are so getting an X," I say. "Not playing by the rules."

He stops what he's doing and it's a little bit excruciating that he stops. I want to cry, but at the same time, I did tell him to.

He picks me up.

"What are you doing?" I demand.

He carries me across the room. A strange sound comes out of me, something between a scream and a laugh.

He tosses me on the bed like I'm a rag doll—five stars for that being totally sexier than it sounds—and then crawls over me, pausing midway. Strong hands grip my thighs and press them apart.

Suddenly, I'm lost in the crazy pleasure of his tongue.

I'm dying, reeling, shoving my hands into his hair like an octo-banshee.

He holds my thighs with an iron grip that feels a little dirty, like he won't let me go now. He would if I asked, I'm sure, but the sensation is that I'm this caught animal, punished with pleasure by the beastly tongue of Malcolm Blackberg—that's the madness that is taking over my mind.

If he keeps going, I won't have my senses anymore.

I should stop him—it's too good, and if he keeps going, it'll be too late to stop him.

"Maybe we should transition..." To regular sex, I mean.

He growls and holds me more tightly, and it just makes everything dirtier and better.

And suddenly something flips because the way he's licking

me now, I can't let him stop. I would have to kill him if he stops. It's too good. And I'm just on the verge of coming.

I'm gasping, right on the knife edge.

Then he slides a finger inside me. I'm reeling.

"Don't stop," I gasp. He is so incredibly wicked, the way he holds me with one massive hand and invades me mercilessly with his finger while stroking me with his muscular tongue that feels like it has some kind of space-aged guidance system that tells it just where and how hard to go, a system that is so advanced it must never fall into enemy hands because it could be used to take over the universe.

But right now, his advanced-guidance tongue is taunting and plying my pussy with pleasure, pushing the good feeling higher and higher, like pushing the most delicious boulder of pleasure up the side of pleasure mountain, higher and higher, and any moment it's going to come crashing down with total glee.

At this point I'm basically writhing under his diabolical ministrations. He squeezes my thigh, he licks me once more.

Then stops.

"What are you doing?" I protest. "You can't stop!"

He presses a kiss to my belly. "Do I get a tick?"

"No fair!" I grab his hair and twist and try to make him return to business, but he won't go.

"Oh my god!" I'm panting.

"Do I get my tick for today?"

"I can't give *ticks* for sexual favors," I gasp. "That would be so..."

"Inappropriate?" He kisses my mound; his lips frustratingly near my pussy. "So inappropriate." His words are warm heat, so close and yet so far.

I cry out in frustration, but he won't relent.

"Fine. You get a tick."

"If I lick your pussy some more I get a tick?"

"Yes," I say. "Yes!"

And then he's back. Finishing what he started, only it's better now—because of how intolerable it was that he stopped, and all my nerve endings were straining for his tongue to go back, the proof that absence definitely makes the pussy grow fonder.

He gives me a few more expertly placed, scarily-advanced-intelligence licks, and that's it—orgasm comes over me like a zillion spinning stars.

I'm gasping and panting.

He keeps me flying, lick action grinding to a halt as I freak underneath him on the bed. He kisses his way up my totally pleasurized and still-shuddering body.

"That was so not fair," I say, unbuttoning his shirt with trembling fingers.

"I know," he says. He yanks down my bra and kisses my breasts. I half sit up and pull it off for him myself, tossing it aside. I'm down this road so far, nothing really matters.

"My little country mouse," he says into my nipple. "You have no idea how sexy you are when you're making demands. You just have no idea."

I'm feverishly undoing his belt—in for a penny, in for a pound, or more specifically, in for Malcolm's underwear, in for my hand around his cock. I groan, because he's warm and heavy in my hand and utterly perfect in every way. "Your penis is very you," I say.

"I'm glad. I'd hate it to be not mine. Any other cock would not fuck you properly."

"Need you in me now," I say.

"Say it again, this time with that witchy look," he says.

God, this man. He makes me feel new. I give him the look

that I think he means. I'm about to repeat what I said, but I decide to surprise him. "Fuck me now, Malcolm."

He growls. A condom wrapper crinkles.

I fumble with his buttons.

"Country mouse, so careful and gentle," he says in his sexy accent.

It feels like a challenge or an insult, maybe both, and there's only one way to answer—I rip open his shirt.

"Fuck," he says.

"Uh, sorry..." I mean it, actually.

He laughs, and then I do, too. How do I feel so comfortable with him? I press my hands to his chest as he enters me, thick and huge.

"Fuck," I gasp.

"Too fast?"

"No, I meant, *fuck yes.*" That is totally what the witchy-look girl would say. I grab ripped shirt fabric, pulling him to me. He pushes into me again and again as I consume his skin with hungry palms.

And at some point I'm on top of him, moving on him. He grasps my nipples, scissors-style, between his fingers. He just holds them gently but firmly, but it creates this wicked tug as I move over him, a tug that I'm free to exploit, and I go for it, just taking the nipple action as I take my pleasure from his body.

It's midnight and there's no yesterday and no tomorrow and I've gotten lost with the villain in my story.

I've eaten the croissants and all the cheese and crackers and at this point I'm moving on to the chocolate cake. I'm plowing through the cake, plowing through the ice cream, and maybe even some bruschetta. I'm consuming everything delicious about him. It's ludicrous that I'm going to come again, but I know that I will. I'm feasting on the whole world.

We come very nearly together, or more, I come, and then he

starts when I'm coming down—enough that I feel the exciting vibration of his orgasm inside me.

Afterwards, we collapse on the bed. And I look over at him. And I run one finger down his cheek.

And for a second we feel like partners, balanced evenly on a fulcrum, perfectly in sync in this one true moment.

22

Malcolm

NOT WANTING or needing things is a bit of a superpower when you're a child, and even more so when you're an adult—especially when you combine it with being a known bad guy.

But lying here with Elle, feeling this strange sense of peace with her, I have this troubling sense that I care very much about her.

An outlandish amount, actually.

She's different from everybody else—better, somehow, or maybe just more interesting and exciting. Certainly hotter—no other woman is even in the same ballpark of hotness. And then there's the easy way we fit. How is it that things can be so easy?

And there's the way she looks at me. Like I'm somebody good.

I'm a bit conflicted about it. She's dead wrong, yet at the same time, I'm soaking it in. I'm a pirate, hoarding the glittering jewels of her regard, burying them deep.

And it's not enough. It may never be.

I can't allow myself to be cut off from her—that's what I'm thinking right now.

I love how I feel around her, I love the way she looks at me, I love the secrets in her eyes, and the hidden bravery in her heart. I love the way her nose curves and the freckle next to her mouth. I love the way she juts out her chin when she's trying to be bold. I love the way her pale brown hair glitters gold in the sunlight. I love that she can't be bought. As if she's priceless.

She's a bright thing that I didn't know I craved, the essential cherry on top of my hierarchy of needs.

She's also temporary. We're well over halfway through her program. What happens when it's over?

What happens when she goes back to Trenton. Or worse, takes on another client? Somebody else to create a ridiculous program for. Somebody else to believe in.

But for now, she's here.

I plaster on a cool smile and turn to her, expecting to see her all sated and happy, being that we just had the best sex ever.

But she looks horrified.

Something unpleasant grips my chest.

"Oh my god." She sits up and smooths her hair. "This can never happen again."

"But it was so good," I say, with a lightness I don't feel. "What's the problem?"

"The problem is that last I checked, I had a moral code that didn't involve giving check marks in exchange for sexual favors!"

"Moral codes are so boring," I say.

"Don't do that," she says. "Please, just don't."

"Don't what?"

"You know, your whole...enchanting darkly alluring thing."

"You don't like my enchanting darkly alluring thing?" I say.

"Don't be funny, either. Don't you see a problem here?

Making you do sexual favors in exchange for check marks instead of making you watch the video?"

"Personally, it was one of my favorite sessions so far."

"Not funny," she whispers. She looks like she's going to cry. This really is serious.

"It wasn't literally sex in exchange for anything. We were just joking—"

She shakes her head, having none of it. Her eyes begin to fill with tears. My heart hitches.

During negotiations, I always know what to say to pull a person toward a given goal, a given destination.

What do I say when a person herself is the goal? When she is the destination? Her feelings, her well-being.

I should reassure her and comfort her, but I'm not sure how. Comforting and caring about a person might be one of those use-it-or-lose-it muscles. Howie would know.

"I know this program isn't important to you, but it's important to *me*," she says.

"Elle." I sit up, brush a bit of hair from her forehead. "It doesn't matter what you do. Your empathy program was doomed from the start. You have to know that."

She starts to cry.

My gut clenches. Why is she crying? I don't want her to cry. Crying rarely moves me, but Elle doing it feels like a knife. I try to think how I can get her to stop. I settle a hand onto her shoulder. "Hey," I say. "It's just a job."

"It's not just a job," she sobs. "Haven't you been paying attention? It's more than just a job. It's a whole..." She waves her hand, as if it defies description. "The whole building and the people and everything."

"Buildings come down," I try, "and they go up."

She presses her hands to her face. "I just always let everyone down."

"How can you say that?" I ask. "You're one of the most diligent, hard-working coaches anybody could ever imagine. You passed up a million dollars."

"You don't understand," she sniffles.

"Make me understand," I say. "I can't imagine you letting down anybody. If anything, you're too conscientious. If I ever needed anybody fighting for me, I'd want it to be you," I add. It's the truth, and surprises me. "It would be you," I say.

"You wouldn't say that if you really knew anything," she says. "I have let people down. You have no idea."

"I can't imagine it," I say.

She shakes her head. Somehow I just know she needs to tell me.

Usually I goad people into telling me things because the knowledge gives me power. This is different. I want to be with her in it.

"Tell me, I won't judge," I say. "You couldn't have done anything worse than what I do on a daily basis. And you know what they say about confessing things to terrible people, people far worse than you? It cleanses the soul way better than confessing to priests. Terrible people won't judge you for your transgressions. Terrible people get it."

"For one thing you're not terrible. Also, you don't know anything about me," she sniffles. "I'm not what you think."

"You're saying that you've done worse things than I have? That's what you're saying? Because I'm going to go with a 'highly unlikely' rating on that."

She snorts through her tears. She seems about to speak, but then she stops. Then, "For starters, did you let somebody die?"

"No," I say softly.

"My mother died of cancer," she continues. "You probably know that already."

"Yeah," I say.

"What it doesn't say is that I let her die."

"When it comes to cancer, we usually don't have a choice," I say.

"You don't understand. I was all she had. And it was a weird kind of cancer where I had to fight with the insurance company on getting it classified the way it should've. I was on the internet all the time, and I never knew what was reasonable to ask for from them, or what was extreme. It's complicated, but they pushed back on everything all the time. And she'd get better, and then worse."

"And it was just you," I prompt.

"Yeah. Non-entity dad. My mom loved being on her own. She was a banjo player. The bossiest woman ever, and she did a great job of raising me. So fiercely independent. Anyway, I read about this treatment that was accepting people for trials, it was for her exact kind of cancer. It would've cost something to get her there, to get her in, but I felt like it would help, and they refused, and they kept refusing. They said she was too far gone." She wipes her eyes. "But I felt sure they were on the fence. I felt sure they were thinking about saying yes. I had this relationship with one of the people at the headquarters. I mean, I'd been calling for two years for things when she got bad, and I woke up one day and I felt sure that if I took my savings and cashed in part of my 401K, I could fly down to Texas, and maybe fly both of us down if she was having a good week, and they wouldn't be able to say no—not to her face, and not to my face. I felt sure that if they saw her humanity, they would have to say yes."

"You have a pretty high opinion of people," I say. "I don't think insurance companies operate like that."

"No, I don't think my opinion of people is too high," she says after a bit.

"Okay," I say dubiously.

She gives me a warning look and I raise my eyebrows. Go on, my raised eyebrows say.

"But then...I just didn't. I let the window close. I did nothing and then it was too late."

"They wouldn't have changed their mind."

"You don't know that. If I'd gone the extra mile—going the extra mile makes a difference to people. But part of me wanted her to die. I can't believe I'm telling you this. But she was so sick."

"She was suffering," I say.

"I could've kept going. Going the extra mile."

"It's normal to want people to stop suffering."

"But *she* didn't want to die," she says.

"Do you know how common that is, what you're telling me?" I say. "Aside from the crazy idea of the heroic jaunt to Texas where you would've used the last of your meager savings for nothing?"

"Part of me wanted her to die. Just to have it over with for myself. It was the easy way out."

"Look, you get to hold conflicting feelings," I say. "You get to want to save her and want it to be over with. You get to want her to live and want her to stop suffering, even when she wants to keep on suffering. You get to be messy."

"The treatment saved other people at her stage," she says. "I could've gone the extra mile. I can be persuasive."

"You think you should've gone the extra mile."

"Yes," she says.

I wrap my arms around her, wanting to save her from her guilt, wishing I could. "I've never met somebody so damn conscientious," I say into her hair.

She sniffs softly. "You won't change my mind."

I bury my nose in her hair. I know a black swan when I see one, and this is hers, paddling lazily up the stream. The reason she rejected a million dollars. "Are you going the extra mile to save that building?" I ask.

She pulls back with a wary look.

"Do you think, if you save the building, that will make up for it?"

"Nothing can make up for it," she says.

"But maybe a little bit?" I try. "Saving the building from destruction won't change what happened with your mom, but maybe a little bit?"

"I've learned from it, that's all," she says. "I've learned to go the extra mile. I've learned that it's important to do your best. You of all people should understand. You don't need money. You don't need to work ever again, yet you go around making your deals and turning companies inside out. Why?"

It's not lost on me that she's turning the spotlight back onto me. I allow it. "When I see something that needs to be done, I can't unsee it. I need to act. It's almost painful if I don't. Like an uncompleted melody and you're waiting for that last note, for that resolution. These companies, these buildings, they're like square pegs next to square holes, and nobody doing anything about it. It drives me crazy seeing what could be, what *should* be. It's a type of tension, I suppose."

"Right?" she says. "And when you put things right, the world feels right."

"For a little while," I say.

"It's like with me and the mail..." She turns on her side, props up her head on her hand, and I can see that she's preparing to make yet another confession. And I'm excited to hear it, like a schoolgirl at a sleepover or something.

"Putting the world right, that's how I always felt about the mail," she says. "At the beginning of the day, the mail bag is full of square pegs, each with one specific place to go. Delivering it feels like putting the world right. Getting things where they need to be. It feels amazing."

I love that she's as passionate about putting the mail right as I am about putting the world of commerce right. And now she's a coach, trying to get the big, bad wolves to see the humanity of Little Red Riding Hoods.

"You know if you save the building, there'll just be something else or someone else you need to save. It won't go away until you forgive yourself."

She narrows her eyes and touches the tip of her finger to my nose. "Whatever you say, Chuckles."

I laugh and dare her to repeat it, and she does, and I wrestle her to her back and kiss her.

She looks frail, but she's a fighter. She fights for the mail and she fights for people. And it makes me want to do things for her. Something more than carts of food and carnal pleasures.

In my mind, I run through the things that she's passionate about. Hedgehogs. Is there some kind of a hedgehog zoo in this part of California? They have everything else. She's passionate about her work, of course.

It comes to me, then, that one of my West Coast development partners has a husband who is one of the top executive coaches in the nation. He's a pompous ass, but he's famous among executive coaches. Elle is so invested in her job, she's probably read all of his books. She'd be over the moon to be able to sit down with him.

And his wife owes me. I've made her a lot of money.

A plan forms around having drinks with them. Maybe drinks before a dinner session, because I don't want to share her for an entire night.

I'm thinking somewhere nice—with the best food. And she'll want to be wearing something nice to meet such an esteemed colleague. And I know just the thing.

23

Noelle

DON'T LET him get into your head, that's what the traveling team said, but they don't realize how good it feels to tell him things, how good it feels to imagine he's even just a little bit with you. What would it be like to really partner on something?

I can't believe I confessed about my mother to him; it's something I never told anybody—not even Francine.

But I wanted to tell Malcolm. It felt natural.

I'm hiding so much about my identity, but at the same time, I feel like he knows my heart better than people who've known me for years. I cup his cheek. "Confessing to an evil person. You are so full of shit."

"Didn't it help just a little bit?" he asks.

"You are so full of shit that you're evil," I say.

He rolls his eyes. He doesn't like when you say he's not evil. What does it mean? Is this idea of his that he's evil like a suit of armor? A way he protects himself?

"I like my idea for a new kind of confessional."

"I'm sure it's already on the internet," I say. "I wouldn't want to see it. I wouldn't want to read about the horrible things that strangers have done."

"Me either," he says. "It sounds absolutely tedious." My breath catches as he wraps his arms around me, as he sets his chin onto the top of my head. "Why hedgehogs?" he asks. "Why do you like hedgehogs?"

"Hmmm," I say. Nobody ever asked that. "They're always out there in the dark, quietly industrious. I like their little cone faces. I like that they seem optimistic."

"What are they optimistic about?"

I slide down next to him. "I don't know. Just...life."

His phone alarm sounds. He has a dinner meeting to prepare for. He asks me what I'm going to do, and I mumble something about maybe having dinner, too. My dinner will be the rest of the room service cart.

The next morning, I send AJ his gift card, feeling just awful about it. "He probably won't kill the golden goose," Stella had said.

Probably won't.

I meet the traveling team down in the lobby at the usual place, waiting for our rides to the Kendrick building. I'm bracing myself for when Malcolm appears. I don't want them to notice any kind of energy between us. I resolve not to even look at him.

Malcolm arrives after a bit, and he's perfectly discreet, which is to say, his usual surly self. You'd never know we had mind-blowing sex and shared secrets last night. Or at least, I shared secrets with him.

He's still a mystery. An exciting and forbidden mystery that I should probably steer clear of.

The session is friendly and productive; Malcolm and

Gerrold seem to be inching closer to a deal—that's clear to me during the moments when I'm not debating on the second croissant.

I'm happy for Malcolm, being that this is what he wanted so badly, but I worry about all of the people with their jobs. Is it truly inevitable that they're just out of work no matter what?

He had a certain point about New York being full of rickety fire traps if nobody had ever knocked the building down.

Still.

I catch him looking at me while Gerrold is huddling with his son on something. He glances down at the tray of pastries and back at me, raising his eyebrows.

Discreetly I shake my head, suppressing a smile. I already had one.

He gives me a dark look that thrills me to my toes. He knows I want another one.

I gaze up at the ceiling, but I can feel his eyes on me, and when I look back, he's still watching me. Having his focus on me, it's so strangely gratifying. And fun. I widen my eyes because, he's totally going to get us busted. He narrows his, waiting, waiting. He nods at the croissants.

I stand and grab the tongs—just to shut him down. I put one on my plate, and then, just to mess with him, I put another there. Then I give him the look that he seems to like–the witchy look.

His nostrils expand ever so slightly, as if in a secret inhale. I'm thinking about last night, and so is he. I look around to see if anybody noticed. Coralee did—she's smiling at me, like she thinks it's funny. "I don't know where you put it all," she says.

"I'm hoping it'll go to my hair," I joke.

She grins and goes back to her phone, and nobody else really seems to notice.

After the meeting, I find myself alone with Malcolm outside at the limo pick-up point while the rest of the team uses the restrooms. The air whips in from the bay, salty and fresh, and a streetcar clanks down from the next street over, and I do mean down. The streets here are crazy steep.

"Progress," I say under my breath.

Malcolm's eyes sparkle. "Yes," he says. Just one word, and I wonder briefly whether he's talking about the croissants.

"So, we have a four o'clock session set up," I say. "It's going to be a video session."

Malcolm groans. "I still have to watch the videos? I thought we were past that."

"That is the program," I remind him.

"I thought we'd established a new and better program," he says.

"Nice try."

"Have you even read my essay answers from the other day's session? I don't think you have."

"I shall be reading them forthwith," I say, in my own rendition of his accent, "and I'm quite sure they'll earn you your tick."

He gives me a dark look that I love. "Well, the program is going to have to take place at the Monaco Club."

"What?" I turn to him. "It's an hour of video. And you really have to watch it this time. No multitasking."

"So diligent," he says. "Don't worry, I'll watch it. We'll watch it over dinner."

"Seriously, no more check marks without watching the video."

"Are you sure about that?" he asks smoothly.

"Stop!" I snort. "I mean it. And isn't the Monaco Club really fancy? What will they say about us watching a video at the table?"

"We'll use earbuds," he says.

"But, taking up a table."

"With the money I drop there, we could have a three-day orgy on the tabletop."

"That is definitely not in my coaching program," I say, but the dinner works. I was worrying what I'd eat—I'm probably the only guest in the Maybourne Hotel who's going hungry.

"What do you say? Leave at four thirty? I'm thinking cock-tails first. I have a surprise for you."

"You can't be drunk for the video."

"I don't get drunk," Malcolm says, and of course that makes sense. He's such a control freak.

THAT AFTERNOON, I finally get around to reading Malcolm's answers to the essay questions I assigned the other day. I smile at his praise of Antonio's acting skills. He has kind words for Mia, and it comes to me that they are similar sorts of people, both really blunt and opinionated. But most interesting of all: he has a theory on the dryer-lint bandit. How does he have a theory? I don't even have a theory! The dryer-lint bandit never was caught. I think back through all the videos. Could there be clues? Right in the video?

The box arrives at three, brought up by another room service person who refuses a tip. The name looks familiar. I open it up, and there's one of the dresses I tried on the first night I was here—my favorite of the dresses. I hold it up in awe.

What kind of sorcery did he do to figure out about this dress? The price tag isn't on, but I know it cost an arm and a leg. I can't take it, but I have a feeling that rejecting one of Malcolm's presents is about as easy as defying the laws of gravity, or making time move backwards, or not petting Smuckers when he trots up wearing his little bow tie.

And I love it. There's something else in the box—a book on executive coaching. I frown. Does he think I need a book on executive coaching? Has he figured out I don't know what I'm doing? The cover is a full-length photo of a confident-looking fifty-something man with his hand draped over a podium. The title is "The Executive Power-Confidant." I flip through it, and a card drops out.

We'll be having pre-dinner cocktails with a mystery guest and his wife. Consider this your clue.

I have a bad feeling that this mystery guest is Soren Sheffield. The bio inside the back flap calls him "the world's foremost authority on the art of executive coaching."

He lives in the Bay Area with his wife.

Gulp.

Drinks with this Soren Sheffield?

It's one thing to fool Malcolm, who hates executive coaches, but how will I fool the world's foremost authority on the art of executive coaching?

I grab the phone and try Stella again. No answer. Furiously, I page through the book, familiarize myself with terms.

The phone rings right before I have to start getting ready. "Noelle!" she says, above the murmur of voices in the background. "I teach in five. How are things going with AJ?"

I tell her I've been sending him gift cards. "I hate doing it," I say.

"God, I'm so sorry. He really is such an unbelievable asshole. The product of some really bad judgement on my part. Though, he's hot. I know that's not an excuse."

"It happens," I say. "But I have bigger problems than AJ." I sink onto the bed and pick up the book. "Do you know who Soren Sheffield is?"

"Oh, right, the executive-confidant guy? What about him?"

"Does he know people at the Bexley Group?"

"Hardly," she says. "He's like, famous. A big cheese."

"So, he definitely does *not* know you, right?"

"Not in a million years," she says.

"That's good," I say. "Because I'm going to cocktails with him and his wife and Malcolm tonight."

"Wait, what?" she says. "Soren Sheffield? Like, in person?"

I'm running out of time, so I put her on speaker and shimmy into my dress. "I guess he thought it would be a treat for me to meet him," I say.

"Malcolm is taking you out to cocktails with Sheffield and his wife? Like just you four? What is going on out there? Do you know how many real coaches would jump at that chance? My boss Nadine would die."

"What should I talk about with him?"

"Nothing! Oh my god. Dude, you cannot go," she says. "Might I remind you that you are a postal carrier."

"I have to go," I say. "I said I was going. I can't back out now."

"Then you tell them you have diarrhea," Stella says.

"Diarrhea?"

"It's the best excuse because it's embarrassing. Nobody would say it if it wasn't true," she says.

It's funny that Stella would have this right at her fingertips. I can easily imagine her having an entire hierarchy of excuses. She really isn't the most conscientious person ever. She quit with no notice, after all, just took off to Estonia without saying anything to her job. Who does that? It worked out for me, but it really isn't the most responsible move. And then there's the whole AJ thing. I definitely can't imagine her coaching an executive.

"I can't back out," I say. "Can you give me some hints on shop talk?"

"Yeah, one really good one—easy to remember. Don't do it."

"Just a few lines?" I brush out my hair. My blowout from the morning has gone limp. I grab a curling iron and go to work while Stella freaks out on the other end.

"Listen to me closely, my friend: Do. Not. Talk. Shop. Coaching has its own specific rules and language, and lots of things you would never ever say. The second you open your mouth, you will totally give yourself away. Treat it like, if you're pretending to be a nuclear physicist and trying to fool a nuclear physicist. Do not talk shop."

"What if he asks me a question about my approach?"

"He seems like kind of...full of himself on his Ted talks. So, maybe he won't." She groans. "He might, though. Okay, make sure he knows you do court-ordered emotional intelligence stuff, and he'll know you're a nobody. And if he asks you anything beyond that, just say that everything you do is based on the client. That's a thing in coaching. What is your technique? It's based on the client. What is your program? Based on the client. How do you wipe your ass? Based on the client. Somebody like Soren Sheffield isn't going to care what you do once he finds out you're just the cannon fodder they throw at court-ordered people."

"Good. Thanks," I say.

"Whatever you do, don't say you dress up as a letter carrier. And you can't let him know about those videos. Malcolm may be buying it, but Sheffield never will. You will be automatically busted." She then makes me note down a question to ask Soren that will get him talking. "As executive coaches, we work to provide a safe place where leaders can truly be their genuine selves. Can you say a little bit about how to create that space?"

I have just enough time to send a selfie to Francine of me in my dress before Malcolm knocks. I know it's his knock. I don't know how, it's just this two-way line that seems to connect us.

I swing open the door and there he is, looking gorgeous in a black silk dinner jacket. Except he has this troubled look on his face when he sees me. My heart is beating nearly out of my chest; has AJ got to him?

"What is it?" I ask.

"So serious," he breathes, eyes sparkling. "You just take me by surprise, that's all," he says, coming to me. "Elle." The way he says my name fills me with relief. "Elle." He makes me feel like I'm the most beautiful woman in the world, and I so wish right then that he knew my real name, that he'd look at me like that and call me Noelle. "Elle..." He pulls me to him. We kiss.

I slide my hand down his silky black lapel. "Hey you," I mumble against his lips.

"Ready?"

"Yes," I say back.

"Car's picking us up in back." He leads me down the hall and down the back stairway and to a door I hadn't seen, one that requires a key card. We enter a fancy, secret part of the hotel that has an even more fabulous elevator than the public part.

"Is this a secret celeb elevator?" I joke, but then he tells me that it is exactly that, a convenience for celebrities that allows them to exit discreetly through the parking garage.

On the way to the restaurant, he asks me how familiar I am with Sheffield's work and if I've read his books. I tell him that I'm most familiar with that last book, though I don't add that I just now speed-read the thing like my hair was on fire.

He's clearly excited to introduce me to Sheffield, and I so wish I could level with him—about everything. We've become close in so many ways, and we have a surprising amount of common ground—inside, where it counts—even if we couldn't be more different on the outside.

He'd probably think it was hilarious—given a different set of circumstances.

I stare out the window, feeling nervous. Who am I to pull this off?

I could still say I have diarrhea. I rehearse it in my mind. But suddenly, we've arrived.

The Monaco Club is an upscale hilltop bistro with floor-to-ceiling windows. The front is an elegant cocktail area with lots of candles and chandeliers and green velvet furniture, and the back is a spacious dining room.

I'd be thrilled to be here if I weren't completely freaking out.

Maybe I actually *will* get diarrhea.

We're led to a table next to the window—clearly the best table. Malcolm introduces me to Verlaina Henry. Verlaina wears an elegant turban, plum lipstick, and some very hip-looking bracelets.

"Verlaina and I go way back," Malcolm says.

"Way back," Verlaina says, clasping his hand. She introduces Soren, who has white-gray hair and a linebacker's face and body.

Malcolm gives Soren his hard-sparkle smile where his mouth forms into a gorgeous smile while his gaze sharpens on the person.

We all sit and order. There's a small green crystal bowl on the table that contains a kind of high-end Chex mix, and I really want to empty the whole thing into my mouth, but I content myself with two dainty handfuls of it. Of course, nothing escapes Malcolm's attention. He adds a double bruschetta plate for the table.

Our drinks come. I know it's inevitable that the conversation will soon turn to me, and by way of preparation, I gulp half a glass of bubbly.

But what really comforts me is being with Malcolm. I feel

aligned with him in a deep way, like we can get through anything together. Maybe we can.

Verlaina and Malcolm spend a bit of time catching up, which includes Verlaina informing Malcolm that she's heard the Germantown Group is absolutely not now and never will be for sale. Malcolm simply nods, and then he smiles at me, causing something in my belly to twist with joy.

"Malcolm tells me you're his executive coach," Soren says suddenly.

I smile. "Yes. And I just want you to know, it's such an honor to meet you," I say, adding something about his last book that kind of recaps what's on the back flap. It really did seem like it was probably a good book for the right person. I could see how executive coaching could come in handy for business leaders. Even the biggest business leader on the planet needs a confidant, a wise neutral party to bounce ideas off of. Though I am definitely not that person, and for the record, Stella would not be the person either.

"Malcolm Blackberg getting emotional intelligence coaching," Verlaina says, like it's the hugest joke ever.

"Yes, I'm under a court order for twenty-one hours of soft skills training." Malcolm turns to me. "Elle drew the short straw. But I get to determine where and when that coaching happens. So why not here?"

I shake my head scoldingly. I feel like we're this team, putting on a very specific show together.

"Ah. Court-ordered," Soren says, like that explains everything he needs to know about me. He's trying not to sound dismissive, but his attempt to specifically not sound dismissive makes him sound even more dismissive.

Verlaina grins. "I can only imagine how that's going. What did you do this time, Malcolm?"

"Had a bad employee," Malcolm says. "Threw him out on his ear."

Verlaina snorts and turns to me with a wince. "Teaching Malcolm Blackberg emotional intelligence? I don't envy you."

"Well, we're muddling through," I say.

"You're turning him into a kinder, more evolved version of himself?" she asks, and it's clearly another joke, like nobody could ever do that. I find it sad.

"He's doing very well, actually." I turn to Soren and pull out my question. "I don't want to bore these two with shop talk, but..." I rattle off the question that the real Stella made me memorize.

He gives a long answer.

Luckily, the bruschetta plates have come. There's basil and white cheese and little pea-looking things on them. I take one and force myself to eat it slowly while Soren talks in a slow and sonorous way, like he's making a speech. I make sure to nod and try to look delighted, even though I don't know what he's talking about. When he pauses, I repeat the last few words that he said in a really fascinated way—that's a Malcolm trick I picked up that makes him seem involved while adding absolutely nothing. It works brilliantly on Soren, who runs on and on. At one point I catch Malcolm's eye and he's giving me this friendly gleam, as if to say, I know what you just did. And my heart beats a little harder, because we're all about our secret relationship now.

Another round of drinks comes. Soren is on his third martini, but I'm pacing myself. I'm still really hungry, and I need the shop talk to be over. I gaze out the window. "You know, I've heard that in the Bay Area, you can't legally obstruct another person's view of the Golden Gate Bridge. Is that true, you guys?"

I'm grateful when Verlaina gets onto the subject of tree-trimming. Malcolm sets the last bruschetta on my plate and I just want to kiss him.

Unfortunately, Soren picks this moment to steer the conversation back to me. "What's next?" he asks. "Once you graduate from the court-ordered coaching clients."

My heart races. What would a real coach say? What other kinds of coaching are there? I have no idea. Would he accept "non-court-ordered" as an answer? Probably not. "Umm, I like where I am," I say.

Soren furrows his brow and frowns hugely, becoming the very picture of a man balking. If there was an Irish balking jig, he would get up and do it—that's how intensively he is balking right now. "Court-ordered soft skills coaching? Come on. Nobody voluntarily stays in court-ordered soft skills. Where do you see yourself in five years?"

I'm a deer in headlights. "I'm happy where I am." I stuff the bruschetta into my mouth.

"But if you're as passionate about the profession as Malcolm claims..." He frowns. "Where are you trying to go ultimately?"

I chew, trying to think what to say. "Court-ordered is my thing," I say.

He smiles. "Now give me the real answer." I can feel Malcolm tense up beside me. True, Soren is being kind of high-handed.

"It's my thing," I say.

"How can you say that?" he challenges. "You're working with students who don't want to learn...you're joking, right?"

"No?" I say.

"Court-ordered diversity training, court-ordered sexual harassment training, yes, that's a leveraged place to make a difference. There is understanding lacking in those instances. But come on. Court-ordered emotional intelligence training? Are you kidding me?" Soren's acting almost insulted that I said it, and he's being a bit insulting as well. "Nobody says that."

"Clearly, *Elle* says it," Malcolm cuts in, giving Soren his hard-sparkle smile minus the smile. "So in fact, it seems that somebody does say it."

"I like to take things one day at a time," I try, diplomatically. "Oh my god, have you guys ever seen that show? 'One Day at a Time'? My mom used to love that show when she was a kid. She made me watch a million episodes of it. File under *bo-ring*!"

Soren turns to Malcolm. "I'm just saying that the fact that she chooses the area of court-ordered emotional intelligence shows that she is really just not serious. Which is fine. Certainly no harm in that. My point is that it's like saying, 'I'm really passionate about filmmaking, and I want to rip tickets apart at the movie theater.'"

"Soren," Verlaina scolds. "Maybe she enjoys it."

"Fine, but you don't call yourself a serious filmmaker if you want to stay in the role of ticket ripper. It's adjacent to the business, yes."

Everybody at the table bristles—especially Malcolm, who fixes him with a fierce look that I feel down to my toes. "I can assure you that she's very serious about executive coaching," Malcolm says. "Frankly, I think you could learn a thing or two from her."

"I doubt that." Soren drains his martini and signals for another.

"I doubt it, too," I say quickly. "I really, really doubt it."

"Didn't the woman from 'One Day At a Time' marry Eddy Van Halen?" Verlaina asks, desperately trying to change the subject. We are partners now in desperately trying to change the subject.

"Is that so?" I muse enthusiastically, even though I have no idea what she is talking about. "From the band?"

Malcolm says, "Not only am I learning soft skills from Stella, specifically skills of empathy, but she is responsible for a major negotiation breakthrough."

"She's giving you negotiation tips," Soren says disbelievingly. "You're getting negotiation tips and learning empathy from a first-year court-ordered executive coach. *You*."

"Yes, that's right," Malcolm says.

"That's wonderful," Verlaina tries, lifting her glass. "To each her own."

"Though it's a bit hard to believe, I have to say," Soren says without even looking at me, like the conversation doesn't involve me.

"And I didn't even want to do it," Malcolm says. "I offered to pay Elle a great deal of money to let me do a self-directed curriculum, if you know what I mean." He looks over at me. "She'd do no such thing. She hung in there. Making a difference is more important to her than hundreds of thousands of dollars."

"Really," Soren says.

"Really," Malcolm says. "She's down in the trenches. Doing the actual work."

Actual work?

Was that an insult? I can't tell; my mind spins way more on what Malcolm said, because, hello?! He's learning empathy? Is he actually saying that he is learning empathy? From me?

"The *actual* work?" Soren asks. "As opposed to what, exactly?"

"I'm just saying she's getting results," Malcolm says. "She's doing the impossible, with her very innovative methods." He turns to me. "Maybe you should write a book, too, Elle."

Oh my god, is Malcolm just completely messing with Soren?

"I would never write a book," I say, and then I polish off the last of my drink. "And I'm sure Verlaina is bored to tears of this shop talk."

"Oh come on, now, I can't wait to hear this," Soren says, turning to me. "So what are your very innovative methods, exactly?"

"They're not really that innovative," I say. "I'm sure they seem that way to Malcolm considering he's managed to pay off all of his anger management and soft skills coaches up to now."

"Not innovative? Are you kidding me?" Malcolm says. "For my intro session, she came dressed as a letter carrier. I'm sure that's not a common approach."

Soren looks at me, skeptical. "You dress as a letter carrier? To what purpose?"

Needless to say, the diarrhea excuse is looking pretty good right about now. "I-it was the program that I designed," I say.

"Right. But why?" Soren says. Because apparently that answer doesn't work as well on him as it did on Malcolm. His new drink is delivered.

"It's just the program."

"Seems...odd," Soren says, giving me a quick, efficient frown.

"It's complicated," I say.

"I think I should be able to comprehend it," Soren says, clearly taking insult. My pulse races. I really want to swig more bubbly now, but my glass is empty.

Malcolm cuts in to tell Soren how I'm forcing him to watch video of people whose building is being torn down. "Hours of footage of the people," he says. "The best part is her mail-carrier-themed advice. Like the big dog, little dog thing?" He looks over at me. "And that anecdote about the lost dog? It was brilliant. Absolutely brilliant," he says, going on to explain the way he used it in his negotiation.

Soren stares at me, stunned. "Let me get this straight. You

tell your clients mail-carrier-themed anecdotes and force them to watch video of people on the other end of their business operations? What is the thinking there?"

"It's just...the program—"

"I understand—the program that you designed," he snaps. "But why design the program in the first place? Is there some protocol or rubric that you are drawing from? Or did you just make it up?"

"That's..." My pulse races. "That's proprietary."

"Excuse me?" he says. "Proprietary vis-a-vis the Bexley Partners? I thought you said you designed it."

"Yes, I designed it. It's proprietary vis-a-vis myself."

24

Malcolm

"PROPRIETARY VIS-A-VIS YOURSELF," Soren says.

I bite back a smile. The man is a blowhard.

Which is just one of the many reasons why it's so hilarious that Elle refuses to explain herself to him. *Proprietary.* I want to kiss her. I never imagined our cocktail hour would be quite this entertaining.

"Well..." She shrugs apologetically. "Yeah. Vis-a-vis myself."

"So basically what you're saying is that you want to keep it a secret from me," Soren says. "You don't want me to know. Can I ask you why not?" he demands.

I struggle to keep my face neutral. Usually it's me upsetting people.

"It's proprietary, that's all," she says.

Soren has no idea how maniacally Elle will hold on to what she knows—she's like a little dog, teeth sunk in, refusing to give up her one sure patch of knowledge. I don't enjoy when it's turned on me, but it's magnificent seeing it turned on Soren.

"Let's just drop it," Verlaina says.

"You've told me the technique itself," Soren says to me, ignoring Verlaina. "Are you telling me that the *rationale* is proprietary?" This like it's the stupidest thing he ever heard.

She does her chin-up thing that I've come to enjoy. "I'm sorry, that's proprietary."

"It's not as if I'm going to steal the rationale," he growls.

Elle can take care of herself; that's definitely something I've learned, but I don't like Soren's bullying tone—I didn't appreciate it aimed at the waitperson and I definitely don't appreciate it aimed at Elle.

I turn to the man. Calmly, I say, "If it's proprietary, it's proprietary."

"But it's ridiculous to make such a thing proprietary." Soren says. "It's like making your method for tying shoelaces proprietary. There's simply no reason for it."

"Soren," Verlaina says. "She doesn't want to talk about it."

"Fine. Say you don't want to talk about it, then, but don't claim it's proprietary." He finishes up his drink. "A letter carrier and amateur documentary footage. Not as if I'm going to steal it," Soren grumbles. "I don't do gimmicks."

I give him a cool smile. "Maybe you should try it, Soren," I say. "Anybody can take on the clients who want coaching, but it takes a real innovator to take on the uncooperative clients."

"This is ridiculous." Soren stands and grabs his phone. "You may need a bit more of her emotional intelligence dog and pony show, Malcolm, because those soft skills? Not in evidence." He throws down a few bills and heads out.

Verlaina winces. "I'm sorry. He's been under so much pressure with the new release and everything." She looks from me to Elle. "Thanks for coming out. It really was nice to meet you, Elle."

"You, too," Elle says.

"Soft skills," I growl as Verlaina rushes off to catch up to Soren. "I've got some soft skills I'd like to show him."

When I look over, Elle's beaming at me. "Thank you," she gusts, as though she can't believe how fiercely I took her side. Has nobody ever done that? I move closer to her. "I've got some soft skills that will lay him right out."

Her grin grows even wider.

I say, "I'm sorry I brought you out to drinks with that jackass."

"No, it was sweet," she says. "It was a nice idea."

"He was a jackass," I growl.

She makes a sly face. "Dog and pony show? Do you think he was trying to insult me?"

"I should've laid him out," I growl.

"And let you end up with another court-ordered emotional intelligence coach? No way," she says. "Anyway, I'm sure I was insulting with my proprietary thing. But he made me nervous, like I might say the wrong thing."

"I think he wanted to make you nervous."

She frowns, not liking that.

"But you got the better of him." I lean in closer to her. "It's proprietary."

She smiles her huge smile. "Well, Malcolm, they say that anybody can take on the clients who want coaching, but it takes a real coach to help the uncooperative ones."

I grin, pleased that she enjoyed that.

She grabs my hand like it's the most natural thing in the world. "Those soft skills, Malcolm? Not in evidence!"

"Certainly not," I say. And just like that, we're sitting there, holding hands. And I'm looking at our joined hands. And my heart is racing. And I know I'm falling for her. "I love your dog and pony show," I say.

"Good, because I love doing the dog and pony show with you," she says.

"I want you to do the dog and pony show with me...and nobody else," I say, and it's clear I'm talking about much more than her coaching.

A strange, sad look comes over her face. The look alarms me to the core.

"What is it?" I ask.

"Nothing," she says softly, taking her hand back, ostensibly to fix her hair clip. "And, no, I don't want to...do anything with anybody else but you right now. It's the truth."

"But..." My blood races. "Is somebody else in the picture?"

"No, it's not that," she says, still with the sense of a reservation, a *but*.

"But what?" I demand, then, "I need to know if there are any obstacles to us being together."

I don't like the wary look that comes over her face. It reminds me I'm not in control—not a sensation I'm accustomed to where a woman is concerned.

"Well? Are there?"

"It's not that simple," she says.

"Because of your profession?"

"Sort of...this whole situation—"

"Never mind," I say. "I'm pushing you."

"No, you're not."

"Let's just have dinner," I say. She's stuck with me for the time being. I don't need to push.

"Malcolm—"

"I push people all the time and I don't want to push you. I won't do it," I say. "Look at your soft-skills teaching paying off, right?"

She smiles wistfully.

I spot the host coming for us. "Come on, then." I offer her my arm. She takes it, and we follow him back.

A nice dinner, now. One step at a time. Usually I prefer to root out and demolish obstacles head-on, but that might not work with Elle. She's not a company. There's no backroom leverage to apply. No financial pressure to exert. If she doesn't want to be with me in a real way, I can't force it.

I tell myself that she's probably worried that she'll lose her beloved job. That I can overcome, but what if it's more? I don't enjoy this lack of power, but at the same time, here we are, heading to dinner. We have the whole night in front of us; I can't help but feel happy about that.

My shameless bribery has paid off with a stellar corner table bathed in candlelight.

"Wow," she says. "Nice." She goes right for the menu. I love that she loves to eat. "Another tiny menu with no prices," she says. "A San Fran fashion, huh?"

"See anything you like?" I ask.

"I might like it all," she says.

"There won't be a bad dish on there," I say, signaling the waiters. We order two more drinks and a feast off the menu, including more bruschetta.

"Our favorite food," she says.

Something strange shimmers through my chest at that.

I quiz her about her favorite eateries in New Jersey. I usually quiz people about their lives because it helps me gain control over them, but with Elle, I want to know all.

She doesn't like to talk about Newark, but she comes to life when she talks about her friend group. They all seem to live near each other—maybe in the same neighborhood? I'm glad that she found what she set out to find.

She nearly dies with each plate that comes across the table.

It's not about corrupting her anymore—I can feel her pleasure as if it's my own.

"Thank you again for this," she says, motioning to her dress.

"You look stunning."

She waves it off. "It's not my usual thing, but I really love it. I know I'm not the most fashionable person ever," she says.

"I like the way you dress."

"Oh, come off it," she says. "Nobody likes how I dress."

"I do. You're utilitarian. Taking the decision-making out of dressing saves bandwidth. I admire it. It's what I do."

"That's why you wear your black suits every day? To save bandwidth? So you can save your vast brilliance for the negotiating room?" she asks, grinning.

I reach over and wind a lock of her hair in my finger. "Among other things."

"For me, it's more about a proven outfit. It gives me one less thing to feel awkward about. I'm not good with people."

"I'm not really, either."

"Oh, please," she says. "So what have I been watching in those negotiation sessions for the last two weeks? What was that?"

"Business skills," I say.

"Oh-kayyyy," she says.

"It's true, I'd far prefer to stay away from everyone."

Her gaze locks on mine.

"Except now," I add.

"Okay, then," she whispers.

People think I'm misanthropic, that I don't like my fellow human being. It's more of a chicken and egg thing, though. Not liking my fellow human being came after my fellow human being not much liking me. Elle has carved out an exception to that rule. For whatever bizarre reason, she's decided to believe in me, to think I have a good heart. I find it...compelling.

Every entrée comes with a creative presentation—a squiggle of sauce, or a sprig of something stuck upright in the food like a flag, and she seems to find it funny. And really, it is funny, and we laugh as each ensuing entrée has more extreme artiness to it, which is something I never paid attention to before. We decide the cook is trolling us.

I ask her if she's ever seen the small mammal exhibit at the San Diego zoo. She hasn't. I tell her about the extensive hedgehog display. She looks excited. I'm thinking about a side trip.

We order decaf and three desserts and I watch Elle dig into them with gusto. It's the perfect dinner.

Until I look across the room and see him there.

He's standing next to the host station while his driver/body-guard attempts to land a decent table, because he stays above that kind of thing. Or he might be too drunk; one never knows.

I set down my fork. He seems to be scanning the place. Did somebody tell him that I was dining here, or is it just bad luck?

"What's wrong?" Elle asks.

"Unwelcome visitor," I say. "Whatever happens, don't react. Hopefully he'll just go away."

"Is he a murder hornet?"

"If only," I mutter as he makes his way toward our table.

First thing he does is to set his hand on the back of Elle chair, already going for a fight, I see. I stand, letting him feel my full height.

"I heard you were in town. The Germantown Group?" he asks.

My pulse thuds low and hard. "Is there something you want, or did you just want to ruin our appetites? If so, you're too late. We had a lovely time." There's nothing he hates more than to see me happy.

"I understand they're in a mind to sell," he says.

I sigh as if I'm bored, though I'm anything but. I shouldn't be surprised that he knows about the Germantown Group. He always did have a large network of spies.

"They are well positioned for a takeover and a revamp," he says. "I was thinking I might put in a bid. If they want to sell, they shouldn't sell to a chop shop."

Just like him to use my legwork and intel, and then swoop in for the kill. I smile. You never let him see anything.

He smiles back. We're in a pitched battle, though if you didn't know us, you might mistake this for a happy father-son reunion.

And for the record, my father would chop up the Germantown Group, too, but he has better PR. It's a lot of lies and fake philanthropy.

I can't let him take it out from under me. How did he discover that they were in a mood to sell?

"The look on your face? The acquisition is already paying off." Then he turns to Elle. "Royce Blackberg," he says. "And you are?" He holds out his hand.

"Don't touch her," I say.

Elle frowns at him, refusing to offer her hand and even as he beckons with his, instantly taking my side. The feeling of her being with me without question is almost worth all of this. People never take my side. They never think I want or need it.

Usually I don't.

But this now...it feels amazing. Like we're a team.

"Is this the executive coach?" he asks. "Delivering coaching with a happy ending, from the looks of it. I'd love to arrange a session with your office. Bexley Partners, is it?"

I watch myself move around the table toward him, grab him with brutal force. My arm comes around in a left hook, connecting with his jaw with a satisfying crunch. It's the only hit I get in, because his driver, Steen, and his other bodyguard are on me, one holding me so that Steen can get in a few hits before the staff intervenes.

"I won't press changes," my father says.

"Yeah, you go ahead and take the high road," I say through the pain of my split lip.

"All one can do around you."

I laugh and throw several hundreds onto the table—enough to cover the dinner and a couple hundred extra—something for the staff who has to clean up this mess. "Let's go," I say, taking her hand.

In the back of my car, she presses a green napkin to my forehead and tells the driver to do a pit stop at the drug store.

"I'm fine," I say.

"Yeah, your lip and forehead are only completely split. That guy hit you so hard. It made such a loud sound!" Gently she repositions the napkin. "Who was that?"

"My father and his driver and his assistant, but they're really his bodyguards."

"Wait, that was your father?"

"Unfortunately," I say.

"What's going on? You think he's going to try and steal your acquisition out from under you? Why would he even do that?"

"It's a long story," I say. "We don't have the most harmonious relationship."

"That seems like an understatement," she says.

"I'm much more concerned about how he got his information," I say.

Do I have a spy in my midst? It could be somebody from Gerrold's team, but how would anybody from Gerrold's team know about the animosity between my father and me? Know enough to capitalize on it?

I hate that it could be somebody from my team. I hate the idea more than I normally would. As if the loyalty of my team suddenly means something. What's going on? I hate it—I really do.

Is this soft skills? If so, I'm not loving it.

I want to be alone—I feel this need to get right to work on fending off my asshole of a father from the acquisition and figuring out who the corporate spy is, but Elle insists on patching me up.

She's back from her room, having changed into a tank top and stretchy pants. Does she iterate on this one too? If we were together, would she wear different colors of this same outfit when she comes over? Would she keep a version of this outfit at my place?

"Is that your comfort uniform?" I ask.

"Yes, exactly." She sits me in my bathroom and cleans up my wounds. She has bandages and skin glue that work on my forehead but not so much on my lip. It's ineffectual, but she keeps trying.

I like the feeling of her caring for me, and I encourage her to keep trying even though I know she won't succeed. It's the trying that does something for me. I want to reach out to her as she works on me, just to touch her, or maybe to pull her closer, but I don't want to ask for it. It's not the kind of thing a man like me asks for.

"It's going to be in the paper now, too," I say. "I'll be the aggressor and he'll use it with Gerrold. He wanted this."

"I'm sorry. You were standing up for me," she says.

"And it was worth it. I don't care—I'd do it over again," I say. "It's worth it, even if I lose the Germantown Group. Not that I plan on losing it. I need to figure out his spy and hit back."

"I don't think it's anybody on the traveling team," she says. "At least not the admin group."

"Why would you think that? Everybody has their price."

"They just really believe in you. They're proud of you," she says.

"Now whose soft skills are not in evidence?" I joke.

"I know what I know," she says. "They admire you. They love being able to add insight after the sessions. Those moments when you seem to appreciate their observations—it means a lot to them."

I grunt, like I'm not convinced. Really, I don't know what to say to that. Things are simpler when people don't like you.

"Sooo..." she begins, "what's up with you and your dad?"

"He's just an asshole. But then again, so am I. Peas in a pod."

"You're not an asshole," she says.

"Elle," I say. "My being an incorrigible asshole is the whole reason you're here."

She narrows her eyes. "So...your mom..."

"I don't know. She left when I was ten—moved to Australia. Had enough of the two of us. I'm sure she would've volunteered to be a colonist on Mars if that had been an option."

"Leaving you with that guy?"

"Who could blame her?" I stand and unbutton my now-bloody shirt. "It was good not to be coddled. It suited me. I made a hundred thousand bucks by the time I was fifteen. I hired a lawyer and got emancipated. Left that godforsaken boys' school and came back to the States. He's been after me ever since. I mean, not that he was father of the year before that." I toss the bloody shirt and the T-shirt into the garbage and pull on a dark T-shirt.

"She just left for no reason?"

"Well, she said she was visiting her sister in Australia, but she never quite made it back. She wanted a different life. Away from my father and me."

"I'm sure it had nothing to do with you."

"Dear old Dad had his part."

"You were her son," she says.

"But much more my father's son, unfortunately." I take a strand of her hair between my fingers. "It's so cute that you're looking for an explanation other than the fact that I come from a long line of villains. He's an asshole, and I'm an asshole."

"I won't accept that. That's not in any way true or at all how it works."

"Are you so sure?"

"I know you. I know that you stood up for me," she says.

"Maybe I wanted to get laid," I say, forcing a grin. The bandage over my lip pulls off.

"Malcolm, look what you've done!" She presses it back on the unhurt part of my lip, but the stickiness is worn off. "I have to put on a new one now," she scolds. "And also, I personally know you're a good guy."

"Uh-huh," I say.

She takes a new butterfly bandage from the wrapper, concentrating on the placement, fingers trembling pressing the edges of the bandage flat, repeating the movement way more than she needs to. Is she nervous about something?

Her nervousness makes me nervous. Like something real is happening.

I keep my smirk up, but inside, my blood thunders.

What people don't know about being a bad person is that it's not that hard. When you're already hated, more hate doesn't hurt. Just like if you're wet, more water won't make you wetter. You become immune at some point.

People's glares, once you get used to them, are easy to take after a while, even amusing.

What's not easy to take is a beautiful little rube who believes in me. I don't have a place to put that. I think that I'd have to carve that place out of flesh and bone.

"Hey, I almost forgot—I read your essay question answers."

She narrows her eyes at me. "The dryer-lint bandit? You don't really have a theory, do you?"

"Oh, I absolutely do," I say.

"What?" she asks.

"Do I get a free tick if I tell?" I ask.

"You know that's not the kind of coach I am," she says. "Come on, just tell me."

"Sorry," I say.

"Oh my god, you are terrible!" Then, "Please?"

"Nope," I whisper. Why would I tell her when it's so much fun not to?

"Is it based on something specific, or just intuition?" she asks.

"Of course it's based on something," I say.

"I'll get it out of you," she says.

"Maybe."

Soft fingers brush my cheek. Her gentle touch burns. She has no idea. "You got a good hit in on him," she says.

"I did, didn't I?"

She gazes at me, eyes impossibly green—army green. Because she's a fighter. "The way you hit him," she says, beaming. "Soft skills not in evidence."

I snort. "They won't be when I'm through with him. He expects me to hit back, but insulting you like that? I'm going to go at him so hard. And I'll find whoever he has on the inside and squeeze that person. And I have to get Gerrold to sign before my father gets to him. I have to move fast."

"Do you have to?" she asks naively.

I take a strand of her hair between two fingers. "Should I sing 'Kumbayah' with him instead?"

She says nothing.

It's here that I get a strange new idea. More diabolical than any I've ever come up with. "What if I did something truly drastic?"

She looks wary. "Like what?"

"Really unexpected," I say.

She blinks. "Loving kindness and selfless generosity?"

It's interesting how well she's gotten to know me in this short time. "Loving and selfless might be a bit overboard," I say. "But imagine this. What if I threw in training for the displaced workers? That would clinch the deal and seriously mess with my dad. It would be so unlike me. He'd never see it coming, and he wouldn't be prepared to counter it. The fact is, a few of my segments have expanding coding needs..."

"You would train and place the people who get let go?" she asks.

"Why not?" I say.

"What about the money?" she asks.

"What an interesting question from my empathy coach," I say. "What about the money, my empathy coach wonders."

She rolls her eyes. "You know what I mean."

"Yeah, I'll still lose my shirt offering retraining and guaranteed positions, but if we do a PR angle on it, then the publicity might make it worth it. Which would in turn make future companies more receptive to my bids."

"So you're doing it all for the PR," she says.

"And to screw my father. And because I'm a billionaire who gets to do whatever ridic thing he gets into his head."

She snorts and shoves at my shoulder. I make a few phone calls. I get my HR VP out of bed and pitch it. I instruct him to work up a proposal. I get my PR agency to weigh in.

"This is absolute madness," I say a few hours later when things are in motion. "And it could work. It'll definitely put a ticking clock under Gerrold."

"Look at you being good," she says.

"Yeah, look at me being good," I joke. "How incredibly boring."

"Stop. It suits you," she says. "Also, people will not see this coming."

"I have something you didn't count on," I say darkly. "A destructive secret weapon—yeah, that's right, it's a program that helps these workers thrive in the future economy, and I am going to crush your balls with it."

She laughs and comes and sits on my lap and kisses me. How is it that this is so much fun? This kind of giveaway, I should be weeping.

My phone rings. It's legal from back home, returning my call. I'm running this all through New York—no way can I trust anyone on the traveling team. Who the hell has been feeding information to my father? And did it just start when we arrived on the West Coast? Or has it been going on?

But Elle I can trust. Elle is on my side. I conscript her into serving as admin and liaison, pulling together PDF packets and communicating instructions to the different teams while I'm on with the lawyers.

She goes back to her room and comes back with her laptop. She settles in next to me on the bed and I press my lips to her shoulder, enjoying the silkiness of her skin, and the faint smell of rosewood to the coconut berry, which I think might be her deodorant.

"They'll never expect this," I say.

"'Cause you're sooo evil," she says.

She loves to say that like it's a joke now. Wishing so fiercely with her army green eyes.

25

Noelle

WE'RE WORKING side by side, dreaming up Malcolm's proposal, slowly putting the pieces together.

I was feeling a bit tipsy at dinner, but the crazy drama of the evening got me stone-cold sober, and then there are the snacks and coffee that Malcolm sends for around midnight.

He's developing this without the traveling team. He wants things airtight.

Most of the time he spends on the phone organizing things. It's kind of amazing to be a proverbial fly on the wall and witness him in his element. He runs people hard; he's woken people up all over the globe to pull this together. He has poor social skills, that's for sure, but he is never overtly mean to anyone. And they all seem to want to help.

The traveling team isn't the only group that's proud to be with him—does he even see that? Or does he filter everything through this idea that he's a villain?

I take a short rest and lay my head on his shoulder, briefly closing my eyes. "People say you're a villain, but you're really just niceties challenged," I mumble.

I can feel the gentle shake of his chest as he chuckles at this. "Like a serial killer is letting-people-live challenged?"

"Shut the bruschetta hole," I whisper.

"You should sleep," he says. "You're asleep now."

"I'm just resting my eyes," I inform him. "After which I'll be bright as a daisy."

The next thing I know, I'm curled up next to him with a blanket over me as he taps away on his laptop. I doze off to the soft, baritone murmurs of him on a phone call. The next thing I know, I'm squinting blearily at the red numbers on the bedside clock.

Six in the morning.

My tank top and yoga pants are twisted around me from tossing and turning. I kind of can't believe I put my home outfit on last night; it's not the kind of outfit I wear in front of guys. But Malcolm is different. He feels like my people in a way that other guys don't.

I don't let him know I'm awake, because I'm enjoying listening to him on his calls—he's so blunt with his employees, and they seem to understand that's Malcolm. He doesn't start conversations with small talk. He barks one-word questions. Maybe he doesn't know how. He doesn't soften up his sentences.

Malcolm's an unlicked cub—no mother. A father who clearly despises him.

His harshest phone call is reserved for his security person— he really does seem upset about the mole—his team means a lot more to him than he lets on, maybe even to himself. "It'll be a blockbuster offer," he mumbles softly. "Once I make it, there's no way our mole could resist letting Dad know."

He and his security person seem to be hatching a plan to

flush out the spy. It sounds to me like they're going to do some- thing temporary with the internet maybe or something—I can't tell, but I hear the woman on the other end talking about grab- bing communications that go out as long as the person doesn't go down to the street. There's a backup plan for anybody who calls or texts from the street during the break.

Whatever the plan is, Malcolm seems to like it. As usual, the sign of Malcolm liking something is him turning the gruffness down a notch.

Maybe it's the strange clarity of being in that state between sleeping and waking, but working with him the way I have, and now meeting his dad, I feel like I get him in a new way, beyond what he presents to the world. I see a man who doesn't trust easily. He thinks he's a villain. Maybe that's how he survived.

His mother lied to him. The potential spy in his organiza- tion has him in knots. And what am I doing? Running the biggest deception of all.

I have to tell him the truth before it goes any further. Before he works it out, and before AJ tells him. I have to stop this. I knew it tonight in the restaurant when he asked me about obsta- cles to us being together. I know it all the more so now.

A ball of emotion forms in my throat, like my own body warning me not to do it. As soon as I tell, I'll lose him. More than lose him—he'll push me away as forcefully as he'll reject the mole when he finds them, but the longer it goes on, the worse it'll be—for him.

The building will be done for. It doesn't matter. Somewhere along the line, his well-being has become extremely important to me.

I shut my eyes tight against welling tears. God, what have I done?

I'll tell him after he nails the negotiation—he needs to nail this negotiation. He needs to have this plan go right. It's something nice for him to have. And then I'll tell him.

"About time," he says.

I squeeze my eyes closed harder, willing away the sadness.

"I know you're awake." He takes my hand and kisses it, and then my wrist. I'm still curled in a ball next to him and he's kissing up my arm. And I'm smiling through my tears. Because I'm falling for him so hard, it's crazy.

"Whaaaat?" I say. I wipe my eyes with my free hand as if I'm wiping away the sleep. The fact that this will be the last time we're together makes me feel hollowed out with emotion.

He keeps kissing his way up my arm.

"Are you being funny?"

He plants a kiss on the inside of my upper arm; my skin there is crazy tender under the delicious scratchiness of his whiskers.

"Keep going," I say.

He grumbles and kisses the pillowy billow of skin where my arm meets my chest.

"Were you waiting for me to wake up?" I ask.

"Yes. Would you rather I'd woken you up?" he asks. "You know that I thought about it. I had three dirty ideas for waking you up."

"How dirty?" I whisper.

"Disturbingly dirty," he says. "I'm not a good person, as you may recall."

"I want to know them," I say. "All three."

"In good time." He plants a kiss on the pillow of skin on the front side of my underarm. "This is an underrated spot on you."

"C'mere." I grab his hair, trying to get him away from my unsightly bulgy spot that he has deemed underrated, but he stays and kisses it again.

"I didn't know spots on me were being rated," I say. "Are

there overrated spots? Are my wrists not all that? My toes not living up to the hype?"

"Shut the bruschetta hole."

I snort, loving the way he says that in his clipped English accent. He kisses me again, and then he rolls me up and onto his lap so that I'm straddling him, facing him. He tangles his fingers through my hair.

"Is it all done?" I ask.

"Mostly." He's watching my eyes, holding my gaze. He grabs the hem of my shirt and slowly starts to pull it up, pulling it off. I help him, undoing my bra, lifting my arms. "I do love a woman in uniform," he says.

And then my shirt is off.

And I'm naked on the top, facing him, looking right at him, and he has his shirt off, too, but he's more naked because he just said the L word. Not that it was a direct use, but it was partial use of the L word, and things feel more intense, suddenly.

I joke it off—I say, "Wait until day five of wearing this and you might be singing a different tune."

He isn't going for my joke. The awkwardly serious look on his face tells me that he's feeling this big thing happening between us. It feels good, like promise and excitement.

I make myself remember that it will be over soon. Then his abs harden impossibly as he comes up for a kiss, curling up to me and cupping my cheeks, kissing my lips, then my chest, then my nipple, where he settles in for some seriously sexy sucking.

I reach around and it's only a little bit of gymnastics to grab his cock through his sweatpants. "This part of you cannot be overrated," I say. "It simply cannot be overrated."

He just growls, adding vibrato to the nipple action. And then we shift and we're kissing. And he says, "Can you reach over and get that condom?" He lies back. "On the bedside table. I want you to put it on me. I want to watch you put it on me."

I can tell he wants me to do it sexy like maybe it's a thing with him, a woman preparing him to fuck her or something. I love that it's kind of dirty even.

I smile.

"God," he groans, "you have to do it while you're wearing that witchy smile."

"You think this is a witchy smile?" I ask.

"Mmmm-hmm," he says.

I like that, being that I'm not a witchy person. And it's not hard to keep the smile, because now I'm feeling witchy. I lean over and grab the condom from his little bedside kit that has a sleep mask and other stuff. I rip it open and I scoot down and pull off his sweats. His cock is hard and thick and dusky, and curled slightly to one side in a way that feels really Malcolm. I kiss the tip, just because I really, really want to, and then my whole mouth is on him, and I'm taking him all the way in. I want to feel him inside like this, to know him like this.

"You had one job to do," he says.

I hum my answer really loudly and his body tenses in response, like the hum nearly put him over the edge. He feels sexy and dangerous. Eventually, I let him go and I make a big production of taking the condom from the wrapper. "How do I do it?"

"Just a little air at the tip—"

"No, dude, I was in class that day. I mean, how do I do it sexy for you?"

"Serious and slow. Deliberate."

"But with the witchy smile," I say.

"Yes."

"You are very specific," I whisper, cladding him slowly and deliberately, with my witchiest smile and witchiest vibe—but not like I'm being somebody else, or role-playing. It's a part of me that he brings out.

I crawl over him and settle onto him, dying to have him in me. He moves under me, watching me, entering me slowly, filling me.

I give him a little growl of my own.

"You want a little something extra?" he asks.

I narrow my eyes.

He smiles. "Whatever you were just thinking, you have to tell me."

"All in good time," I say. I'm stoking up a rhythm that I don't think I can ever stop.

"I meant little extra here." He puts his thumb on my clit as he moves, letting me rut against it, rutting into the dampness between us.

"Yesssss," I say, eyes shut tight.

I feel swollen against him, against the knucklebone of his thumb right on my clit, and like every nerve ending down there is exposed and building pleasure. When I open my eyes, I see him watching me, monitoring my reactions, my pleasure, adjusting his thumb angle, minute adjustments like a pilot coming in for a very difficult landing. Because he's like that, seeing people, responding to them.

People don't always see him clearly, the unlicked cub alone in his castle, but he sees them.

He's monitoring my pleasure, trying to give me this, because he thinks I'm a good person who deserves his best.

Desperation flows hot through me as I move on him. I'm desperate for release, my body coiling; my hands greedy for every inch of his sexy body. And then I can feel him starting to come, though I can't be sure, because I am coming, pleasure exploding through me like a thousand secret, desperate fireworks.

26

Malcolm

THE PROCESS of taking seats around the negotiation table has always been a tiresome drama of people finding socially acceptable reasons not to sit directly next to me.

Which means they have to find reasons to sit next to other people.

The drama is mostly a pantomime, with some awkward comments thrown in— "Let me see that..." or "what was your question again?" Or sometimes the comment comes first, and then the shock of discovery—an empty chair right there. "Oh!"

The drama is tiresome, mostly because of the assumption that my feelings might be hurt if I realize that nobody wants to sit near me, whereas I vastly prefer that nobody to sit next to me.

Except Elle.

The not-sitting-by-me drama has become hugely convenient over the past weeks. All Elle has to do is wait and she's forced to sit next to me.

We even laughed about it once. She tried to suggest that

people might truly want to sit next to me, but they're scared of me. I told her to please not be tiresome like that, and she smiled like she does, and I sat there loving her smile and I forced her to agree, at any rate, that it was convenient for us.

Nobody says anything about my black eye and split lip before the session begins, but there are definitely two empty seats on either side of me.

As usual, Elle takes one, settling in next to me. I'm still vibrating from this morning—not just the sex, though that was amazing, and not just because her body is delicious, and not just because of all of the pornographically hot high points of it, of which, trust me, there were many, but it's because of how right we felt. How we worked together, caring about getting it right for each other. It was more than getting off; it was us collaborating on a secret experience.

There are times when I feel like I'm building a private world with her. Nobody ever told me it was like this in a relationship. Nothing could've surprised me more.

I've certainly never communicated with a woman as extensively as I have with Elle over the past three weeks. I never imagined something like that would be a plus.

Even more surprising, considering that the sex was so amazing, it was almost more satisfying to have her sleep curled up next to me. It was something about her presence, or more, the way she seemed to take comfort in my presence, that was deeply satisfying.

So many times I wanted to settle my hand onto her shoulder, but I didn't want to wake her.

There was this photo series of a gorilla that raised a kitten circulating a few years back. The kitten would snuggle with its gorilla parent—it only liked the gorilla; no one else, human or nonhuman—would do. I think it disheartened a lot of people who felt like they had soul bonds with their cats when really, it's just that they're a large mammal that the kitten has become accustomed to.

Not a high bar, admittedly but what do you want from a kitten?

So I could've been a gorilla or maybe a toaster and Elle would've snuggled next to me.

I tried to remind myself of that—that it has nothing to do with me, but it swelled me up all the same. And then that light came into her eyes when she looked at me—the kind of light that wouldn't come into her eyes had I been a gorilla or a toaster—and it was impossible for me to lie to myself and tell myself I didn't care.

So I'm sitting waiting for the session to start and thinking all of these things, and she turns to me like she senses the direction of my thoughts.

I direct my gaze at the croissants and she rolls her eyes.

Then Gerrold is seated. "Somebody had a wild night."

I smile. He's the only one who dared to say anything about my face.

I have the proposals in my satchel, a paper copy for everybody. My lead New York attorney has arrived and my legal team bristles when I introduce her around. I can't imagine the mole being among the West Coast legal team—something like that could lead to disbarment, but I don't mess around.

"We've got some interest from another quarter," Gerrold says.

I can feel my people stiffen. Are they surprised? Is somebody a good actor? Meanwhile, Gerrold's son has an eager look on his face—he reminds me of a dog, trying to contain himself at the kids' table, thrilled at the opportunity to squeeze more money out.

"Is there an offer?" I ask.

"No, but a request to open the process up," Gerrold says.

"You might want to take a look at this first," I say, passing out the packets. I can feel the confusion from my team, but they're trained well enough that they won't show it. They don't even pounce eagerly on the sections that spell out the deal, though that's the area they'll be interested in. I'm sure they're wondering if my black eye is related to this personnel switch-up.

My New York lawyer and I set out the terms, the training, the guaranteed employment terms after training.

It's obvious when Gerrold reaches the important part. Everything about his body language changes. "You'd train my displaced people in coding?" he asks, stunned. "Even the truckers?"

"And their significant others, if they so desire," I say. "It's still a job they can do sitting down."

"Truckers and support staff...coding?" the son asks in disbelief.

"People have displaced coal miners doing it," I say. "It's a skill. Skills are learnable." I walk them through the HR portion of the writeup, all of the success rates and income charts for coders.

Gerrold's team wants the room to go over everything, so we head out for a break.

Walt comes right over. "What's going on?"

"Maybe I had to balance out the badassery of my black eye," I say.

"I could've helped work this up..." He gestures back at the room. He knows somebody had to coordinate the details, and it usually would've been him. "You had New York step in?"

"It was late," I say.

He nods unhappily. Is he the mole, fishing to see what I suspect? Or is he an employee, worried that I'm disappointed with his performance—to the point that I cut him out?

"It's quite an offer," Walt adds, trying for a smile. "Should you be wearing a red suit and beard? Or am I missing something?" He wants to know if it's the gift it looks like. Nisha is there, now, and Lawrence. They've been hovering. They want to understand, too—enough to defy tradition and actually group around me during a break.

"Maybe I just want any other interested party buried," I say.

"Usually you use a shovel," Coralee says. "When you want to bury somebody."

"Instead of a delicious candy treat," Nisha puts in humorously.

"There are intangibles," I say. "If that's what you're wondering."

They all seem to relax at this. Inside knowledge. An angle. That's more like me.

"I know you wouldn't put together a bad deal," one of my West Coast lawyers says, showing he's on the team. Everybody's agreeing that they're sure I know what I'm doing. I wouldn't put together a bad deal.

People break for the bathroom and snacks. Only Elle is left.

"Do you see how people fall all over themselves to show they believe in you?" she says. As usual, she's trying to look at the upside.

"If they didn't believe in me, it would show that they're idiots," I say. "And I'd have to fire their asses."

"So full of shit," she breathes.

I look down, wishing I could touch her. She comes off as a shrinking violet, but she's got grit.

If our mole is going to make a move, they'll do it now. We're both really conscious now of who has gone into the restroom, who has gone to the street to vape or talk on the phone. Nisha wanders up with a sparkling water for Elle and they break off to chat about whatever those two chat about.

I do things on my phone until we reconvene.

Gerrold seems excited about the deal.

I like the other party excited about a deal, but it's usually my goal for them to be excited about a deal that gives me exactly what I want. And it typically takes a good deal of work to get them there. Instead, I've plopped his fondest desire right down on the table in front of him.

In exchange for intangibles.

Yes, good PR has monetary value, but still, it's not me. I've left my comfort zone in the dust to head for the unknown.

Then I feel fingers on my arm, searching around until they find my hand. Elle, grabbing my hand, anchoring me like a counterpart.

The most important intangible.

I don't look at her—I won't compromise her in front of the team, but I'm rocked by her.

And right here, I decide that we have to be done with this ridiculous charade—sneaking around because she is my executive coach. Sneaking around is for children.

I want us to go back to New York and be together in front of the world. I have no doubt that she's concerned about the ethics of our situation. I've been thinking about it a lot, and I have to think that that's the obstacle that plagues her. Becoming romantic with the client would probably cause her to lose her license or certificate.

Whatever it is, it would be so Elle to have it framed and cherish the shit out of it, tell everybody she knows how amazing her job is. No doubt she has all kinds of anecdotes about executive coaching the way she has them about being a letter carrier, being that her nerd streak runs a mile wide. I love that about her. And how it's her way of putting the world in order.

Lucky for us, I've figured out a solution. I need to graduate the program early. That's all there is to it.

I'm broken out of my reverie by Gerrold's new ask. Two days to look through the documents.

"Are you kidding me?" I say. "You want to look this gift horse in the mouth? You really do?" True, I made an unexpectedly gift-like offer, but that doesn't mean I've had a personality transplant. "This is not a complex document. The changes are minimal, and all in your favor. Two hours."

Gerrold's thinking about it, but Junior scoffs.

"Look, you've been sitting with most of it for two weeks. This overcomes one of your main objections, Gerrold, with flying colors if I do say so myself. There are provisions for mediation in case of road bumps. Two hours, take it or leave it. I'm not trying to squeeze you here, but I'm not going to twiddle my thumbs. I want this deal done. I want my team back in New York. This is my final offer and it's a pumpkin at four, got it?

Gerrold is nodding. Junior's piping up; he wants more investigation into this offer. Gerrold asks me to walk with him while his legal looks at it.

So we walk. We follow Vallejo toward the water.

I decide to level with him. I tell him my father wants his company. I let him know that my father will look a lot better on paper, but it won't be real in the end. I'm pre-empting it with something concrete, with the best thing he's likely to see. I tell him that even my team is surprised by the seeming gift of it. I tell him that there's a PR angle in it that may or may not happen. I tell him that I think he should take the deal.

"I appreciate your speaking plainly," he says.

We walk for a bit in silence.

I'm feeling bad about the historical retrospective, now—the way we shined on his ego. He wants to be a good guy and he is one, and I played on that. He's about my father's age, and for a second, I wonder what it would've been like to grow up with a guy like this.

The offer is signed not two hours later.

Before we are even out of the building, my security head pulls me aside and lets me know that it was the son who was courting my father; they caught him putting in a call to my old man down on the street. He'd even forwarded him the PDF to look at.

I'm happier than I should be that it's not my people.

"Do you want us to tell Gerrold?" my security head asks.

"He knows. On some level, anyway," I say.

I get my admin to find us a nice table for eight somewhere. We're gonna do some celebrating, and then I'll leave and they can all get drunk and dance. But they won't be taking Elle. I've got after-dinner plans for her.

Noelle

I GET to the restaurant early. It's one of those glam hotel lobby places that make you feel like a princess.

I have a cocktail with Nisha while we wait for our people. Nisha is speculating wildly about Malcolm's black eye. "He's gotten into things with strangers before," she says, "but usually it's somebody he knows, and I'll bet you so much money that they deserved it. He doesn't go for people who don't deserve it."

I nod, feeling bad having to pretend that I don't know. The pretending has to stop. Not just with her.

I try not to think about that. We'll have a nice dinner with the gang. I'll tell him right after.

"Coralee thinks it's connected to the generous offer," Nisha continues. "Like something happened. What? But it could be really good PR. That has to be what he's going for. It's not like the court-ordered coaching suddenly gave him a heart. No offense, but wouldn't you just keel over?" She turns to me. "Oh my god, that was kind of offensive, wasn't it? I didn't mean like it's ineffective—"

I'm laughing. "No offense taken."

Nisha and I talk and laugh, and at one point I'm thinking I need to invite her over when this is all finished, maybe for one of our fifth-floor dance parties. Then I remember there won't be any more of those. The building is going down in sixty-some days.

The rest of the traveling team arrives minus the legal people. There's some vetting thing they have to hammer out. The team is excited to be going home.

"I honestly thought we'd be here forever," Walt says. "I thought I was going to have to miss the Voidz concert."

People are talking about what they're gonna do when they get back to the city. When they ask me, I say I'll be mostly looking for a new place and getting ready to move.

"A better place, I hope," Nisha says.

"I hope so," I say. But no place can possibly be better than 341.

More people arrive. Apparently we're supposed to start with the apps and the drinks and not wait for Malcolm.

"He usually swoops in for the entrée," Lawrence says. "Quick cameo."

We file in to the restaurant and order all the outrageous things, and it's fun. The traveling team is totally fun.

I text Malcolm at one point. Just a frown emoji, like where is he?

He texts back—an upside-down frown emoji, which is so him. It's him doing the right thing for the wrong reason. It's him throwing the best party he knows how to throw—a party he mostly isn't there for. An upside-down frown as a smile. It's sweet and sad and it makes me want to go find him and forcibly snuggle him.

It gets late. We start in on our entrées. Where is Malcolm? I would have thought he'd stop in at least by now. I keep thinking about AJ—what if AJ got to him?

"Maybe he's huddling with New York on something," Walt says.

"It's weird that he wouldn't come at all," Nisha observes. "He's the one that gathered us."

"I hope he didn't get into another fight," Coralee says.

People resume eating. Conversation goes back to normal. I text Malcolm a question mark. Nothing comes back.

I'm getting a bad feeling about this.

Right before dessert, Walt eyes the group of us. "I'm thinking another round, full dessert service, and then dancing it off at that place on Mission Street."

"I've got an early flight," Coralee says.

"I'm out, too," I say, over the protests of Nisha. "I slept for shit last night," I add.

Back at the hotel, I go straight to Malcolm's room. I have this terrible feeling he's found out. Or what if AJ got to him? I need to tell him.

Nervously, I knock on the door. This is the right thing to do. If I'll ever have a chance with him in the future, I have to be honest with him now. How did I let it go on so long?

The door swings open, and Malcolm's broad smile tells me he doesn't know. "What's wrong?" he asks.

"You didn't come to dinner or answer my text."

"You texted?" He pulls me in. The door shuts behind me. In a jokey voice he says, "There is *something* you can assist me with."

I roll my eyes. "Shut." I make a little hand motion that means hole and also bruschetta, and I walk in. There are papers strewn all over his desk. A printer is spitting out hard copies of something. "It's ten at night, dude, and you just closed a deal. Is this more about Germantown?"

"No," he says, stepping between me and the papers.

"Is it a secret? A secret for *moi*?" I tease.

He smiles, and it makes me smile. I'd wanted him to see us as humans with hopes and dreams—that was the extent of my plan. I'd never imagined how important he could become to me. How his hopes and dreams might become intertwined with mine.

"Look, I need to tell you something."

"Oh, I think I know what you're going to tell me," he says.

My pulse is racing. "You do?"

"I've missed my video session. I understand that you might feel compelled to give me an X for the day. We know how stringent you are about those rules."

"No," I say sadly. "That's not it." I take a deep breath, unsure how to begin.

He's gathering up his papers and collating them. "That's right, you're not going to give me an X. I'm making sure of that." He spins around. "I'm expecting a passing grade, in fact, because what have I done? Completely nailed this course." He shoves a bunch of papers into my hands.

"What is this?" I ask, clutching them, not reading. They look legal. Did his lawyers figure out a way to get him extricated from the coaching?

"It's my extra credit assignment."

I furrow my brow, confused. "What extra credit assignment?"

"Don't you remember?" he asks. "One way I can get a pass out of the class? I'm tired of this, Elle. Take a look. Let's end this charade."

I glance down and read the first line. "A proposed offering plan relating to the conversion to cooperative ownership of the apartments in this building has been submitted to the Department of Law of the State of New York..."

Cooperative ownership. "What..." I ask, heart racing. I scan down and find the address—341 West 45th Street. Our building. Everything in me begins to vibrate. It's everything I wanted.

And the worst thing, too.

"Before you freak out." He takes the papers and shows me the payment part. "I'm converting it to rent-to-own if they can't pay up front, which I'm assuming most of them can't, because let's face it, if they could, they wouldn't be living there. It's actually a good price. We'll courier it to the residents tomorrow, but I think it counts to get me out of class today, don't you?"

I look up, mouth hanging open. Yes, I said that. I'd forgotten. The pie-in-the-sky ask.

"I can see you're stunned. I'm fine if you want to give me more postal anecdotes. In fact, I rather like those, but I draw the line at more of that insipid video."

The words on the document blur and bend. It's everything I'd wanted. Everything I'd never hoped to dream.

A legal contract for us to own our apartments.

He'll sign it and send it around to us, and if we sign, it'll be binding. There's probably some percentage of us who need to agree to make it legal, but who of us wouldn't?

Once it's all signed, it's final. He couldn't take it away.

I sink onto the bed, mind spinning. I could have this—*we* could have this—me and my girl squad and everybody else.

"You're a hard audience. Look—this is the best part." He takes it from me and turns to the next part. "Look who's running the place." He shoves it back into my hands.

It's John and Maisey. He somehow found out their last names—I suppose because he's the landlord. He's put them in joint charge as the first presidents of the cooperative board.

I'm holding onto that document so tightly, it's a wonder my fingers haven't pulverized the paper.

He pretends it's about getting out of watching any more of the video, but he's doing it for me, and maybe even a little bit for my neighbors. The detail about John and Maisey gives him away. This is Malcolm, tentatively opening up his heart.

"Malcolm," I whisper.

I can feel his confusion. "What's wrong, country mouse?"

Hopelessly, I shake my head.

"Wow," he says, "you really had your heart set on showing me those videos, didn't you? I'm sorry, I really am, but a man has his limits."

"Don't be funny," I gust out.

"But I thought that was one of my selling points," he says softly. "My darkly acerbic yet strangely compelling wit."

I shake my head.

"You don't like it?" he asks, meaning the contract. "Personally, I think it demonstrates an almost psychotic level of empathy."

I look up to find him smiling, searching my face.

His tone changes, turning serious now. "You know this has to end. This sneaking around, this pretense of coach and student. I know what your profession means to you, and I don't want you to be crossing ethical lines and jeopardizing your career, but this thing between us deserves better, don't you think? Let's see where it goes. You did say that I get to graduate if I promise not to tear the building down. Surely you remember..."

"I remember."

"I had my designer look into an alternate way to do the parking ramp entrance, and he worked it up. And yes, it's not the best in terms of aesthetics, but there is an unexpected convenience factor to re-orienting the ramp. And you know me, just another billionaire who does whatever ridic thing that flies into his head."

Malcolm. I think he has never been more lovable.

All I have to do is to hold my tongue for a day or so, and we'll have what we want. I can just imagine my people's faces when they see these papers. They would be beyond amazed. I can see Mia laughing her head off. *Little Noelle!* Francine would be wide-eyed with shock—*these apartments can be ours? We'd never have to leave?* Jada would be like, *No way!* She'd practically yell it, and that would make it so incredibly fun. Willow would just laugh, loving it. Tabitha would make more hot pink Barbies. Lizzie would bake up a mean batch of cookies shaped like our building.

For a moment I allow myself to enjoy the daydream of it.

But what about Malcolm? I can't do that to Malcolm. My belly twists in a knot.

He kneels in front of me. He takes the papers from my hands. "What's going on, Elle?"

"I'm so sorry, Malcolm. I'm just so sorry. I've let this thing go on way too long."

"What thing? What are you talking about?"

I suck in a deep breath. "I'm not an executive coach."

He does this amused smile-frown. "What?"

"And my name is not Stella or Elle."

He's frowning now. "What are you talking about?"

"My name is Noelle, and I'm a letter carrier," I tell him. "I live at 341 West Forty-fifth Street."

His dark brows draw in, expression mystified. "What?"

"I was going up to talk to you about our building that first day when we met in the lobby, but they wouldn't let me up. So I came back in my letter carrier's uniform, knowing I'd be more likely to get in to see you. I got stuck in the elevator with your real coach. She was hating on her job..." I tell him about our conversation, and how I encouraged her to quit coaching and follow her dreams.

His usually warm brown eyes are cold. His voice is eerie-soft. "And you decided to impersonate her."

"No, I didn't *decide*, it just happened. She gave me her card to stay in touch. Your people made the assumption and—"

"So...this whole thing was always just about the building," he says.

"No, don't say that. It started out that way, yes—"

He drags in a fitful breath. "All this time, it was just you trying to get me to halt the demolition plans."

"You know that's not true," I say. "It's not!"

"All this time," he bites out, words hard as diamonds. He plucks the papers from my hands. Everything about him is different, now. His expression is tormented; his eyes shine with misery. It's like an out-of-body experience, facing him like this.

"Listen, Malcolm, it was real—my feelings for you, all of it —" My words die in the face of his furious anguish. In a small voice, I say, "It was real."

He stalks to the window, looks out over the city, the small sheaf of papers in his fist. His silence cuts deeper than any blade could. I'd prefer thundering rage—anything but this—him back in his angry and desolate ice castle.

Because of me.

"You have to believe me."

He turns around. "Do I? I have to believe you? And why should I?"

"Because I wasn't lying about you—how I feel about you."

Malcolm

"OUT," I point at the door, stunned at the steadiness of my arm. "Out."

She stands there, blinking. Caught out.

The one person who looked at me and saw something more than a villain. Or so I imagined.

"I'm so sorry," she says. "Malcolm..."

She's babbling on, but the whoosh in my ears drowns out her words. Like a fool, I let her in. I thought she saw something good, somebody worth caring about.

I thought she saw somebody worth sticking around for.

Now I want to burn down the world.

"Go," I say.

"Malcolm," she says, wringing her hands.

The longer she stays and pretends to care, the more it hurts. It never was true or real—I just very badly wanted it to be.

"You might want to hurry," I add. "The eviction and demolition timetable seems to have been sped up. The building comes down in three weeks."

"What?" the blood drains from her face. "I thought we had nine or ten..."

"Not anymore," I announce with a calm that I don't feel. I'm raging inside. I'd tear down that building with my bare hands, brick by brick, if I could.

"Please, you can't—"

"Can't what?" I ask. "Oh, dear. Am I displaying a lack of empathy?"

"I get it, you're angry, but we'll all be on the street! This isn't you."

"That's where you're wrong—it's exactly me." Again, I point at the door. "Should we make it two weeks? Or are you going to get out?"

"No, please—" She backs toward the door, begging me with her eyes. She lets herself out. And I'm alone with our crumpled dreams in my fist.

NEWS FLASH: When something's too good to be true, it probably is. This is a lesson I learned early on, but not well enough, apparently.

I'd planned to stay in town a couple more days, working with my legal team and Gerrold's team, but I have to get out. I have to get away from this place.

Not an hour later I'm on my jet, heading back east, just me and the flight crew. They'll have to double back to get everyone else.

So be it.

I gaze out the window as we rise above the cloud line, relieved to put distance between me and the coast.

All I feel is empty, now.

And coldness.

And a little bit of hate.

I hate the rush of excitement I felt whenever she'd walk into a room. I hate the wonder I felt when she turned down a million bucks. I hate that I ever found her refreshing.

I don't hate that I hit my father on her behalf, because any excuse to hit my father is a good one, but I hate myself for how deeply I absorbed her tenderness afterwards. Thinking it was about me.

Like a fool. I hate feeling the fool.

I hate that it's not even a good building. Could it not at least be a grand building? She screwed me for it, after all.

I hate that I'd started to look for hedgehog things, that I even began to like hedgehogs, just because she liked them.

So that's one silver lining—I can go back to hating hedge-hogs. They really are unpleasant, stupid creatures, what with their ridiculous fur, not that you could even call it fur. What was it she said that she loves about them? Their optimism? They have *quills*, for crissake, always at the ready, prepared at any moment to prick people. Not exactly a sign of optimism.

I hate that John and Maisey might have been in on it. I find that I very much hate that idea. Was any of it even real? John's flowers in those coffee cans, were those just props? Their stupid bike rack meetings? The bullshit with the dryer-lint bandit?

I hate that I had my architects redesign the building and the whole complex in a completely substandard way, and that when it was finished, instead of being disgusted with myself, I felt happy about it, imagining those ridiculous people being happy about it.

I hate how much I loved her shy bravery. Her steadfastness. Her passion. Her loyalty. Her sense of humor.

I hate that she made me feel like I was more than what I thought. Like *we* were more. Like I wasn't alone.

I hate that she made me happy.

I'm back in my office the next day, handling all the things I should have been paying attention to while I was dealing with the Germantown Group and wasting time with Elle—or whatever her name is.

Walt strolls in at around three, fresh off the plane. He's got packets and schedules. He's been coordinating with the city guys. I ask him how the flight went, and he seems surprised by the question. It isn't the kind of question I typically ask, and being that I'm in the habit of not lying to myself, I'm fully aware that I want to know if she was on the plane.

"Good," he says. "Very smooth."

It's rather maddening that he doesn't simply tell me, so I follow up my question with another seemingly casual query as to whether everybody made the flight, jokingly asking if we'd left anybody behind.

I finally get the information that I want—it seems Elle—or rather, Noelle, "Made her own way home."

"Made her own way home?" I ask.

He shrugs; apparently that is the extent of his knowledge. So she didn't take the company jet. As if that would make up for things.

I waste additional time imagining her doing standby, floating around the airport like a ghost, dreaming of almond croissants. Because if there's one thing I know about her, it's that she doesn't think ahead when it comes to food, constantly showing up places hungry. I once saw her eat a piece of fruit out of the lobby fruit bowl. What the hell was she spending her per diem on all the time we were there? That I'd like to know.

My PR team comes in. They're excited about these new developments. The boss of the group, a woman by the name of

Wynn, is especially thrilled with the ambitious employee retention and retraining program.

"People retrain work forces all the time," I grumble. "It's not that much of a coup."

"But *you* never do that," she says. "It's unexpectedly positive. The unexpected is always newsworthy, and accelerating a positive spin on a positive story is far easier than putting a positive spin on something outlandishly negative."

I smile, and she gets this worried look on her face. "Not that you always have outlandishly negative things to spin."

Just before the end of the business day, I get notice from Corman's lawyers' office that Bexley Partners has marked my training requirement as satisfactorily completed.

29

Noelle

I RETURN home to discover that news of the accelerated eviction timeline landed well before my standby flight touched down at Kennedy.

"What happened?" Francine asks the second I walk in the door. "They took away our ninety-day move-out window. We have less than a month!"

"I am so sorry," I say, dropping my bags. "He found out. Everything."

"Oh my god. Was he angry? Are you in trouble?"

I wrap my arms around my middle, feeling utterly exhausted. *Trouble* isn't the word. *Crushed* might be more like it. *Destroyed. Guilty.* What have I done?

"Honey!" She comes to me and wraps me in a hug. Being that I have my arms around myself, it's more like she's hugging a mummy or maybe a large cocoon. "Whatever it is, we're all in on this together," she says, though that's not true anymore. We're getting dispersed like milkweed seeds in a tornado.

I mumble a mummified thanks.

"How did he find out?" she asks, letting me go.

I wince. "I had to tell him."

"Oh, no," she says. "What happened?"

"Well, you know, it was going really well."

"You were getting him to watch that footage and everything," she says.

"It was so beyond that." I give her the whole story. The thrill of our sessions. The magic of our secret relationship. The sense of getting to know him, like finding a counterpart out in the world. Of falling for him so hard, my head spun.

She blinks, stunned. "Sooooo...it wasn't a fling. You were in a whole actual relationship with him."

I nod.

"He seems so, opposite of you."

"Not in the important ways." I sink down to the couch, exhausted. "For this little window of time, this span of a few weeks, Malcolm and I were in tune with each other in a way I never knew. You just can't believe how we clicked. I know that's a surprise, considering who he is, but I got to see this side of him that nobody else sees. And I loved that side of him. I loved all the sides of him."

"But, Noelle—he's throwing us onto the street," she says.

"I know."

"So...maybe you're better off without him?" she says. "As in, good riddance?"

"You don't know how bad I hurt him. I should have told him the truth as soon as things started happening, but I didn't. I slept with him and got close to him. I let him fall for me while I was lying to him. The thing is, this is a man who doesn't open up to people—not ever. He doesn't need anybody. He doesn't let anybody in. Except me. And now he thinks I was lying the whole time. Which I was."

"But you told him in the end."

"Too late."

Softly, she says, "People make mistakes. You have a good heart, Noelle—if he knew you at all, he'd know that."

I shake my head, picturing the misery on his face. The desolation in his gaze.

"You went out there and you tried so hard to save our building," she continues. "You went out on such a limb for the people you love..."

"And I got us all evicted sooner. So..."

"I'm so sorry." She disappears into the kitchen. I hear our candy drawer open. She comes back with a full bar of chocolate almond toffee.

"Thanks," I say, ripping it open, though I can't imagine how I could eat.

"We're proud of you," she says, sinking down onto the couch next to me. "I mean, you had the papers in your hands. Oh my god, can you imagine? Rent-to-own condos and not being kicked out ever? But you were right to tell him. None of us could really be a hundred percent behind getting the building in a deceptive way. Even from Malcolm Blackberg."

I break off a piece and give it to her. She takes a bite. "Yum."

"Francine, I know you're still imagining it," I whisper. "Rent-to-own condos and not being kicked out ever."

"I am. But still, you couldn't."

"Yeah, I couldn't," I say. "That and five bucks will get me a shitty frappuccino, huh?"

Francine snorts softly. "Still, to throw us on the street to punish you? I mean, even John and Maisey? Who does that?"

"Malcolm," I say. "When you rip out his heart."

30

Malcolm

ONE OF THE biggest mistakes I see out in the business world
is people not having the stomach to do a thorough post-mortem
when something goes wrong. I'll be the first to admit that it's not
easy to look a failure square in the eye, but it really is necessary
if you're ever going to get anywhere.

Elle, of course, is a spectacular failure, a situation where I
didn't see something that was right in front of my nose.

This is the reason that I give myself when I ferret out her
mail delivery route. I need to understand this whole thing, right?

It is the reason I give myself for deciding to do my work at a
window table in a café on one of the streets her route takes her
through. I take calls and type memos, keeping my gaze vaguely
on the scene in front of me. After three hours of sitting there, I
finally catch sight of her walking along in her blue uniform and
summer shorts.

I can't tell her mood from her stride—I don't know why I
thought I would.

She stops to talk to a shopkeeper, talking and smiling and backing up, trying to keep the conversation short while trying to be so polite. Comfortable in a uniform.

I think about the butterfly tie. I never did get to pull it loose. Probably for the best.

I thought that we had time. I imagined that once she wasn't my coach anymore, we could officially date. I imagined finding a place to set down my chopper near her home in Jersey—that's how we'd have shortened the distance at first, until I prevailed upon her to move into the city. But what do you know? She's already living here—at 341 West 45th.

Is this kind of post-mortem helpful to me? No.

Yet somehow I keep on.

A thorough post mortem is the excuse that I give myself when I order my accountant to send me a fully detailed itemization of her per diem. What was she spending her money on? The accountant I talk to tells me he'll get the message to the per diem accountant. Apparently my corporation employs one accountant who deals exclusively with per diems.

There's no real reason for it but my car naturally goes past her place when I'm en route to certain destinations—my driver has a whole rubric of shortcuts that sometimes involve 45th Street. I make a point to neither stop nor encourage his driving past her place.

But when he does drive past her place, it's only natural that I look at it. Though I have to admit that I find it a bit maddening that I don't know specifically which window is hers. I'm already looking at her building, why prevent myself from knowing this last detail?

So I have somebody on my real estate team bird-dog that information—apartment number and window location.

It turns out that knowing which set of windows belongs to her and her roommate, Francine, is not in any way helpful. In fact it only leads to more questions. When the windows are dark, I wonder if they've moved out, or are they just out for the night? And if so, what are they getting up to?

When the windows are lit up, I wonder if it's her alone up there, and what exactly is she doing? Is she with some guy? Showing him hedgehog things?

Now and then I see people out front with boxes. I suppose it's only natural; last week they thought they had ninety days to vacate the premises; now they have less than a month. No doubt my acceleration of the timetable has them scrambling, putting down deposits on whatever shitty flophouses they can find.

I try not to think too hard about that. Or to wonder where John and Maisey might end up.

Elle—or rather, Noelle—begged me not to punish the rest of the people in her building, and it's exactly what I did.

In my initial rage I assumed they were all in on making this stupid film for me, and I hated the idea of it, but upon rewatching the few videos that I'd had to download on my machine, it's clear that these people aren't acting, that they're regular people in a documentary most likely created to commemorate their stupid little building.

Were they angry with Noelle when they learned that she had that contract for saving their homes in her hands? That they would've been home free but for her fit of conscience?

One evening, sitting alone in my penthouse in front of the spread my chef has left me with, I start entertaining the idea of restoring their ninety days. Moving up the demolition date was a rash, overly emotional decision; the project doesn't need to kick off that quickly.

I decide I'll do just that in the morning, first thing when I get to the office. It feels like the right decision, and I eat with a kind of gusto I haven't felt for a long time. It's not just for John and Maisey—there are those first-floor twin boys who love their school. Mia, the cat suit one. Antonio.

I wake up some hours later and think about sparing the entire building. Just keep it as a rental property, if nothing else. The idea gets my heart pounding dangerously hard. I'm imagining the relief and happiness that they would all feel. The relief and happiness that Noelle would feel.

My delusions of saviordom fizzle out the next day in my office when I open up my inbox to find an email from my accounting team, getting back to me on Noelle's per diem itemization. It turns out that she was using the $150 daily stipend to buy Amazon gift cards and sending them to a man named Allen Junior who lives in New Jersey.

My blood boils at this news. I can barely see straight, barely think straight. She was taking the money that my firm was providing her for her daily living expenses and sending it to some guy?

I grit my teeth. Is this her boyfriend, then? From his picture he's quite the looker. Was he in on the whole thing? Questions spin wildly through my mind. I can't do my work with all of these angry questions, so I get my private investigator on the phone and set him on Allen Junior, because I just need to know.

31

Noelle

I REPEAT my story up and down the hall. My friends are supportive of my decision to tell him the truth, even though... ouch! And also there's the stunning revelation of my fling with the big bad Malcolm Blackberg. How could I be with somebody like that? People are angry at Malcolm, and though they don't say it, a few of the people I don't know as well are frustrated with me.

Maisey, the person who might just have the most to lose, turns out to be the most understanding.

I'm telling her about what happened, explaining in my usual way which amounts to me saying that I couldn't do that to him. I'm practically begging her to forgive me, when she stops me cold. "A building is just a collection of bricks," she says. "It would've been wrong to keep the building through deceit. You have to look at yourself in the mirror. We all have to look ourselves in the mirror each day."

"It's not really even like him to kick us all out," I say. "I saw his beautiful heart. And then I whack-a-moled it right back into its hiding place."

"You still believe in him," she observes.

"I suppose I do," I say.

"Does he know?" she asks.

"It doesn't matter," I say. "You didn't see the devastation in his eyes. He's not a man who lets people in. But he let me in, and I hurt him."

She nods. Later on, there's a baggie of caramel corn tied to our doorknob.

Sometimes I sit around crying. I'm sad about the building, yes. But really, it's Malcolm. The whole world felt better when I was with Malcolm.

Francine and I spend the week packing everything up—quietly, not even playing music. Usually we would have something fun on, but not now.

When I'm not packing or desperately scanning rental listings, I'm back on my route. It's never been more comforting to be a letter carrier than now, because it's a task I can perfectly and fully achieve. Every envelope and package in its right place. No room for error. No room for destroying others or being destroyed.

32

Malcolm

IT DOESN'T TAKE long to find Allen Junior, aka AJ.

Three days later, he's in my office. It's not that my guy forced him to come up, but he makes it clear what a dim view I take of employee embezzlement, and how, if I were to become annoyed, I could bring charges against accomplices. But for now I simply want to talk, and he assures Allen Junior that it would be in his best interests to indulge me.

I could bring charges of all kinds, but I'm kicking her out of her home early and that's more than enough. Far too much, but I can't keep thinking like that. I can't keep waking up in the middle of the night thinking about that.

I need to see what kind of person Noelle would send money to, that's all.

I need to see what kind of man she is so infatuated with that she would go without food—literally go hungry—so that she could send him gift cards. Maybe it's masochistic, but I just need to see, and as we've already established, I'm a billionaire who satisfies every ridic whim that flies into his head.

Allen Junior has perfectly blow-dried hair that forms a kind of a helmet around his pretty-boy face, and he wears several woven bracelets. He's trying to pass the blame off onto Noelle before he's even sitting down.

"I didn't know, man," he repeats. "I didn't have anything to do with her whole stupid scheme. None of it was even my idea."

"But you were working together, were you not?" I say.

"We weren't working together at all," he insists.

"You are a boyfriend she's sending money to," I say. "I think that qualifies as working together."

"I'm not her boyfriend—I never even met her!"

I stroll around my desk and over to his chair. I grab the arms and lean down, get right into his face. He's denying knowing her? Noelle prizes bravery and loyalty—how could she be with such a coward?

"Lie to me again," I say, "and you won't like the result."

"I'm not lying!" he exclaims. "Why are you mad at *me*? She's the one who was committing fraud all over your ass. She's the one that took my girlfriend's place. In fact, I am as much a victim as you are. She was impersonating my *girlfriend*. She's a complete scam artist. And then when I found out, and informed her that I didn't think it was cool, she offered to buy my silence. I was like, seriously? But she wouldn't take no for an answer."

I stand. "She offered to buy you off?"

"I confronted her on her deception when I found out about it, and she said, 'look, this rich guy is paying me a sweet per diem—I'm going to turn it into gift cards for you.'" He shrugs. "I honestly didn't even know it was illegal."

I stand, pulse racing. I take a few paces, thinking. This doesn't sound like Noelle.

True, she was passing herself off as something she's not, but other than that, she was honest, conscientious. I think of her in those meetings, salivating over the pastry tray. Not wanting to take more than her due.

Paying somebody off with gift cards? Not Noelle's style.

But this guy?

I give him a hard look. "Keeping in mind that I had a private investigator on you, I'd like you to answer that question again, and this time truthfully."

"I *am* being truthful." He pops right up out of his chair, as if he's outraged at the very thought. But his denial is thin. Weak. I've been in enough business negotiations to know a weak denial when I hear one.

"Come on, *she* thought it up?" I ask.

The look on his face tells me I'm on the right track.

"Look, I just want to know," I continue in a friendlier tone. "Be honest with me about what happened, and we can part ways. Lie to me, and I *will* press charges. Now, which one of you came up with the idea that she should be handing over her stipend in exchange for your silence?"

He takes a few beats too long to think about it; that alone tells me what I need to know.

"Well, maybe it was my idea," he says. "But she was the one pulling the scam on you, and I had nothing to do with it."

"So you figured it out," I say.

"Purely by accident."

I nod. And he calls her. Blackmails her. Noelle is such a Girl Scout, she was probably scared to death of this guy. My accountant had said she used only little bits of her per diem at first, far less than any of the rest of the team; some days she used none of it, and then suddenly she was sending him gift cards. The timing makes sense now. She was trying not to take too much at first, and then this one blackmailed her. Scared her enough that she gave him all of her lunch money.

Something dangerous stirs in my gut.

"And what was she to live on?" I ask. "Did you inquire as to whether she had any money for food? Did it ever occur to you that she might've spent every penny she had on a sick relative or something, and that the per diem was all she had to live on? Did it occur to you that she might be going hungry because of you?"

"Maybe she should've thought about that before deciding to pull a scam," he says with a sniff. "Maybe the little bitch'll think twice next time she decides to—"

My fist finds his jaw before his sentence is out. He staggers briefly, then comes at me with a roar. He's about my size, but I'm a lot angrier. I block his blow and shove him off.

He wants to come at me again. "Do it," I taunt. "I'll give you a free one." I drop my hands. "Go ahead." I want to hit him some more—I just do. It's wrong but I can't stop thinking about Noelle, staring at that pastry tray. Eating hotel fruit-bowl fruit. And this jackass making her give him the per diem. Squeezing my girl for her lunch money.

I want to do some damage. And I think he knows that I could.

"What the hell? I told you the truth," he whines.

"She didn't have anything to eat, asshole," I say. "And if you give me or her any more trouble, I am going to haul your ass to jail so fast you won't know which way is up."

My security guy comes in. "Need any help?"

"Get him out," I say.

The irony of my behavior doesn't escape me. I'm the one tossing her out onto the street. AJ only made her miss a few meals.

33

Noelle

NEW YORK IS A MASSIVE CITY. Manhattan itself
—massive.

Even so, I feel him out there. I'm sure Malcolm doesn't live
anywhere near where we live, but still.

Sometimes when I'm looking out my window at the scroll of
street traffic, I feel sure that he's down there.

His limo looks like anybody else's limo, but still I sometimes
think that I see his. Maybe it's stupid, but we spent those weeks
together and I feel so connected to him. It was more than getting
to know each other; he brought out a new side of me; a side of
me that I don't show other people. A side of me that I don't even
show myself. Me as a woman who says real things and asks for
what she wants. A woman who has the affection of the most
amazing guy in the world.

Meanwhile, my friends and I are freaking out. We don't
know where we're going to go. All the good places are snapped
up; who can get a decent apartment in less than thirty days?

John's moving in with relatives. Maisey has a sister upstate. Antonio is talking about taking a room in a house of guys that he's not a huge fan of, but beggars can't be choosers.

Francine and I take the train out to Queens to investigate a large Airbnb rental for some of us who haven't found places yet.

We walk around it and decide that the picture on the website made it look 30% nicer than it is in real life—that's the way we'll put it to Jada and the others. We decide that the neighborhood is probably good enough as long as there is no nighttime walking, which sucks—in our Hell's Kitchen neighborhood, we know everybody, and you can walk any time of night and feel safe because there's always a whole lot of people out and about. Even at three in the morning, there are cars and people right there. Everything is lit up.

But on the upside, the Queens place has room enough for six of us; it'll make a decent temporary place while we hunt for apartments.

Francine and I stop in at their little neighborhood coffee shop and try out their frappuccinos, which are a little bit better than the corner deli ones in our neighborhood. We agree that that's an upside.

We pick out a nice window table and admire the excellent table availability factor as compared to Manhattan coffee shops, where you have to show up at six to get a table, and table-less people are always hovering around like vultures. It's disconcerting when you're trying to read or have a conversation.

I wander over to the pastry case up at the checkout counter. I've been meaning not to do this, promising myself not to do it, but here I am, doing it. I spot two of the biggest almond croissants and ask for them to be put on plates. I pay and bring them back to our table, setting one in front of Francine.

"That works," she says.

I take my seat as she bites in.

"Yum," she says. "An hour extra of dance practice? Worth it."

I pick up the croissant from my own plate. I rip off the end of it and put it in my mouth. It's not as delicious as the ones in San Francisco. Nothing is as delicious as it was in San Francisco.

"And I spy another upside..." Francine says, pointing out a couple of hot guys up at the barista bar behind me.

I twist around like I'm looking at the menu. "Sigh," I say.

She holds up her phone. "Lemme get this for Jada and the gang. Highlights of the neighborhood. Lean to the right and smile."

I lean to the right and make a lemon face.

"Hellz yah." She sets down her phone. "The blue-shirt one seemed like he was looking at you."

"Not interested," I say. The idea of being with a man who's not Malcolm makes me feel ill.

"It might be good to get back out there," she says. "Get back on the horse that threw you." I'm just shaking my head. Francine glares at me. "Noelle, the man is a jerk. You deserve better."

"You wouldn't say that if you knew," I say.

"I can't believe you still believe in him. You're loyal. I love that about you." She licks a smidge of almond paste off her fingers. "But not everyone deserves your loyalty."

"He's punishing all of you for what I did, I get it. He's tearing down our building when he has a perfectly viable alternative," I say. "But if you'd been there...yes, I was deceiving him, but at the same time, I was more honest with him than I've ever been with anybody, and I think that went both ways. Maybe that's not an excuse. All I know is, I can't stop thinking about him, wanting to make it right. How messed up is that?"

"Messed up doesn't matter to the heart," she says.

I snort. "You totally have to put that on a motivational poster." I raise my hands, making a little frame, like that's the poster. "Messed up doesn't matter to the heart," I say.

Francine jabs the air with her spoon. "I would definitely wear a shirt with that saying."

"If he was walking through that door right now? The first thing I'd feel is happy. Just pure freaking happiness. Even imagining it right now, I want it to happen. I want to see him again." I shake my head.

Francine smiles wistfully. "It's a saying for a reason, you know."

I tear at the flaky pastry.

34

Malcolm

I'M BACK on the West Coast the next week, managing the takeover and absorption of the Germantown Group into my operation while overseeing my New York office and a number of other projects.

My PR people want me to do interviews about this takeover and retraining program. Hell no.

I offered training to displaced workers; I didn't get a lobotomy. I still don't like talking to people. I really don't like people thanking me for things. People who thank me for things —I just want them out of my face.

During one of those trips out to San Francisco, I get a very bewildering lunch invitation from none other than my father. I'm wary, considering we hate each other. But curiosity gets the better of me, and I go.

Dad is in a mood like I've never seen. He tells me that he's been going to AA meetings, and he wants to apologize to me. I don't know what I like less—people thanking me for things or the idea of my dad apologizing after all these years. It's so much easier to hate him.

Hate is always easier.

I lean back and cross my legs, stir my coffee drink, contemplate walking out, not letting him have the satisfaction of even apologizing to me. I don't want to give him anything.

But for whatever perverse reason, I decide to hear him out.

He tells me that he stopped drinking after our fight at the Monaco Club. Does he want an award?

"I want to make amends to you for letting you think you had any part of Genevieve—your mother—leaving," he says.

I don't want to talk about my mother. I never want to talk about her. "And this matters why?" I snap.

"I need you to know—*I* pushed her away," he says. "*I* was the bad guy. I told you she didn't want us, that we were too much for her to handle, but it had nothing to do with you—it never did."

I act unfazed. I've learned never to give my dad anything, any edge, but I can barely believe my ears. This guy, apologizing to me? Claiming full responsibility for driving my mother away?

The central story of our family was that she wanted to get away from the pair of us. That Dad and I were two awful peas in a pod. The story is a part of me, like a tree, growing around a wire, absorbing it in.

"I made you share the blame," he continues. "I made you an equal bad guy because I couldn't handle it. And you took that to heart, and you had that personality change when she left, became sullen and angry. Anyone in your position would have felt like that, having the two of us for parents. A better father would have told you that she loved you."

"We both know that would've been a lie," I say. She never tried to contact me—no cards, no calls. Not to mention an apology.

"She had her own problems, her own issues, but I was a bully to her. A monster—not physically, but..." He shakes his head.

I look away. As if that excuses her. It makes it worse that she left me with him.

"And I made a ten-year-old boy share the blame, like we were a pair of assholes she couldn't deal with anymore. But you were a good kid before all that—you should know that. I always thought it was weird that you didn't remember, but I'm telling you now—you were an outgoing boy, a generous friend to Howie, a good boy to your mother, and I was one shitty-ass husband."

I suppose this is the place where I say a weight lifted from my chest, but I just feel numb. I'm not in a mood to forgive either of them. "So what is it you want from me?" I bite out.

"Nothing. I'm not one of those losers who think making amends means everything's okay. It won't make me less of an asshole or change what a bastard I was to you that whole time, but I thought you'd want to know. I thought it might be useful."

I look him hard in the eye. I have no words. I throw down some money. I get out of there and walk.

The afternoon is foggy and cool, the streets filled with people rushing back and forth. Loud music blares from a passing car.

All this time. Does it matter? I don't want it to matter.

I walk and walk, as if that might allow me to put it all behind me. The utter anger that I have at this man and a mother who left without looking back. At life.

I took his bullshit at face value. I blamed myself. An asshole from a long line of assholes. Maybe I should feel different now, but I don't. What do I care? Things turned out fine.

Still.

The time that I spent with Noelle showed me that I'm

missing something, that there's some essential way in which I haven't joined the human, world—the whole experience of togetherness and sharing and having each other's backs and all of that. And the darkest thing that's rattling around in my mind is the question--what if I never can have that? What if I'm broken beyond repair?

It's here that I wish I could call her.

I'd tell her everything he said. I'd tell her my fears. She'd rise to my defense and fight for me. She'd find examples that I might not have thought of. She'd fight for my heart. She'd be on my side.

It's too late for that, now.

35

Noelle

THE LOBBY of our building was glamorous way back when. Nowadays you might describe it as faded glamour; possibly even seriously wrecked glamour or maybe glamour after a seventy-year bender.

But we love it all the same.

There are these amazing pink-and-rose-colored marble tiles lining the lower part of the walls; above it is cracked vintage plaster, soaring up to extravagant crown molding, and of course, the lovely chandelier.

But at the moment it's the rose tiles that we're focusing on, or more, the tiles that Vicky is focusing on. With a crowbar.

It's sleeting out, fitting weather for our sad project. I've taken the day off—I won't have too many more days with these women.

I wince as Vicky shoves the metal thing behind one of them, grunting, trying to pry it free.

Ancient plaster cracks.

The pink tile pops off the wall and lands on the floor, and Vicky lands on her ass right next to it. Smuckers barks wildly.

"Are you sure we can't help you?" Lizzie asks. "We could all get crowbars!"

"I'd be happy to do it," Antonio says. "I could do it with one hand."

"No, I don't want these tiles getting cracked. I got this." She holds the tile up like a trophy. It's small—maybe a foot by a foot. "Francine, tile number one."

Vicky has an ambitious plan to turn the tiles into serving trays for each of us so that we have a beautiful piece of the building to keep with us always. We each got to choose two tiles —there are Post-it notes with our names all over the walls.

Two marble tiles will form the base of each tray, with silver metal edging all around. The trays could be used probably for a lot of things, but considering this group, they'll be cheese-serving trays.

Francine goes over and grabs it and holds it to her chest. "Pink tile, you have seen a lot of me coming and going around here. Some of it quite triumphant, coming in after yet another amazing freaking dance rehearsal, though there have definitely been times of me stumbling in at three in the morning with a questionable bag of food or possibly an even more questionable dude. But most of all you've seen me coming in and out of here with my absolute best friends in the world, and the absolute best neighbors any girl could ever have."

"Francine, god!" Mia says, holding a prosecco bottle by the neck. "Motherfucker! I don't know if I can handle any more of these tearful goodbye things. I'm gonna cry for the next five hours!" She splashes some more of the bright, bubbly liquid into her cup.

"That's more than enough day drinking for you!" Jada grabs the bottle from Mia and pours the rest of it into her own cup.

"Also, I need more. I have a bad feeling that this is going to be an extremely tearful goodbye thing." She narrows her eyes at Vicky.

"What?" Vicky protests. "So you can make a tearful goodbye movie, and I can't do a tearful goodbye cheese tray project?" She starts crowbarring yet another tile off the wall. "Screw that."

"I didn't say you couldn't make tearful goodbye cheese trays," Jada says. "Your tearful goodbye cheese trays are going to be amazing. It's just that they're tearful."

Maisey writes Francine's name on the underside of the tile. She hands it to Lizzy, who puts it in a cardboard box.

It's afternoon, but the sky is dark as midnight. Horns bellow from the street. Sleet ticks at the door.

Vicky is still going at the second Francine tile—it's a really pretty one where the lines in the marble look like a vajayjay.

"You girls are free to make all of the tearful goodbye things you please," John says in his rumbly voice. "I think it's very important to commemorate..." He waves a hand around in the air, indicating the building, indicating more than words can say, and then he looks over at Maisey, and my heart lurches.

John chose two of the most worn tiles next to the elevator frame. I think he likes the story they tell, the way they show that humans lived in this place together. Waited for elevators together. Now they'll be cheese trays.

Vicky's artisan friend, Latrisha, who once created an elaborate throne for Smuckers—long story—designed the serving trays. They're going to be so cool, but it would be way cooler if the tiles were staying put on the wall and we were staying put in our homes.

Eventually, all of our tiles are in boxes. The wall looks like a sad checkerboard. I go over to Vicky. "Do you really think you can make all of our cheese platters sometime this decade?"

"Maybe?" Vicky says dolefully.

"No more crying," Jada says from where she's lying on the floor, crying.

I sit on the floor next to Francine, whose black ballerina bun is halfway down. I look around at my friends, this family that we've created. "What have I done?" I ask.

"No more of that," she says.

"We could have kept our homes, but I chose him," I say. "And he won't even see it."

"Well..."

"Don't say it," I say, meaning her messed up love saying.

"I wasn't gonna," she says. And then, "If you could do it all over again, would you still come clean with him?"

"Yeah," I say. "He deserved to know. Kicking us out like this, it's not who he is deep down. He's a good person with a beautiful heart."

"Oh, come on, just say it, Noelle." She turns to me. "You loved him a little bit."

I stare down at my hands, pink polish starting to chip. "No," I say. "I loved him a lot. I loved that man a whole freaking lot."

Francine sighs and lays her head on my shoulder. "And now it's too late."

"Yeah," I say. "If only he could see the truth of it all." Then, "Wait, what?" I sit up, dislodging Francine's head.

"Hey," she says.

"Screw that," I say.

"What?" she says.

I stand. Everybody's looking at me now. "I have to go," I say. "I have a message to deliver. A truth bomb. To Malcolm Blackberg."

"But the weather. It's sleeting, out there," Jada says.

"Severe storm warning," John says.

"You'll never get an Uber in this mess," Francine says.

"People!" I put up my hands. "Think who you're talking to." I run up and grab my raincoat and the rain visor I sometimes use on my route. I head down and make Francine give me her bike keys.

I ride, flying past snarled traffic, sleet and rain pelting my cheeks. I know the exact route to take. This is my town.

I get there in no time and lock up.

Blackberg, Inc.'s fortress isn't so daunting this time around. I push in the doors, head around the black marble boulder, and march right up to the executive elevator. A pair of people regard me with suspicion. Maybe it's because I'm sopping wet. I don't care.

"You need a lanyard for this elevator," the man says.

"Like this," the woman says, showing me her own lanyard. But they've already used theirs to call the elevator, so I don't really need one.

"I'm going up there without one," I inform them both.

The man looks over at the security guard, who seems distracted. He could alert him, but he doesn't. He's responding to the conviction in my voice, I think.

When the elevator door opens, I stroll right in, like I own the place. I stab the button for the sixth floor. "Floor?" I ask them.

"Fifth," the man says, all scowly.

"Same," the woman says, joining him.

I hit five. The elevator begins to move. We ride in awkward silence.

"You need a lanyard," the guy says.

I ignore him.

Lawrence is at the front desk when I get off. He straightens when he sees me, looking pleasantly surprised. "Elle," he says. "Umm... Hi!" It's pretty obvious that he knows my secret—I wasn't a real coach. "Didn't think I'd see you here."

"I know, right?" I say. "Is he back there?"

"Well, yeah..." Lawrence says.

And suddenly Janice is there. Janice from the second floor. "You're not going back there," she says.

"I am," I say. "I have to." I head around, marching right back there.

She follows behind. "This is trespassing."

I burst through one door, and then another. She's telling me to stop. Which I do when I get to his closed door. I knock. "Malcolm," I call out.

She has her phone out. "I'm calling security."

There's this silence where I think he might ignore me. I imagine security throwing me out into the driving rain before I can get to him.

But then the door is open and he's standing there, hair unruly, gaze intense.

"I alerted security," Janice says.

"Un-alert them," Malcolm says. "It's okay, I've got this." He waves me in, and I enter the cool, gray world of his office.

I hear the door shut behind me.

I turn, and there he is, leaning back against the doors.

It feels so good to see him—just good, deep down in my heart, though keeping my distance from him is painful. I hate that I can't go to him, hate that I can't press a hand to his cheek, press my lips to his.

"I know you're probably still angry," I say. "I know what I did was wrong. I was so stupid, Malcolm. I know I should have told you when things changed between us. But I want you to understand a few things, right here and now—"

"Like what? That you'd always dreamed of a place like that building?" he says.

"Well, yeah—"

"And you were home free?" he says, closing the distance

between us. "And you could have taken those contracts and signed them? And it all would have been yours, but you gave that up?"

"Umm..." I say, pulse racing.

"Were you going to tell me that you gave up what you most wanted in order to try and make things right with me? Because that's what I've been sitting here realizing."

"Malcolm—"

My heart pounds as he reaches up and brushes a bit of still-damp hair back behind my ear. "It took a few days of calming down for me to see what was in front of my face. More than a few days, actually. The eviction is rescinded as of today—I need you to know. Not only that, but I sent a courier over—I doubt they've gotten there yet. Traffic out there is snarled. Nobody's getting anywhere."

"A courier?"

"There were papers involved—signed papers. Hold on—I have copies."

"Signed papers?" I breathe.

He grabs a sheaf of papers from his desk and presses them into my hands.

"What is this?"

"You know what."

The condo documents. "Why?" I ask.

"This is what I want for you. No strings attached," he adds. "This is legal as soon as it gets signed. My signature is already on the set that I sent over. Legal. Un-take-backable."

36

Malcolm

HER EYES LOOK as big as saucers. She says, "I don't know what to say."

"No words needed. Just signatures."

She studies my eyes. There's a new confidence in her—a sense of strength that I can't quite put my finger on. "You sent a set of these papers over with a courier?"

"I know you came over to tell me something, but hear me out," I say. "I reacted like a madman. I'm sorry."

"You were hurt," she says. "I lied. You trusted me and I broke that trust in the worst way. I pride myself on honesty—"

"Well, I didn't listen when you tried to apologize. I didn't let you explain."

"Well, I pretended I was your coach," she says.

"Well, I threw you all out on the street—"

"Well, I—"

I go to her, press a finger to her lips. "You think you can one-up me on throwing you out on the street?" I ask.

She grabs my wrist, pulls my hand away. "Well, I fell in love with you," she says.

"What?"

"It's what I came over to tell you if you'd let me get a word in edgewise," she says.

My pulse rages in my ears. "That you love me?"

"Yes," she says defiantly, keeping hold of my wrist.

"Say it again."

"I love you," she repeats.

I swallow back the dryness in my mouth. I never imagined anybody saying that to me—not ever. I never imagined myself wanting to say it *to* anybody. Those three words belong to other people—not me. Not ever me. But I take her hands, gaze into her eyes. "I love you, too," I say.

"You do?"

"I do. I love you. I know—stunning, huh? I'm the guy who stalks around alone, hating everybody. But you make me want to be part of the world of people doing all the stupid stuff together, like skating at Rockefeller Center and having jokey theme songs and choosing favorite animals. I know that probably doesn't seem very huge to you, but I never wanted that before. I can't promise my favorite animal would be a hedgehog, of course."

"Oh my god, Malcolm," she says, blinking away the tears.

"No, listen, here's the thing—I can't promise that I'll stop being a villain altogether, but I'll always be your villain. What do you think?"

"I'd be honored...for you to be my villain."

"I don't know what to say now," I confess. "I'm not used to this much sweetness. It might be too much sweetness right now."

"Poor baby," she whispers, beaming at me.

"Maybe this is a good time to let you know that I punched AJ this week. Several times."

"Wait, what?" Her lips part in shock. "You punched AJ?"

"It felt good."

"I don't understand..."

"I followed the money and I tracked him down. He tried to tell me that the gift card scam was your idea, but I could see clear as day how it worked."

"You punched him."

I lean in. "Nobody steals my girl's lunch money."

Noelle squeezes my hands, and it's everything. "I can't believe you punched him," she says.

"Not that I plan to make a habit of punching people—"

She puts on her witchy face, and it does something to my body—to my whole freaking soul. She says, "Empathy skills definitely not in evidence." Then she leans in to kiss me. I haul her body to mine and kiss her for everything I'm worth.

I can feel her smile through the kiss. A million different plans for us spin through my mind. The way we can spend this night. The way we can spend the weekend. Things we can do. "Let's get out of here," I rumble.

"Wait, what about my peeps? We have to tell them before they tear apart any more stuff."

"What do you mean, tear apart?" I ask.

"Do you have your car? Is it near?"

I pull out my phone and text my driver. Five minutes later we're in the back seat of my car. Rain pelts the roof and creates rivulets in the windows, lit bright with the kaleidoscopic colors of Fifth Avenue.

"So, holiday celebrations and theme songs are stupid?"

I pull her into my lap and kiss her. And we're stuck in traffic talking about everything.

I tell her what happened with my dad. I update her on Germantown. She catches me up on her life back at work and a strange project that involves tiles and cheese trays. She fills me in on gossip about the building, including Maisey and John. People in the building have been playing cupid—a bit too much, according to her. "But they have time now," she says.

Eventually we're there. The lobby looks like somebody took a sledgehammer to it. People are gathered around some sort of desk, some sitting on boxes. From the looks on everyone's faces, they'd like to take a sledgehammer to me.

Clearly the courier isn't there yet.

"You guys! I want you to meet Malcolm," Noelle says. "And before you say anything, there's no more eviction. In fact..." She waves the papers. "We're going condo!"

Her friends gather all around us. People are wary, but if there's one thing I know how to handle, it's wary people. I walk them through the papers.

"Whoa!" Mia says. "This is amazing."

Kelsey is the first to grab and inspect the documents. I know all of their names at this point, except for the drunken woman with short blonde hair, who I suspect was the cameraperson.

Maisey comes up to properly introduce herself. "We sincerely appreciate this."

"I'm sorry for what I put you all through," I say.

"We'll be fine," she says.

"How do we know you won't change your mind again?" John rumbles, coming up next to Maisey. In person, he's everything that I thought he would be.

"Once you sign it, it's binding—a binding contract. I can't change my mind again. And I've already signed it, so the ball's in your court."

Francine, the dancer, reads over somebody's shoulders. "These are generous terms," she says. "Thank you."

"We'll need to have a lawyer look at it," Antonio says.

"I'd suggest it," I say. All they have to do is stay there and pay their rent a few months more, and they own it. But they have options to get out of it, too. It is very generous.

Somebody shoves a plastic cup of champagne into my hand. A little dog in a bow tie comes up and barks at me, and everybody seems eager for me to pet him, so I do.

Francine comes up to me. "Thank you, Malcolm," she says. "Welcome." She sticks out her hand and we shake.

"To what?" I ask.

Her eyes just sparkle.

Noelle clutches my other arm. "All the stupid stuff."

That night, Noelle and I go out to a three-course dinner at one of my favorite spots near the park.

We have plenty of bruschetta. We talk about our time in San Francisco. It's pretty hilarious, what she did, and now that we're no longer at odds, we rehash every little session. I tell her exactly how crazy I thought her program was. She tells me how close she always felt to being busted. I tease her about the secret of the dryer lint bandit. Eventually I put her out of her misery and reveal that it's whoever lives in apartment 512.

"Jada?" she says. "Jada's the one who made the film. She lives in 512."

"That makes perfect sense." I explain that the footage seemed to be edited to show the door to apartment 512 right after the dryer-lint bandit was mentioned.

"Oh my god, you're right! It's Jada!" She's on her phone, texting Francine, probably.

We spend the next few weeks doing what we want. It feels like making up for lost time. One of my first acts as Noelle's boyfriend is to buy her some actual butterfly ties, not the clip-on kind, either, and implore her to wear one of them on one of our dates.

She is confused about the gift. "They are beautiful," she says sweetly. "You found one with little hedgehog faces."

"But?" I tease. "Are these the wrong kind?"

"Well, I love them because you picked them out," she says. "But you know I wear clip-on ties. These are impossible to tie right. I end up wasting so much time. They're the most time-wasting thing ever."

"And you lose the sense of uniformity."

"Yes, exactly," she says. "And why in the world would you want me to wear a business outfit for dinner at your home?"

"You'll see," I say.

She thinks I've lost my mind. It's a thought she often has about me, and I'll take it. I think we're all a little bonkers in the end.

That night at my place, in front of a roaring fire as the leaves are falling all over Central Park, I reach over and take her drink from her hand, setting it on the table. Then I reach up and slowly untie her tie.

"This," I say. "I've been wanting to do this ever since I met you," I say huskily.

"Hmm," she says, starting to unbutton my shirt.

"No, wait," I say. "Let me do it."

She stills. Smiles.

Slowly I draw it away from her prim little collar.

"Am I supposed to look witchy?" she asks.

"No, just regular and serious," I say, continuing on.

She gives me a prim face that is only a little bit exaggerated, but it's still hot to pull the butterfly tie free from her collar. It's sexy as hell, in fact. I hold it up, letting it swing free, and then I toss it over my shoulder.

She gets this mischievous look on her face. She leans in and whispers, "Guys are so weird!"

"Oh, *guys* are weird? *Please*," I say.

And then she comes to me, laughing, and tries to wrestle me to the floor, and I let her.

EPILOGUE

Seven months later—the following spring.

Noelle

MALCOLM HAS HAD workers restoring the lobby to its original glamour all winter. And not just putting tiles back up and restoring the chandeliers to their former glory, but really beautifying the place.

But he's also had something going on up on the roof for some time. I didn't realize it—we all thought it was just a place for staging, a place to hold materials for the other parts of the project, but now? It seems it's something more.

Because it's one of the first nice spring days in the city, and he's called for us all to gather on the roof at seven in the evening.

"Have you not gotten anything more out of him than that?" Francine asks, brushing on her mascara.

"Only what you know. Supposedly we can bring dates. Vicky and Henry are coming, too. Theo and Lizzie."

"They don't even live here anymore," Francine says, twisting the cap back on.

I shrug. "Malcolm has been bromancing with Henry ever since Max's New Year gala. I don't know where the rest of them figure in. But I kind of think Henry is in on it. I think they did something up there."

"Got it!" Francine beelines back into her room.

"What's wrong? What are you doing?" I ask.

Francine comes out in a sassy little white sheath dress with flower sequins. She twirls around. "I smell a rooftop cocktail party coming on."

I look down at my yoga lounge-around outfit. Francine points into my bedroom. I go in and change into my going-out skirt outfit and we head up.

The elevator lets us off in the weird half-floor at the top of the building that seems to serve very few functions aside from being a storage place that you pass through to go up to the roof. John and some of the other residents are sitting on crates. Apparently the door is locked. Maisey comes over and asks me if I know what's happening. She's wearing her daisy pin.

"Total secret—from me, too," I say. "You're the tenth person to ask. I thought it was a staging area for the lobby reno."

More people gather. Finally the door opens, letting bright fresh sunshine into the dim space. "Come on up," Malcolm calls from the other side.

I'm the first to step up onto the roof.

My jaw drops. There are trellises and seating areas and raised garden beds, ready for planting. There's a little shelter with outdoor couches where you can sit outside, even when it's raining.

Jaunty lights zigzag overhead, little white orbs against the royal blue evening sky.

I go over and grab Malcolm's hand. "What have you done? It's magical," I say.

Everybody else has reached the roof by now, squeeing and wandering around.

He shrugs. "Well, once the majority of the units are turned over to owners, this'll be all of your responsibility. I wanted to leave it in good shape."

People are crowding around, thanking him, pointing things out to each other. He's shrugging it off. He's still not good with thanks. With praise. With affection.

Except from me.

Max and Mia arrive with a catering crew and suddenly it really is a cocktail party. Caterers ferry around trays of sparkling things and finger food.

Jada is filming. An old friend of Malcolm's named Howie shows up with his wife and twin daughters, all the way from California.

At some point, John and Maisey discover that one of the raised planting beds incorporates four of John's old coffee can planters. Maisey touches John's arm. He turns to smile at her. A number of us exchange excited glances.

There are more effusions for Malcolm once people have drinks in them, and I can feel him turning a little bit rigid.

I grab his hand. "Enough!" I announce. "Malcolm's hitting his kumbaya limit here." Everybody laughs, even though it's not really a joke. I pull him to the edge. The sunset is an orange half-orb over jagged building tops.

"This is terrible," he says. "I have thoroughly ruined my reputation as a villain, and it's all your fault."

"Oh, don't worry, Malcolm. The night's still young. There's plenty of time to earn an X for bad behavior. Maybe several Xs."

He raises a dusky brow. "What did you have in mind?"

I smooth my palm over his silky lapel, thinking about wearing a non-clip-on butterfly tie. "That's proprietary."

~ *The End* ~

ACKNOWLEDGMENTS

Writing a book can sometimes feel like a fun skip in the park... and sometimes it can feel like rolling a super-heavy boulder up a steep cliff. I could never have finished this book without the people on this page—you all dropped down out of the sky, got in with me shoulder to shoulder, and helped me roll that boulder up the hill when I most needed it, and you also skipped with me, and I am so, so, sooooo grateful.

In the general order of their helping...

I want to thank Pippa Grant for thinking up this title (SO much better than the one I had!) A massive thank you to Molly O'Keefe, who helped me make Malcolm and Noelle's interactions waaaaaay better, like seriously. Thank you so much to Joanna Chambers: your ideas on how to get the psychology right were absolutely golden. Kisses to Toni Anderson because your thoughts on the big blow-up...omg I can't imagine this book without them! Mad, mad love to my amazing Minneapolis writing group, Elizabeth Jarrett Andrew, Terri Whitman, Marcia Peck, and Mark Powell—you had so many thoughtful insights that enabled me see these characters in stronger relief and inspired me push this story to a bold new level. Deepest gratitude also to Jenn Stark for the wonderfully witty blurb magic and ending ideas...that shall remain proprietary. And to my pal Rachel Grant...you made so many great tweaks, including reminding me to unmask the dryer-lint bandit! LOL. Massive gratitude to Sunny Lee-Goodman for the insights on the corporate coaching profession and some really fun ideas for how to incorporate the info. You rock!! (Any coaching missteps are me taking my own creative license.) Thank you to Sandy Waters for the *Forza*, to my sister, Sharon Kimmel, for the cheese tray keepsake inspiration, and to Melissa Gaston for all of the amazing hand-holding and advice and graphical genius moves. Major hugs to Michelle Catalano for the future cover, Judy Zweifel for the proofreading, and David Ball for the USPS insights. Thank you also to Courtenay Bennett for the fantastic read-through and so many catches and artful re-wording ideas, to Nina of Valentine PR for the smart guidance and cheerleading, and to Joan Lai for late-breaking catches. Big, wild gratitude also to the Fabulous Gang for being amazing, fun readers, and for giving me my happy place on the internet. Crazy thanks to my awesome ARC gang—It means everything to have you in my corner, pulling for me. Hugs!!

And finally, thank YOU, random reader reading these acknowledgements (pinky shake! I love reading the acknowledgements, too!) I just want to take this moment to thank you for reading my book. It seriously means the world.

ALSO BY ANNIKA MARTIN

Stand-alone romantic comedy (read in any order)

Most Eligible Billionaire

The Billionaire's Wake-up-call Girl

Breaking The Billionaire's Rules

The Billionaire's Fake Fiancée

Return Billionaire to Sender

Just Not That Into Billionaires

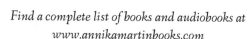

Find a complete list of books and audiobooks at
www.annikamartinbooks.com

ABOUT THE AUTHOR

Annika Martin is a New York Times bestselling author who sometimes writes as RITA®-award-winning Carolyn Crane. She lives in Minneapolis with her husband; in her spare time she enjoys taking pictures of her cats, consuming boatloads of chocolate suckers, and tending her wild, bee-friendly garden.

newsletter:
http://annikamartinbooks.com/newletter

Facebook:
www.facebook.com/AnnikaMartinBooks

Instagram:
instagram.com/annikamartinauthor

website:
www.annikamartinbooks.com

email:
annika@annikamartinbooks.com

Thank you for reading!

xox Annika

CPSIA information can be obtained
at www.ICGtesting.com
Printed in the USA
BVHW050351040123
655462BV00013B/1192

9 781944 736217